Doing
Scary

Donald M. Bell

Clink
Street

London | New York

In loving memory of Miracle Ray-Ann Bell, my warrior princess who fought for every breath she took in her short life.

Acknowledgements

While writing is a solo endeavor, authoring a book requires a unique set of partnerships that merit acknowledgment. At the community level, I would like to thank the three spiritual communities that helped mold me: Covenant Blessing Fellowship, The Family of Faith and New Testament. Special thanks to Bishop K.C. Ulmer, D. Min. Ph.D. for his timely counsel; Jim and Phyllis Hamann for being a counterweight of positivity and encouragement that love can last a lifetime. The Covenant Mothers: Patricia Ashley (in memoriam), Ramona Clark, Gloria Gunning, Claudia Hughes, Fern Johnson, Estella Roach, and Gwen Tucker for always having my back. And the Covenant Blessing Fellowship staff for their support.

Thank you to my support crew: all the people who read then reread, processed and reprocessed with me through the various incarnations of the book you now hold in your hand, several of whom I must mention by name: Melanie Austin (in memoriam), Angela Birdsong, Morgan La Royce, Robyn Stokes, Kors Vandiver and Dr. Krishna Smith.

Thank you to the Holt family, Eric and Cyndi Shanklin for your steady stream of encouragement and support. T. Faye Griffin: thank you for coming out of retirement to get this thing to the next level; your polish as an editor gave me the courage to ship. Huge thanks to Falana Monroe, the rocket booster who helped me escape the gravitational pull of ADD to put this thing in orbit; it is your turn to show the world how brilliant you are! To the hundreds of people who granted me a backstage pass to the darkest hours of their lives: thank you for trusting me and taking a hit for the team. It is your stories of defeat and triumph that inspired me to write this book.

To my friend and brother Ted - thanks for your friendship, support, and transparency.

Special thanks to David and Gloria Gunning for your unconditional love, unlimited support and your abiding faith in my calling to reach people.

To my wife Michelle, thank you for keeping me focused on the finish line. To my children Alexandria, DJ, and Donalin – whose curiosity about the characters helped me trudge through the tedium of writing through the seasons of self-doubt – thank you for your love. Honor and love to my mom (Mary Frances Bell-Bagby) and dad (David S. Bell) in Memoriam, thank you both for your sacrifices. A final word of thanks to my stepfather, William Elmo Bagby whose love of words, gift for storytelling, affection, and discipline emboldens me to Do Scary; I miss you Pop.

CHAPTER ONE

The Rare Bean Prologue

Found in the Westside District of Los Angeles County, the Rare Bean (RB), a classic SoCal adaptation of the French coffeehouse, works for the same reason the other idiosyncrasies of living on that side of town works—no one challenges the delusory charm of things that work. No one wants to burst the denial bubble that envelops his own neighborhood. No one would dare ask how a building that once housed a fast-food restaurant, and sits at the end of a strip mall one block east of one the busiest stretches of freeway on the planet, can be touted as a French coffeehouse simply because of a few tables and chairs placed at the entrance and called a "patio area."

Locals would never ask perplexing questions like: How can a place adorned in a toneless palette of gray and brown, with a pop of mortuary green, encourage customers to lounge for hours in extra double-small industrial steel and wood furnishings, then be marketed as "your living room away from home"? How can it get away with serving 20-ounce, 675 calories drinks laden with enough sugar and caffeine to mimic a crack cocaine high? Or why it is that a place promoting itself as a second office has neglected to install any task lighting? And what about the hordes of people who gather at a place in an environment designed to promote community and human interaction, yet wear headphones and stare at screens who clearly preferring the warmth and affection of their own virtual communities to a real one based on the number of people wearing headphones and staring at screens?

Providing the soundtrack for the whole soul-numbing

experience is the house blend of neutered R&B and faux-rock leaching from the ceiling, at such a passive aggressive level you can't actively listen to it for over ten seconds. The array of products on the wall from the entrance to the cashier makes the place feel more like a theme park souvenir shop than a chic coffeehouse.

Also, missing from the Rare Bean's take on the French coffeehouse, the mouthwatering welcome the aroma of fresh-brewed coffee extends to customers when they enter. Like the effect the colors have on the eyes, the seats have on your glutes, and the music has on the ears, the acrid smell of volume-brewed java offends the senses. The stench of coffee manufactured by the gallon rather than by the pot to satisfy the procession of cars snaking their way through the 24/7 drive-thru fills the porous fiber of everything it contacts.

A mixture of apron-clad Millennials at opposite ends of their generation and the career spectrum make up the staff. There are the brooding lifers who, like the coffee they serve, come in various flavors of bitterness, and translate the orders of those who don't speak fluent coffeehouse with contempt. Alongside them are the spirited part-timers, a mere semester away from a degree that ends in "-ology" instead of "-ing." They welcome every patron with a greeting devoid of warmth or eye contact, then administer an oral exam before taking your order: "So, how's your day going?" The exchange of forced pleasantries that follows ends abruptly the moment it appears the dialogue might escalate into full a conversation. "So what can I get for you today?"

From 4:30 p.m. until closing the place bustles with a steady stream of Westside refugees fleeing the tyrannical demands of clichéd lives. There are the stay-at-home moms wearing the latest incarnation of mom jeans—yoga pants, a couple of fathers in their usual off-work attire consisting of cargo shorts, graphic T-shirts, and flip-flops getting in some quality time with children. There is the work-dudes who gather in clusters of three to five young men standing in line enthusiastically discussing the latest reboot of the next Marvel Comics movie. They are adult adolescents with "-ing" degrees like engineering, decked out in hybrid outfits of jean-slacks, a dress-casual shirt and sneaker-soled dress shoes. Seated at a table along the front window is the female counterpart of the work-dude—the girlfriend. There to catch up with other girlfriends, she sits in a cell phone induced trance broken only by the squeals and long, enthusiastic embrace of the arriving girlfriend whom she hasn't seen in "Foreverrrrrr."

Other partakers of the evening festivities include the "Seekers": groups of teens or seniors in search of the Holy Grail of the coffeehouse—a full-sized table near an electrical outlet. On the fringe of the cast of regulars are the "Outsiders." Outsiders are hardcore Westsiders who refuse to buy into the hype of the latest trends. They would not think of being seen inside such a trendy place as the Rare Bean despite the fact they produce sixty-eight percent of RB's revenue. Instead, they rely on a mix of friends, relatives, and drive-thru access to get their fix. Outsiders love the perks of living on the Westside but hate to admit it. Outsiders are quick to tell people they live on the Westside, but make it clear that they are not "Westside-ish."

CHAPTER TWO

Owen Thinks Something Is Up

An "Outsider" of the highest order, Owen Bryant entered the Rare Bean for the first time. While scanning the room for a table, he became self-conscious about the stares he drew from the regulars who scrutinized him like a parole officer walking into a biker bar. He made his way to the lone vacancy, the bistro arrangement off the main room generally shunned by the regulars. Even though Owen was the only African-American in the place not wearing an apron, he knew none of the glances in his direction had anything to do with the color of his skin. He knew how race worked in a progressive environment like the Westside. It factors into everything, but isn't an issue in anything.

Even though Owen struggled with being alone in public, he had grown comfortable being the lone black in a room full of his colleagues and peers. You could even say he'd learned to work it. From scholarships to prestigious schools to internships at Fortune 500 companies, he had stockpiled degrees in math and economics; he then converted them into a small fortune on Wall Street by his thirty-first birthday. Straight out of Central Casting, his looks and mannerisms made him the perfect token. His slight frame and boyish "I can't believe you're that old" face with its vague ethnic features, along with his accent-free, newscaster voice, intelligence, and nerdy ways caused the Caucasians in the room to feel their acceptance of him was progressive without having to leave their comfort zone. For Owen, being able to check "black" in the ethnicity box without being urban gave him an advantage. Even though he had mastered the art of being the lone black in a room full of colleagues and peers, he had not mastered the art of being alone.

But it was the clothes he wore not the color of his skin that really grabbed people's attention. Westsiders cast a suspicious eye on anyone who appeared to flaunt their success after business hours—no matter what their race, creed, religion, or sexual orientation. The precision tailoring and drape of the fabric was all any onlooker needed to confirm that Owen had breached the social contract. Wearing an Armani custom after hours was an act of rebellion (even if the suit was, in fact, a high-end knock-off crafted in boring beige). Only one person on the planet had enough pull in Owen's life to talk him into venturing inside the Rare Bean during the rush-crush hour wearing a designer suit accented with Detroit Gator shoes and a monogrammed, cuff-linked shirt—Sage Elizabeth Bryant-Cole.

Sage, also known as "BC" (before Cole) to Owen, was his first cousin and best friend. The nickname was Owen's subliminal reminder for her husband, Roman, that his friendship with Sage predates their marriage. Thirteen months ago, Sage and Roman moved to "The Coast," a band of small cities between the Westside District and the Ocean. The sworn enemy of Westsiders, "Coastals" live in what they dubbed, "The True West." And unlike their Westside neighbors, Coastals have no problem flaunting their success and wealth. Whether it's a new body created by the latest fad diet or exercise regime or a supercharged Bentley, Coastals want everyone to know four essential facts about their lives: how exclusive it is, how fashionable it is, how expensive it is, and how well-connected they had to be to get it that way.

Despite his misgivings about Sage's insistence they meet at such a trendy spot, the Rare Bean provided the perfect backdrop to plan the next bi-annual Bryant family reunion, especially considering the level of delusional buy-in a person had to maintain to even get an invitation to an official Bryant family event.

For the fifth time in ten minutes, Owen glanced at his aging smartphone trimmed in electrical tape as he tugged on the oversized collar of his starched shirt. His tie felt like an anaconda around his neck whose grip tightened with every sigh of anxiety and frustration. "Can't she be on time for once in her life?" he ranted inwardly, even though Sage wasn't tardy. In fact, she had another forty minutes to spare before he could send a formal "You're late…again. Where are you?" text. Typically, it was Owen who arrived thirty to forty minutes early for everything.

To quell the dentist office waiting room level of anxiety he felt whenever he sat alone in a public place, he decided to get a refill. Eager to report his findings to Sage, he stood in line with one eye focused on the table where he'd left his stuff, and the other on the tinted glass at the entrance. He kept one hand on the phone in his pocket in anticipation of Sage's usual, "running late be there in a few," text.

Owen had just told the barista to hold the whipped cream this go around when Sage strolled through the double doors held open by one exiting gentleman and another just arriving. Like a model strutting her stuff on the catwalks of Milan or New York during fashion week, minus a half-foot of stature, Sage confidently crossed the room in his direction. One of her sculpted arms supported two bulky designer tote bags, the other a small matching purse. The latest iPhone dwarfed her fresh from the nail shop, French tipped right hand, while the left clutched a large cupful of green sludge so thick the humongous straw pointed straight towards the ceiling without a lid. Without having to turn around, the sudden pausation of sound and movement along with the slack jaw leer of every man sitting along the back wall facing the entrance told Owen it was Sage.

Sage didn't merely walk into a room, she changed the atmosphere of it. Her complexion radiated the golden-brown splendor of a biscuit baked to perfection giving her the bronze glow of a woman who had run the gauntlet of make-up counters at a high-end department store. Not a hair of the tight, swept high ponytail resting on her left shoulder was out-of-place. The black Diane Von Furstenberg classic wrap dress hugged her curves like a fresh layer of asphalt at Daytona. It paid homage to a figure sculpted by the denial of red meat, dairy fat, and high-fructose corn syrup then refined by Zumba, Pilates, CrossFit boot camp, and the occasional spin class. Her body, beauty, fashion, and charm provided the place setting for a pair of rainforest green marble eyes so brilliant, even the most lustful of men kept eye contact despite her ample cleavage. From behind Sage had a walk that shifted zip codes with every step.

By the time the room absorbed Sage's entrance, Owen knew the room was about to lose its equilibrium as it entered a polarized state Owen called "the Sage effect." On one side there were the haters, women whose instant disdain for Sage approached Darwinian levels. On the other side, there were the men—straight and gay—who were dazed by her style and flow. When it came to having an opinion about Sage no middle ground existed. People either adored her or resented her long before they could get to know her.

Sage excused her way to the front of the line where Owen stood, passed a host of stares out the corners of eyes and comments made under breath. When Owen turned she gave him a kiss on both cheeks. "Hey Sweetie, look at you in your Armani all dressed up like a big boy," she said, flashing an affirming smile as she tightened up his tie. Owen relieved the fashionista of one of her totes as she shifted into verbal overdrive.

"You will not believe the old pictures I found for the souvenir book. This, this right here is going to be so next level, no one can touch it. Even Aunt Zara will be left speechless. I just hope Tracey doesn't get mad when we put the picture of her and Gram wearing matching Easter Bunny sweaters in the book. I'm still laughing. Oh, and for the record, I'm not late. Per usual you're early and anxious about having to wait alone. In fact, I would have been early had the line at Jojo's Juice Box not rounded out the door into the parking lot."

"You do know they sell bottled green goo here?" Owen said half-jokingly.

"Oh, you mean that fauxganic kale smoothie they are trying to pass off as healthy? You do know a sistah did her research."

For as long as Owen could remember Sage's fear of the 40 by 40 curse (the forty pounds Bryant women put on by their fortieth birthday, mostly on their hips), had fueled her obsession with health and fitness. Part of the Bryant women legacy was the act of letting themselves go, and Sage wanted no parts of it. But Owen didn't want to sit through another one of her diatribes on the dangers of aspartame. He had hoped that foregoing his usual sneakers and sweats for the suit she had made for him would distract her enough to get through their planning session before noticing how uncomfortable he felt in his skin. Despite his sullen mood, he felt gladdened to see his cousin so light-hearted. Six months ago, the always-together Sage began committing what she called "fashion felonies" like wearing nail polish that clashed with her outfit, going out in public with nothing on her lips, and wearing jeans without the proper accessories on a regular basis. Her refusal to "add the finishing touches," as she called it, grew out of the despair she felt after finding out her husband Roman was a serial cheater.

It was six months to the day that the revelation of her husband's infidelity left Sage's marriage dangling by a thread. Since then, Owen had detected a noticeable change in her attitude as she emerged from her funk. She looked and sounded more like her old self despite the burden she'd borne. Given the way Bryant women could nurse a grievance into full-blown bitterness with a minute amount of provocation, it was amazing how it hadn't set up shop in her heart as it did with her cousins and aunts. Sage's radiance left Owen awed. She had not just survived the ordeal, she'd figured out a way to thrive in spite of it.

Gone were the waves of disdain across her forehead he feared might become a permanent cluster of worry lines, a graph of the emotional rollercoaster of success in the board-room and misery in the bedroom that had become her life. The torment she'd endured left no discernible mark on her countenance. The withdrawn blood-spattered eyes she blamed on an extended allergy attack were bright and engaging again. *How is this possible?* Owen wondered. He hoped her ready smile meant she had turned the corner, and wasn't faking it just to get through the evening as he was.

Owen remembered how dumbstruck Sage's response left the family when Aunt Zara told the family he and Sage would oversee charge of planning the biannual Bryant family gatherings moving forward. Sage, the genteel family standard bearer of class and decorum, wore a scowl worthy of her father, retired Marine Corps Sergeant Major Horace Bryant. Her obsession with the planning and execution of the Bryant reunion began the year of the Universal Studios versus Disney World debacle. That year the Sergeant Major canceled their plans to take Sage to Disney World for her 16th birthday in order to attend the Bryant family reunion at Universal Studios three months later. The cancellation of her birthday celebration broke her heart. Owen knew something apocalyptic must have occurred when Sage raised her hand and asked, "Why do we waste our time and energy planning a bi-annual family reunion that lasts one week, when all we are going to do is complain about it for next two years?"

The something turned out to be the unexpected revelation that her husband hadn't had just one affair, he'd had a string of them interspersed with scores of sexual liaisons.

Sage and Owen grew up more like brother and sister than first cousins. Because of the sibling bond they shared Owen might have tried to step to Roman when he first learned how he had dogged Sage, if it hadn't been for her constant reassurance that she would be okay. (Of course, that and Roman's size were the deciding factors.) At six-foot-five inches with the body fat of a thoroughbred, Roman was a legit eight inches taller and 70 pounds of shredded muscle heavier than he was.

Owen grabbed his drink and motioned Sage over to a table he'd saved. She plopped down on the chair and tried to arrange her things on the small round surface. Realizing there wasn't enough room to dig through the cumbersome photo albums, she went on to item two on her agenda.

"Let's start with what you found," she said.

"Well, it looks like the best deal will be the Mission Inn," Owen said pulling out his notepad. "They can give us thirty percent off the regular rate if we reserve a block of at least twenty-five rooms, which shouldn't be a problem. We'll only be minutes from the park where we want to hold the picnic. The only drawback is it puts us a few miles from the location we want for the banquet. But with the money we'll save we should be able to get everything catered."

When he looked up Sage was leaning back in her chair with her arms folded staring at him with the same hawkish glare that served as an early-warning system every time the idealistic but clueless Owen was about to "step in it."

"You're kidding, right? Seriously? The Mission Inn?" Sage was incredulous. "Um, bad enough we nixed the destination reunion everyone wanted. How am I supposed to sell our people on a two-and-a-half-star motel when everyone knows where I work and how I get down? The instant they find out that not only are we not going to some tropical island, but we'll be staying at a motel that boasts free Wi-Fi, we'll be excommunicated from the family."

"Free Wi-Fi? That's a huge exaggeration," Owen said, trying to defuse the bomb he inadvertently lit. "I don't see why we can't have it at your spot. I'm sure your employee discount would more than keep us within budget."

"Seriously?" Sage raised one eye at him.

"Yes, seriously. Why can't we have it at your place?" Owen replied, with his arms dropping to his sides in frustration.

Sage responded by counting off with her fingers, "Because one, some of yo' people are too country and the rest of are too entitled. Two, I like my staff. And three, I want to keep my job! How about you kick in some of that Wall Street cash you're sitting on and we go to the Bahamas and call it a day?"

Owen ignored Sage's Wall Street comment.

"I admit it won't please the most discerning of our relatives, but the location and price are too good to ignore," he snapped back.

"Ha! Discerning? You are much too gracious. Some of our kinfolks are snobs. Love them, but they are on the snooty side," Sage said, sneaking a glance around the room before pressing the tip of her nose skywards. She chuckled hoping to lighten the mood.

"Are you done embarrassing yourself?" Owen said.

"Okay, okay, sorry, O.B. I didn't mean to get you all worked up about it," Sage knew how he could get when anyone talked about his money.

She ventured on. "What happened with The Grand? They were going to give us a discount. The manager over there owes me big time."

With just the mention of The Grand, the hotel where he and his wife Lia were married, Owen's shoulders slumped and the hold on his cup turned into a death grip. Noticing the earnest look Owen gets when championing a cause had given way to a blank stare, Sage leaned forward, reached through the piles of photos to touch his hand.

"I know you O.B. What has Ms. Lia done now?" her eyes searched his.

Owen shifted his gaze away from her and focused on the cardboard sleeve around his cup. He cleared his throat to try and overcome the sudden dryness in his mouth as he processed the conflicting thoughts racing through his head. "I should tell her; she would understand, – Of course, she would. Maybe too well," he reasoned. knew he needed to talk to someone. Still, he wasn't ready to admit failure, not even to someone as close to him as Sage. Beside there was the concern over how his marital troubles might cause her to doubt her own circumstances.

He closed his eyes for an extended blink. When he opened them, he leaned in and said: "That's just it. I don't know what's going on. Or at least I'm not a hundred percent sure," he sighed.

Even though Sage heard Owen she did not grasp what he said.

"It's Lia. She's been acting distant. I think something's up."

"There's always something up with Lia," Sage tossed a dismissive wave in his direction.

Owen, feeling forced to declare his suspicions more clearly leaned in and whispered emphatically:

"I mean like seeing someone else, that kind of 'something's up.'"

Immediately he pushed back from the table to put some emotional distance between him and the words he'd just spoken. Sage grabbed his cup before its contents damaged the memories strewn about the table.

"Owen, no," Sage said in a drawn-out whisper. Her own heart-numbing feelings of isolation and horror were instantly resuscitated. Owen's disclosure was the last thing she expected or wanted to hear.

She, too, began to try and put some emotional distance between herself and Owen's revelation. A barrage of thoughts hit her all at once.

"Get it together sister. Suck it up, it's not about you it's about family. Stop acting like such a girl. This isn't the time for all that. Press on. Get over yourself. Owen needs you." A few of the lines were borrowed from lectures she received as a child from her father.

"I am so sorry, O.B. Here I am going on about hotels and pictures while your marriage is in crisis," she said, finding her voice at last.

Owen placed his other hand on top of hers. "Don't worry we're going be fine. Lia and I just need to get through this rough spot." He hated burdening Sage like this.

Sage sat up to attention. "First of all, it's not okay. And two,

14

families worry about each other, it's what they do; and no one does worry better than Bryants. You worried about me when I was going through, now it's my turn to worry about you. End of story."

Knowing how much he despised being on the receiving end of help, she wasn't sure if he would be open to what she knew she needed to share with him. Still, the counseling she had received over the past few months taught her that the earlier you start doing truth the better.

"Can I ask you a few questions?"

Owen barely nodded, reluctant to probe his situation even with his lifelong confidante.

"Did she admit anything?"

"No. I haven't said a thing to Lia since I started putting two and two together."

"Then your marriage is in limbo."

"Meaning what?"

"Meaning you're at the point in the relationship where a spouse suspects something's going on but can't, or won't, confirm it because they're afraid to deal with the answer."

Owen bewilderment took over his face.

"It's an extremely dysfunctional space for a marriage to be in. It gets worse the longer you wait because the only thing a couple stuck in limbo can do is escalate and entrench the fear and manipulation between them. Owen, you have to confront Lia. It's the only way the two of you can move on with your life."

"Move on? You already think I should divorce her?" Strangely, Owen found himself on the defensive.

"No. When I say move on I'm not talking about divorce. I am talking about the two of you working your way through a process that puts the two of you back in charge of your lives as individuals. Then you can honestly look at your marriage," Sage explained. "Trust me on this O.B. I know what I'm talking about. I'm not doing well because my marriage is doing better, my marriage is doing better because I'm doing better. You know what a mess I was when I first found out Roman had cheated on me. Look at me now." Sage leaned back with her arms wide open.

"It took the implosion of my marriage, a whole lot of support, tears, and counseling, along with a bunch of frank conversations between me and Roman before my heart began to soften. I'm not saying things are great. Lord knows I still have a lot of ground to cover with my heart and with Roman. But what I am saying is, I've come to accept the 'You are here' point of my journey, and because of it I am in a much better space than I was even before I got married. Does that make sense?"

Owen nodded his agreement. He had noticed how she looked and sounded more like her <u>before Cole</u> self recently. Marriage to Roman had caused the little girl with the big personality in her to shrink. But now, though she was distressed by the news about his marriage, he hadn't seen Sage this light-hearted and self-assured since their college days.

She leaned in to grasp her cousin/brother's hand again. "All I'm saying is, it's a process—a process where you're going to have to lay aside your pride and anger and let someone walk with you through it. Otherwise, the pain-induced delusion will overwhelm you—not to mention the denial."

"All right, all right." Reluctantly, he absorbed the reality that for a change he would be the one receiving help, not extending it. "Tell me what I need to do," Owen sighed heavily.

Before she could get a word out, the clunking sound of chairs being placed on top of tables and the intense smell of pine-scented floor signaled that the coffeehouse was closing.

"I left my car at the Park and Ride lot and took the Green Line over here," Sage said, while Owen helped her pack her things. "Why don't you drive me back to my car so that we can chat some more."

"Sure, there's no way I'm letting you take the train this late at night." Truth was, he welcomed any delay in going home face the inevitable.

CHAPTER THREE

Form Follows Function

Sage placed the last of her belongings in the hatchback of Owen's 10-year-old hybrid between two trunk organizers that looked more like the cubby holes you might find in a day-care facility. She then settled in for the twenty-minute ride to her car. The interior of Owen's car was as immaculate as the day it left the showroom; the only thing missing was the new car smell. The same could not be said for the coat of paint on the outside which resembled a pair of acid wash blue-jeans.

Knowing Owen's propensity to shut down, Sage pounced. "To start, you are going to need real help." She wanted to give him as much information as she could in their short drive. "I can share the stuff I've learned to get you going on the right path. But at some point you're still going to need to see somebody like Roman and I did to help you sort through some of this stuff."

Owen mumbled and nodded. His clenched fists at ten and two on the wheel, along with his thousand-yard stare, told her he'd about checked out of their conversation. Still, she pressed on. She knew she would have to make it quick if she wanted him to reengage.

"Coach Perkins taught us that we needed to rebuild dignity before we could even think about rebuilding our relationship. He had to hammer that into me because I was ready to either go straight to a lawyer's office or renew our vows. I was way ahead of where I needed to be."

"Coach?" Owen perked up a bit at the mention of this title.

"Yeah, Coach. At least that's what I call him because he's like a life coach, even though that's not what he does for a living.

Roman found him, long story. When Roman suggested we talk to him I was still too angry and proud to talk to anyone, let alone a stranger. I was sure anybody Roman wanted to talk to would be on his side. Boy, was I off," she chuckled at the memory of how tight she was during those initial meetings.

"Coach Perkins helped us connect with the real Roman and Sage—the good, the bad and the ugly so we could address our real strengths and weaknesses. I'm not saying we've gotten our stuff together and all is forgiven in the Cole House, but we're making progress."

More attentive now, Owen signaled to get off at the next exit. Although his interest was now peaked, he wished they were having this conversation via text so he could hide his despair. In attempt to keep his composure he became preoccupied with adjusting and checking the mirrors.

"I don't have time to see anybody," he said at last. "We're in the thick of planning next year's summer program at The Center. We got new interns that need to be trained. I need to sort this it out on my own first before I invite a stranger into the process. Besides, I still haven't confirmed if Lia is cheating or not. What if it's nothing?"

It saddened Sage to think how much Owen sounded like her when she first suspected Roman was being unfaithful. She had made excuses and rationalized until the situation blew up in her face. "Here's the thing I know now that I didn't know then— something was definitely wrong with my marriage. Either the bond between us was so broken Roman felt the need to have an affair or it was so broken I felt the need to imagine he was having an affair. It doesn't matter how you slice it, you are going to have to make time to deal with your marriage."

"Thanks for understanding," Owen sighed. Concerned that he'd dragged Sage into his mess then shut her out again left him feeling conflicted.

"Why don't you just tell me some of what he taught you?" Owen asked to appease Sage.

Sage grabbed her phone out of her purse and tapped the

screen twice to pull up the mobile notebook containing her counseling notes. She scrolled through the app menus.

"Ah, I got it. *Form Follows Function*," she read. "Wait, the best way to explain this principle is on paper." After digging through her purse again to find a pen, she then grabbed a menu from the glove compartment. Flipping it over, she began to draw four shapes at the top of the page.

"Okay, look at all the shapes. Tell me which one would make the best table?" Sage shoved the menu in Owen's face while he stopped at a light.

Four worry lines appeared above Owen's eyebrows as he gazed at the defaced menu. Owen did not understand why Sage just put graffiti all over his Shin Shin Chinese Takeout menu, or what any of it had to do with his current predicament. But out of deference for his cousin who was clearly trying hard to help, he would be polite and play along. Although hastily drawn and somewhat rudimentary, the four shapes staring back at him amid the rice and noodle dishes were obvious.

"The shape that looks like a deformed capital 'T' at the bottom next to the Kung Pao chicken."

"Exactly," Sage chirped, a little too excited for Owen. Sage knew something he didn't. "Now which shape would make the best ball?"

"The circle right here just below the Egg Foo Young," Owen said, then mouthed the word "Duh."

Ignoring his sarcasm, Sage continued. "Exactly. Which would make the best house?"

"The pentagon, naturally," he said, growing impatient. "Look Sage, if there's a point to all this I need you to make it."

"The point is—form follows function," Sage said, tapping on the menu. "Structure matters because it determines what you can do with it. What if you made a ball in the shape of a pentagon and then tried to play basketball with it? You would be chasing that thing all over the court. Ignoring the form follows function connection between structure and function can create all sorts of problems...even in relationships."

Sage had Owen's full attention. She grabbed the menu and scribbled three more drawings next to the appetizers. When she handed it back to him, three triangles adorned the entire side from pot stickers down to egg drop soup.

"Imagine all these triangles are slides. Now think about little Kiki," The mention of their cute 4-year-old cousin brought a smile to Owen's face. "Would you put her on a slide shaped like a triangle at the bottom?"

"No, of course, not," Owen imagined the tiny girl careening down the death trap such a steep slide would make.

"Why?" Sage asked.

"Because it's dangerous. The angle is too steep, it's too tall and too narrow. She would get hurt and Children Services would get involved."

"And what about the middle triangle?" She pointed to the shape resembling a triangle laying on its side.

"That wouldn't work either. It's too short and too wide to slide on. You would have to scoot across it to make it work," Owen beat Sage to the punch and motioned toward the last triangle. "And let me guess, this triangle is just right," he mimicked Goldilocks of the Three Bears fame.

"Yep. And that's when you get to go 'Wheeeeeeeeeeee,'" Sage squealed throwing her hands up.

"Uh, you all right?" Owen said.

"This is next level stuff, O.B. You don't understand how helpful this one principle was for me," Sage said, her tone sober. "As juvenile as this may seem, these diagrams showed me how important the structure of my relationship with Roman was to our satisfaction with our marriage.

"To experience the 'whee effect' you need the right blueprint for your relationship, one like the diagram at the bottom shows—a blueprint where the reward you get out of the relationship more than compensates for the danger and work it takes to stay married. If you want to fix your marriage then you and Lia need to change the structure of your marriage."

Owen remained silent. Her words were beginning to

make sense. His nod of approval spurred Sage to seize the opportunity to continue. "If each one of these three triangles were blueprints for a slide, only one of them would result in an apparatus a sane parent would let their child use—the one that doesn't require a lot of danger and work." Pointing at the other triangles Sage said, "The other two represent danger and work. Owen, it's the same in a marriage. It's the structure that determines whether a marriage works. It doesn't matter how sincere or loving two people are if they don't get the structure right. It doesn't matter how much love a couple has for one another at the start of their marriage, if it's full of danger and work their love for one another will lose its resiliency. A good blueprint for a marriage, like a good blueprint for a slide, is structured in a way where what you get out of it more than makes up the danger and work of being together."

Owen relaxed his grip on the wheel as the implication of what Sage was saying soaked in. *"Yep. Danger and work describes my situation to a T. It's been one thing after another ever since we started hanging out,"* Owen thought. Her crazy relationship with her ex, her family, her out of control spending, her lack of focus, in addition to her insecurity around his devotion to his work and family were just a few of the things Owen had to deal with over the course of their relationship. As far as he was concerned, helping Lia get her life on track had become a full-time job.

"You get it, right? It's the structure that delivers the results. And when you play with the structure, you create complexity, and with complexity you get more danger and work. It took me a minute, but I got it. Roman's affairs were a symptom, not the disease."

"Mm," was all Owen could utter, still engrossed in his own internal narrative.

"Bad people don't create bad marriages—bad patterns do," Sage quipped.

Owen pulled into the parking lot. "If you want to follow me

home we can finish talking there. Roman will be there, but he'll give us the space to talk if we need it."

"Give" and "space" – two words Owen never thought would find their way into a sentence with Roman's name attached to it. *"Dude must be desperate to keep Sage,"* he thought. He would find it funny if he weren't so numb. Although Roman had cheated on Sage, Owen admired him. He possessed the charisma to lead men into battle and women into sin. It was his college roommate that began calling him, "Trojan Man." Most people assumed it was a play on the name Roman or reference to his devotion to the school's iconic mascot. Only his roommate and a few of his frat brothers were aware of how he'd earned the nickname.

"I have no problem talking to you, but let's pick this up tomorrow. I'm not ready for prime time, and I would hate to lump Roman and Lia into the same cheater's club," said Owen.

Sage winced at the mention of Roman's unfaithfulness. As many strides as they had made, she remained sensitive when it came to talking to others about their struggles. Even so, she knew a part of owning the cost of putting her marriage back together meant embracing the shame that came with it.

"Okay. That's fair," Sage conceded

CHAPTER FOUR

Sage and Roman Talk Limbo

Sage inserted her key into the lock with care, trying not to jingle them too much. Roman had a big day tomorrow, and although she wanted to talk to him, she was hoping not to startle him awake. The tangy sweet aroma of barbecue sauce met her before the door opened. Earlier, she had been perfecting the pulled pork recipe she learned from the new chef she'd hired.

She smiled at the thought of how supportive Roman had been. He even handed out cards to many of his high-profile boosters. It was quite a turnaround from the days he insisted what she did was only a hobby.

All was dark and quiet in Sage and Roman's expansive new home, except for the pulsating greenish glow from the clock on the microwave and the muffled sounds coming from their bedroom. The sound caused her heart to race and a familiar lump of distrust rose up in her throat. She was done with trying to be quiet. After taking a few deep breaths to bolster her courage to face what she might see, she charged through the door.

"Hey Babe," Roman said. His tall, athletic frame rested against a mountain of decorative pillows on their four-poster bed. He grabbed the remote to mute the sound on the TV. "I thought you would still be out."

Sage was glad she had taken the time to look around the room before shouting "I bet you did." She was still adjusting to not viewing him through the lens of his affairs. When she glanced around and saw the high school football footage playing on the large flat screen, she realized she had no reason to be suspicious.

"No, Owen gave me a ride to my car," she avoided eye contact. Even though she understood coming to terms with her humanity was part of the cost, she hated that she still so wary. Next time when faced with the unknown she would choose to think the best.

"So how is Owen? Still trying to perform miracles with those delinquents?"

Roman loved harassing Owen about his work with the kids from The Center because Owen took the work and himself so seriously. One of Owen's biggest pet peeves was the prejudice people showed towards his kids based on their address.

"You better be glad he's not here to hear you dis his kids. Well, not that it matters considering all the stuff he has on his mind."

"Is Lia on his case again? She never gives that brotha a break."

"Owen thinks she might be on someone else's case."

"What? Not Miss 'I'm-just-sayin'-if-he-cheats-once-he'll-cheat-again' Lia? Not the woman is who is still giving you grief about your decision to work on our marriage?"

"Yes, the very same. But to be fair it is only alleged cheating at this point. Owen suspects something is going on although he has no proof."

"If Owen suspects she is cheating, then she is. Well…well…," Roman didn't try to hide his amusement at the prospect of Lia falling from grace. "So, while she was telling everybody how trifling I was, she was doing her own dirt." Sensing the glee he was deriving from the situation might not be sitting well with Sage he switched gears.

"Did you tell him he needed to find out for sure?"
"Yep."
"Did you tell him to confront her?"
"Yep."
"Did you tell him…" Roman stopped mid-sentence when

he noticed Sage was tugging on her right ear. Borrowed from the Carole Burnett show, tugging on her ear was the gesture they decided on to alert him whenever he cut her off or didn't give her a chance to contribute to the conversation. They both found gestures worked much better than her saying something to make him stop. It was Coach's idea and again he was right.

"Sorry, my bad. You know I'm still a work in progress," Roman said. He grabbed her playfully around the waist and pulling her closer to him until the back of her head rested on his expansive shoulders.

"You have the floor and my undivided attention. Please, tell me what happened to Owen."

"Yes, you're a piece of work," Sage said, laughing while she nudged herself away just enough to turn around and face him.

"Hey..." Feeling a burning question forming on his lips, he caught himself about to interrupt again, so he grabbed a throw pillow and placed it over his mouth. His big, brown puppy dog eyes pleaded for forgiveness.

Sage cut her eyes back at him before clearing her throat. "I was about to say I'd be happy to tell you all about it after I text Owen the link to Coach Perkins' audio on the three types of relationships." She jumped up to retrieve her phone from a bag she'd left on the kitchen table. She stole another glance at her husband with the pillow covering his mouth and had to laugh. Something she thought she'd never do again.

CHAPTER FIVE

Three Types of Relationships

Owen had just grabbed a glass of milk from the fridge and returned his secret stash of Oreos back to their hiding place when the buzz of his phone signaled an incoming text message. Lia had been on a no-sugar kick for the past few months, and when Lia was on a kick, he was the one with the imprint of her size 9.5 designer shoes stamped all over his lifestyle. He considered leaving the cookies on the countertop with a trail of dark chocolate crumbs just to provoke her. Nevertheless, he'd resolved to act like a responsible adult no matter how she provoked him.

Slumping down in the oversized leather recliner in their living room, he picked up the remote from the end table. He was in no mood to check his messages, but the sound of his phone vibrating against the recliner's cup-holder interrupted his new evening ritual: watching sports highlights on a 30-minute loop until he dozed off or Lia came home. His heart sped up at the thought that it might be Lia. Although they hadn't spoken much the past two weeks, she texted him on occasion with clipped, assistant-like requests: "Pickup clothes from cleaner, thnx," "We need toothpaste," and "Visa expires in 2wks – U need 2 call them 2 c what's up."

"Here's the link to the lecture I told you about," the text read. Intrigued, Owen clicked on the link, navigated to the audio, and pressed play on the mp3 entitled "The Three Types of Relationships." Coach Perkins engaging delivery and explanation of the three relationships archetypes instantly got his attention. After three minutes, he paused the recording so he could take notes. Like Sage's playground geometry lesson written on the back of a Chinese restaurant menu, he had no idea how predators, prey, parasites and host could help him with his marriage. The more Owen listened, the more the haze surrounding his marriage lifted.

"Man, this thing is all jacked up," Owen said to himself as he began to accept the notion of his marital problems being connected to the physics of their marriage and not the chemistry between them.

When he finished listening to the lecture, his head was spinning and his tablet full of notes.

"Three Types of Relationships," the heading read. Underneath it he'd written: "The Predatorial Relationship" – driven by the practice of loveless order. Theme: battle over voice and choice. "The Parasitic Relationship" – driven by the practice order less love. Theme: battle over needs and deeds. "Partnership Relationships" – driven by loving order. Theme: authenticity and honor. The idea of three types of relationships wasn't exactly an alien concept to Owen. Although he knew what predatorial and parasitic relationships were, he had never heard them used in the context of human relationships. Still, it made perfect sense, especially the parts about the parasitic relationship—excuses, demands, scapegoating, and an ever-changing set of rules. He realized how accurately it described his marriage.

Reclining back in his chair, Owen inwardly questioned himself: "Why didn't this bother me before? Am I blind, ignorant, or both? What's wrong with me?"

Though he had been going to bed earlier than normal, his suspicions about Lia had exhausted him. His body got the sleep it needed, but his mind did not get the rest it needed. His imagination had him running scenarios around the clock trying to figure out Lia's end game. The energy he had once put into taking care of Lia was now diverted to catching her. Even his efforts to catch her reflected the enabling tendency of the host archetype. Owen did not want to hold her accountable for any indiscretions she may have committed because whatever she was caught up in, he was sure she was a victim in need of rescue, not an accountable adult.

The idea that his wife was a damsel-in-distress surfaced the first time they met. Despite being a striking 5'11½" in flats, Lia got Owen's attention when she fled the room crying while they were watching a movie in their upper-level Psych class. A few moments passed and it was clear to Owen that the always engaging and upbeat girl had experienced some sort of meltdown. He went out to the quad in search of her. When he caught up to Lia she told him how she'd just been worked over by her mixed-message sending, wannabe player of a boyfriend. Thinking she needed a friend to help lift her spirits, he made up his mind on the spot it was going to be him. In Owen's world being a friend meant anticipating and taking care of every need. The only relationship he had with any reciprocity to it was his relationship with Sage, and even their relationship had its own unique dynamics. At first, Owen's eagerness to be there for her made Lia uncomfortable. But once the awkwardness faded, Lia came to enjoy and expect the attention.

Owen rubbed his temples as he closed his eyes, and said aloud, "And I have been taking care of her ever since."

According to Coach Perkins, in a parasitic relationship, one partner was a parasite and the other the host. Owen went over the notes he jotted down under the heading: Criteria of a Parasite and began to make notes in the margins:

—unstable (check), chaotic (check), making everything about their needs and everyone else's responsibilities (check, check and double check).

"Well, we know who the parasite in the relationship is," he murmured. Next to the definition Owen wrote "LB" followed by a star.

Feeling emasculated at the thought that if Lia was a parasite, he might be the host, his inner conversations grew more intense. "I know I'm not the hardest brotha on the block, but I'm nobody's punk. Or am I? Am I a punk? Is that how Lia sees me? Is that why she's coming home later and later?" His eyes feel to Coach Perkins's description of a host: over accommodating (yep), overwhelmed (uh huh), overextended (absolutely), burnt-out (most definitely).

His hand shook as he wrote the initials "O.B." next to "Host" and drew a circle around it. "I guess the shoe fits," he said aloud, releasing a dejected sigh. Rubbing his eyes, he snapped off the lights. "Damn!" he exclaimed as he headed down the hallway.

Upon entering the room where he and Lia had shared so many loving nights, his eyes fell to the bed. Planting himself face down on the plush comforter he wondered aloud: "Where the heck could she be?" The notion the night had just begun seeped to the surface of his consciousness. His eyes rolled back and he drifted off to sleep.

CHAPTER SIX

Something Is Up

When the lane departure warning system on Lia's Lexus LS informed her she was drifting, it just as easily could have been her conscience letting her know how much her personal life had drifted over the past six weeks. Heading home to a husband who had been waiting up hours for her, Lia had spent the evening in a hotel with a man she'd waited years for.

The insistent dinging of the alarm awakened her from the trance, interrupting the reminiscing about her time with "her man." "Whew, almost missed my exit," Lia said as she hit the turn signal and dug the heel of her Baretta Studded Red Sole pump into the accelerator. The 430 plus horsepower hybrid engine cleared its throat and leaped from the fast lane of the 405 to the Sunset exit, masking the impulsivity of the driver. From the BMW trailing her, she looked like a woman in control, making moves.

"Mmm...Did I tell him I'd be meeting a client or that I had an event to go to?" Lia thought. She and Owen talked so infrequently it was hard for her to to keep her stories straight.

Whatever it was it was quick and to the point. In the beginning, the lies were unnecessarily elaborate. Whenever someone asked Owen if worried about guys hitting on his wife, he laughed. The thought of Lia having an affair never entered his mind. But not because men didn't find her attractive—they did. At a hair under six feet, with a fitness model's body, all wrapped in Texas femininity and approachable class, Lia had no problem getting men to notice her. Owen laughed because he believed she lacked the initiative and follow-up necessary to pull off an affair. Until today, only four things had ever held his wife's attention for more than a nanosecond: the Dallas Cowboys, school, fashion, and social media.

The guilt she once felt following her rendezvous with Casey had been replaced by an indifferent stream of lies, she now told with little to no effort. At this point she didn't even care if they made sense. The hardening of her heart toward Owen had made her reckless. As she had done in the past, she'd adapted. The only sin her conscience was bothered by was her lack of feeling guilty. Countless details meant limitless opportunities to forget what was said. It was much better to be brief.

Headed north on Sepulveda, she checked her gas gauge before making the left onto Casiano Rd. There was half a tank remaining. *"Gotta love these hybrids,"* she thought. The LS wasn't just any Lexus, it was the $119,000 crown-jewel of Lexus luxury and technology. And being a hybrid gave her hippy-elite clients the impression she was concerned about the environment. Before buying it she caught a lot of flak for driving a Range Rover with its obnoxious gas mileage. The day luxury car companies started making hybrids she jumped for joy. Good gas mileage meant fewer trips to the gas station, a plus when you have as much going on as Lia did with the public relations firm. She had begun to attract some serious clientele while trying at the same time to keep her man happy, and her husband in the dark. There was precious little time for anything else.

With her game plan set, Lia pulled into the driveway.

Her strategy was to hit the door with a flash bang of complaints about having to work late, traffic and such. She reasoned that before Owen could collect himself enough to ask where she'd been, she could pin him down with a series of complaints about how unsupported she felt. "He'll never know what hit him," she mused to herself.

CHAPTER SEVEN

The Discovery Phase

Like a parent waiting for a child who'd miss their curfew after borrowing the car, Owen awoke between the second and third beep letting him know Lia was home. He rolled over to look at the clock to take note of the time—a record at 2:40 a.m. "I don't have the energy to deal with this tonight," Owen said to himself, turning back on his side.

Convinced it was better to handle things in the light of day Owen fell back to sleep. A few minutes later he was startled by a whoosh-thump noise that sounded like a light saber being fired up down the hall. The house groaned and sputtered until the water heater accepted its fate and delivered warm water to the far end of the house.

His stomach sank just as he jumped out of bed at the realization there only one reason Lia would need to take a shower in one of the guest rooms before coming to bed, and it wasn't because she didn't want to wake him.

"Oh, hell no! Un-freaking-believable! Un-freaking-be-believable!" Owen repeated while making his way down the hall where he was sure Lia was washing away her evening's indiscretions.

"I may be a host, but I'm not going to be punked in my own home," Owen thought.

He'd barely grasped the doorknob when he heard Lia's phone buzz. He hesitated for a moment. Would she tell the truth if he confronted her? She obviously hadn't been a portrait of honesty throughout their marriage. Owen did a U-turn back up the hallway. He squinted, scanning the darkness for

her purse. Before the next message could come through he entered her security code: TXSGRL.

"Sweet dreams Lili. Maybe next time you can work it where we can do breakfast?" The speech bubble said mocking him. Even though Owen didn't recognize the number, there was just one person who called his wife "Lili"—her ex, Casey Lynch. The guy she had an on-and-off again situation with before she and Owen met.

Overwhelmed, Owen braced himself against the wall and staggered to the couch.

He tried to wrap his mind around it. Hadn't Casey dogged her out her first two years of college? By the time Casey was finished with Lia, she was questioning her sanity. "There's no way she would..." he muttered aloud.

Owen cocked back his arm, intending to smash her phone against the bathroom door where the shower was running, but his "host" tendencies surfaced. He lowered his arm. *"Maybe I'm overreacting? There may be someone else who calls her Lili— perhaps someone innocent,"* he thought, giving her the benefit of the doubt. While trying to gather himself he considered giving her a chance to explain before he jumping to a bunch of unfounded conclusions. As the last ounce of fight drained out of Owen's heart he scrolled through the thread of texts trying to identify this unknown person.

There it was. Right before his eyes was a six-week thread documenting all the lurid details of Lia's entire affair with her ex-boyfriend Casey.

Mt me at the Grove.

> I'll see you there; I can't wait.

> You deserve the best. Need u to come b4 6:30

> I can't. He's still here.

>Ditch him. U know what to do.

Scrolling through the texts, it was clear to Owen that Casey was the culprit, and he was the "him" who got ditched.

On the verge of tears, Owen slumped down to the hard-wood floor he'd recently restored at Lia's insistence.

"What the hell," Owen mumbled, "I'm screwed."

Lia opened the bathroom door and strode confidently toward her bedroom drying the huge mounds of curls on her head with an oversized Turkish cotton bath towel.

"Good, he's still sleeping," Lia thought, believe it was Owen snoring she heard as she came through the door. Convinced he was none the wiser, she'd planned to slip into bed unnoticed, then claim she had gotten home around 12:30 or so. Still there was a part of her that wanted to wake Owen so she could confront him about not checking on her or waiting up—all things he did gladly prior to this season of their marriage.

With the covers tossed and the room dark, it took a minute for her to realize the bed was empty.

"Where is he? His car was out front when I pulled up..." With the flick of the switch the recently installed LED lighting illuminated every corner of the room. Terror- struck by the loss of cover the darkness provided, Lia spun around to see Owen filling the doorway. He emanated a presence considerably larger than his slender 5'7" frame would warrant.

"Don't you know what's done in the dark eventually comes to light?" Owen said as he tossed her phone past her and onto the bed. His tone was menacing.

"What the heck is wrong with you? Are you trying to give me a heart attack?" she gasped.

It took her a moment to realize what was happening before the abandonment issues from childhood kicked in. She wanted to play it cool, but couldn't. The coldness permeating Owen's being drew out a fight in the usually passive Lia, which was as rare as a politician admitting to lying in order to get elected. Like a mongoose staring down a cobra, Lia was in survival mode and it was time to fight. She told herself that he couldn't possibly know everything.

"Explain," he said, pointing to the phone partially hidden by the comforter.

"Explain what? You're the one who ought to explain. Sneaking up on people in the dark."

"Me sneaking up on you? You're the one trying to wash off another man's funk at 2:40 in the morning before trying to creep into bed with your husband," Owen countered, pointing at her.

"What did you just call me?" she shot back even though Owen had not called her anything.

Not backing down, Owen glared back at her in defiance.

"Oh no, don't go mute on me now. If you are man enough to come in here all Seal Team Six on me, then man-up and say what you got to say. But watch your step little man because I am not the only one in this marriage who been keeping secrets."

Paralyzed by rage over the "little man" comment, he continued his stare down through blood-shot hazel eyes.

"I'm going to bed. It's late, I'm tired, and you're just being trifling," Lia blustered, breaking the stalemate between them.

Owen brushed past her, grabbed the phone off the bed, navigated to her messages, then shoved it in her face. "So, this is what you mean when you say you have to put in extra work? You've been screwing around behind my back with that good-for-nothing ex of yours. Casey Lynch is the reason you've been ghost around this house isn't he? Admit it!" Owen yelled, pushing the phone closer to her face.

Lia slapped the phone out of his hand causing it to sail across the room where it crashed to the floor. Her face contorted like a witch casting an evil spell as she pointed a finger at him and roared: "Don't you ever shove nothing in my face! What the hell is wrong with you?" Taking a step back she continued, "You want to know what's been happening? Then, open your damn eyes! While you've been focused on at-risk kids at The Center, you've completely ignored our at-risk marriage, so someone picked up the slack. What did you think would happen when you're never around? You got time for everyone else—your family, friends, the kids at The Center—but when it comes to me it's 'Sorry, change of plans,' 'Something came up.' What? You didn't think I'd eventually come up with a plan of my own? Oh, and don't get me started on the all-female, all blond interns with their Stepford wives-in-training flow. Looking like sister wives. What's up with that?"

"I didn't think your backup plan would include acting like some trailer park skank from *The Jerry Springer Show*," Owen responded.

"How else am I supposed to act when I'm treated like a prostitute by my own husband? You only touch me on the very rare occasions when you want sex. We only talk when you're complaining, mostly about money. Aside from the occasional beat down, which uh...you know better to even try it, what's the difference between the way you treat me and the way a ho gets treated by her pimp? Think about it. When's the last time you took me somewhere special or bought me something nice to show me how much you love me—not to prove to yourself how loving you are?"

Owen stepped back and glared at her. "Wow," he said under his breath. Coach Perkins was right. He was a full on host. Owen spun toward the closet with Lia hot on his tail. He pulled out a garment bag and the small carry-on he used for business trips and threw them on the bed. Dashing back to the closet, he quickly emerged with enough clothes in his arms to last several days.

Lia watched Owen stuff the clothes into his garment bag. Blinded by her adrenaline-fueled rage, it hadn't dawned on her that he was packing to leave. Ever since they met in college he had always been there for her no matter how she treated him. Tonight was different. Something had broken in him. When he emerged from the closet the second time, he had two things in his hands that let Lia know he was serious: his toiletries bag and his emergency credit cards. She hovered over him as he sat down at the foot of the bed to put on his shoes.

"And where do you think you are going this late at night?" she demanded. "So that's it? The conversation gets a little rough, and you bail on me?" she mocked.

He ignored her as he bent over to tie his shoes. When he'd finished he looked up and calming said, "Whatever you need to tell yourself to be the victim in this." Rising to his feet, he grabbed his bags and headed toward the front door. As Owen passed their wedding picture hanging on the wall in the hallway, he paused long enough to put his fist right through it. The last sounds Lia heard was Owen cursing as he slammed the door, followed by the sound of rubber being laid down in the driveway.

"Well, that didn't go as planned," Lia said with a shrug. Even though her husband was barely out the driveway all Lia could think about was Owen leaving the front door unlocked, the fact he took her car and the prospect of moving Casey in.

Lia picked up her phone to see whether it was damaged. Not only was she tired, but tomorrow was going to be a long day. Her fingers flew across the keypad.

Babe, he knows.

> Good. No more sneaking around.

CHAPTER EIGHT

Sage and Roman Become Collateral Damage

Sage was halfway through her cooldown on the elliptical when her phone started its spastic dance. She glanced at the clock on the wall—4:47 a.m. *"Must be someone from corporate,"* she thought. After a slight hesitation, she grabbed her phone.

"It's official," the text from Owen read. Intuitively, she knew what he meant. Stepping off the elliptical with two minutes and forty-seven seconds left on her cool down, her thumbs flew into action.

>"What happened?"

>"She came in at 2:40 this morning. Headed straight for the guest room shower to wash off the filth. Her phone blew up. I check it and there it was. "

>"Did you confront her?"

>"Yes. It got ugly."

>"Let me call you from the car in 30 minutes."

>"K."

#

Roman sat up in bed when he heard the front door. All Trojan Man cared about was Sage "keeping that body right" as he put it. "I am not trying to be married to one of your aunts," he would say when she over did it on the sweets. On the other hand, he didn't like the idea of his wife leaving the house before sunrise just to work out, which explained why he insisted they move into a gated community with a modern gym.

As she entered the room, Roman held his arms out motioning her to give him a hug. The glimmer in his eyes, the turned-up smile on his face, and the strategically turned down sheets suggested he wanted more than a hug.

Sage darted to the right and headed directly for the bathroom. "I don't have time to fool around with you this morning, Mr. Man. A sister got to get to work," she tossed the words over her shoulder in a stern yet flirtatious voice.

"All I want is a hug. Can't a brother get just one hug?"

Sage considered granting his request until she realized the non-early rising Roman managed to take a shower, shave, brush his teeth, and straighten up the room while she was gone. Definite signs a brother wanted more than "just one hug." Not wanting to say no to her husband yet frantic to call Owen, she decided the best thing to do was to tell Roman what was going on.

Reticently she walked toward the bed. The moment they made eye contact he could tell something was up. The last time he'd seen anything close to the look in her eyes she was confronting him about having an affair with a woman named Sheila. Despite Sage's willingness to take him back, and the reality that he'd been faithful to her since then, he continued to think of himself as a cheater. As she drew closer, he scrolled through every imaginable scenario that might be a problem. Was he about to be falsely accused? Had someone from his past resurfaced?

"Well, it's official," she spoke softly. "Last night, Owen found out his gold digging wife has been cheating on him."

"Man, that's a shame," Roman said. The mix of relief and earnestness in his tone caught Sage off guard. Again, he extended his arms for a hug. This time he wasn't trying to meet his needs, he was attempting to meet hers.

"Are you okay?" Roman whispered, holding her in his arms.

For the next 20 minutes, Sage lay in his arms downloading all the random thoughts and emotions flowing through her head as he just held her and listened. Caught in the blissful intimacy of a moment rarely shared between the two of them, Sage forgot she'd left Owen hanging.

"Oh my God," Sage spurted out. "I got to go!"

She bolted for the bathroom. Halfway there she made a sharp pivot back towards the bed, kissed the dumbfounded Roman on the forehead, and then made a mad dash for the shower.

"I don't want to leave Owen hanging. I told him I'd call him in thirty minutes, forty minutes ago!" she yelled over the running water.

Roman sat up on the bed surrounded by decorative pillows of every imaginable shape, size and firmness. They gave no comfort. He wondered what effect Lia's affair and Owen's despair would have on his on-the-mend relationship. He worried that watching Owen go through the discovery phase might change Sage's outlook about their marriage. Would she question the viability of her own marriage? Would it wipe out all the progress the two of them had made?

Even more distressing was how his assessment of the parasitic dynamic between Sage and Owen would play itself out. If there was one concept Roman learned from Coach Perkins that he clearly grasped and assimilated, it was an understanding of the three-archetypical relationships of the Predatorial, Parasitic, and Partnerships.

Not only did it give him clarity about his marriage—which he realized was predatorial considering the level of antagonistic control exhibited between, he and Sage— it also gave him insight into other relationship structures. He could see the predation between coaches and players, and the parasitic bond between the NCAA and athletes, as well as colleges and their alumni.

Over the past four months, Roman had observed and reflected on the interactions between his wife and her cousin–brother–best friend. He'd noticed the antagonism built around the dual themes of needs and responsibilities. Namely, Owen's parasitic neediness coupled with Sage's endless array of responsibilities of the host to meet those needs. He concluded that Sage and Owen's relationship was impenetrably parasitic.

Their relationship was a powerless exercise of one-sided love, driven by a narrative steeped in victimology that dated back to their childhood when Sage's father, a Marine Sergeant Major gave her the command to "keep an eye on your younger cousin. He's family." Eager to please her father, the newly commissioned Sage took on the role of the surrogate big sister/mom with all due diligence. An assignment Roman recognized had expanded in their adulthood to include his wife's management of Owen's personal and professional relationships.

Though Owen loved Sage a great deal, his love for her remained powerless because it never manifested itself in mutual accountability. Roman was aware of Owen's proclivity for allowing Sage to take on the emotional burden of dealing with the problems he didn't want to talk about, particularly those about Lia.

With his eyes mindlessly fixed on the black screen of the seventy-inch TV monitor on the wall, the picture in Roman's head was coming into focus. Sage was about to head down another rabbit hole with Owen. A journey that would mean neglecting the work she needed to do in their marriage.

The more time Roman spent ruminating, the more anxious he became. To relieve the emptiness he felt in the pit of his stomach, and the dryness inside his mouth, he tried to re-engage Sage as she appeared from the bathroom. But it was too late, Sage was already in her "Hurry-up No Huddle Offense," a term Roman borrowed from the world of football to describe the frenzied, no time to talk, abrasive, "I've got to go" single-mindedness that possessed she whenever she went into mission mode. Before Roman could produce enough saliva to speak, she was on her way out the door.

"I'll bring you to speed tonight when I get home. Love you. Bye," Sage said, cutting off the lights and exiting the room as though it were empty.

Roman sat on the edge of the bed in the darkened room. Emptiness gave way to the dull ache of impending trouble ahead. His mindless stare became a fixed gaze. Concern for their marriage had morphed into seething anger, but it was not directed at Sage as one would imagine. No. Roman's anger was directed at himself. He'd let his guard down. The rejection and shame he felt that very moment came from within. He had committed an act of self-treason.

"This is what happens when you're vulnerable. You get punked! he reasoned with himself.

#

Oblivious to the emotional state she had left Roman in, Sage barely gave her phone enough time to sync with her car audio system before she'd issued the command "Call Owen's cell." Before the phone could ring on her end, Owen picked up.

"Hey, you alone?"

"Yep."

"Good...I wouldn't want to give Roman another reason to clown me."

"It's not like that. When I told him he genuinely seemed grieved."

"You told him already? I wanted to keep this between you and me."

"Yes, I had too. It's a long story."

"So, what did he have to say about it?"

"That's too bad."

"What else did he have to say?"

"Nothing, he asked if you were all right, then asked if I was all right."

"That's it? "Roman the Orator" didn't have anything else to say?"

"Come to think of it, no. All he did was listen," Sage said wistfully.

"Wow."

"Why are you so fixated on what Roman had to say?"

"No reason," Owen said. He didn't want to disclose his respect for Roman's professionalism even though he thought Roman was a dog.

"Enough about Roman. Tell me what happened with Lia."

Owen recited the whole sordid mess.

By the time Owen finished, Sage was pulling into the parking structure of her office building. "I've got to get to work. We'll have lunch so we can do some more processing." Processing was Sage-speak for rehearsing the countless reasons why he and Lia should have never married in the first place.

Out of a small measure of embarrassment, and partly to punish Sage for telling Roman, but unable to say no, Owen said. "Let me check my schedule. I will call you later."

#

He was still fuming when the phone in Sage's office rang for the third time. Rather than holding his growing resentment about the dismissive way he felt handled earlier until she got home, he was calling to allay his concerns about the effect Owen and Lia's situation might have on their fragile relationship.

"Hey Honey, can't talk. Got a lot of work. What do you need?" her hurried tone on the other end of the line only stoked his resentment.

"Can we do lunch? I need to run some stuff by you," he asked, with as much meekness as he could muster. Roman was trying to strike a balance between sharing his heart and sounding like a punk.

"As much as I love seeing your handsome face and that chiseled body, I can't. I want to leave my schedule open in case Owen wants to do lunch to do some more processing. You know how he depends on me when it comes to his relationships. Oh, you won't believe how Lia reacted when Owen confronted her. It's so next level you won't believe it."

When Roman didn't respond, Sage broke the awkward silence. "Is that it? Because I've got to go. I've got work to do."

"Yeah, I guess," Roman said. He struggled to maintain his composure. What Sage meant as a compliment made him feel objectified. Her focus on his looks was well-meaning, but it only made things worse.

"Okay, got to go. Love you. See you tonight." Sage hung up the phone unaware of the Hulk-like rage stirring in Roman.

CHAPTER NINE

Roman Reaches Out
to Coach Perkins

Roman pressed the home button on his phone, "Call Coach Perkins" he said, careful to take some of the boom out of his voice. Roman never texted Coach because he thought it disrespectful. In fact, he never called him "Coach." It was Coach Perkins or sir, always.

"Hey Coach Perkins, do you have any time for me this afternoon? I need to bounce some stuff off you."

"Sure, if you're down to make a few runs with me, we can talk in the car."

"No problem, I wasn't going into work."

"Great. Meet me at my house in, say, forty-five minutes?"

"Okay see you then, sir...and thanks."

"No problem, Big Man. Oh and leave the Trojan gear at home. I want to keep this run under the radar."

It wasn't hard for Roman to guess they were going to roll through the O.C. at some point, and Coach Perkins did not want their time together compromised by the untold number of middle-aged, Trojan faithfuls living in Orange County. Being with Roman in Trojan gear in the O.C. was like watching an episode of Shark Week. First, they pick up the scent, then they gather and the next thing you know you have got a full-on feeding frenzy, grown men body checking one another to get a selfie with Trojan royalty.

"Things are finally looking up," Roman said, as he holstered his phone.

Making a run with Coach meant it was more than a road trip. It was a therapeutic journey. The first time they met,

Coach invited Roman on one of his epic runs. He discovered Coach's vehicle was more of an office. The passenger seat served as the chair where a therapist would typically direct you to sit in by saying, "Make yourself comfortable," right before things get real uncomfortable. During these three to four, sometimes five-hour road trips, Coach Perkins helped Roman, and others like him, overcome the messes they had made of their marriages. He called it "changing the narrative."

"Yeah, this is just what the doctor ordered," Roman nodded in approval.

#

Unaware of the anger and rejection fermenting in Roman's heart, Sage texted him to let him know she might be late in anticipation of hooking up with her cousin after work since they did not have a chance to do lunch. Unfortunately, Roman didn't receive Sage's message as the act of consideration she intended it to be. Quite the opposite, he went into internal dialogue overdrive.

"First she blows off lunch with me for a lunch date that didn't even happen. Now she's putting our marriage on hold for dinner with her boy Owen. What? Am I'm supposed to wait by the phone and..." he started to text then deleted it. *"I knew she was going to take her eye off the ball,"* he thought. *"She married the wrong brotha if she thinks I'm going to sit around waiting for her like I'm some punk while she plays Rescue Ranger to a grown man who can't handle his business. Oh, I don't think so – she must be crazy. I don't know what she's thinking...I don't have to eat alone. I got plenty of female friends with husband issues who would love have dinner with a brotha."* In the middle of the diatribe going on in his head, his phone flashed a message across the screen reminding him to breathe. It was a meditation app he'd installed last week to prompt him to meditate in the mornings.

But Roman was all too familiar with the toxic cocktail of emotions brewing in his heart. He knew he needed something a little stronger than deep breathing to process what he was feeling. He needed to get with someone who could help him sort things out before "Trojan Man" decided it was time to make someone pay for his feelings of rejection.

#

Sage tapped the home button on her phone. It was close to lunch and she still hadn't heard from Owen.

"Are you okay? What's up with lunch? Are we still on?" Knowing Owen's inability to turn down a free meal she button the text with: "My treat."

Forty-five minutes later , the response came: "I've been busy all morning. Let's reschedule."

"What are you doing after work? We could hook up then."

"Let me check my schedule," he replied in a move he employed whenever he wanted to punish someone out of anger or avoid them out of shame. It wasn't even midday, and he had used this strategy on Sage twice. The first-time Owen used this strategy to avoid conflict with Sage was during his courtship and subsequent marriage to Lia. It was his way to prevent the shame and anger he was made to feel for marrying someone who had not received the Bryant women's stamp of approval. During a Bryant event, Roman stayed long enough to engage anyone he and Owen's father dubbed Lia the "anti- Sage."

Despite being almost six-foot-tall tall, and having a yoga fit physique without ever taxing a sweat gland, Lia did not have the confidence of a model like Sage. Her matching dark maple brown skin-tone, hair, and eyes gave her a monotone look that she could quickly convert from unassuming to exotic with a couple of passes of her fingers through her thickset naturally curly hair, a few swipes of her Dior "Wonderland" lip gloss to her full lips, and several strokes of MAC "Purple Times Nine" eyes shadow to make her lips shimmer and eyes pop. Her thick, yet refined Texas accent coupled with her guy-friendly, easy going manner ingratiated her to everyone she met except the Bryant women. All but one of them found Lia to be a little too country for their taste. The lone holdout was Sage's mother. It was Sage's mother's identification with Lia (not spite as Sage assumed) that fueled Mrs. Bryant's fondness for Lia. She was also the only other Bryant woman in the family who knew what it was like to take on the burden of the Bryant name.

CHAPTER TEN

Flashback to the First Meeting
With Coach Perkins

For a second Roman thought he had parked in front of the wrong house when he spotted a root beer brown truck backed up against the garage door at the end of the long driveway. "He did it," Roman thought when he saw the new registration sticker on the window. Every time they passed a quad cab on one of their runs, Coach would threaten to buy one before talking himself out of it with a bevy of reasons—too much gas, my kids are almost grown, no one needs a truck as big a yacht, etc. In Roman's eyes, it was the one area in Coach Perkins's life he seemed indecisive, until today.

Once past the gigantic steel sculpture in the driveway, Roman's heart began to warm in anticipation of the iron-like "I got you" embrace awaiting him on the other side of the door. From the first time Roman met Coach Perkins he's been greeted with a big hug along with whispers of encouragement: "Welcome to my home," "Good to see you," "You look well," or a "Hang in there." The words were sweet, refreshing, and always spoken in due season.

He first met Coach Perkins while working to recruit his son, Jr. Even then Coach Perkins embraced him as though he was family and whispered, "Welcome to my home, young man." Eleven months later, Roman would tell you those were the most significant words a man had ever said to him, not because it led to him landing a five-star recruit, but because of the impact a routine business trip would ultimately have on his personal life.

In the middle of Roman's pitch to the family Coach

Perkins told Roman, "I need you to make a run with me." The next thing he knew the two of them were headed down the highway. With a slight lean in his seat, his left wrist resting casually on the steering wheel and eyes firmly fixed on the road, Coach talked to Roman without taking his eyes off the road.

"Roman, how long have you been a Trojan?" he asked.

"About five years as a player, three years as a Graduate Assistant, and nine years as a scout slash recruiter."

Coach Perkins paused for a moment. "What's that, about eighteen years you've devoted to helping the Trojans build a championship program?"

"Yes, sir," Roman responded, confused.

"Eighteen years, that's a long time to devote to one cause."

"Yes, sir," said Roman. He tried not to show that he was still unsure where the conversation was going.

"What do you think I have been doing for the past eighteen years?"

"Building your business, sir," his bewilderment rapidly growing.

"No, like you I've spent the last eighteen years building a championship program of my own."

"Your consulting firm, sir?" Roman ventured.

"Roman, I have spent the last eighteen years training my son to be a champion—as a son, student, athlete, citizen, man, a potential husband, and father. In the same way, you've walked, talked, and dreamed Trojan football for the past eighteen years, I've spent the last eighteen years training Jr. to become a man I would be pleased to call "son," and a person his family could be proud of."

"Do you understand what I am saying?" he asked, taking his eyes off the road briefly to search his passenger's face. Roman nodded with hesitancy and replied, "I think so, sir..."

"Let me explain it this way. You're recruiting my son because you believe he is a good fit for your defensive scheme as well as your program. What I'm looking for is the same thing, a football program compatible with my program. You follow me, Roman?"

"Yes sir," Roman said. "You are looking for a school where he can develop both as a player and as a man."

"Exactly."

"Coach Perkins, let me assure you, if Jr. signs with us I will personally look out for him," Roman said. His confidence fully restored.

"Do I have your personal word on that?"

"Yes sir, you have my personal word."

"Don't take this wrong young man, but how do I know if I can trust you? How do I know if your word means anything? How do I know if you're the type of man who'll say anything to get what he wants?"

"Sir, in my profession your word is all you have. If I say I am going to do something, then I am going to do it. I have to. This job is how I put food on the table and clothes on my back. You can check with any of the parents or players I have recruited. I've delivered on every promise I've made. You can even check with other recruiters. Word is bond with me."

"I appreciate your professional integrity, but that's not what you promised. You said you would take a personal interest in my son, and that I had your personal word on that. For that, I'd need a personal reference from somebody with intimate knowledge of how you handle people in your personal and private life, someone like say your wife. I have spent the past eighteen years surrounding my son with men and women who took a personal interest in him. No offense but I am not about to blow that on smooth talking brother who looks good in a game day Polo shirt. So Roman, here's the five-star question: If I called your wife right now and asked her how well I could trust you based on the way you have handled her heart, how would she answer?"

Like a car barreling down the highway that had drifted across the median into oncoming traffic, Roman's personal and private worlds slammed into one another. With the sudden fury of a head-on collision the conversation went from a simple dialogue to horrifying spectacle. They were no longer talking about the character and athletic skills of an eighteen-year-old, high school football player. With one question, the conversation turned into a discussion about a lot of things. They were now talking about the character and relationship skills of a full-grown man in his mid-thirties, what it meant to be a husband, honor, real love, disappointment, unfulfilled potential, and a whole host of issues that, in truth, turned out to be a conversation about one thing– manhood.

Roman had no problem selling the program, but selling himself was another matter. Caught off guard by the ease with which Coach Perkins put the spotlight on his personal life, he could do nothing but sit there dumbfounded. He stared down the road with an uneasy grin on his face and his 6'5" frame hollowed out like a jack-o-lantern. It was trick or treat come early for Roman.

Coach Perkins let the big man steep in a state of self-awareness for a full ten minutes before he broke the silence.

"Am I to assume by your current body language and lack of response that Mrs. Cole would not give you a ringing endorsement?"

Roman descended deeper into his seat and sighed, "Let's just say I haven't put the same effort into my home as I've put into building a championship program on the football field."

"Why not?"

Still struggling to wrap his head around what just happened, Roman began to writhe in his seat. "It's complicated, sir," was all he could get out.

"What does that mean?" Coach Perkins asked, pressing Roman for a more enlightened answer. "Does Mrs. Cole love you? Do you love her? Is she good to you? Does she take good care of you?"

"All the above, sir."

"Then what's so complicated? How hard can it be to be a

good husband to a good wife, unless that's not what's in your heart? Is it?"

"Yes sir, it is. At least, I think it is."

"Then why isn't it happening, young man?"

"Like I said, sir, it's complicated."

"But why is it complicated? That's the question you need to answer for yourself."

"It just is sir. It just is," Roman mutters, now staring out the passenger window.

Coach Perkins then informed Roman that his son would not be joining the Trojan family in the summer.

"Not because your wife wouldn't vouch for you as a husband. Heck, a lot of wives wouldn't. Early in my marriage my wife wouldn't have vouched for my character, for different reasons I suspect. Young man, I don't have a problem with a person who makes mistakes in his personal life. I don't do morality I do opportunity. What I have an issue with is the fact that your wife is giving you a chance to get it right, and all you're doing with the opportunity is making excuses. And you don't even want to put the work in to identify the problem. I'm sorry, but I can't place my son in the hands of a man who makes excuses when he should be making changes. I need to know I'm placing my son in the hands of someone who is willing to put in work for the people in their care. Not to be too harsh young man, but it's time to put away childish things and start putting in the work necessary to save your marriage."

For the rest of the ride the two men sat in silence intermittently interrupted by Coach Perkins singing a combo of Gospel and 70s funk songs under his breath. Upon arrival back at the Perkins home, Roman bolted from the car. In the time it took him to lay his jacket on the back seat of his SUV, the older man was standing behind him.

When Roman extended his hand, Coach Perkins put his arms around him and drew him into an embrace and uttered the words that changed Romans life: "It's not complicated young man—it's just scary. And you don't want to do the scary that comes with doing right."

Loosening his embrace, Coach Perkins then grabbed Roman by the arms before he could turn away. Fatherly concern was on his face as he peered into the towering man's eyes. It was as though he were looking past his shame-riddled, damaged soul.

"You've run out of time to grow up. It is time to step up," he said firmly.

"Yes sir," Roman said as he climbed into his gold-colored SUV.

CHAPTER ELEVEN

Coach Perkins Schools Roman
On Difficult Conversations

"Boy, a lot sure has changed since that first ride," Roman thought, as he strode up the Perkins' walkway. The tearing sound of the weather seal on the front door brought him back to the moment. Although the 6' 5" former athlete stood three inches taller than Coach Perkins, he felt small in his presence. Not in a shaming way you might expect given the way their first encounter ended, but in the way a son's perception of his father looms large in his psyche. In the middle of their embrace, Coach Perkins whispered, "No need to get discouraged, God is still in control. Nothing's changed. The struggle is a part of the process."

"I know," Roman whispered back. He turned his attention to the new whip in the driveway. "So you finally broke down and did it. Rims, grille, and all," he said with approval and amazement.

"Yes I did," said Coach Perkins, as a Cheshire Cat grin broke out on his face.

"What about the gas, the size, the insurance?" Roman mocked.

Quick on his feet as ever, Coach Perkins poked back playfully with: "I discovered it wasn't complicated, it was just scary."

"Touché," Roman laughed. "Why did you back into the driveway? Trying to show off the chrome grille to the neighbors, huh?" he teased.

"No, I was trying to spare you some embarrassment when you pulled up."

"What do you mean?" Roman said, taking the bait.

"Look at the back window."

Roman read the sticker prominently displayed on the back windshield: "Cardinal Dad. Oh man, that's cold," he shook his head.

"Hey, I didn't want that to be the first thing you saw when you pulled up," Coach Perkins said with an "I gotcha you" grin on his face. "It is also one of the reasons why I didn't want you wearing your Trojan gear. We wouldn't want anybody posting pictures of you wearing Trojan gear rolling in a Cardinal truck."

"You know you're wrong."

"What's wrong is what those stickers cost. I'm learning there is an enormous difference between a full-ride and a free ride. What's up with all the hidden fees they never tell you about?" Coach Perkins said, suddenly serious.

"I would ask you how Jr. is doing there, but you already know I keep close tabs on him."

"Sounds like you've taken a personal interest in my son."

"Yes sir, I got to honor my word, especially when his dad took a personal interest in me."

"You ready to roll?"

"Yes sir, let's do it."

Coach Perkins hung a left out the driveway towards the freeway.

#

With the 400+hp engine tamed by the cruise control, the new plush leather "therapy chair", Coach Perkins 15 minutes into his customary gangster lean, and the road clear for miles, it was time to get down to business.

"So, what's going on in Roman and Sage's world? Coach Perkins asked, catching Roman off guard.

"How did you know it was about Sage and me?"

"Because it's the only time you use the 'Bat Signal.' That's not a criticism, it's a compliment."

"Thanks...I guess."

"So tell me what's going on?" The coach was nothing if not direct.

"Well...last night...It was this morning..." Roman searched for the right words. "Sage found out her cousin Owen's wife has been cheating on him. She's gone into 'got to be there for Owen crisis mode,' which means our marriage gets tossed aside like last year's Christmas presents so she can be there for him," Roman rubbed his head as his voice faded.

"Have you talked to her about it?" There was no judgment in his confidant's "let me state the obvious" tone.

"I tried to...twice. But she's already gone into her 'hurry-up, no-huddle offense.' You know how she gets."

"Yes, I do. I also understand how you respond to feeling neglected, and that's not a good look either. First you withdraw, and then you start to nurture your pain until it becomes a full-grown grievance. Then presto, it's the return of the Trojan Man."

"Mm...Yeah, you're right, but..." Roman sighed.

Seeing that Roman was about to go victim on him, Coach Perkins played the "Son card." Whenever it reached the point where he thought a man needed to step-up, a combination of the Brooklyn and the father in Coach Perkins would bubble to the surface, and he'd call a brother "son."

"C'mon son, you got to talk to her. Bottom line is neither of you can afford to camp out in that neglected and abandon space you retreat to."

"Got it," Roman answered, rubbing his hand from the top of his head down his face.

"So how do I have this conversation with her when I don't think I have the right to ask her to stand down? Owen was the one who had her back when she was dealing with the hell I put her through? How do I say: 'Sorry about your cousin, but I need you to keep your eye on the ball'? How do I say something so self-serving without coming off as selfish and insensitive?" Roman asked.

"You can't. There's no way you're going to avoid looking selfish and insensitive. Still, it doesn't mean what you have to say is not valid, necessary, and loving. The fact she may struggle with it is on her; the fact you think you don't have the right to ask is the cost of your past behavior. Look, the goal is not to make yourself appear loving and sensitive, the goal is to be sensitive even when it sounds unloving and insensitive. There is no smooth way to do rough, no cute way to do ugly, and no easy way to do hard. Roman, it's not about appearance, it's about authenticity."

"Yeah, but what if I get frustrated...say something wrong... Or the situation escalates and gets out of hand, you know...?" Roman countered.

"Then the two of you will have to grind it out until the two of you figure it out like every other couple fighting to make their marriage work. Working through issues in a hostile, chaotic, environment is the hard work people say they know it takes to make a marriage work but usually aren't prepared to deal with at the level it requires."

Coach Perkins could tell when Roman was attempting to hide behind a smoke screen of the hypotheticals. He changed tactics.

"Son, this is the hard work the two of you have avoided your entire relationship. When a couple first gets together the love they have for one another produces a storehouse of grace that allows them to grow up and become close. If they don't take advantage of the opportunity, they run out of grace. Once they've wasted the time they had to grow up, they have to step up. Son, guess what time it is for the both of you?"

Aware that Roman had heard enough raw truth, Coach Perkins backed off to let him process the depth of what he was saying. A few moments passed.

"I get it. I need to embrace the scary. But how do I do it without making the situation worse? You know our flow when we get frustrated with each other," Roman responded, the defeat in his tone palpable.

"Okay good, you're committed to the process. Let's talk tools in the toolbox."

"Here's the template I follow when I have something difficult to process with my wife. It's an amalgam of insights I've gained over the years through experience, training, and a whole lot of trial and error in running my consulting business," Coach replied.

"The first thing I do is get my head and heart right to have the conversation. Prepping the mind for the awkward conversation you know you need to have will save you a whole lot of heartache. The goal is to take ownership of the situation before I run it by her. When people try to share their unprocessed concerns and emotions with others, the conversation turns into a series of back and forth accusations and blame where no one feels heard.

"I see," Roman said, encouraging him to continue.

"My goal is to gain as much clarity and ownership of the issue as possible about what's going on with me. Ultimately, I want the conversation to be as authentic an experience as I can make it.

"The second thing I do is sift through and identify all the feelings I have around the issue I want to discuss and actually 'feel' those feelings. If a person doesn't get in touch with and take ownership of their feelings, those feelings will take ownership of them. It's like having a child. If you neglect that child it grows up to be a problem you can't ignore.

"That's what happened to me. Like most of the men in my generation, I was taught any display of emotion was a sign of weakness, unless you'd just vanquished an opponent. Only then could you shout, cry, scream or just act a fool because you were doing it in a heroic and manly way. So, I spent the bulk of my life suppressing feelings, becoming more and more resentful."

"You suppress your feelings?" Roman blurted out, shocked that the man he'd come to know as the most comfortable man in his skin on the planet actually suppresses his feelings.

"I used to," Coach Perkins chuckled. "Until somewhere around my late thirties, it hit me, I wasn't running from my feelings, I was running from the authentic me. I wasn't suppressing my emotions; I was rejecting my humanity. Every time I tried to avoid a feeling, I was sending myself the message that I didn't deserve to experience that area of my life. And by extension, I was also telling myself that I wasn't worthy of people making an investment in getting to know me.

"Through meditation and much prayer I learned to embrace who I am by embracing what's going on with me without filtering it through the shame we inherited from Adam and Eve.

"And that's what I'm saying to myself by avoiding the conversation I need to have with Sage so I don't seem selfish?" Roman interjected.

"Exactly. Avoiding your feelings has a shaming effect," Coach Perkins continued.

"The second thing I do to prepare is an exercise I came up with called 'Scaling the Narrative.' Its designed to rein in the stories people tell themselves about what they think is going on. All you have to do is answer five questions about the story you're telling yourself as honestly as you can."

Roman pulled out his smartphone to take notes. "What are they?" he asked.

"The first question is meant to challenge the facts surrounding the story I am telling myself. 'On a scale of one to 10, how accurate are the facts I'm relying on to form my narrative?' The second question challenges my emotions. Using the same one to 10 scale ask: 'How emotionally invested am I in this situation?' The third question is intended to challenge my assumptions: "How compatible with the reality of the situation are my assumptions?" Coach Perkins said, rattling off each question.

"Slow down," Roman said. His sizable fingers flew across the digital keyboard on his phone.

"The fourth question I ask..." Coach Perkins continued at

a more deliberate pace, "challenges my expectations—'How legitimate are my expectations of myself and others when I consider the reality of the situation, and the personalities and skills of everyone involved?' This question is undoubtedly the question I struggle with the most.

"The fifth and final question is about my conclusions. To check those I ask: 'How reasonable are the conclusions I've drawn about myself and others when I reconsider the facts I have relied on, my emotional investment, my assumptions, and the legitimacy of my expectations?"

"Question five is more of a summary question?" Roman asked.

"Yes. Now, the third thing I do to prepare is I try to identify and own any problems with the choices I've made in response to the choices of others," the coach continued. "The key to this part of my preparation process is to own the problem. Truth is, people make choices that work for them. If we don't like those choices, then it is our problem, not theirs, even if they are supposed to love us. It's our responsibility to address the problems we have with others first through dialogue designed to create awareness, then through changes in our response to their behavior—that is, if they are unwilling to partner with us around a solution. To own a problem, you must reject the role of victim.

"Which brings me to the final step in the preparation process. Once I am done accepting, feeling, scaling, and owning, I 'frame the future.' Framing the future is where I identify the changes I would like to see going forward."

"Whew, that's a lot of work," Roman said. He appeared dazed as he looked over the notes he had feverishly typed.

"Yes, good preparation always is. Do you need a minute before I go on?"

"No, I'm good, go on."

"Once I have laid the groundwork for sharing my concerns, there are two things I want to be mindful of while I share those concerns. First, am I speaking the truth in love? And secondly, am I leading with my heart and following up with my head?"

"Speaking the truth in love is a concept I got from the Bible. There's a passage in Ephesians that talks about the role 'speaking the truth in love' plays in the maturation of a relationship. To do it you approach love and truth as a 'both and proposition," and not an "either or proposition." Not to get too deep here, but a Christian philosopher by the name of Paul Tillich said, and I'm paraphrasing, people who choose love over truth end up in relationships driven by powerless love, which I call a 'parasitic relationships.' And those who choose truth over love end up in relationships driven by loveless power..."

"Are what you call predatorial relationships," Roman finished Coach Perkins' sentence.

"That's right. Telling the truth in love nurtures the bond between a couple because it provides both spouses with an opportunity to get to know each other's heart which gives them, and the relationship, a chance to grow.

"Another thing telling the truth in love does is influence the way we communicate truth. When the things we share are not only motivated by love but are shared in a loving way, it places boundaries on our tone and delivery. The love we have for our spouses should motivate and restrain the way we communicate with our spouses. Everything we say needs to be said with enough grace to express our sincere desire to build and not tear down."

As Coach Perkins spoke, it was clear to Roman that he was in the zone. He thought this is what it must be like to be raised in a house with a father invested in you. Roman placed his phone in the cup holder and hit record on his voice memo app because he didn't want to miss a word.

Without missing a beat, Coach Perkins continued, "When people do not tell the truth in love, the truth eventually becomes weaponized, something used to score points rather than to share a point of view."

Roman nodded. He wasn't listening so much as he was experiencing the moment of being related to like a son.

Like an auctioneer, Coach Perkins was on a roll.

"Leading with my heart and following up with my head is one of those activities more easily said than done because it requires two of the most demanding activities humans can engage in—sharing our heart while being an engaged listener. Before someone can connect with your perspective they need to connect with you as a person. Leading with your heart places a premium on connecting at the core level before trying to connect with them on a rational level. It's what cognitive psychologist call a 'bottom up process.' To avoid rejection people often share their analysis instead of their heart. Presenting what is on your heart sets the stage for open communication. Remember, you're not opening the floor for debate, you're opening your heart to stimulate dialogue."

Again Roman nodded, taking it all in. Deep in his heart Roman craved not only the wisdom being shared, he also craved the sharing process.

Coach Perkins continued, "The more points of connection created between the two of you, the more positive influence the two of you will have on each other.

"Once you've done the heart work, you can make the transition to the head work. This is where the active listening kicks into gear. At the same time you're processing what Sage is telling you, you must manage the conversation that's taking place in your head. An active listener tunes out the internal and external distractions. The only thing you can't ignore about your internal state is the level of provocation being triggered by the conversation."

Coach Perkins paused to see if Roman was managing to keep pace.

"Early in my marriage," Coach Perkins went on, "my wife might say something that I'd filter in a way where I'd snap inside and then escalate the situation instead of diffusing it.

"To become an active listener, I adopted some of the

principles of Change Theory called "Appreciative Inquiry" or AI. AI is based on the notion that the best way to approach a person is to appreciate them and to explore with them in a way that affirms and strengthens the capacity of the relationship. AI requires an attitude of receptivity and legitimate interest in your spouse. At its core, AI assumes that the best way to resolve issues in a sustainable way through discovery, not enforcement."

Coach Perkins took a breath and said, "That's a summary of my process, thirty-five years in the making. Now...tell me what you heard?"

Roman reflected for a moment. "I need to love Sage enough to put the work in to share my heart, then receive what's in her heart. Like you always say, it's a First Corinthians 13 thing."

"That's it. Any questions?"

"No, I think I caught the spirit of it."

"Awesome, let's find a place to eat."

For the rest of the trip, Roman and Coach Perkins spent time enjoying each other's company in a way that simulated a maturing relationship between a father and son despite the mere 14 years separating them.

#

While Roman's spirits were being elevated by his time with Coach Perkins, Sage's spirits had plummeted back to earth. The jolt of adrenaline she'd felt over the prospect getting together with Owen was quickly wearing off. She wondered what was going on between them. She scrolled through the recent thread of texts between the two of them. "Can't get with you tonight...I got a lot on my plate...Maybe later this week?" Owen's text read.

She entertained the thought that Owen might be avoiding her. And she did not like it one bit, which meant someone was going to have to pay.

CHAPTER TWELVE

Roman and Sage Round One

It was a quarter to eight in the evening when Roman's key hit the door, and it would be a quarter after two in the morning before his head would hit the pillow—the exact amount of time it took for his faith, progress, love, commitment, and ultimately his manhood to be tested. Arriving home with his head clear and his heart softened, he had decided to take a day or so to prepare to share with Sage the things that were in his heart. But he had no clue how much pent up animosity awaited him on the other side of the industrial-sized, black lacquer double-doors that served as the entrance to the dream home Sage dubbed "the Magic Kingdom."

He barely got through the door when he caught a glimpse of Sage's silhouette at the head of the dining table where she nursed a cup of what he assumed was her favorite Oolong Peach tea. Halfway down the hall, he caught a whiff of the trouble that had been brewing all afternoon. It was one of the three smells from his childhood he swore would never emanate from his house. It wasn't chitlins. Although they topped the list because they're chitlins, and chitlins smell like chitlins. And it wasn't the unfiltered Camel cigarettes his uncles Richard, Ron, and Riles smoked by the carton whenever one of them needed to crash at their big sis's crib long enough to allow "you know…a brother to get back on his feet" after they got out of jail, left rehab, or was put out by one of the multitudes of aunts Roman acquired. Getting back on their feet might take anywhere from three months to an entire year. To avoid the three flights of stairs it took to smoke outside, they would light up in Roman's room while he was at school. By the time they found a new aunt or wound up back in jail, his room had ingested so much second-hand smoke that everything he owned reeked to the point his friends started calling him Joe Camel.

As bad as either one of those smells might have been, this odor was something worse. It wasn't Oolong tea Sage was sipping from her pink and green Minnie Mouse-Walt Disney World souvenir cup—it was coffee. The aroma of coffee had a strange effect on Roman. The odor had had a similar effect on Roman as fireworks might have on someone suffering from PTSD post deployment to a war zone. It evoked the darkest emotions of his childhood—the smell of cheap bourbon mixed with a few ounces of coffee to settle his mom's jitters, the nauseating pungency coming from the La Coffee packing plant in the afternoon when beans were ground for the next day's delivery, the musk of the coffee Ms. Irene served when his mother picked him up from the babysitter's house in the evening after work. Just one whiff of the offensive liquid could deport him back to a childhood full of trauma and loss.

Sage not only knew this, but she'd weaponized it. When she brought coffee into their house it wasn't mental lapse, it was an open declaration of war. It was an act of treason, an emphatic statement that said she wasn't looking for a fight she wanted to engage in mortal combat.

Roman bent over and leaned to one side to let his backpack he'd slung over his left shoulder slide to the ground. By the time his body returned to its upright position he could feel it happening—the telltale swimming in his head, the wave of hot flashes, the intensification of his heart rate and respiration, tingling feet, a flush of irritability, and the sudden awareness of the emptiness in his stomach. These were all signs of Roman's body lurching toward a state of fight or flight. He took a deep breath to steady himself. But the moment he regained his bearings, Sage was all over him.

"So where have you been all day, Mr. Roman? I thought you

were supposed to be taking it easy today? 'Hang out – kick it around the house.' Isn't that what you said?" Sage put the cup to her lips taking a mocking sip.

"Do I smell coffee?" Roman countered, his eyes fixated on the cup. The wisdom gleaned from hours spent with Coach Perkins that afternoon turned to vapor. It was too late. There was blood in the water and the sharks were circling.

"So what if it is? I'm supposed to deny myself because you've got issues? I don't think so homie. Since I never know when you're coming home because you decide when you want to go radio silent on me, I decided to have a cup of coffee to help me wait up for my loving and faithful husband."

"What are you talking about? I haven't done that in months," Roman said, advancing toward the silhouette down the hall like a soldier on patrol.

"So where were you Roman? I called you several times," Sage said, honing in her cross-examination of Roman.

Not liking where the conversation was going Roman fired back: "I had a couple of runs I had to make. And I thought you said you were going to dinner with Owen. I wasn't expecting you till late."

"Hmm, I'll bet you weren't. Owen had something to do, which is something you would've known if you had answered your damn phone any of the eight times I tried to reach you," Sage barbed.

Roman tried to regain the moral high ground by advancing on Sage's position while fighting the urge to run down the hallway and slap the cup of coffee out of her hand.

"Hey, first off, you might want to check your tone. I'm not one of your employees, and my momma didn't raise no punk." Roman stepped into view to continue his barrage. "If I'm not mistaken, the last time we spoke, I was trying to connect with you and you were rushing me off the phone—'Got to go bye.' He punctuated the point with air quotes and mimicked hanging up a phone. "And let me see if I got this right, Owen flakes out on you twice and I am supposed to sit around waiting for you to call or come home like I'm a rescue dog waiting for my master? Please…give me a break."

Seizing the opening Roman left, Sage jumps to her feet, points an index finger right between his eyes and blares: "Why not?! That's what I did for years while your sorry behind was running the streets chasing tail."

The situation had escalated from something one might see on the Military Channel to something seen on the Discovery Channel or Animal Planet. Even if Sage didn't mean to be so cutting, it was too late. The savagery of her comment, along with its condescending delivery, crossed a line that triggered the predatorial reflex in Roman. It wasn't personal. It was worse; it was primal. They sized up one another like two apex predators about to get it on because one of them had strayed into the other's territory. Sage's need for safety and unresolved issues of rejection had encroached on Roman's need for security and shame.

Exposed and vulnerable, Roman retreated into his alter ego, Trojan Man. Although Trojan Man made his official debut in college, he'd been hanging around for years. When he felt alone and unprotected in the aftermath of the abuse he suffered as a child, he'd fantasize about what it would be like to have a big brother who would take care of him. Over time, this big brother became more and more of a fixture in Roman's inner world. By the time Roman reached 12, his big brother fantasy was so well-defined it had morphed into a role model he sought to emulate to protect himself. Trojan Man became a suit of armor Roman wore to protect himself that became a catch-22. The empowerment Trojan Man could project to others reinforced the disempowerment that haunted Roman as a child. The problem was the big brother Roman conjured up to protect him turned out to be the person who was most disgusted by his inability to defend himself.

If Roman did not step up and handle his business, then Trojan Man would. At stake was his future with Sage. If Trojan Man was permitted to respond to her blatant act of aggression, then the battle would go to another level. Roman would win the fight between him and Sage, but he would lose the war for his marriage because his manufactured personality fights dirty. He is an emotional counter puncher who specializes in lightning fast comebacks with the brutality leaving the carnage of a train taking out a car stuck on the tracks. Since Roman's freshman year of college Trojan Man was responsible for verbally annihilating anyone who dared to come after him, which is what Sage had done with the coffee and her comments.

During a session with a therapist they saw a few years back, Sage accused Roman of flirting with a coworker. Trojan Man delivered a response with all the authority and effect of a clinician diagnosing a patient when he countered: "I believed my wife and Owen might be engaged in a latent emotionally incestuous relationship that has borderline features more deviant than any flirtations on my part that she has conjured up in her emotionally insecure imagination." It left Sage devastated and the therapist speechless. If Roman were unable to rein in his manufactured persona, and Trojan Man was allowed to return verbal fire, one could bet it was going to be a kill shot, aimed right at Sage's heart, executed with the precision of a long-range sniper. Such a response would be quick, clean, and final. Trojan Man would speak his peace after which, he would rise from his camouflaged position, turn and walk away.

As sensitive as Roman's manufactured persona Trojan Man was to being called out in public, Roman hated it even more because of how deep his shame ran. For all the rage Trojan Man carried around, it was a drop in the bucket compared to the dark abyss of shame in his soul.

The only advantage Roman possessed over Trojan Man was the capacity to count the cost. Every word Trojan Man uttered was notoriously short-sided. Were Trojan Man allowed to respond to his wife's comment their marriage might not survive the evening. While the battle for control of Roman's soul raged on, Sage did something that tipped the scales in Roman's favor. She began to cry, but not in the near-hysteric way she had done in past arguments. This emotional outburst was different. There was no sound just tears, a drop or two then a torrent. Standing there frozen, just three feet from the man she loved with a passion deeper than she had ever known, with a look in her eyes that measured the distance between them in light years, she made no effort to wipe away the tears streaming down her face.

Although it was something he had never seen from Sage, it was a cry he had experienced before. Once he and several players from the '95 championship team visited a 14-year-old Trojan fan named, Brandon, who was in a hospice facility, It was arranged through one of those organizations that helped grant wishes to kids who are terminal. Brandon was in the final stage of a battle with an inoperable brain tumor. When the players walked into his room dressed in Trojan gear from head to toe, all the emotional depleted Brandon could do was cry. Like Sage, he made no sound, no movement, just tears and distance in his eyes that said: "I've lost hope." In Brandon, Roman saw a lot of what he wished he had growing up such as a loving family and courage. Roman checked on Brandon every day until he got a 6:30 a.m. phone call from the teen's mom saying the boy had passed sometime during the night. The three weeks he'd gotten to know Brandon were so profound, Roman secretly placed his single most prized possession in Brandon's coffin—his National Championship ring.

Roman had experienced the same level of grief the last time he saw his father. It occurred on his tenth birthday when his dad, a self-described player/hustler, dropped into his party and barely fifteen minutes into his visit told Roman he had to go handle some business. Lil Roman begged him to stay at least until they cut the cake. When he started to make a scene, his father grabbed him, pulled him to the side, and told him to stop acting like a little punk in front of his friends.

As his father pulled off in a candy-apple red and black,

two-tone '86 Riviera convertible with yet another stepmother riding shotgun, Roman stood on the sidewalk with tears running down his face trying his best not to look like a punk. It was the last time Roman would see his father. Later that same night, six bullets fired from the gun of either a jealous husband or a dope dealer (depending on who you talked to) would end his father's life. To this day, his mother swears the woman in the car with him set him up. It was also the last time anyone would see Roman cry. He'd spend the next 27 years proving that he wasn't a punk.

It's hard to say what would have happened had those tears not started to fall from those green eyes that were the centerpiece of Roman's attraction to Sage, but they did, and it worked. Her blunt honesty followed by her extreme vulnerability neutralized the toxic mix pulsing through his heart. The toxic brew of shame and rage that had a Hulk-like effect on Roman was counteracted by a sudden vulnerability that neither he nor Trojan man knew how to handle. Out of sheer primitive instinct Roman reached out to her. He pulled her close wrapping his massive arms around her with the dexterity of a seasoned midwife swaddling an infant in a blanket, and like a newborn she bawled uncontrollably. For several minutes, she vacillated between a wail and a soft sob until her body fell limp in his arms from exhaustion. Time paused as they stood between the dim light of the dining room and the dark shadow of the hallway. They swayed back and forth ever so slightly to the unexpressed rhythm of their love for one another. For the first time in their relationship the only thing between them was silence broken by an occasional sniffle.

Roman mindlessly scanned the dimly lit room as though he'd find a clue that might help him understand what had just happened.

"What's going on, I thought we were doing okay?" Roman asked, summoning enough courage to go deeper.

"We're okay. I'm not. I'm a mess...I can't help but wonder if someday I am going to wake up and you're going to say you're done. Ever since we met I've done everything in my power to keep you. I have obsessed about everything: my body, my clothes, my conversation, our home– everything. I love you so much and I don't want to lose you." The sincerity in her voice rang loudly in his heart.

Roman took a deep breath and stepped back. He searched her eyes as he tried to take it all in. "Let me tell you something. From the day I met you, I wanted to spend the rest of my life with you. The thing I worried about the most is if I was man enough to do it, knowing my history. I've always worried that my lack of character would someday catch up to me. I was afraid I would either sabotage our relationship or you would figure me out and leave me. It wasn't until Coach Perkins and I hooked up that I began to believe that I had the capacity to love you the way you deserve to be loved. I know I can be that man. I know I have given you the message that I expected you to work hard to keep me, and I apologize for that. But now...I'm not asking you to work to keep me; I am asking you to work with me. I want us to work together as we move forward. I am not going anywhere, and this time, I am not just saying it to make you feel better. I'm saying it because I know it." Roman got on his knees as though he were proposing, took Sage by the hand and said: "Mrs. Sage Renee Bryant-Cole will you partner with me?" Caught off guard by the tenderness of his gesture, she smiled and laughed through her tears.

"I think I can do that," Sage replied happily.

Back on his feet, he took Sage by the hand and walked her to the couch where they poured out their hearts to one another for the next few hours. It was during this conversation that Sage realized that finding out about Owen's situation triggered the shock response that Coach had explained to them.

"It's like hearing about Owen's situation hit the reset button on our progress, "Sage confided in Roman. "It's like I am back in the discovery phase."

#

Exhausted from the emotional energy they'd spent the night before working through their smoldering issues, and the energy spent making up, the two early risers didn't stir until well past 9 a.m. Sage lay there still studying her husband's face as he slept. Moments later, Roman awoke to her fixed gaze.

"I'm sorry about last night," Sage whispered as she gently stroked his strong jawline.

"I'm sorry too," Roman whispered, drawing her closer to plant a series of soft kisses on her forehead ending with a soft kiss on her lips.

"It's not your fault, this was totally on me. I lost it yesterday when Owen blew me off for lunch and dinner. As much as I said I wanted to be there for Owen I must admit, my motives weren't altogether pure. A part of me wanted to be there to support my image of myself. "His rejection was more than I could stand."

"I see," said Roman. "You were feeling if Owen could abandon you in a time of crisis, and he's a good man, what hope do we have?"

"Yes," Sage said with a nod, "I know we've been doing well the past few months, but sometimes I wonder if it's just because we have not had to deal with anything. I worry that you're going to get frustrated and leave."

With affection in his eyes, "Guess what? What do you think we're doing right now?"

A slight smile broke across her face as she acknowledged the obvious, "We're going through."

Roman rose from the bed, bent over, placed both hands on her cheeks, kissed her softly on her forehead and said, "It's not complicated, it's just scary," before heading to the bathroom to get ready for the day.

After his shower Roman crossed through the dining room on his way to the kitchen to make his protein shakes. From the dining table he grabbed the half-full coffee cup that set off the previous evening's events. Standing over the sink for several minutes, Roman rinsed out the cup with attention to detail that bordered on OCD. As the warm water coursed over his hands, his mind drifted to what Sage had said about Owen's character. Why was Owen avoiding Sage? Although Owen's situation had come close to destroying his home, Roman couldn't help but wonder how he was doing. Things must be truly sorry if he's ducking Sage. In less than a minute, Roman decided to swing by The Center. Maybe he could talk Owen into reaching out to Sage before she's suffered irreparable damage to her heart.

CHAPTER THIRTEEN

Owen's Surprise Number One

On the way over to The Center, Roman realized he might be getting in over his head. What exactly would he say to Owen? It's not like they were 'boys.' In fact, the longest conversation they'd had to this point took place when Owen reached out to Roman for help when a small D3 school in Idaho was recruiting a kid who graduated from Owen's mentorship program. It was during that conversation that Roman came to admire the deep commitment Owen had for the kids in his program. Oddly enough it was the same conversation that Owen also came to realize and respect Roman's deep commitment to children. During those conversations both gentlemen got to see the non-Sage filtered side of each other. It produced a mutual respect neither of them could voice to the other.

The first thing Roman noticed when he pulled into the parking lot was the LS sitting in the director's parking spot. Who would park in Owen's spot? he wondered, confident that Owen would never spend that kind of cash on a car— even if it was a hybrid. Once in the gymnasium, he spotted Owen working on his jump shot on the far-left court.

"Still trying to work your way onto somebody's roster?" Roman yelled halfheartedly across the court.

Without even looking up Owen said, "Just trying to stay sharp. You never know when a team might need somebody."

Before Roman could reply, Owen looked across the courts where he recognized the 6' 5" silhouette across the gym.

"I bet you never thought you'd see me here," Roman said as he approached Owen.

"Would've bet my life on it. So...what brings you to this side of town?"

"Just thought I'd check in," Roman said with a wide grin.

"Real talk?" Owen asked, with an incredulous look on his face.

"Yes. I know I give you a lot of grief about working with underprivileged kids, but the truth is, I've bragged to people about the work you do. I think it's admirable. Honestly, Owen, without guys like you in the community, I wouldn't be able to qualify two-thirds of my recruits."

Still shocked by the words coming out of Roman's mouth, Owen extended his hand. Roman accepted the gesture, and shaking it slowly looked downward to meet the shorter man's gaze. "Thanks, man, I appreciate that."

In an unprecedented move, Roman pulled Owen in closer, patted him on the back, and whispered in his ear, "You're a good man, Owen. You're a good person."

For the next 25 minutes, the two men shot baskets and engaged in small talk, neither of them knowing how to deal with the sizeable elephant in the room. At last Roman said, "So...at what point are you going to talk to your cousin?"

"Oh, so that's why you're here. Sage sent you," he said, thinking it would be just like his cousin to overstep her bounds.

"Really man, when is the last time Sage talked me into going anywhere I didn't want to go? She doesn't even know I'm here. The truth is I'm not sure how she's going to react when she finds out I came to see you," Roman chuckled. "I've always had the feeling that even though she says she'd like for the two of us to develop a friendship, she'd live to regret it."

"As paranoid as that sounds, you might be onto something," Owen cracked a smile.

"Yeah, up to this point it's just a theory. This morning I decided I'd test it. So here I am— no games, no hidden agendas— just one brotha checking on another brotha."

"Real talk, I'm okay."

Roman stepped behind the three-point line, chuckled, and let the ball fly. He hit the three with a swish before responding.

"Real talk, you're not nor should you be. You just found out your wife is having an affair, and you won't speak to your best friend in the whole world about it. Unless you have resilient super power I do not know about, you can't be doing ok. Hey, I'm not saying you have to talk to Sage or me. But you do need to talk to someone, and by someone, I mean someone not toxically connected to the situation."

"What do you mean toxic?" Owen's interest piqued.

"It would be easier for me to draw you a diagram than to explain what I mean," he said looking around. "There's got to be a grease board in one of the locker rooms."

"What's up with you and Sage and the drawing thing?" Owen fires back.

"Can we help it if we're visual learners?" Roman kept his tone light.

"We can use the big dry-erase board in the conference room," Owen gestured for Roman to follow him toward the massive blue steel doors.

Once they were in the conference room, the two men walked towards the dry-erase board.

"It figures you would have the fresh see-thru glass boards," Roman said, picking up the black marker.

"The interior designer chose those; I had nothing to do with it," Roman's remark put Owen on the defense. "If it were left up to me, we'd have bought chalkboards."

"Hey man, I'm not hating. I'm congratulating. I'd love to have one of these babies in my office. So how much of the material on the link Sage sent you have you gotten through?" Roman asked.

"I'm clear that I'm in a parasitic marriage where I'm the host and Lia is the parasite."

"So you've figured out how you got here, and you have identified your 'You are here point'. Good. The next step is the 'What do I do now?'"

"Should I stay or should I go, hmm...Thank you, Captain Obvious," Owen bristled.

"C'mon man, The Clash? You need to spend more time with the brothas. What do I do now is not about the long term, it's about the here and now. Here's what you need to do while you decide what you're going to do...Once you and Lia both acknowledge that an affair took place, the two of you will enter the 'discovery phase' of your recovery process."

"Okay, what's that?" Owen lowered his guard.

"The period where the one cheated on learns the intimate details of what's been going on in their marriage."

"You mean in the affair, don't you?"

"No, I mean in your marriage," Roman stated in a firm voice. "Without context an affair is nothing more than an act committed by two consenting adults. It becomes something when it takes place in the context of marriage making it one of the dynamics within the marriage. It's not the problem, it's a symptom.

"No pun intended, but there's no way to divorce what's been going on in your marriage from Lia's affair. Like it or not, her affair is a statement about the health and condition of your overall marriage. She didn't step outside the marriage to cheat, she did it inside of it."

"Ouch, that's harsh," Owen winced.

"All I'm saying is a lot of the stuff you are going to learn about Lia's affair is going to enlighten you, revealing the depth of issues in your marriage," Roman assured him. Although Owen was still skeptical about the methods being presented by his cousin-in-law, he was willing to hear him out.

"Discovery is all about gathering all the information that will lay the foundation for the rest of the recovery process. It makes this the most important part of the recovery process because it sets the trajectory for your future—with or without Lia. Blow it and you can wind up in a whole world of unnecessary hurt."

"Take it from me, cheaters don't suddenly become

forthcoming just because they've been caught. Unless Lia is different than most, she's not going to disclose the details, they are going to leak. Once I acknowledged I had cheated on Sage, my need to run game at the same level lessened. It was like I had exhaled. But that's when the magnitude of my cheating began to come to light.

"Just know every time a new detail of Lia's affair gets exposed it is going to feel like someone tearing a scab off a wound that's barely starting to heal. And for Lia, it's going to feel like two steps forward three steps backward."

"Man, that sounds painful. I'm not sure how much of that I'd be able to take" Owen confessed.

"Yeah, I feel you, but that's why it's called the discovery phase. You'll discover the cost of the neglect and start face the reality of what's been going on in your marriage and your life," Roman restated.

"Shouldn't Lia be the one taking on the burden of cheating on me? Isn't she the one who needs to make it up to me?"

The flash of indignation on Owen's boyish face caused a laugh to escape Roman's mouth. Not wanting Owen to feel as if he were taking his plight lightly, he was immediately sorry.

"Yeah, if life were fair that's how it would work," Roman continued, care to maintain a serious tone "But it's not and it doesn't. I hate to be the one to break it to you, but taking on the burden of what's been going on between you and Lia is a team sport. Both of you will need to own up to the life you have chosen to live as individuals and as a couple. That includes all the pre-cheating that took place in your marriage before the affair.

"You'll need patience before you can have enough clarity to build the conviction to stop living in compromise about what you want, and what you're willing to pour into your marriage. It's no joke. Terminating or saving a marriage isn't for the soft. Committing to a path of vulnerability will expose you to stuff that's going to require a bold response. But that's the only way I know. You have to come out of denial, stop living in compromise, and take actions your family and friends may not support. Feel me...?"

"Mm..." Owen nodded, eyes blinking.

"Trust me," Roman said with his hand over his heart. "At some point the people closest to you are going to be asking the same types of questions about your marriage they are asking about Sage and me—'Why is she wasting her time trying to work on a marriage with a cheater who's been so serial with it, his middle name should be Kellogg?'" Roman said in a high pitch voice that mocked some of the family gossips.

"Wow," Owen was surprised by Roman's 'Hi, my name is Roman and I am an adulterer 12-step level of transparency.

"If Sage hadn't gone through the discovery phase, we wouldn't be together today. And that's for real, real talk," Roman was emphatic.

"Oh, there's one other thing that needs to take place during discovery. You're going to need to develop the ability to see things from an allocentric viewpoint," Roman added.

"Okay, I'll bite. What's allocentric mean?"

"It's an SAT word that means seeing things from another's point of view. And from what little I know about you bro, that's going to be the hardest part of the process."

"What are you trying to say?" Owen said, half-joking, half-offended.

"I'm saying despite our differences, we are both two very opinionated brothas who struggle with the point of view of others. And to make matters worse, one of us is a baller who doesn't have to be bothered if he doesn't want to."

Owen hedged, "Man, it's not like that."

"That's your opinion," Roman immediately countered. "I'm sure you are going to go with that. All kidding aside, the real reason why you are going to struggle is that your sense of what's happened in your marriage is going to be shaped by the pain you're feeling. To get past the pain you are going to have to expand your view of the situation to embrace Lia's view of your marriage. You're going to need to cultivate space in your perspective for her thoughts and feelings as well. The bottom line is, to relieve the pain you're going to have to expose yourself to more pain," Roman answered.

"How is that?" Owen said, the indignation returning. "She cheated on me. She's the one who needs to understand my perspective, not the other way around," Owen argued.

"While what you said is true, it only matters if you're opening up the floor to debate a moral argument about who's right and who's wrong, which one of you is the good guy, or who is the victim and who's the perpetrator? But that's not what we are talking about here. What we're talking about is what it is going to take to fix your marriage."

"So you're saying I'm supposed to let her get off scot-free just to save my marriage?" Roman could detect that Owen was building a wall of justification brick-by-brick. Before responding, he took a deep breath and searched for his inner Coach Perkins.

"See, this is why I said you were going to struggle with her perspective. Like me, you are going to get stuck on the hamster wheel of who's right and who's wrong. Let me tell you something you need to wrap your head around sooner or later. Your wife cheated on you for reasons that are legit. Right, wrong, real, or imagined, she did it for reasons that are true and rational to her whether they are factually unsubstantiated or morally flawed. And if the two of you don't address those reasons, and you get back together, it won't be a question of if one of you is going to cheat, it'll be a question of when. Listen man, I'm not suggesting you let her off scot-free. I'm saying neither one of you should get off scot-free. And that's straight word."

"I hear you. But I'm concerned about sending the wrong message. The last thing I want to do is to legitimize Lia's complaints. That'll just give her license to cheat," Owen reasoned.

"Going after the moral high ground is the worst thing you can do. Moralizing the situation is just going to escalate the bickering. Take it from someone who knows, you'll end up going back and forth with no end in sight.

"What if I asked you to validate your passion for the kids you work with through my ethical lens? Can you imagine what it would feel like if you had to justify your passion for your work to someone who doesn't share your passion?" Roman asked, trying to get Owen to step outside of himself.

"That's what Lia's been doing for the past four years with all her questions and comments about the validity of my work," Owen answered.

"How do you feel when she does that?" Roman asked.

"Frustrated as hell."

"Okay now, think about the passions Lia has had that you have asked her to justify because they don't make sense to you. How do you think it makes her feel?" Roman countered.

"Yeah, but I didn't cheat on her. I wouldn't exactly compare working with at-risk kids with making the greedy richer."

"Maybe it's because you've been more dismissive of her passions than she's been of yours…just saying."

Unable to come up with a response to Roman's statement left Owen slack-jawed.

"Speaking from experience brotha, it's hard to share your heart with someone who wears a crown and a halo. When Sage and I started dealing with our issues, I struggled because I didn't think I had the right to complain about anything considering the way I'd treated her. I engaged in a lot of self-check. Even though there were things about the way she treated me that made her a co-conspirator in my doggish ways. It took us a while to make the connection between her dismissiveness and my silence, which lead me to search for validation outside the home. Once we began to honor each other's real stuff without judgment, our relationship began to move forward."

Owen sighed, "Man, that's a hard pill to swallow."

"Yep and you better do it quickly if you want to save your marriage."

"Listen man, what Lia did wasn't a crime committed against you, it was a conspiracy carried out by the two of you. You may not want to accept this, but for Lia to cheat on you there's stuff you had to do to help facilitate the process."

"Like what?" Owen asked.

"Like not holding someone accountable when they come home six hours after getting off work. Like letting it slide when they go on a business trip, and don't check in the whole time. Like tolerating lies because you don't want to fight. Letting them have too much privacy and being glad when they are gone because you don't have to deal with them...just to name a few."

"Wow," said Owen, overwhelmed. "What if you don't want to seem jealous or controlling, so you let some stuff slide?"

"Then, you need to stop worrying about your image and start worrying about your marriage," Roman replied bluntly. "Your wife is cheating on you with another man, and you're worried about looking jealous or controlling? C'mon bro, snap out of it. It's time for you to stop hosting her foolishness."

He sat down on one of the brown upholstered chairs strewn about the conference room. Seated in the chair backward with his arms folded across the top of the back of the chair he stared at the gray flooring. Roman stood at the board his arms at his side, still clutching the marker in his hands. He looked at Owen in a way that he hoped communicated he was there for him. Yet, he could tell by the Owen's expression he was engaged in an internal dialogue and had most likely checked out of the conversation both emotionally and mentally.

"Did I push too hard? Have I been too confrontational?" thought Roman. The blunt force trauma he had inflicted on Owen's psyche was harsh and exactly what was needed to penetrate the labyrinth of his denial package. It consisted of all three levels of denial Roman had learned from Coach Perkins: 'Hear no evil' (the denial that problem exists), 'See no evil' (the denial of the impact of the problem that exists), and 'Speak no evil' (the denial of the need to do anything about the problem that exists).

"I got it, I got it. It's a conspiracy," Owen said, snapping out of his trance. "A lot of this is not on her. It's on me. What else do I need to know about the discovery phase?"

Relieved to see him engaging the conversation again Roman said, "It's not on you, it's not on her, it's on the both of you. To put it back together, the two of you will have to work... together, as a couple."

"Got it, as a couple. What else can you tell me?" Owen asked, suddenly energized.

Roman told him, "There are two other components of the discovery phase we need to cover. The first are the Three Levels of Revelation, and the second is Quarantine Mode."

"What are the three categories of revelation?" Owen asked.

Roman drew three columns on the board. Atop the first column he wrote the heading "Context," on the second, "Connection," and the third "Consequences." He turned to Owen who was still seated and said, "These are the three categories of revelation. Everything you'll learn about yourself, Lia, your marriage, and the whole sordid affair will fall into one of these categories. Context is what you learn that helps you put the affair into the larger framework of your marriage. These are the influencing habits and patterns of behavior that have had a toxic influence on your relationship. Connection is what you learn about yourself and others, discoveries that reveal the real level of intimacy and connection between you, your spouse and those in your support community. The consequence category encompasses all the details about the affair that involves the penalties and cost of moving forward. So, let's say you're going to divorce Lia, that decision will come with its own set of costs and penalties. But say the two of you decide you want to try and work it out, that decision will come with an entirely different set of costs and penalties. The key to this process is having enough information to make a decision you won't regret later."

Roman began listing words under each column that described each category more fully. When he finished Owen pulled out his phone and took pictures of what was written on the board.

"Man, this is good stuff," Owen said, taking pictures from every imaginable angle and distance.

"Any questions?" Roman asked.

"Not at this point," Owen said, distracted by the board. "I want to make sure I got it so when I sit down to process it my notes are thorough" quickly following up with, "That's not to say I won't have questions. It just means I don't have any now. I'm sure I'll have plenty of questions later. Give me a few days to sit with it."

"No rush man," Roman said, his hands motioned the gesture to slow down.

After Owen finished taking pictures, he grabbed the black eraser on the ledge at the bottom of the board and thoroughly erased it. "What about this "Quarantine Mode"?

Concerned Owen might be a little too enthused, Roman suggested they hold off on the explanation of the Quarantine Mode until Owen had a chance to process what they'd already covered.

"You're probably right," Owen said with resigned disappointment. He carefully placed the marker back on the ledge of the board.

"Cool," Roman said. "Let's hook up later this week. We can go over the Quarantine Mode then, provided you don't have questions about the discovery phase."

"Cool."

Glancing down at his watch Roman replied, " Cool. Alright, let me check my schedule when I get to work. I'll have an answer for you by Wednesday morning, but I'm thinking Thursday morning should work."

The two men made their way across the gymnasium floor. "So what are you going to do about Sage? Roman asked. "You are aware you are going to have to talk to her about this at some point."

"Yeah...just not now. No way."

"I get where you're coming from. Nevertheless, it needs to

be soon." He fully understood Owen's hesitancy. While he loved his wife dearly, he knew her Miss Fix-it mode would be more than Owen could handle at present.

Arriving at Roman's SUV in the parking lot, Owen stopped and looked at Roman earnestly, "Can I get your personal advice on something?"

"Sure," Roman said. "It's the least I can do after I did a drive-by on you."

Testing their newfound openness, Owen said, "When I first blew Sage off it was all about me feeling played. The truth is I was just too embarrassed to talk to her. Now it's not so much about the shame, although a bit of the residue remains. It was more about what affect my situation with Lia might have on her. I'm just not sure if this is a healthy situation for her to be in the middle of—especially when I consider the situation the two of you are still in, not to mention the fact she didn't like Lia from the jump..."

Roman stopped him down with an assuring chuckle, "I got you."

"Is it wrong for me to think this way?" Owen asked.

"No, I believe that you're using wisdom."

"But how do you tell your best friend 'I don't need your support because I got this?'"

Roman thought for a minute. "Let me handle Sage," he responded finally. "I need time to process how to go about it. In the meantime, I think you are going to need to have a conversation with her on a superficial level just to let her know everything is cool between the two of you. Afterward, you'll need to tell her this is something you're going to have to handle with a different flow than you usually use."

"Yeah, yeah," Owen said. "I got it, cool," nodding his head in agreement.

Satisfied Owen heard him Roman said, "I got to run," a moment of awkwardness followed as the two men struggled to come up with an appropriate goodbye befitting their new level of bro-ness. When Owen stuck his hand out to shake

Roman's, the big man grabbed it and pulled Owen close to him and patted him heartily on the back with the other hand to acknowledge their new state of bro-dom.

"Thanks for checking on a brother."

"It's all good. Don't trip. We all got our burdens to bear. A few months ago, someone had to check on me. Today was my day to pay it forward."

Roman hopped into his Escalade and rolled down the window. "One last question man, who parked their new LS in your parking spot?"

"Me," Owen answered without lifting his head.

"That's you? That's you?"

"Yes, it's me."

Roman smiled broadly putting the giant SUV in gear, "You know you're going to have to explain yourself the next time I see you. I'm not hating. I just want to know the story behind the purchase." Having gotten the last word Roman accelerated out of the parking lot, "Peaaaaace..."

CHAPTER FOURTEEN

Owen's Surprise Number Two

The clock on the wall flashed 11:45 even though the watch on Owen's arm read 12 p.m. He had intentionally set his wristwatch ahead 15 minutes as he despised being late. He got up from his desk and headed towards the break room across from his office, where two bags of leftovers from Shin Shin Restaurant awaited him in the refrigerator. He carefully measured servings from the six a la carte boxes onto a white plate reminiscent of the industrial strength ones found in a school cafeteria circa late '70s. No disposable plates for this environmentally conscious kid who grew up four blocks downwind of a landfill. He hated how they leaked when the teriyaki sauce soaked through the bottom of the plate.

He leaned back against the counter with his back to the microwave. The combination of the high-pitched growls and hums of the microwave set Owen's mind adrift. As his food spun round and round, he thought about the upcoming afternoon staff meeting, his talk with Roman, the state of his marriage, as well as, the state of his life. Startled out his trance by the harsh, sustained beep coming from the microwave letting him know his food was piping hot on the surface but cold on the inside, much like his marriage. He hit reheat button a second time, then made his way back across the hall to his office where he grabbed a Diet Mountain Dew out of the stash he kept in his office mini-fridge.

Two-thirds of the way through the meal another buzzer went off. This time it wasn't the microwave sounding off, it was the buzzer at the rear loading bay reverberating throughout the building. *"That's odd,"* he thought, *"There's nothing scheduled for delivery."* Owen grabbed the lone sheet of paper off the massive white oak desk crafted from recycled material from an old yacht to check if there were something he'd missed. Everything seemed to be in order. He wolfed down the rest of his meal, grabbed the can of Mountain Dew, and headed to the end of the hall to check the security monitors at the reception desk. Owen rushed down the corridor as the crescendo of the buzzer signaled the impatience of the person on the other end.

"Coming, coming," Owen said impatiently. Leaning over the side of the receptionist desk, he checked the small bank of 12-inch monitors that cycled through the facility every several seconds. He waited for them to cycle back around to the rear of the building. Despite the high definition clarity of the video feed on the monitor, he could not believe his eyes. There she was in hi-def. Glory! It was the absolute last person he'd ever thought he would see at the rear entrance of The Center—Lia. If Roman's visit was a 9.0 earthquake, then Lia's appearance was the tsunami that followed. Lia was not a "use the back-entrance person." There's nothing subtle about this Texas native. Everything she did, from her clothes to her conversation, was large out there for the world to see. she did not have an ounce of shame in her body. Lia did not like parking in her own garage because it meant she would have to enter the house through what she called the "servant's entrance." But there she was at the loading dock, leaning on the buzzer like a delivery driver behind schedule trying to collect a bonus.

Because he had never buzzed someone in through the rear entrance, Owen fumbled around for a few moments attempting to figure out how to work the intercom to let Lia know he was working on buzzing her in the door. Meanwhile, she continued to press the buzzer. Frustrated, he decided that a diagonal run across the entire facility to the rear entrance might be quicker. For the 11 minutes and 15 seconds it took to make his way to the loading dock, Lia kept her finger on the buzzer. He made it to the rear of the facility out of breath. And Lia was out of patience. Whatever civility she might have brought to their first conversation since he'd left home had been wasted on the buzzer.

The moment the door opened Lia pushed her way past Owen. Once the door shut behind her, she started in. "How come it took so long to let me in? I'll bet you did it to punish me," she rolled her eyes. "Something could have happened to me while I was out there waiting."

Owen tried to explain himself to her to no avail. Before he could offer an explanation, she was on to another complaint. "Why is it so cold in this place?"

"The system is automated. It shuts down when it detects an area is not being used. It's warmer up front."

"Uh, then why are we standing here?"

While escorting her to the front of the building the complaints continued one after another. She found fault in the look of the building, the color scheme, its size, the artwork, etc. In the ten minutes it took to reach Owen's office, he was in full host mode and entrenched in his old habit of vacillating between appeasement and defensiveness. It wasn't until they walked passed the conference room where he and Roman talked a few hours before, that Owen snapped out of host mode.

Upon entering Owen's office Lia immediately began to survey the room, "This is nice," she said. "What do you use this room for?"

Momentarily stunned, Owen eventually found his words, "This is my office."

"Your office?"

"Yes, my office," he said with a "how do you not know this" tone. Suddenly, he realized that Lia had never been inside his office. In fact, she'd only been to The Center four times. Once for the opening dedication ceremony, and a second time for Owen's cousin's graduation which was held in the gymnasium. Her other two visits where the day the mayor brought a resolution to honor Owen's service to the community, and when then-presidential candidate Barack Obama came through for a tour of the facility. "So, who put this together for you? It's way too big and way too sweet for you to have done it."

Not wanting to make things worse between them, he avoided telling her that his office was hooked up by a designer with Sage's input.

"What do you want Lia? It's clear from all the complaints you've spewed since you hit the door that you didn't come to apologize."

"Apologize? Uh…" Lia sneered as she took a seat on the large brown leather sofa, pulled out a notepad, and began to rattle things off a list she had prepared. "I need to know when you are coming to get the rest of your stuff out the house? How much money you are going to give me to take care of things? Also, I need your key to the house and the Lexus. Oh, and here's the information to the kennel where I put your dog."

"My dog?" Owen said, in shock and disbelief, "Scarlet is our dog. We got her together."

"No, she is your dog. You are the one that wanted a dog. I don't have time to take care of a dog."

Owen snatched the paper from her.

"So?" Lia's tone remained calm and matter-of-fact.

"So what?" Owen could do little to mask his bewilderment.

"What are you going to do about my finances and your stuff?"

"Are you on crack?" Owen was infuriated. His voice now escalated an octave higher than normal. Breathing deeply he moved closer to looked directly in Lia's eyes.

"Just so we're clear—If we don't get back together, I won't be the one moving out the house. You will. Did you forget you signed a pre-nup? So I don't need to come and get anything. Furthermore, I'm not giving you a dime. Your business clears $140,000 a year—off my connections I might add. That's more than enough for you to survive off until this thing is over. As for the car, you can take it. The only reason I drove off in it is that you blocked me in. Just use your key and take it and leave me the Prius."

"You're the one who must be on crack if you think I am supposed to survive off what I make. That's my money. You're the one who's always told me that my business was just a hobby, and that the money I brought in was small change. Who knows? Maybe a judge will decide that your airtight prenup isn't so airtight after all, and rule that I was defrauded into signing it."

"I'm done talking about it. Are you going to take the Lexus and leave me the Prius or what?" Owen said bluntly.

"Fine. I'll take the Lexus. Just give me the key."

"Why?"

"Because I lost the other key."

"Then what key have you been using?"

"You never drive the car, so I took your key."

"So, this is the only key? Do you know how much money it would have cost if you'd lost it? I can't believe you," he blasted her. "I need to take the car to the dealer to have another key made. You can follow me in the Prius. We'll swap cars after they sync the new key."

"That's not going to work for me because I have things to do and the Prius is at the house," Lia said as the two of them reached the parking lot.

"What car did you expect me to drive if you took the Lexus?"

"I didn't think you needed a car since you practically live here."

"How do you expect me to get to the Prius if you take the Lexus?"

"I'm sure one of the doe-eyed honeys that work here would love to give you a ride…home," Lia snarked, but leaving herself wide open.

"You're the only one giving rides to people," retorted Owen.

Not to be outdone, Lia fired back, "You're the one with all the hot twenty-something's running around him all day with half their booty hanging out of their shorts!"

"Wait a minute – if the Prius is at home, how did you get here?" ask Owen, choosing to ignore that remark.

Lia hesitated for a moment, "I took Uber."

Owen knew she was lying. Her hesitation and her body language gave her away. *"It had to be Casey. Who else would she be able to talk into driving her from the Westside all the way to Compton?"* he thought.

Having deduced that she chose to use the back entrance to avoid being seen getting out of her lover's car, he decided on a frontal attack.

"I can tell you're lying. Casey brought you here didn't he?"

"What if he did?" she said in defiance, "I had to call some-one since you left me without a car."

Her brazenness made Owen so furious he didn't know what to respond to first: the fact that she claimed he left her without a car or the fact that Casey had been to their house.

"You mean to tell me that you asked that trifling negro to pick you up at my house?" he yelled.

"Like I said, so what if he did? You're the one that aban-doned me. Just because you don't know how to take care of me don't get mad if another man knows how to get the job done."

"Unfreakin' believable!" muttered the words repeatedly as he paced fully engulfed in rage. Across the parking lot he noticed a vehicle out of place parked across the street. A 2009 White Range Rover with limo tint and 24-inch gold spoke rims. It didn't take Owen long to conclude that the dark figure sitting in the driver's seat of the vehicle was Casey. He thought for a moment about his next move. As he considered whether to go over and snatch him out the car or walk away, an eerie coldness enveloped Owen's heart and dissipated the heat that had been generated by his anger. He refused to handle Lia from what he felt was a position of weakness—from his emotions—instead, he decided to approach the situation from a position of strategy and strength. He would speak the one language Lia understood—money.

For several years before he became the founder and director of the 100% Community Center, Owen worked on Wall Street. Recruited right out of college with degrees in mathematics and economics, he earned over 25 million dollars as Senior Equity Trader in Derivatives at AEG.

"Not only am I not going to have a key made for you, but you're also not getting the car back. I'm canceling your credit cards too. Let's see if another man can handle my business better than me," said Owen, squaring off his shoulders.

"You...Uhh..." At first Lia was dumbstruck. She then let loose a blood-curdling scream to raise the dead. Like a child, she clinched her fist and stomped her feet in a tantrum worthy of any two-year old.

"You need to leave before I call the Sheriff and have you escorted off the premises. So walk on across the street to that gas guzzling ghetto bucket your broke wanna-be baller man is sitting in and leave. I'm done hosting your foolishness."

Comforted by the notion he had set Lia straight, at least in his mind, Owen turned his back on her and headed back to The Center.

"That's okay, I know you don't think this is over little man. But I know a little something about the law too," she called after him. "Just wait little man, just wait!" trying unsuccessfully to regain her dignity. Owen disappeared into the building.

Once inside, he watched the security monitors to confirm his suspicions. When the cameras cycled back around to the front of the building, he caught a glimpse of Casey getting out of the white Range Rover as Lia approached it. The couple embraced for a few moments. Which felt like a lifetime as he watched his wife being comforted by another man. After they drove off, Owen dragged himself back to his office where he collapsed on the couch and wept.

CHAPTER FIFTEEN

Guess Who's Coming to Dinner

Around 2:45 p.m. The Center comes alive. The ambient light provided by the clerestory glass placed throughout the facility takes over the lighting duties, filling The Center with natural light. The strategically placed windows and skylights bathe the courts lined with recycled rubber with inviting warmth. Giant ceiling fans that look like propellers taken from vintage bombers produce a hum heard throughout the facility. The sound of bouncing balls, tennis shoes skidding across the courts, along with the symphony of conversations driven by kids using their outside voice provides an energy and buzz that reverberates throughout the building.

These are the sights, sounds, and smells that typically draw the socially awkward Owen out of his shell, but not this afternoon. Feeling more than a little guilty about the way he handled Lia, trying to process Roman's intentions, as well as the information Roman and Sage shared with him over the past two days, Owen was trying to recover from the emotional roller coaster that shaped his day when his cell phone rang. He glanced at the caller ID with a weary "What now?" look. A picture of a Roman soldier stared back at him.

"Hey Owen, it's Rome," Owen was slightly irritated by the cheerful voice on the other end of the line.

"One visit <u>and</u> a call? People are going to start to talk," said Owen, his sarcasm thinly veiled. Roman ignored the comment and got right to the point.

"I figured out how you can address the issue with Sage. Come over for dinner tonight and let her download. We can go over the rest of the discovery process, which includes Quarantine mode. Then, you can tell her you need to handle this with a different flow."

"It sounds great, but I have not processed the discovery phase yet. Can we do it tomorrow or the next day?"

"Trust me, you'll be able to process both at the same time."

"The truth is I am not having a good day," Owen revealed, still not used to confiding in Roman.

"What's wrong? When I left, you seemed fine."

"Yeah, that was until Lia came by to pick up the car and to ask when I was moving out."

"What? Wow, she's got a lot of nerve. What did you say? Please tell me you're not moving out and that you didn't give her the car."

"I'm not and I didn't. I was all prepared to give Lia the car and even to change my schedule to have a key made to replace the one she lost. That was before I looked across the street and saw Casey waiting for her..."

"Let me guess," Roman interrupted, "A white Range Rover, 24-inch gold Daytons on it that looked like a prop out of the original Jurassic Park."

"Yep, how did you know?"

"I saw Casey at Seals Car Wash a few months back. When they rolled his ride around to the drying area, several of the brothas standing next to me laughed out loud. One of them said, 'What kind of Jerry Springer Show ghetto-centric negro puts Dayton rims on a Rover?' Everybody who saw it clowned him. I hid in the back so he couldn't see me. The last thing I wanted was people thinking we were boys."

"Yeah, right. So you see why I don't want to come to the house tonight?" Owen was grateful that Roman shared his disdain for Casey.

"No, I see why you need to come to the house this evening. Owen, you need to go into quarantine mode right now. This is going to happen one way or another. I've already had to talk Sage out of doing a drive-by twice this afternoon."

"Got it. I'm there. What time?"

"Around seven, seven thirty."

"Cool, see you then. Later," Owen responded

Once Owen hung up, Roman wasted no time calling Sage. Roman nervously tapped beats with his thumbs on the steering wheel as the phone rang. He was relieved when she answered with a loving "Hey baby, what's up?"

"I need to run something by you, but I need you to hear me out before you comment."

"Okay."

"First, I went to Owen's spot this morning to check on him. We talked, he shared some stuff with me, and I shared some stuff with him about the discovery phase. I've invited him to dinner tonight so the three of us could talk and he agreed. So, he'll be at the house between seven and seven thirty. That's it, what do you think?"

A few seconds of silence passed while Sage processed the shock of Roman taking it upon himself to drive to The Center to check on Owen, the fact that Owen opened up to Roman (and not her), and the jealousy she felt about it, not to mention the joy she felt about Owen having a man to talk to. His coming to the house left Sage feeling a whole other range of emotions. Underneath Sage's joy was the usual anxiety she always felt about hosting someone for dinner on short notice—even if that someone is family.

"You can comment now," Roman said. Her silence was making him nervous.

"I am just stunned. I don't know if I'm more shocked you didn't tell me you were going to talk to Owen or that the two of you had a decent conversation-"

Roman interrupted, "Yeah...on that I'm invoking the rarely used 'Six Hour Amnesty Rule.'"

The 'Six Hour Amnesty Rule' was an agreement Roman and Sage made with each other to give him a chance to come back and tell the truth if he failed to be forthcoming. If he confessed within six hours of lying or withholding something, he would be given amnesty on the lying but not on what he lied about.

Sage was reluctant but agreed.

"Thank you for the grace," he said. "What's the other thing on your mind?"

"Prepping the house for a guest and figuring out what to serve." He could hear the anxiety in her voice.

"He's not a guest babe, it's Owen. Tonight is not a night for you to go all OCD with the house any more than you normally do. Remember, it's about Owen, not your reputation. And since I am the one who's technically hosting him, I am going to handle dinner."

"Whoa! Now I know I'm in Bizarro-world," Sage was only half joking.

"Hey, don't hate," Roman chuckled. "I can handle this. I know how to order food. And while I'm not a gourmet chef I do know how to whip up a couple of edible dishes that are quite pleasing to the palate."

Sage was reluctant but resolved. "All right, I'm going to let you handle it. If you run into difficulty, I can always run by Chipotle on my way home."

"Having a backup plan is not letting me handle it, especially if you're going to worry about how it's being handled. Having a backup plan communicates your level of mistrust which is why I've let you handle the hosting logistics in the past. Babe, I'd appreciate it if we could agree that moving forward you'll give me a full chance to fail or to surprise you. If I can't deliver I promise I will own up to it/ I'll even let you say, 'I told you so.' Deal?"

Surprised by how all-in Roman seemed to be, Sage gave another reluctant "Okay."

"On that note of agreement, I will see you in a few hours."

"Yes, love you, bye."

He hung up with a smile.

CHAPTER SIXTEEN

Dinner at The Coles'

The combination of an early sunset and the shadows cast by the 6,500square foot tri-level mini-mansions on the two-block long slope made it seem like night had already fallen on the Cole house. Concerned about the time, Sage jumped out the car carrying several bags with big red bull's-eyes on them. The smell of curry greeted her as she made her way down the hallway. "Roman must have gotten take-out," Sage thought. "Good. There is no way he could pull this off by himself."

Content with the notion she was right and Roman was wrong, Sage decided she wasn't going to say 'I told you so.' After all, he tried. Shifting her attention to savory aroma emanating from the kitchen growing stronger with each step, she wondered where he'd gone to pick up the food. As she made a right into the great room comprised of their kitchen, a casual dining area, and family room, Roman was setting the table with his back to her. He turned just in time to see her place the bags on the massive white and gray granite island that helped frame the kitchen area. After stepping out of her heels, she walked over, threw her arms around him, and gave him a big kiss.

"I'm sorry," Sage said.

"No problem, for what?"

"For not being here to help…What did you order for dinner? It smells awesome. Don't tell me you decided to try something new," Sage asked, scanning the room for take-out containers.

"It's Honey Curried Chicken, and I didn't order it, I made it," he replied, trying not to be offended.

"You made it? Wow, it smells delicious," Sage said with a mix of awe, disappointment, and concern.

"I told you I know how to cook," his agitation growing.

Amazed, Sage tried to open the oven to peek. Roman quickly ordered her to close it.

"You'll dry out the chicken if you lift the lid," he said authoritatively.

Roman didn't know whether it was true or not. He was merely repeating what his mother always said when he tried to open the oven.

"Okay, okay," Sage said. "I wouldn't want to mess with the genius at work."

"Ha-ha, So what's in the bags?"

"Oh, just a few things we were out of."

"A few things, huh?" Roman smiled to himself.

"Yes, a few things," Sage said defensively.

"Like what?" Roman asked.

"Paper towels, cleaner, diet Mountain Dew, and a few other miscellaneous items," Sage replied.

"It's a shame you wasted your time. I'd already stopped and got the paper towels you like for the bathroom, along with the cleanser that won't trigger Owen's allergies, and the Mountain Dew he drinks."

"Well, seems like you've got everything under control," Sage said. There was slightly detectable tension in her tone.

"Yep," Roman said. "So relax, I got this."

"Just one last question," Sage said as she scanned the room. "Why aren't we eating in the dining room?"

"Because it's a formal setting that seats twelve. There's nothing about that table that says casual conversation—not even at Thanksgiving."

"Got it, got it, just asking."

Sensing that a tiny seed of tension was rapidly growing, Roman walked over to Sage as she unpacked the shopping bags and put his arms around her from behind.

"I do have this part under control," he spoke softly, his lips brushing her ear.

Sage spun around and asked, "What's the goal for tonight?"

"It's simple. We want to give Owen a chance to share his heart, and if there's enough time afterwards you and I can go over the quarantine mode with him."

"What's your goal for tonight?" he asked.

"I just have a lot of questions. There so much I don't know," she responded with equal softness.

Roman worried that Sage's need to know details might overwhelm their guest.

"I know you have a deep love for Owen and a deep appreciation for details, but can we go easy on the questions tonight. Let's let him tell his story at his pace," he cautioned, trying to strike a balance between begging and insisting.

At 7:15 exactly the doorbell rang. When Roman opened the door, there was Owen with a 24-can box of Mountain Dew and Dad's Root Beer in one hand, and a bag filled with French Vanilla ice cream in the other.

"I know you and Sage don't drink the hard liquor, so I brought my own (holding up the Mountain Dew). The root beer and the ice cream are for the float stash you keep in your office fridge outside," the ever-punctual, and prepared, Owen whispered.

Roman grabbed the two cases of sodas from his wife's cousin and invited him in. As they moved down the lengthy hallway Owen explained that he didn't want to be too early or too late, and how he decided to split the time since Roman had been vague about it.

"Don't sweat it, man, you're right on time. Dinner is almost ready," Roman reassured.

"Whatever it is, it sure smells good. Sage must've put in work."

Roman laughed, "She sure did."

After Roman sat the two cases of soda on the counter, he turned gave Owen a big hug. "Welcome to our home," he said, emulating his mentor Coach Perkins.

"Thanks," Owen reeled from how surreal the moment seemed.

The two men sat on two of the eight stools lining the enormous custom kitchen island, where Sage did most of her entertaining. With one stool in between them and drinks in hand, they enjoyed the organic feel of a conversation destined to change the moment Sage entered the room and "the Sage effect" kicked in. At 7:30, Sage entered dressed in one of her "this old rag" outfits she wore when she hosted an evening that she wanted to go well without looking as if she was trying hard.

She greeted Owen with a hug that screamed "Sorry to hear about your loss," Throughout dinner, she could barely contain her eagerness to revel in the drama of Owen's marriage.

#

Alert to the tension created by Owen's reluctance and Sage's anticipation, Roman moved the conversation to the living room where it would be easier to have eye contact. The three of them made themselves comfortable on the unexpectedly comfortable formal couches: Owen with his Dew, Roman with his root beer, and Sage with her tea. The tension in the air thickened.

"The reason I called this meeting is to get a progress report on the planning for the family reunion. Roman began in a serious tone. "It seems like the two of you have been slacking off the last couple of days and I need answers." This was met with laughter from both Owen and Sage. His ploy had worked. With the impeding tension broken, he directed his attention.

"Seriously, the primary reason I wanted this meeting to take place is to give you a safe place to download. Piggybacking on what we talked about earlier, I think you and Sage need to connect to hash out some of the feelings the two of you are processing. Depending on how long that takes, I figured

Sage and I could go over some of the 'quarantine mode' stuff," Roman ventured.

Owen slid to the edge of the love seat, hunched over with his elbows on his thighs, and positioned his knuckles under his chin.

"I guess that's my cue to start. So where do I begin?" he said, taking a deep, but shaky breath. "Well, on the night I found out Lia was having an affair, I left the house. I was so amped that I decided to head to work early. It was around 5:30 in the morning, so I crashed on the couch in my office. Right now I'm staying at an extended stay hotel off the freeway by The Center, that covers where I have been physically. Where I am emotionally, that's a whole 'nother matter," he said, his earlier breakdown fresh on his mind. He paused to gather himself before continuing.

"I was doing much better after Roman's visit. It was the first time I felt like I was starting to gain some perspective. Then Lia dropped by The Center and everything went south after that. It was one thing to find out via text she was cheating, and quite another thing to have it thrown in my face—especially at The Center, a place I consider a refuge for the community. The last thing I want is a bunch negative energy flowing through the place. It took her violation to a depth of treachery that, frankly, I'm not sure I'll be able to forgive." Owen paused again to collect his thoughts.

"She came to The Center? For what?" Sage took this opportunity to chime in.

"She wanted to know when I was moving out and how much money would I be giving her?" Owen answered sullenly.

"I can't believe her," Sage said, her astonishment genuine.

"That's not the half of it. She came with Casey," Owen added.

"No!" Sage's hand flew up to cover her mouth that gaped with amazement. In a flash Sage began an epic rant about Lia: the way she treated Owen in college, during their engagement, when they first got married, etc.

Owen took his usual seat in the front row for the lecture while Sage climbed on her "I knew there was something up with this chick when I first met her" soapbox. This toxic pattern had existed between the two of them since they were children. And it was about to go into overdrive and threaten the entire evening if Roman did not put a stop it. Whenever Owen had a problem with someone he would share the details with Sage. In turn, she would take ownership of it and do all the condemning, labeling, and strategizing Owen would never do because of his need to preserve his image as a good man. Per usual, it was up to Sage to say all the "mean," "vicious," and "judgmental" things that the "patient, kind, loving and compassionate" Owen would never say.

Roman formed a "T" with his hands signifying a timeout. "Okay, let's not turn this into a bash Lia session." He shared his belief that their time together would be more productive if Owen could say what was on his heart without being interrupted.

"I know. But I get so mad when I think about the way she's treated Owen," Sage agreed, still managing to have the last word.

Roman countered, "It's okay to be mad. But now is not the best time to process your anger. You and I can hash that out later. Right now, let's allow Owen to download his stuff."

"You're right, you're right," Sage said, turning to Owen. "Sorry, please continue. I won't interrupt again."

Amazed at the frankness of the dialogue between Roman and Sage, he had to ask: "Is this the way the two of you talk to each other?"

"What do you mean?" Roman and Sage said in unison.

"Like that, you just say what is on your mind?"

"Yes, it's how we deal with our issues," Roman replied adding, "It hasn't always been like this. For years I walked on eggshells. Something would bother me and I would keep it hidden because I didn't think Sage cared about what was going on with me, or I thought she was too fragile to deal with the raw truth."

"Playing emotional hide and seek was part of the dysfunctional way we communicated. It helped me stay in denial, and helped Roman to justify his behavior," said Sage, reinforcing her husband's comments.

"Lia and I have never had a conversation where I felt comfortable to tell her what was on my mind, let alone my heart," Owen said, his words coated in a measure of admiration and envy.

"Hopefully, that will change for you as we spend more time together and you download some of the stuff you've been carrying," Roman assured him.

The big man's heartfelt affirmation caused the floodgates to open. Owen began to share the emotional details of his relationship with Lia. He spoke of just how deeply in love with Lia he still was and the hurt he felt when he saw Casey embrace her. He also shared how weary he had become being on the emotional roller coaster that had been their relationship since college. He talked about how frustrated he was with her lack of gratitude.

True to their word, Roman and Sage listened quietly and intently as he disclosed the affect being with Lia had on his sense of manhood. For years he told himself that it felt like he forfeited his manhood to be with her. He related how he would repeatedly get mad at the way he was being treated, then set a mental boundary on her behavior only to cave. No matter what she did to him he would always look past it. Over the past few months, Owen had found himself between an emotional rock and a hard place. On the one hand, he could not imagine life without Lia, but on the other hand, he did not want to be bothered with her either.

"Even now I do not know whether I am crying because I miss her, or if I am crying because I can't stand her. That's where I am emotionally," he admitted, summarizing the random feelings he struggled with.

Sage tried to comfort Owen with clichés and criticism; "You are better off without her. Everything happens for a reason..."

As soon as Sage paused Roman cut her off, fearing the conversation was drifting. Roman did not trot out the tired "It's going to be okay" that is typically used to try and lift people's spirits. Instead of attempting to comfort Owen, Roman wanted to affirm and encourage him to embrace the distress he was feeling so he could get in touch with the resentment that had developed in his heart over the last couple of years.

"As I sit here experiencing what you just said, I hear a lot of anger and frustration along with fatigue. I also understand the pain and shame of rejection that comes when you love someone who doesn't seem to love you as much as you think you love them. If I were to describe what I just heard in one word, it would be: lost."

Owen slid back on the love seat to contemplate Roman's summary.

"Yeah, lost. That's it...that sums it up exactly. I'm just lost, and I've been lost for the past several months, heck, maybe for the past several years."

Worried that the often-melancholy Owen might slip into depression, the ultra-upbeat Sage said, "How can you be lost? You've got an excellent education, you've made lots of money on Wall Street, and now you're devoted to a line of work you find meaningful."

"Yet the woman I've pursued nearly all my adult life is so dissatisfied with me she would rather be with a man who serially abused her."

"Yeah. That's because Lia is either too blind, too stupid, or too hurt to recognize and appreciate real love."

Roman stepped back in to reel in the conversation.

"When I say lost, I'm not talking about somewhere on a graph that charts success. In fact, achieving "success" is one of the ways you get lost. Pursuing things that make you successful in the eyes of others at the expense of your personal dignity is the actual definition of what it means to be lost to me," Roman leaned in. "For me, being lost was pursuing extramarital affairs at the expense of my dignity. For you, Owen, it's been the pursuit of Lia at the cost of your dignity. And for you baby, it was putting up with my disrespect at the expense of your dignity. So when I say "lost" I'm not talking about failure to achieve your goals; I'm talking about the inability to maintain self-respect."

"But I don't want to be lost. I spent my entire life strategizing and planning my every move so that I wouldn't be lost. Yet here I am," Owen agonized.

"Yup, here you are lost," Roman said.

"You don't have to rub it in," Owen shot back.

"Yeah, why so harsh?" Sage concurred.

"I apologize if I gave you the impression I was rubbing it in. I'm just affirming where you are and your right to be there. Unlike the two of you, I don't think it's a bad thing to be lost. I believe that it's a bad thing when you don't know you're lost. Acknowledging the extent of the loss is the first step to finding your way back. It may sound counterintuitive, but being lost is the 'You are here' point on the map that allows us to explore our options. Without it, we are lost, even when we know where we want to go. Like Coach says, 'God doesn't waste his power on our fantasies.' All I'm trying to do is help you discover the most significant place on your map Owen that's your personal 'You are here' point," Roman explained.

As the conversation moved forward, Owen began to understand the real meaning of loss. He found encouragement in knowing that feeling lost wasn't some final place of emotional exile, and that the sense of loss he felt was an appropriate and natural reaction to the loss of his marital reference points.

"The more missteps and compromises you acknowledge, the more you'll realize circumstances haven't conspired against you. It was the collective choices you and Lia made that brought your marriage to this point." Roman continued his impassioned explanation. Even Sage had to sit up and take notice of her husband's grasp on Coach Perkins' material.

As a mathematician, Owen recognized the real variable in his marriage wasn't Lia's mood, it was his response to her moods that was going to determine his level of contentment moving forward. He had been convinced that it was up to him to begin engaging Lia from a place of authenticity, not image, if he wanted things to change.

CHAPTER SEVENTEEN

Sage and Roman Introduce Owen to Quarantine Mode

"Whew, it's 9:15. Let's switch gears and talk a little bit about quarantine mode." It appeared to Roman that Owen and Sage had moved past the awkwardness of their estrangement, and both were ready to continue the discussion.

"Yes, I'd like that," urged Owen. "I was intrigued when you said I needed to go into quarantine mode after my confrontation with Lia."

Roman suggested they move the conversation to his office. He led them across the patio through a breezeway towards two sets of French doors trimmed in nautical gray. At the end of the path was the entrance to what was supposed to be the place where either of their mothers would stay when they could no longer live on their own. Instead, the 1400 square foot space had been converted into the ultimate man-cave/office, but it wasn't because he didn't like the idea of his mother-in-law living with him. On the contrary, Roman had an unusual amount of affection and respect for Mrs. Bryant, who reminded him of the only source of warmth and carrying from his childhood; Mrs. Lamberson, his third grade teacher. It was Sage who insisted they have those rooms converted so she would never have to deal with a mom she had no reason to dislike, but didn't respect nor want to be bothered with either.

As they crossed the threshold into Roman's office, Owen realized he was about to get another lesson on a dry-erase board. At the back of the room was two 4' x 6' dry-erase boards. On the board to the right was covered with Xs and

Os, as well as arrows and notes, reminiscent of something you'd find in a coaches war room.

On the board to the left was the phrase "Quarantine Mode" in big bold letters across the top. Just beneath that were several evenly spaced color-coded columns, each with its own meticulously written heading.

"I should've known," Owen said with a smile.

"Can we help it if we're visual learners?" Roman responded.

Owen took out his phone as he made his way toward the board. He snapped several pictures—first, a close-up of each section followed by several shots of the whole board. When he finished he took a seat on the stool next to Sage.

"I am ready to roll. Give it to me," he said eagerly.

"In a medical setting," Roman began, "we know that a quarantine is the separation and restriction of contact with a patient for a period to contain the spread of a disease. The separation and restriction of contact also prevents a compromised immune system from being further compromised. Quarantine mode used in the context of dealing with an extramarital affair is more of a psychological quarantine that performs the same functions for the emotions as a medical quarantine performs for the physical body. It is the intentional separation and restriction of your focus, actions, and communication with yourself, your spouse, and others to constrain the trauma created by an affair.

"In a marriage with issues like a cheating spouse, the interaction of the couple, and everyone else involved, is usually charged with toxic levels of transference—transference is the 'unconscious redirection of feelings from one person to another that spreads and escalates the drama within the marriage, eventually spreading it among family members and friends. Going into quarantine mode protects everyone involved from the toxic leakage of the unresolved issues, hurt and pain associated with the affair—directly and indirectly.

"Likewise, it limits actions of well-meaning family members and friends who would emotionally hijack the situation to make it about themselves. That does nothing but infect the couple with the toxic pain and bitterness of their own unresolved stuff.

"All that drama floating around changes the trajectory of recovery because it polarizes and provokes people unnecessarily. People get distracted in ways that prolong or hinder the recovery process. In the same way people say it's the cover-up not the crime that creates the problem, it's the drama that arises after the affair that makes it an even bigger deal. That's why sometimes it's family and friends who wind up with irreconcilable differences even if the couple reconciles."

"*That's deep,*" said Owen. He could barely mask his astonishment that these words were coming out of the mouth of a man whose indiscretions were legendary in their family. But Roman appeared to be a new man. Owen reasoned there had to be some validity to what he was saying.

Roman pointed to the board where he'd written the objectives of Quarantine Mode:

Objective Number One: Adopt an attitude that promotes authentic expression from a place of personal dignity, creates healthy boundaries, and initiates the process of coming out of personal compromise.

Objective Number Two: Limit the opportunities for the unnecessary escalation of drama and hostility by breaking the non- productive habits and patterns that foster an atmosphere that hinders authenticity.

Objective Number Three: Clarify the choices you have arrived at and present the options as you see them moving forward.

Objective Number Four: Create a flow that prevents the frustration and burnout that can occur as things leak out.

Sage added a word of warning, "Doing the stuff that needed to be done to manage myself in quarantine mode was harder than dealing with the fact that I had been cheated on. The things Coach challenged me to do at the time were counterintuitive to the Bryant way of dealing with things. You'll have to watch out for the emotional cross-contamination that can take place when those of us who have not fully recovered from our own emotional trauma catch wind of what is going on and want to 'help'. Another thing to remember is you are only doing this for a season. All the behaviors are short-term, small-scale actions that serve a larger purpose. It's not a permanent change. Although, there are a few things I have implemented on my job."

"So how long does this last?" Owen inquired.

"Until your reflex give way to reflection and reasoning and you start to come out of the discovery phase," Sage looked to Roman who was nodding his agreement.

"How will I know when that happens?"

"You'll know you're coming out when you start to put the affair in the broader context of your overall relationship," Roman added.

With most of Owen's preliminary questions answered Roman began to go into detail about quarantine mode using the columns he'd written on the board. He expounded on several areas vulnerable to toxic transference in a relationship where an infidelity has taken place.

Careful to be very clear, Roman explained how each area of the Quarantine Mode can be affected by the situation. He spoke of how a "quarantined attitude" promotes a mindset that fosters personal dignity. How "quarantined access and affections" create healthy boundaries, the role "quarantined actions" play in the de-escalation of hostility and increased clarity, the crucial function that "quarantined attention, assessment, and assets" play in the prevention of burnout and frustration.

"Any questions?" Roman asked.

Owen wanted to spend time processing before he asked any questions. And though he need time to process what he learned, there were a few things that resonated that he wanted to implement right away.

Roman sat down on the third stool he'd arranged in front

of the board. Up close he considered the wear and tear the
past few days had on Owen's face. He decided not to press for
a response. Instead, he suggested that Owen spend the night
in the guest bedroom rather than make the long drive back to
the extended stay hotel. Sage immediately cosigned the invitation saying it would only take a moment to change the linen
and get things ready.

"We know you keep a change of clothes in your car," she
kidded gently.

But Owen was still not comfortable being on the receiving
end of help from others, even people close to him.

"There's no need to go through that. The hotel is right off
the freeway," he said, begging off.

Roman shot it down with a quick, "It's no problem. I
already changed the linen and got the room ready. And this
saves us from having to wait up until you got to the hotel and
let us know you arrived safely. This way we can all just go to
bed." Too fatigued to counter Roman, Owen consented. Sage
quickly took Owen by the hand as she led him to the sanctu-
ary of their guest room.

#

Beneath Sage's concern for Owen driving late at night was her
desire to get some time alone with Owen, and to check on the
prep work Roman had done in the guest room. After helping
Owen get settled, and critiquing the job Roman did in prepping the guest room, which was surprisingly on par with her
a three-star hotel level, Sage sat at the foot of the bed.

"Well," Sage probed.

"Well, what?" Owen evaded.

"I know you're tired, but I thought you might have a
few issues you weren't comfortable talking about in front
of Roman that you'd want to process with me." Sage could
hardly mask the pride she took having the only backstage pass
to Owen's life.

"No," Owen said pensively. "I pretty much shared everything that was in my heart. Roman and I are cool. There's nothing about what I'm going through that I'm not comfortable disclosing it in front of him."

"Oh, so one conversation and the two of you are homies now?" Sage fired back in a mocking tone.

Irritated by her comment and not in the mood for her possessiveness, Owen said nothing. Unable, or unwilling, to read the expression on Owen's face she plowed straight ahead.

"Are you sure there's nothing you want to share?" It was like a parent asking a child if anything happened at school after getting a phone call from the teacher.

At this point Owen realized Sage was on a fishing expedition of some sort. This conversation wasn't about his need to process what was going on, it was about her need to process what was going on. It was about her need to protect the unique relationship they'd shared since childhood. Although she had always told Owen he needed a few strong men in his life, now that it was happening it was freaking her out. She was jealous of Owen and Roman's newfound closeness.

In the back of his mind, Owen was aware he would eventually have to tell Sage he didn't think it was wise for her to be so close to his situation. After going over the access and affection section of the Quarantine Mode, he was even more convinced he needed to establish clear boundaries between Sage and his current situation, especially considering her long-standing dislike of Lia, the still raw state of her recovering marriage, and the obvious way she seemed to be marking the territory around their friendship. The only problem was he was still not ready to have the conversation with her. He told himself it was mainly because he was too tired, and he did not want to create a mess Roman would have to spend the rest of the night cleaning up. The real problem Owen had with telling Sage to back off was he never liked playing the role of the man in the black hat. He hated the idea being seen as the villain.

He reasoned the wisest thing to do was let her vent her

frustration without feeding into it. Then, in the morning, he would tell her at breakfast when Roman was present to back him up. He imagined hopefully that Roman would take some of the pressure off him.

"All our lives we have shared everything with each other. I know it was difficult for you when I blew off lunch and dinner when this came to a head." He hoped giving her a little nugget would appease her until morning.

"No biggie," Sage tried to play it off with her go-to phrase and a smile that looked more like a grimace. She was not happy about the way Owen had treated her, but being the ulti-mate friend/teammate she would never confront Owen (or anyone close to her for that matter). Sage dreaded confronta-tion. It wasn't that she didn't get angry, she didn't like being out of control.

Like many people who take on the role of "prey" in a pred-atorial relationship, Sage had spent most of her childhood and the entirety of her marriage saying, "No biggie." Starting with her Sergeant Major Marine father who was seldom present and never engaged. Sgt. Maj. Bryant taught her at an early age that one must be able to sacrifice their wants and needs for "unit cohesion" and the "sake of the mission." Lost in all this discipline and decorum was any notion of mutuality. It was only Sage being asked to be a good soldier. By the time she was a young adult in college, she had mastered the art of min-imizing her wants and needs. She'd learned how to play off the insults, inconsideration, and outright disrespect of family, friends, and coworkers with a salute and a smile. In fact, the only two people she never had to handle in this way were Owen and his mom, Aunt Rosie who is her Dad's little sister. The "Sage" of her generation, Aunt Rosie had been raised by a father who was equally awkward with the emotional needs of a daughter as the Sgt. Maj. was with her.

The only intimate moments Sage could remember sharing with her father were tied to Father's Day and his birthday. On those occasions, Sage would bake a German chocolate cake from scratch just for him. Although Big Mama Bryant had handed the recipe down to all the Bryant women, Sage was the only one among her aunts and cousins willing to study at the feet of the master to perfect it. Once Sage discovered the road to her dad's heart went through his stomach, she built an express lane. Sage became a gourmet chef by the age of 23. By 28, she had an MBA degree in hospitality management from the University of North Texas in Denton. At 36, she was one of the youngest managers of a five-star hotel and resort in the industry, and one of only a handful who was African-American and female.

"Did you just drop a passive aggressive 'no biggie' on me?"

"No...I mean, yes," She knew she couldn't fool one of only three people (on earth who could interpret what, "No biggie," meant in Sage-speak. Aunt Rosie, and recently Roman, were the other two.

Recognizing how deeply he'd hurt Sage by his blowing her off, Owen extended a heartfelt apology. He owned up to his sense of shame and even confessed his avoidance of the "I told you so" he knew she harbored, but would never verbalize. To that Sage reassured him that he had no reason to be ashamed; he wasn't the one that cheated.

The two of them talked for another 25 minutes or so until Owen started to snore mid-sentence. Sage put a blanket over him as she had done many times when he arrived at her home late to spend the night because his dad had to rush his mom to the ER.

Standing in the doorway about to turn the lights out she looked back over her shoulder at her cousin. She didn't see a millionaire, a philanthropist, community leader, or a meal ticket – she saw the one boy who did not mind playing dolls with her or letting her play basketball and Sonic the Hedgehog with him and the guys. She saw her friend.

#

Roman sat up in bed wondering what was taking Sage so long. It had been over 45 minutes since he had left the two of them.

"I must have done some job getting the room ready for it to have taken this long for you to come to bed" Romans said with a note of sarcasm as she entered the room.

"No, you did a good job. Owen and I had a little catching up to do."

Knowing Sage's need to preserve her role as Owen's most intimate confidante, Roman said, "Please tell me you weren't water-boarding your poor cousin for more information?"

"No, he had a few things he wanted to share with me that he wanted to keep between the two of us," Sage said, rolling her eyes.

Too tired to challenge what he thought was a factually malnourished assertion, a moniker he sometimes used for "lies," Roman decided to drop it rather than to have the fight they were eventually going to have to have over Sage's involvement in Owen's situation.

CHAPTER EIGHTEEN

Breakfast at the Coles'

With little more than four hours of sleep, Sage still managed to get in her work out and prepare a breakfast, the likes of which should only be eaten by someone who worked in the fields all day. It was a fusion of clean cuisine and country comfort: turkey links, fresh fruit, nonfat yogurt, and gluten-free bran-muffins lying side by side with thick butcher cut slabs of maple bacon, buttermilk pancakes, eggs, grits and pork chops. As the two men made their way into the kitchen from opposite ends of the house, they were greeted by the symphony of smells that one might encounter at the most exclusive of bed and breakfasts. Overwhelmed by the sheer magnitude of the spread, the men asked in unison, "Who else did you invite to breakfast?" Sage laughed, "Nobody."

"There's no way the two of us are going to be able to eat all this food." Roman was as serious as his eyes were wide.

"Well, do your best," Sage said, "What you and Owen don't eat I will take to Mr. and Mrs. Hilliard up the street.

"Good, because you know my position on wasting food," Owen chimed in.

"Yes, we know O.B.," Sage said, rolling her eyes. "Roman, will you bless the food? But before you do I'm invoking the never used by me, Six-hour Amnesty rule. When I came to bed last night, I said something to you that was what you would call 'factually malnourished.'"

"I know," Roman said. "All is forgiven."

"Thank you, Sweetie," Sage replied with a flirtatious grin.

"You guys are weird with all your diagrams. And now

rules? Owen commented, taking his place at the kitchen table.

"Hey, we do what works for us," Roman said as he grabbed Sage and Owen's hands and bowed his head to pray.

Even though Roman outweighed Owen by almost 70 lbs., Roman tapped out first. Despite his massive frame and muscular build Roman was not much of an eater. He was on the chubby side as a child until he hit puberty around age 14; that's when everything changed. In two summers, he went from a fat kid to a grown man capable of growing a full beard. At 17, he was a teenager trapped inside the body of a 6' 3½" 235 lbs. stud linebacker. And as the quintessential high school jock, he lived up to the cliché.

Every guy wanted to be him, and every girl (and a few women) wanted him—including Mrs. Irene, the 29-year-old wife of a neighbor, who used her close friendship with his mother to emotionally and sexually molest Roman. In six months, she turned a withdrawn, 17-year-old virgin into a sexual surrogate for her absentee husband. To compound the abuse she perpetrated against Roman, Mrs. Irene mocked his lack of sexual prowess. To keep Roman from telling anyone how she repeatedly raped him, she'd turn the tables on him and accused him of being a womanizing predator who, in fact, seduced her. Her schemes against the youngster also included reminding him that if his mother were ever to found out, she would realize he was just like his father and disown him. With no one to protect him from or help process the abuse, Roman internalized it in the same way he did his relationship with his father; he entombed it in a vault of denial, anger, and shame.

To live in this state of denial, Roman had to externalize the source of his pain to avoid the process of having to look at himself. He developed controlling, confining, and forceful tactics that mimic that of a predator to prevent the women in his life from saying or doing anything remotely emotionally provocative.

In the same way that many predators in nature must

establish and defend their territory from intruders, emotional predators exhibit the same territorial behavior. Roman lived in a state of denial, driven by the delusion of control and prevention, operating under the assumption that his safety depended on his ability to restrict the power and freedom of the ones he deemed responsible for his discomfort. Namely, his mom, dad, Mrs. Irene, Sage, and anyone else he perceived as a threat to order. To maintain a sense of well-being, Roman remained vigilant in suppressing and controlling Sage's free expression of emotions.

It was this mindset that gave birth to the Trojan Man persona. This false persona acted as armor, a sort of emotional avatar whose duty it was to keep anyone from getting too close to Roman's vault of denial. It was also his duty to see to it that the sensitive chubby kid who made up the bulk of Roman's authentic self never got mocked, teased, hurt or taken advantage of again. Especially by females whom he believed always had the upper hand because of, as he put it, "their manipulative nature."

To carry out these duties Roman's Trojan Man avatar employed a series of strategies. The mainstay of which was a toxic combination of disarming charm, intimidating sarcasm, and blunt force verbalizations. All these strategies were employed to achieve an objective: dominate everyone's sense of reality. When a person has practiced emotional avoidance all their life, they find it incredibly difficult, if not impossible, to endure the pain associated with the maturation process. Instead of learning to deal with their pain by "processing their feelings," "grieving their losses," or "working through their stuff," they get to manage people and circumstances which they find easier to deal with than their feelings. Managing things and people rather than feelings fosters the development of a predatorial approach to relating to others that relies on coercion instead of intimacy.

In the world of emotional avatars, there are only winners and losers, which makes partnership impossible. One of the major drawbacks of Roman's use of the Trojan Man avatar was the eventual need to employ an additional strategy to protect the avatar who was supposed to protect him. Because the avatar itself is fictitious, it cannot do intimacy. It can neither give nor receive real love. It also has to be protected from the prying eyes of the people who want to be close to you. Over time Roman became entrenched in the denial he walked in, and in the shame that imprisoned him. This created a love–hate relationship between Roman the person and Trojan Man the persona.

Twenty minutes later Owen tapped out after he polished off four more pancakes, three sausages, and one bran muffin more than Roman. Owen was one of those people whose metabolism ran so high he could eat any quantity of whatever he wanted without gaining an ounce. Everything he ate seemed to go in one end and come out the other ounce for ounce. Consequently, Owen could consume all the junk food he wanted without a care in the world. Unfortunately, the same thing was true about Owen's emotional digestive process, especially when it came to relationships. He struggled with processing and holding onto the insight he had about the behaviors and patterns of himself and others. He seemed to be in a constant state of what the Bible calls "ever learning but unable to come to the knowledge of the truth." It wasn't because Owen lacked the necessary IQ points; he was on the borderline of being brilliant. He could process complex math equations in his head with relative ease. His deficiencies were not academic. His shortcomings were in two distinct areas of emotional intelligence: self-awareness and social skills. Although Owen would score high marks on empathy, motivation, and self-regulation on an emotional intelligence test, his self-awareness and social skills score would be barely measurable.

The lack of self-awareness and limited social skills go all the way back to his childhood. A few years after Owen was born, his mother Rosie found out she had lupus. At only 31, she struggled to manage her husband, health, house, and a newborn. Six months after his birth she had been diagnosed with postpartum depression signaling the onset of intermittent bouts of melancholia. These depressive episodes went on for the greater part of nine years, which was around the time Owen's mom found a pharmacological and therapeutic approach that helped her manage her health as well as come to terms with her limitations. The sad reality of his first ten years is that both his mother and father were emotionally unavailable to the young Owen. Not because they were bad or neglectful parents, they were both loving and compassionate people who were simply too overwhelmed to be attentive parents. As his dad explained on several occasions, it was a good thing that Owen was so low maintenance as a child because "Rosie and I were in over our heads in those early years."

At the time of his mother's diagnosis, lupus was considered a death sentence. People with the disease seldom lived more than five years past their diagnosis. Owen's family felt compelled to rehearse this inevitability. Believing his mother was living on borrowed time, he grew up deeply terrified he could lose his mother at any time. This resulted in his profound fear of being rejected or abandoned.

Because Owen carried himself with an air of maturity beyond his years, his parents never questioned the level of responsibility they expected him to shoulder for his mother's care. By the time his parents developed the coping skills to manage their house and his mom's health issues, the concrete around Owen's personality had hardened, along with his heart in many ways. He had already internalized the message that his needs weren't a priority, and his call to life was that of a good boy—translation: selfless caretaker.

Adopting the role of devoted caretaker, Owen consistently subordinated his wants and needs: first to his parents, then to his friends and family. He constantly suppressed his negative emotions to maintain his idealized view of himself. Unlike Roman's dreaded emotional avatar of "Trojan Man," Owen actually idealized his false persona of the selfless caretaker. Whereas Trojan Man kept people at bay, Selfless Caretaker strived to draw people close, thereby becoming the ultimate host.

The main drawback of being a host is the constant need for reassurance. By the time Owen reached his teens, his fragile identity was utterly dependent upon an endless stream of affirmation, accolades, and affection. Like a functional addict he'd mastered the art of hiding his addiction to flattery and constant reassurance behind a veil of humility that now might be showing signs of wear.

CHAPTER NINETEEN

The Shelia Incident

The two men sat at the breakfast table like two lions that just gorged themselves on the carcass of water buffalo. Meanwhile, Sage was packing up the leftovers with the efficiency of a takeout restaurant, complete with printed labels that identified ingredients in case of food allergies. The whole time she was instructing Roman on the delivery and set up of the food at the Hilliards' house.

"How long do you think the Hilliards have been married?" Roman asked.

"Let's see Mrs. Hilliard told me they got married six months after her eighteenth birthday, and she turned 78 a month ago that's... ah?"

"59 years and 7 months," Owen said without pausing.

"Now that's deep," Roman remarked. Owen's lightning speed was impressive. "I don't know which is more amazing, watching you calculate all that in your head, or the almost 60 years of work of the Hilliards have put in."

"Trust me, it's the 59 years and 7 months, not the math. How does a couple stay together that long?" Owen pondered out loud.

Directing his gaze at Owen, Roman said, "I imagine for them it would have been easy. They were high school sweethearts in a small town who grew up together without the internet. All they have ever known is each other. No one got divorced back then. If you married someone, it was for life."

"Umf..." Sage put her cup to her mouth to stifle a snicker. "That's what you think," she said under her breath, unaware that she'd been heard.

"Is there something you want to share with the class?" Owen said. He was eager to hear some juicy gossip.

"Well…let's just say it's a good thing that Nadine was down for the ride till the wheels fell off because Eddie was hell on wheels when they first got married."

"Chairman of the Deacon Board Hilliard? You're kidding, right?" Roman said, jerking his head back.

"Yep," Sage said as she continued packing the food without looking up. "He was a total player back in the day," she added.

"Now that you mention it, I can see it. He does have that Billy Dee Williams vibe with the deep voice and the tailored suits and Gators he rocks. And his jewelry is straight out of the old-school player's handbook," Owen smiled at the thought of the diamond-encrusted ring that Deacon Hilliard donned on his pinkie finger.

On cue as if she had just read his mind, Sage lifted her hand in the air and jutted out her pinky finger. This made Owen laugh out loud.

"Oh, and don't forget the pocket watch with the thick gold chain, and the blinged-out cross over the tie," he added. "And if it's cold, a real player must have the overcoat draped, not worn, over the shoulder, along with the fedora hat cocked ever so slightly to the side." He was on a roll.

"Wait! Wait! Let's not forget the pièce de résistance, the Pierre Cardin cologne circa 1972," Sage said, pantomiming spraying cologne over herself.

"That's enough you two," Roman said in a righteous tone. He had always admired Mr. Eddie, as he called him, for being "a man of God" who walked with integrity. Listening to Owen and Sage mock him was unsettling at a deep level because it brought up memories of his father.

"Why are you spreading gossip about Mr. Eddie?"

"Oh…it's not gossip. These are facts. I got them straight from the horse's mouth," Sage said, responding to Roman's rebuke in a defiant tone. "They shared their story with me the night I confided in her after 'the Sheila Incident.'"

"I didn't know you talked to her," Roman averted his eyes from Sage's gaze and began to fidget with the salt shaker.

"I spoke to the both of them that night; I had to talk to someone. They're the main reason you did not come home to an empty house the next morning," Sage added.

"What's the Sheila Incident?" Owen regretted asking the question the moment the words passed through his lips.

With her hand clamped over her mouth as though she was trying to push the words back in, Sage looked at Roman. Signs of terror were on her face as she mouthed, "Sorry, it slipped" to Roman, who stared back blankly.

"It's okay. The Sheila Incident officially refers to the way Sage found out I had cheated on her," His voice monotone as someone resigned to his fate.

"You told me he confessed and that's how you found out," Owen said bewildered.

"That's true. He did confess," Sage said, trying to close the Pandora's box that she'd inadvertently opened.

"It's okay. I don't mind telling him if you don't," said Roman to Sage.

She nodded her agreement.

"If this is something the two of you aren't comfortable sharing, I don't have to know," Owen assumed he'd get it out of Sage when Roman wasn't around.

"You've been open with me about your stuff, the least I can do is be open to you about my stuff," Roman said. "Sheila is the name of one of the women I had an affair with, and the one that ultimately told Sage I was cheating."

Finding her voice again, Sage offered, "It wasn't that she told me, it was how said."

"Yeah, it was how she did it," Roman said, his jaw clenched and disdain in his voice.

"All right so, which one of you is going to tell me how it went down?" Owen asked, shifting eye contact back and forth between the two of them.

"I got this since I am the one that created the mess," Roman said to Sage.

"You sure?"

"Yeah, I'm sure." Roman sat erect in his seat. He leaned forward and placed his forearms on the table to support his well-developed but now limp frame. After clearing his throat a couple of times to steady himself, he began.

"Before I tell you how it happened, I need to give you some of the back story," he said by way of introduction. "A little over nine months ago, I went to recruit this kid out of Pasadena. He was one of those hybrid linebacker/D-ends who specialized in sacking quarterbacks."

"Let me guess, his mother's name was Sheila?" Owen interrupted

"Just let him tell the story O.B.," Sage said, knowing Roman's reluctance to share his "personal business" as he referred to it.

Roman continued. "Towards the end of the home visit the dad ask me to take a ride with him. During the ride he asked me why should he trust my words since most recruiters are little more than used car salespersons? My response to his question changed the whole dynamic of our conversation, as well as my life, marriage, and future. I gave him my personal word I would look after his son. Again, he said, 'How do I know if I can trust your word?'

"Thinking I was about to close the deal I told him, 'You can ask any parent, kid or school official I've dealt with if I am a man of my word.' That's when he flipped it on me." Roman recounted how Coach Perkins had pointed out that Roman's professional reputation was not in question, and how he asked for a personal reference from Sage.

"He said, 'Here is the five-star question: If I called your wife and asked her about the level of trust she would put in your word based on how you have treated her, what would she say?'"

"Oh man," Owen said, his fist to his mouth half shocked and half amused.

"I was shocked," Roman said. "I just sat there. I couldn't even make up something because the question came so out of left field. He knew by my body language, and the fact that I was speechless, that my wife wouldn't vouch for me. Then he completely knocked me off my game by asking why hadn't I been a good husband. I couldn't admit to how much of a dog I was at the time, so I gave him some lame excuse about it being complicated. That's when he flipped it on me again."

Owen's amusement dissipated as Roman told of how Jr.'s turned down the offer for his son to join the Trojans team in the fall—not because Roman wasn't a man of his word, but because his wife was giving him a chance to fix their marriage and he wasn't taking it.

"Without missing a beat he told me he couldn't put his son in the hands of a man who made excuses when he should be making changes."

"I don't get it. What did he mean by that?" Owen was genuinely confused. What did one have to do with the other.

"He wasn't bothered by the reality that I'd been a dog for most of my marriage as much as he was bothered by the fact that Sage was giving me a chance to step up and be a man, and all I did with the opportunity was make excuses."

"Oh, I see. Wow, that was cold-blooded," Owen said.

"The cold part was how he handled me after that. He didn't say it in a condemning way, he just said it in the way I imagine a father would have told his son if he were disappointed in him, which made it made it more painful. I couldn't even be mad at him. Honestly, I would have preferred he had just called me a dog and been done with me. "

"Yeah, I'll take anger over disappointment any day of the week.

"Especially since we were still thirty minutes away from his house."

"Oh man, how did that go?" Owen cringed.

"It was brutal. It had to be the longest 30 minutes of my life, and yet what made it so amazing was his attitude towards me never changed. It was weird. It was like: This is true and this is what I think about. Let's move on."

Roman continued, "When we got back to his house, he walked me to my car, grabbed me and put me in a big old bear hug, then whispered in my ear: 'It's not complicated, it's just scary.' I kick myself daily for not heeding that piece of advice."

"You've talked to him since then?"

"Oh yeah, we've talked a lot since then. He's the man that saved my marriage. He told me I needed to have a conversation with Sage where I put all my cards on the table, apologize, and ask if we could make a fresh go of it, but only if I meant it. At the time, I was carrying around way too much shame to have a conversation as open and authentic as the one he was encouraging me to have. I also didn't think there was any way Sage would, should or could forgive me if she knew a fraction of the stuff I'd pulled over the last several years. I still had a truckload of ego to protect and a lot of game left in me. Instead of dealing with the situation head on, I decided to do an end-around. I made a clean break from all the side chicks.'

Sage broke her silence. "You know I hate it when you call women side chicks, side or otherwise. It's demeaning to women—even to home wrecking skanks."

Roman promptly apologized for momentarily forgetting his wife's aversion to the term. Owen waited patiently for him to continue telling the backstory of the Sheila Incident.

"My plan was to make a fresh start on my own without having to ask for forgiveness or face what I had done," Roman resumed. "Honestly, I was already tired of the entire running around even before my first encounter with Coach Perkins. That conversation with him just solidified it. Well, almost solidified it. I hadn't quite hit rock bottom yet."

Roman sighed. "I called them up and one by one I told them I'd "found religion" so to speak, and I wanted to work on my marriage. All of them seemed cool with the idea. Heck, one of them said she thought it was God at work. Told me she'd be praying for us. She even encouraged me to start going to church."

"See that's why I can't get into the whole church scene," Owen interjected.

"Down boy," Sage said quickly, daring Owen to make another comment with her eyes. "You know how I feel about you talking about the Lord's house and His people. I'm not trying to have this house struck by lightning."

"Uh-hm," Roman cleared his throat. "The only one that didn't take the news well was this chick... uh, woman that I'd been seeing off and on from back in the day named, Sheila. When I told Sheila, she went all fatal attraction on me. She accused me of making promises to her that made her put her life on hold. She started talking all this crazy stuff about how I'd seduced and deceived her. She ranted, but I kept my cool and stayed on message like a politician: 'It's over... Sorry you're disappointed...I love my wife...I want to be with her...I apologize if that's the impression I gave you but...'

"When the conversation ended I had a sinking feeling I was in for some drama. Something told me to come clean, confess my sins to Sage, and face what I had coming. Even then Coach Perkins' baritone was in my head like the voice of God. I could hear him saying 'Put your cards on the table.' Call it fear, shame or denial, I knew what to do but I couldn't. I just couldn't. Instead, I called my boy Mitch who knew a brother who'd also messed with her back in the day. I asked him what he thought her 'freak out potential' was."

"Freak out potential?" Owen asked.

"Sorry man, I forgot who I was talking to. It's a term a few of my boys and I came up with to describe the cost of being with a girl who's clingy, jealous, controlling, full of drama or just plain crazy. If one of our boys wanted to mess with someone, we'd ask him 'What's her freak potential vs. her freak-out potential?' In other words, 'What's the chance of getting caught up in some drama over the girl when you're done?'" Roman explained.

"Got it, got it. It's a cost–benefits analysis," Owen said, nearly salivating. "Wow, that's a new one. I can't wait to drop that on the kids at The Center." He was always on the lookout for ways to keep the kids engaged during math tutoring sessions. This page from Roman's playbook was something the teens could relate to.

So, what <u>was</u> her freak out potential?" Owen urged Roman on with the story.

"According to my boy Mitch, he said his homeboy would put her at a level nine, on the border of being a ten. He told me to watch my back because she tried to set up his boy in some mess with a wannabe thug from Springdale West in the L.B."

"If at level nine you need to watch your back, shouldn't that be considered a level ten?" Owen asked.

"Level ten is harm brought to your doorstep that creates collateral damage. For a brother who's a real player, getting hurt for running game is just the cost of doing business. You get your story right, you go home, and you up your game. But if some chick you've been messing with brings it to your door step, that's a whole 'nother situation altogether-"

Knowing Owen's unhealthy fascination with all things 'hood, Sage intervened to try and refocus them.

"Uh...Owen is not the little homie, Roman, and you're not an OG. He doesn't need you teaching him about a game you've retired from and one he'll never play."

Duly chastised, Owen asked, "So, what did you do?"

"I implemented the slow fade," Roman continued. "Don't call, don't respond, and eventually she'll get the message. She didn't know where I lived, so she couldn't bring it to my door-step. I rarely go into the 'hood except to get a haircut, to get my car washed at Seals, or to check in with a few of my boys who didn't make it out, but are still good people-"

"Okay, okay! Enough of the player talk. Get on with the story, Roman." Sage's face was now set with a church mother glare.

Owen, completely engrossed, also egged him on. "Weren't you worried?" he asked.

"No, not a bit," said Roman. "Thinking I'd put Shelia in

the rearview mirror, I instituted 'Operation Dedication.' We moved into a gated community where Sage was closer to her job. I started spending more time at home. I worked on my communication skills and all kinds of relationship stuff. I'd made up my mind I was going to put the same amount of energy into saving my that I'd put into jeopardizing it. Things were going smooth, real smooth for the first two months. At least, that's what I thought."

This was Sage's unspoken cue. "Even though he was doing a lot of the things that I'd asked him to do, I wasn't buying it," she said picking up where Roman left off, "I thought something was going on. I thought Roman might be planning to divorce me. So, while he was doing his 'Mr. Lover, Lover' routine, I was waiting for the other shoe to drop. Well…it didn't take long because not long after that I…"

Roman interrupted Sage mid-sentence. "Do you want to share this part of the story or do you want me to finish it?" he said almost tenderly.

"I think I need to tell it to do it justice; I am the one who withheld what happened from him," Sage's tone matched his.

"But I am the reason it happened."

"I need to do this so I can own and grieve it," Sage countered.

Sensing Sage's resolve Roman leaned back in his chair and said, "Go for it."

Owen was completely mesmerized by their display of selfless communication. *Could this be real?* he wondered.

Sage took the seat next to Roman and slid closer to him. She positioned herself directly across from Owen. Simultaneously, Roman leaned back further to put his arm around her, allowing her to get even closer.

"Well," Sage took a deep breath and clutched the linen napkin on the table. "It was a Tuesday morning," she exhaled. "I got to the office about 8:30 a.m. and was going through my messages when I came across a voicemail from a woman named, Sheila."

"No! She didn't leave a message, did she?" Roman motioned

with his free hand for Owen to hold his questions and let Sage tell her story.

Sage continued, "The message said, 'Hi Sage, my name is Sheila. You don't know me, but I'm an old friend of your husband, Roman. I'm getting married next spring and Roman recommended I call you to check on the availability of your facility sometime in late April. Again, my name is Sheila. I can be reached by cell at blah, blah, blah.' Long story short, I thought even though I didn't oversee the special events and catering department anymore, I would give her a tour of the place before handing her off to our event staff. Thinking I was doing a favor for a friend of Roman's, I decided to give her the VIP tour. I comped her lunch and spa treatment before we met up for the tour of the grounds."

"Man, that's bold!" Owen hated to interrupt, but could not contain himself.

"Oh, that's not the half of it. This skank went over 750 dollars for lunch and spa treatment before she had me take her on a full tour of the facility: wedding suite, private villas, ballroom...the whole nine. From the ballroom I took her to see the garden where Roman and I got married."

"It was already set up for the three weddings we had scheduled for Friday and Saturday. To close the deal, we take people through the big automated glass doors that lead to the garden area and walk them down the aisle to paint a picture of what their magical day will be like" Sage continued, reliving the moment. "We were walking down the aisle, I'm thinking I'm closing the deal, and she's nodding like everything is okay. We get to the end of the aisle where we are standing in the archway of flowers. I turn to her and asked: 'So what do you think of our facilities?' And while standing at the altar where Roman and I got married, this woman proceeds to tell me that she's been having an affair with my husband for the past three years. She goes on to say she has tried to break things off with him for the last two months so he could work on his marriage, but Roman kept calling her and begging her to take him back. She said he'd even promised to leave me if she would take him back," Sage paused to steal her emotions. Roman rubbed her arm in an effort to assure his wife the memory she was reliving was just that—a memory.

"Stunned, I stood there," Sage continued. "Shelia kept talking. She told me she decided to say something in the hope that Roman would stop harassing her so she could move on with her life. She then apologized for the affair, claiming she didn't know Roman was married when they first hooked up. By the time she found out he was married, she'd already fallen in love and did not want to lose him but wanted to do the Godly thing."

"When I finally opened my mouth, all I could say was, "How do I know you've even met my husband?" She told me she knew everything about Roman, me, and our marriage. 'I know where the two of you live, where you shop, and where you go to church. I also know what he likes to eat, what he wants in bed. Hell, I even know what you like in bed.' Then, she said the one thing that let me know she was telling the truth: 'I also know you have scaring due to fibroids and can't have children. I know Roman won't consider adoption because he doesn't want to raise someone else's problems.' Well, that's it, Owen. That's how I found out my husband was cheating on me," She wiped her moist eyes.

"You're telling me this wench came to your job, ate a comped lunch, got a spa treatment to the tune of almost 1,000 dollars, and let you give her a tour of the facility, all while pretending like she was looking for a place to have her wedding? Then tells you, at the altar where you got married, that she'd been having an affair with your husband?"

Unable to speak, Sage nodded as she dabbed at the tears flowing down her cheeks.

"Wow, you got to be a straight up sociopath to do some heinous stuff like that!" Owen felt indignation at as he took in the sheer magnitude of Sheila's boldness. "What did you do after she dumped all that in your lap," his morbid curiosity spurred him to ask.

"Ironically, to steady myself I sat down on one of the white wooden folding chairs on the front row...right where Roman's mother sat at our wedding. I was so stunned I couldn't say anything. I was in shock."

"You didn't say anything?"

"No, not a word."

"Man...She's lucky she wasn't dealing with any of the other Bryant women. They would have had plenty to say." He pictured white chairs and colorful words flying at Sheila's head.

"Oh, I had plenty to say. I just couldn't get it out. Believe me, I've replayed the conversation over a thousand times in my head. I still can't believe I let her punk me at my job!" Sage had to admit she was still bothered by how weak she had been.

"So how did the conversation end?"

"I do not know if she felt sorry for me or what, but she said she was sorry again and left. I called security to make sure she left the grounds. I sat at my desk staring out the window for what seemed like hours. I couldn't stop crying. Finally, I collected myself and went home. The next morning when Roman walked through the door after a scouting trip, I asked him who is Sheila? That's when he came clean about everything. It took us about two weeks to separate the lies Sheila had told me about their relationship from the lies Roman had told me about our marriage," She glanced out the corner of her eye at Roman. She could see him struggling to keep his composure.

Roman caught a glimpse of her peering at him. He muttered a faint "Excuse me," and hastily got up from the table before hurrying out the room. For the next few minutes, Sage tried to make small talk with Owen, even though she wanted to go and check on Roman.

"You know it's okay if you go and check on your husband" Owen said.

"Do you mind?" Sage asked, ever the gracious host.

"Go ahead," Owen said. He shooed her away with his hands. "I need to get going anyway."

CHAPTER TWENTY

Sage and Roman Round Two

Sage made her way back to their bedroom only to find the lights out and the blinds closed. Roman sat on the edge of their bed with his head in his hands. It was evident to Sage that he had been crying.

"Are you okay, Honey?" Sage asked.

"I don't know," Roman said without looking up. Sage joined him on the side of the bed.

"What's wrong?" her tone gentle as she put her arms around his broad shoulders.

Overcome with shame, Roman could barely stand Sage's ever-faithful presence, let alone her touch. He recoiled as though driven to respond out of some primitive instinct. Somewhere deep inside of his damaged soul a voice was screaming: "You're not worthy. You are just like your dad."

Rather than respond to his rejection of her touch as she had done in the past, she moved in even closer and contoured her body to every open space of Roman's slumped frame. The moment he felt the warmth of her body the emotional dam inside him burst. The heart he had maintained at slightly above freezing was thawing, not only towards Sage but himself as well. All the years of hiding his pain behind a wall of power, posturing, and pretense had taken its toll on Roman. The shame he had managed to keep at bay had pierced the barrier between his head and his heart. And like a tidal wave, it took out every landmark of normalcy in Roman's life. All the distractions in his life that made him emotionally unavailable disappeared in an instant and now, only the "scary" he and Coach had talked about was left.

For the rest of the day, Roman checked out for the most part. He remained hold up in his office: no food, no film study, no phone calls, no conversation. The Trojan covered smartphone that many believed was an extension of his right hand spent the entire day on the bedroom nightstand. In fact, it was so out of character for Roman to not answer his phone, several people called Sage in a panic wondering if something had happened to him. Sage told them he was fine, and that he was just exhausted from all the traveling he had been doing and needed to catch up on his rest. Covering for him in this manner made Sage feel uneasy.

#

In all the years they dated, he'd never been like this. No matter what was going on in his world, Roman always had the ability to play it off, to never let them see him sweat. The gregarious always-outgoing Roman had done something he'd never done before—he turned inward to deal with his shame. It was his way to deflect and distract rather than lash out. And as much as it pained Sage to see him like this, deep inside she judged Roman for being weak. She could not help herself. It was one thing if Roman were having a moment, it was quite another if that moment turned into hours, days, or weeks.

As the afternoon wore on it became more difficult for Sage to hide her anxiety. By early evening, her intermittent gentle check-ins on Roman turned into a full-fledged challenge. By 7:30 that evening, Sage had enough. She walked into the room where Roman lay on the couch with his back to the door. Standing in the middle of the room, she issued the following edict: "I don't know what's bothering you, but you need to stop PMS'ing over it and snap out of it! This little phase you're in is not attractive, let alone manly. Stop feeling sorry for yourself and pull your head out of your butt!"

There! It was straight out of her Sergeant Major Dad's playbook, "Motivation 101." To hear him tell it, if you sincerely want to motivate someone, nothing beats shame. Sage had resorted to the same tactics her dad used on her when she was a child and he would say: "Now you're just acting like a girl. Pull your head out of your behind and snap out of it." In the same way he attacked her femininity, she'd just attacked Roman's masculinity.

"*Where on earth did that come from?*" Sage wondered as she stood there as though a dispossessed spirit had uttered the words that had come out of her mouth. Unfortunately, there was no time to process it. If she heard it, Roman heard it.

Before she could try to take it back, Roman was on his feet, headed out the door across the courtyard with the dexterity and speed of a Bengal tiger. In an instant he managed to extricate himself from the couch, get around her, and make his way to their bedroom. In what felt like only a few minutes to Sage, Roman re-emerged from the bedroom looking and smelling like a man going out on a date. Wherever he was going, it looked like Trojan Man was driving. Wearing a pair of high gloss Kenneth Cole shoes, slate gray slacks, and a gray and white linen shirt Sage has been particularly fond of, he walked by her without saying a word.

"What's going on?" she said, grabbing his arm to get him to stop and talk.

"This is me snapping out of it," he said seductively.

"Where are you going?" Sage asked, rushing behind him.

Roman spun around. His face wore a sinister grin she'd never seen before. He looked her in the eyes and said, "I'm making a Tampax run."

"What does that mean?"

"You figure it out! I'm too unmanly, unattractive and PMS'ing to explain it to you!"

As he put his hand on the doorknob she pleaded, "Roman stop, we need to talk." But, to no avail, Roman was on anger autopilot. When the big black doors eclipsed the last sliver of light from the porch, Sage was in an absolute state of panic. "*What have I done?*" she thought. Of all the remarks she could have made, she unfortunately chose to push Roman's most well-worn button—his manhood.

"*Stupid, stupid, stupid,*" she muttered to herself.

It didn't take long for her to do the math. She was more than aware of the damage that a well-groomed, good-smelling, well-dressed, hurt and angry Roman could do on a Saturday night in a city brimming with lonely women who had no problem taking advantage of a vulnerable marriage.

CHAPTER TWENTY-ONE

Mrs. Bryant-Cole vs. Mrs. Bryant

After her numerous texts apologizing to Roman went unanswered, Sage needed to talk to someone. Whether out of desperation or some primal instinct, she did something she never imagined herself doing—she called her mother. Their relationship wasn't bad as mother–daughter relationships go, it was just shallow (more like half an inch thick and 100 miles wide). Sage often said of their relationship that the only reason she wouldn't label it as superficial is because "the first five letters of the word spell: super." And theirs was anything but. They could talk about anything while never dealing with anything.

Mrs. Bryant was equally shocked that her daughter chose call her to share something personal. After Sage explained to her mom what happened, Mrs. Bryant laughed in that soft, passive tone that thoroughly irked Sage growing up. It was as if she knew something that the rest of the world didn't.

"What's so funny Mom" Sage spoke in a monotone voice—a sign of her own passive-aggression.

"You are so much like your father," Mrs. Bryant answered in a laughing whisper.

"How's that?"

"You think love is something you can pull off without dealing with feelings."

"Oh please, Dad deals with his feelings just fine," Sage fired back.

"Okay, but you asked."

"Listen, Roman is the one who struggles with his feelings not me," said Sage.

"Is he now? Are you sure about that?" There it was again, that all-knowing tone.

"What are you trying to say?" her voice raising octave. "You don't think that I deal with my feelings?"

"Oh, you deal with them well enough. I just don't think you process them well," Mrs. Bryant answered.

"No offense Mom, but how about you?" Sage purposely baited her mother.

"None taken. What about me?" her tone remained inviting, but camouflaged.

"You don't process your feelings at all. So maybe I got this swallow your feelings thing from you," her tone now sarcastic and unapologetic.

"Some stuff you did get from me, and I am quite proud of that. But some things you got from your dad, and that's the part that worries me."

"Mom you never express any of your feelings. At least Dad tells you what's in his heart, everybody talks about how open he is!"

Again Mrs. Bryant laughed at the childlike defiance in her daughter's tone. "No he doesn't, Sagie. He tells you what's on his mind, that's not the same as saying what's on your heart. Ask your dad what he feels about something and he'll tell you what he thinks, knows, or believes. In all the years I have known your father, he's never started a sentence with 'I feel.' I think you're confusing openness with unfiltered impulsiveness, intimidation, and stubbornness seasoned with cluelessness.

"As for me," she sighed, "I have always shared what's in my heart. Just not with people like you or your father. I only share my feelings with people who are emotionally safe. My girls, Tina and Rachael are where I go when I need to vent, my old pastor and his wife when I need to be affirmed and challenged, and occasionally my therapist when I need a little confidential objectivity to sort things out. Things like the first few years of my marriage when I had to decide if I was going to stay with your dad or not."

"What!" Sage gasped, "Wait a minute! You see a therapist and you thought about divorcing my father? I don't believe it."

"I had to. Who wouldn't have? Look Sagie, I know you think your dad walks on water, and in your eyes he can do no wrong but, despite his saintly qualities as a father, he was hell to deal with as a husband. Back then he was even more of a jerk and a bully than he is now, though he's gotten a lot better over the years. Living with him was no walk in the park back then. He and I had to work through some things. He's matured a whole lot since the early days." Sage couldn't believe what she was hearing. She had never heard her mother speak so bluntly about anything.

"How come this is the first that I'm hearing about all this?" Sage was torn between being afraid of her mother's answer and needing to hear it.

"Like I said, you struggle with dealing with the feelings of others, which is why I don't share what's on my heart with you. Every time I've tried to have a serious conversation with you about something that makes you uncomfortable, you'd either shut down or become dismissive. I wasn't about to waste my time trying to get through to you...one Sargent Major in the house was enough. You've been like that ever since you were a kid," Mrs. Bryant exclaimed.

"C'mon Momma," Sage said, reacting to what she felt was a clear insult.

"Okay, Sagie. But you did ask."

"So, what else have you been keeping from me that you think I can't handle?" Sage dared her mother to validate her point.

"Are you sure you want me to give you an answer considering all the other stuff you got going on right now?" Mrs. Bryant cautioned.

Sage placed the phone on the kitchen counter, hit speaker, stepped out of her shoes, took a step back, folded her arms and with all the confidence of a bully about to take another kids' lunch money declared, "Oh yeah, I'm sure. Go 'head. Now is as good a time as any."

"Mmm," Mrs. Bryant said, pondering where to start. Sage could swear she could hear her mother smirking through the phone.

"Well let's see," she began. "I know you don't respect me because I didn't pursue success at the level you thought I should have. This despite the fact I have two master's degrees and a Ph.D., and you only have one masters degree."

Mrs. Bryant continued, as though she was calling the roll in one of her classrooms.

"I know you think thirty-eight years of teaching in the 'ghetto' as you put it isn't an achievement, even though you're on the board of Owen's non-profit, in the same neighborhood, working with the same 'at risk' children. I know you think I'm weak because of the way I let your father run over me. I know your greatest fear is winding up as weak and pathetic as you think I am. I know your number one goal in life is your dad's approval."

Mrs. Bryant could imagine the wheels in her daughter's brain spinning and paused a few seconds to allow Sage time to catch up. Her silence signaled that she was either in shock or attempting to process. "Is that enough or do want me to go on?"

Feeling like someone who just had all the buttons pressed on the elevator to their reasoning, Sage was rendered speechless.

"I respect you," Sage muttered. Collecting herself, she continued: "I always tell people what a strong black woman you are."

"Save it Sage! I thought we were doing truth," Mrs. Bryant replied, with that smirking know-it-all laugh Sage despised.

"No, seriously. I am always telling people the story of how you just about raised me by yourself, at the same time you finished your education," Sage said, going all in.

"I don't doubt that you say it, I just doubt that you tell it from the perspective of a daughter who's proud of her mom's accomplishments. Do you want to know why I didn't advance in my career? It's because the man I fell in love with and married, your father, would not have been able to handle it. If I had pursued my career, he would have had to change his, which would have devastated him because unlike him, I have always had options. I could have done whatever I wanted to do. Your father, on the other hand, is a different story. The military or law-enforcement were the only options for a person as emotionally unavailable and rigid as your father could work in and be successful. He was too mathematically challenged to be a successful engineer or accountant."

Sage could hear her mother sigh heavily on the other end of line as Mrs. Bryant continued, "As much as I wanted to pursue my career, I wanted my marriage to work more. I also wanted to be there for you. I made sacrifices that matched my priorities. My lack of talking about it reflects my acceptance of my choices which I deem as a strength, not a weakness. Every year my principal asked me if I was ready to come out of the classroom. Even when I retired I had people ask me if I would be willing to take a run at a spot on the school board.

"Oh, and here's another truth for you," Mrs. Bryant lowered her voice as if to reveal a secret. "Your father being in the military served my purpose as much as it served his and the Marines. Even though I'd always envisioned myself marrying a man who would be more involved in the daily running of the house, it would not have worked out well for any of us. Trust me, it was better he was gone for long stretches of time. It allowed me to raise you with a reasonably soft heart towards others. The last thing the world needed was a Jr. Sergeant Major."

"Wow," Overwhelmed by her mother's confession, Sage slumped over her phone.

"Sage, the only truth about your momma you need to come to terms with is the fact I made choices that required me to make sacrifices, not compromises. On the second date of our courtship, your father got all worked up over a conversation we were having. I waited for him to finish his point then told him that there were eight things he needed to know about me if he wanted us to spend the rest of our lives together: 1) The Lord gets ten percent of everything I make. 2) Don't ever complain about the things I spend my money on once the house is taken care of—especially if I'm sharing what I bought with him, 3) Keep all that Bryant drama out of our house. 4) If he ever puts his hands on me in anger I'm out, 5) If he ever calls me out of my name, I'm out, 6) If he tries to intimidate me or 7) cheats on me, I'm out, and lastly, 8) He needs to stay in shape to keep momma happy. Do that and we would get along just fine. Not once has he ever challenged me on any of the standards I asked him to abide by, which, by the way, is why we are together to this day." Mrs. Bryant said.

"Wow...okay...okay..." Astonished, Sage searched for words. "My world has officially been rocked. That explains a lot—like why he yells at everyone else in the family but you? I thought it was because he thought you were too weak or fragile to take it."

"Yep, that's also why he hits that gym every day. Baby, that isn't a Marine thing, that's a momma thing! Now that's your momma's version of who she is and what she is all about. I chose my love for my husband and the love I have for you over my – (quote) – potential. If that makes me a bad role model in your view of female empowerment, so be it. I may not have been a good role model, but I was a damn good mother and wife," Mrs. Bryant said proudly, her voice cracking.

Sage's eyes welled with hot tears. "That you were and that you are Momma," she managed. "All I can say is, wow. While Dad and I were playing checkers, you were playing chess," she chuckled, not unlike her mother.

"What can I say? I just took the strategy and effort I would have put into building a career and applied it to raising a daughter who could have a better career and what I hoped would be a better marriage. I had such high hopes for you and Roman," she sighed. "He's good for you."

"What do you mean by high hopes?" Sage asked.

"Sage, the man I met and fell in love with was bitter about a lot of things, which is why he thinks he has the right, as well as the duty, to be mean and nasty to people. The man you met and fell in love with is wounded, not entitled; trust me there is a difference! Roman is a nice guy with a broken heart and an orphaned spirit who needs to be challenged and affirmed by another good man, a man who knows how to honor a woman's femininity and not exploit it. Then, he needs the love and affirmation of a woman who embraces her femininity instead of rejecting it," Mrs. Bryant said.

"What are you talking about he has an orphaned spirit? What kind of spiritual mumbo-jumbo is that?" Sage said. She instantly regretted the flippant way she posed the question. Either Mrs. Bryant didn't hear it or simply chose to ignore it.

"Roman is a half black and half Cuban male whose father died when he was ten—and on his birthday no less—who was raised by a black single mother in a predominantly Mexican neighborhood," Mrs. Bryant was well aware of Roman's background.

His birth certificate reads: Raymòn Rogelio Guevara. He'd changed it when he turned 15 to "Roman Augustus" because he thought it sounded strong, and too the last name "Cole" to honor his mother, Nicole. Not only did he reject his father's last name, he also rejected his mother's last name. It said a lot about his perception of the men in his life, and of himself.

"You don't think a man that wounded might have some identity issues?" Mrs. Bryant said with a hint of frustration and sarcasm directed at Sage.

"Then if that weren't enough, the only affirmation he has gotten from men occurred when he was taking the head off a quarterback or the drawers off some floozy. Your husband isn't a dog, he's a boy trapped in a man's body searching for a father."

"Oh my God, Mom, you did not just say drawers and floozy?"

"Well, that's what we use to call them. I know what they're called now, I'm just not comfortable with all that foul language," Mrs. Bryant was embarrassed she had even gone that far.

"Let's say you're right and that's what he needs long term. What do I do about tonight?" Sage's question had notes of desperation all over it.

"Listen. This evening you sent the same mixed message to your husband that many women send to the men in their lives. On the one hand, we tell our husbands we want them to be open, vulnerable, and to share their feelings. But when they do, we flip out because they're now appear weak. Then what do we do? We turn on them because their weakness makes us feel vulnerable," Mrs. Bryant explained.

"Mm" was all Sage could say as she began to connect the dots in her head. *"For the past 10 months, I've been looking for a sign that Roman felt my pain and when he final showed me a sign I attacked him for being weak,"* she thought.

"Understand what you did Sagie. You put a good-looking, articulate, well-dressed, sweet smelling man on the streets with his pride wounded and something to prove. What do you think is going to happen given his history?"

"What do you mean his history?" Sage was incredulous. She couldn't help but be defensive about the insinuation of chinks in the armor of the three men in her life: Roman, Owen or her father.

"Girl, please! Remember we're doing truth tonight. Now is not the time for you to go Bryant on me. It doesn't take a rocket scientist to figure out what a man as fine and insecure as your husband does to be affirmed when he doesn't have positive role models in his life."

"You're right. What would you do at this point?" Sage conceded.

"Hold on, let me savor the moment for a minute. My daughter has asked me for my advice, "Thank you, Jesus!" she shouted into the phone. "Now, here's what you do. Call him, don't text him. Then, tell him you were wrong, wrong on two counts. The first thing you did was send him the message his home wasn't a safe place for him to be emotionally vulnerable. Then, you tell him the second mistake you made was sending a man that fine out on the town, looking and smelling that good, without you on his arm to make other women jealous. Finally, you ask him if you can meet him somewhere for dinner, drinks, dessert, coffee, a Slurpee, or anythang. Yes, I said 'thang.'"

"That won't work. Roman's not into all the flirty stuff, he's pretty straight forward."

Mrs. Bryant laughed again, "Whew, there's still so much Momma needs to teach you. You think he left the house looking and smelling good because he wanted to feel pretty? No, he's looking for a woman to glue together the shattered pieces of his ego you crushed. Call him before you make your third big mistake of the day."

"Okay Momma, I'll do it, I'll do it."

"Don't do it for me, do it for your marriage. Trust Momma on this. This old lady knows a lot more about this stuff than you think she does."

"Thanks, Momma. I'll call you tomorrow to give you an update. Oh, and don't think I didn't notice what you did with the Bryant name," Sage said.

"You knew what I meant, though. Oh, and Sagie," she measured her words carefully, "Use your sexiest bedroom voice when you talk to him, not that customer service-white girl voice you use when you answer the phone at work. Tonight, you need to embrace your ethnic feminine side."

"All right, that's enough sister-sister for one night." Sage couldn't believe her face was actually turning red.

"Hey, as you guys say, Momma is just trying to keep it 100. Besides, you called me I didn't call you."

"Okay Momma. Thanks so much." Sage quickly grabbed the phone off the counter and cupping it in both hands put it close to her mouth. "I love you Momma, and I'm sorry for being such a butthole all these years."

"Love you too Sagie. Bye-Bye," Mrs. Bryant said. A smile

of accomplishment spread across her face as she hung up the phone.

Despite her reticence, Sage took her mom's advice and called Roman immediately, and to her surprise he picked up on the second ring. Startled that he picked up the phone so fast it took her a moment to summon her sexy voice. Once she got it going, she worked it like a rented limo on prom night. It took only ten minutes for her to get Roman to agree to meet her at an Italian restaurant in the Grove.

As soon as she got off the phone with Roman she texted her mom—"You were right. Thanks again." Within minutes her mother responded. "Learn to embrace your femininity. It's the only tool a woman can use to get a romantic dinner out of a husband when she's the one who did wrong. Don't forget to spend the rest of the evening reaffirming his manhood. You need to fill the shame hole you dug in his heart with honor and affirmation."

#

When Sage's face appeared on his phone – Roman felt like Captain Kirk after spending too much time on a strange planet – all he wanted Sage to do was beam him up. In the past hour and half sitting at the bar trying to watch sports on the big screen, he'd experienced the zombie apocalypse that is the dating seen. Already he had been hit on by four women desperate to buy him a drink, one dude wearing eyeliner who tried to get Roman to buy him a drink. As much as he wanted to punish Sage by not answering the phone the truth is his passion for hanging out in bars was as extinct as the jerry curl.

After exchanging "Hey's" and a few awkward moments Sage broke the silence.

"I apologize for wanting you to be vulnerable, then turning on you when you were," She then asked if she could make it up to him by taking him out for dinner. Throwing on her

I-got-a-date-with-my-man dress and a fresh coat of red high gloss polish on her nails to match, she headed out the house.

#

Once they were seated Sage reached across the table resting her hands on his hands.

"I am so sorry."

Roman smiled back and said, "No biggie," Then leaned across the table and kissed her.

CHAPTER TWENTY-TWO

Lunch Number One:
The Forgiveness Phase

A few days after his dinner with Sage, Roman met Coach Perkins for lunch. He filled him in on his short-term lapse back into Trojan Man. Coach Perkins shared the how and why Roman and Sage's conversation escalated.

"Forgiveness and mercy play a vital role in the recovery process. Without them, long- term relationships are unsustainable because everything we say and do would eventually become tainted by unresolved grievances we have toward one another. Forgiveness and mercy address the grievances within the relationship by demythologizing the stories we tell ourselves about the level of grievance that has taken place.

"The goal is to take the focus off the things we think should have happened, be happening, or need to happen, and put the focus on what is happening. It demythologizes the marriage by confronting the 'should-driven' narratives that birth the unrealistic expectations. Those stuck in grievance tend to stay in conflict. When we practice forgiveness and mercy it helps us make the transition from posturing to a partnership."

"Isn't forgiveness and mercy the same thing, sir?"

"Sort of, but not quite. Forgiveness as I define it is the process we use to come to terms with the humanity of our spouse. In it we address the mythology about our spouses regarding their character and capacities that hinder us from embracing their authenticity. Forgiveness occurs when we release our spouse from the condemnation we held them in because they have not met our expectations about who we think they need to be."

After placing his order, Coach Perkins continued. "Forgiveness in this context addresses the evil intent we create when we turn our spouse's behavior into a story that explains a spouse's intent, as if we read their mind.

"So, you're not talking about letting stuff slide or giving a person another chance?" Romans inquired.

"No, I'm not. Real heart level forgiveness releases a person from the indebtedness created by all the 'shoulds' we bring to the table about our spouses' duty towards us. Most of us forgive episodically."

"What's that?"

"It's when we let stuff slide repeatedly without ever dealing with the question of whether the expectations we have placed on our spouse even make sense based on who we know them to be. To fully forgive someone, a spouse must come to terms with the personality and character of the person they married, not just their behavior— that means the humanity of their spouse and all the nuances that go with it. Holding them to standards they can't keep is unloving, no matter how pure the motive or how good the standard because it requires them to forfeit their dignity."

Roman was beginning to get a clearer picture of what happened over the weekend. "I see. That's what Sage was struggling with when she told me to snap out of it."

"Exactly. In the same way she was bullied and shamed by her father about not being weak, she was trying to bully and shame you into meeting her expectations of a strong man."

"We absorb this stuff from our parents and pass it on is what you are saying," Roman surmised.

The waiter arrived with their entrees and the two men took a moment to savor a few bites before continuing their discussion.

"At the onset of the forgiveness phase, all the judgments and the blame is laid at the feet of the other spouse. At this point in the process neither spouse can see the conspiratorial dimensions of their enabling within the marriage. The repeated shortcomings and failings of their spouse are usually the only things we see. Psychologists call it a "self-serving bias" where we get trapped in a tendency to interpret situations within our marriage in a fashion that places our intent and behavior in the most positive light. Meanwhile, we interpret the intent and behavior of our spouses in a more negative light."

"Guilty as charged, sir. You should have heard some of the conversations that went on in my head early in our marriage."

Coach Perkins laughed, "Don't forget I have heard some of the recent ones. Selfishly, we think we're the ones with all the goodwill, putting in all the work, being understanding and cooperative while we think of our spouses as saboteurs of the process because of their lack of character, goodwill, and/ or effort.

"So how do you keep from getting punked by a spouse who takes advantage of the situation?"

"Accepting the humanity of your spouse doesn't mean you are letting them off the hook," the coach offered. "You aren't giving them a license to continue cheating or to attack your manhood. Nothing could be further from the truth. All forgiveness does is accept a person for who they are and release them from the judgment of who we think they should be. It doesn't release them from their responsibilities. What gives a person license is when you keep giving them opportunities while expecting change without coming to terms with who they are. In fact, the whole notion that one person can hold another person responsible for their actions when they don't want to be is one of the biggest relationship myths there is.

"The scary reality is, the only thing that you can do with someone who either can't or won't keep a standard, is get rid of them or keep giving them chances until your heart becomes so hardened and bitter you become numb. The more you and Sage come to terms with who you married, the more your relationship will repair and strengthen. Think for a moment...when did things go left for you and Sage the other day?"

Unsure of how to answer, Roman paused for a moment "When Sage went off," he said.

"Yes, but deeper than that it occurred when she judged you after she lost patience with you. Did any of that motivate you to change? No. In fact, being judged by her motivated you to act out rather than to opt in. Ok, here's another question: When did your marriage start to improve?" Coach Perkins paused. "Answer: When Sage knew and accepted you as being a cheater and the two of you began to address the cheating?"

"I get it," Roman exhaled, "I have to accept how hurt she is and she has to accept how hurt I am before we can address the hurting we've caused each other."

"Could not have said it better myself. The objective here is simple: soften the heart enough to create a level playing field and take the frustration of unrealistic expectations and the shame of judgment out of the equation. Forgiveness is accomplished when the two of you can acknowledge each other's strengths and weaknesses without all the judgmental blaming that recycles the shame in the relationship causing you to compete for the moral high ground."

"You want to know what's ironic about this whole blow-up? The grief that triggered it arose out of the remorse I felt for what I had put Sage through. It was the first time I'd made an actual connection with the depth of pain I'd caused the women in my life. Most of my life, I have handled my relationships with females from a Darwinian perspective–survival of the fittest." This confession made Roman feel as though weights from the weekend fiasco had been lifted from his shoulders.

"That's going to be a big part of Sage's struggle to come to terms with your humanity. When you didn't play it off, it scared her. She married you expecting you to be daddy-strong. But don't worry, the two of you will soon make the transition into the Mercy Phase. In fact, you're already dealing with issues associated with it. But that's going to have to wait for next week. Coach Perkins motioned for the waiter to bring the bill. "Right now I've got some errands to run for the Mrs. Gotta love the ladies," he joked.

CHAPTER TWENTY-THREE

Owen Goes Straight Out of Compton

Having processed several elements of the Quarantine Mode, Owen made appointments with his doctor to have blood work done to make sure he had not contracted a disease from Lia's extracurricular activity. He also arranged a meeting with his lawyer and his financial advisor to see what kind of hit he would take if he and Lia were to divorce. The way Owen dealt with money was one of the few areas in his life where his behavior was more predatorial than host.

With the meeting with his lawyer and financial advisor going well into the afternoon, Owen decided to skip his doctor's appointment to get back to The Center. On the way back to the facility he called Sage to tell her how both meetings went.

"The bad news is my personal life is a mess. The good news is I saved a bunch of money on my Lia insurance" mimicking the tagline from the Geico Insurance commercial.

"That's not funny O.B."

"I know, I know."

"So, what did they say?"

"The most I'll have to pay is about a quarter of a million dollars and some spousal support when it's all settled."

"That's great! It beats the twelve million you know she would try to take. I'll bet you're surely glad you took their advice and got Lia to sign that prenup."

"Uh… about the prenup…I have a confession to make. I lied back then. I'm the one who told them I wanted a prenup. I told them to put something together that was as ironclad as they could make it," Owen confessed.

"No. Not Owen the philanthropist!" said Sage.

"Yeah, it was my idea. When I told them what I was trying to do they volunteered to take the hit. I didn't want anyone to think I was 'that guy' you know M.O.B. (money over bitches)."

"Hey, I don't care how you did it or why you did it. I'm just glad you did it."

"I hate to admit it, but me too. If Lia thought it was my idea I would have never heard the end of it. But I needed her to relinquish any claim to any of the assets I'd accumulated before our marriage, including any profits, interest or other income derived from them moving forward. After watching my dad struggle under the economic weight of taking care of my mom in those early years, I just couldn't take the chance. It's not like I haven't been generous towards Lia."

"Absolutely. Lia came up," Sage added.

What she didn't know is Owen usually purchased those big-ticket items through his corporation to feel good about himself as a provider, like the Lexus he leased for Lia. It also served as a tax write-off. In reality there was no way he was going to let anyone jeopardize his ability to take care of his parents or run The Center.

"I understand. You don't have to convince me. When will you get the results back from the doctor?" Sage said, moving on to the next item on the list.

"I wasn't able to make my doctor's appointment because my meeting with my financial people took so long."

"So when are you going to get that done? Don't be fooling around with this, you know I'm going to stay on you until it's done."

"Yes Mother."

"You know I hate when you do that, Owen," Sage responded in an even more motherly tone. "So now, what's your next move?"

"I'm going back home tonight. My lawyer said that I do not want it to look as though I abandoned her."

"Oh wow! That should be interesting. Does she know you are coming home tonight?"

"No," Owen snickered, now feeling himself and some of the anger he'd been sitting on. "I am just going to surprise her."

"Do you think that's a good move? What if you are the one who gets surprised?"

"Oh, then it's on!"

"Owen don't invite trouble. Call her and tell her you are coming home," Sage pleaded.

"Hey, that's my house, and until we get divorced she's my wife. I wish he would come up in my house trying to regulate. I'll…"

"Owen stop acting all 'Straight out of Compton.' There's nothing gangster about you, so stop trying to sound all hard; this is me you're talking to."

"I mean it, Sage. If this is how it has to go down, then I am prepared to defend mine—by any means necessary."

"How about using the one weapon that works for you—your brain? Call her, Owen. I mean it," Sage's maternal instincts had kicked into overdrive.

After a few moments of dead air, Owen suddenly broke into a rap.

"Some fools have to learn the hard way. When you test the best, bring a vest, cause a brotha like me ain't afraid to make a mess. Step to me and I'll show you how a real G relieves stress, then leave it to his momma to identify what's left."

Horrified by his language, Sage protested in frustration. "Have you lost your mind?! Listen to yourself. I don't know whether to laugh or cry. You sound like one of those white guys Roman listens to on ESPN who's always quoting rappers to show how down they are. O.B., you were raised in Torrance. That is South Bay not South Central. Dude, you're tripping. I can see the Getty Center from your backyard. What's gotten into you?"

"You think I'm playing? You think I'm playing?" Owen bellowed into the phone. His hand trembled as he hung up.

#

Sage dialed Roman.

"Hey, what's up baby?" Roman answered.

Sage quickly explained how her phone call with Owen had upset her, and how she believes he's looking for a fight to prove his manhood.

"I'm sure of it. Owen's got to be feeling like he got punked out of his house. I'm sure he feels the need to mark his territory," Roman said, mentally reviewing the chapter on revenge from the player's handbook.

"But that's not who he is. He is a thinker, not a fighter. You should have heard him trying to sound all hard. And the language! Ugh…it was just vulgar," Sage protested in frustration.

"Thinker or not, he's still a man. And as a man he feels like he has to handle his business."

"I could see that if he were the size of say you or Uncle Robert."

"If he were my size he wouldn't need to look for a fight, he'd have nothing to prove," Roman explained. "It's because he isn't big he feels the need to prove something."

"I don't get it?"

" If you were with Casey and Lia was my cousin, who do you think Lia would be worried about?"

"Oh, she'd be worried about Casey definitely."

"Why?"

"Just look at you." She imagined her husband's sturdy 6'5" frame.

"Right. Because you have no doubt I would be able to handle him. Therefore, I'd have nothing to prove. The more you expressed concern about Owen's safety, the more you validated his need to defend his household."

"Oh shoot! If I had known I was talking too much, I would have kept my mouth shut."

"I'm not even going to touch that. Just remember it came out of your mouth, not mine."

"I know I walked right into that one. But I thought the whole Napoleon complex thing was psychobabble."

Roman tried not to break a smile as he thought to himself: "How could you not know it's true when the dad who raised you has a Napoleon complex?" Instead he said, "Trust me it's a real thing."

"What do I do now that the horse is out the barn?" Sage asked.

"We can swing by his house and say we are dropping off the sunglasses he left our place. Or you can call Lia and tell her he's coming home and you do not want any mess. It's your choice."

"Let's just go over there, that way I'll know everything will be cool."

"You got it," Roman said, "We just need to get to there at or before the time that Owen does. I'll meet you at home and we can ride over there together."

"That won't be a problem. You can set your clock by the time Owen arrives home."

"Wait. What if Lia calls us out on our pretense for coming over there? The glasses thing is kind of weak."

A deep furrow appeared across Sage's brow. "What do we care?" she replied emboldened by the fact that they would be on this mission together. "She's the one cheating on her husband. She's hardly in the position to claim the moral high ground."

CHAPTER TWENTY-FOUR

Owen and Lia Round Two

Turning onto Owen and Lia's block, Roman could tell that there was trouble brewing. Outside their house a white Range Rover with gold Daytons was parked in front of their Lexus. Yelling from the house could be heard as they pulled into the driveway. Roman threw the car into park and hurried towards the house without opening Sage's door. When he got to porch, the door to the edifice was ajar. He knocked hard then proceeded to walk in, calling out: "Hey it's us—Sage and Roman."

He followed the voices into the family room where he found Casey and Owen wrestling on the floor. Casey was on top of Owen while Lia stood by yelling "Stop, stop, stop!" Before Casey realized that he and Owen were no longer the only men in the room, it was too late. Roman had picked him up and slammed him so hard on the tile it produced a thud that echoed through the foundation of the house. Thunderstruck by the explosive power Roman had just unleashed on Casey, the whole house seemed to stand in frozen awe. Even Casey's writhing on the floor didn't produce a sound. Not since the last bowl game Roman played in had any of them witnessed the raw power he possessed and, even then it was at a safe distance.

As the shock and awe of what just happened began to wear off, Roman and Sage helped Owen to his feet. Owen's heart was pounding so hard Sage could feel his pulse through the sleeve of his sweatshirt.

Quickly surveying Owen for injuries, she asked, "Are you all right O.B.?"

"I'm okay, I'm okay," he assured her.

Using the cabinets along the wall to brace up, Casey made his way back to his feet. It was clear his back was not the only thing hurting him. His pride had taken an even harder hit. The trash talking, in-your-face hustler, who was fond of intimidating women, waiters, and men of smaller stature, did not say a word. The hit Roman put on Casey was so devastating his whole body felt concussed.

"What happened?" Roman turned his attention to Owen.

"I'll tell you what happened," Lia blurted out. "After my devoted husband abandoned me, he suddenly decides he can just pop in anytime he wants, without calling, and start messing with one of my guests. Then you come busting through the door like you're the Hulk and attack my guess from behind."

At that point, Roman had heard enough. He turned toward Lia and calmly said, "I wasn't talking to you. I was talking to the owner of the house–Mr. Bryant. If I wanted to talk to the tenant, I would have directed my question to you. But don't worry, you'll be able to give your victim's impact statement when you repeat this over and over again to anyone who'll listen." Knowing Roman's capacity to inflict psychological harm with his tongue was greater than his ability to inflict physical harm, Lia chose to retreat. Instead, she chose her second favorite attention seeking behavior—the dramatic exit.

"Are you going to let this womanizing jerk talk to me like this?" When neither Owen nor Casey came to her rescue, she stormed out the house leaving Casey behind.

"I will own being a womanizer and a jerk if you will own any of the terms that describe a woman who brings home strays like a skank, slut, ratchet, ho, or..." Roman clamored down the hall after a fast stepping Lia.

"Roman, don't!" Sage stopped him before he resorted to using the B-word.

After Lia slammed the door, Roman turned to Owen and said, "Don't you think it's time for Lia's guest to leave too?"

"Definitely," Owen said. He squared his shoulders and took a step forward.

With all the tone and authority of a cop on a disturbing the peace call, Roman turned to Casey and said, "It's time for you to raise up the dog, before I have to go Ivan Drago on you and break you."

Trying to recover what little pride he had left after being body slammed, Casey lashed out, "I'm out, but I'll be back with a U-Haul truck when Lia divorces you and takes this house, that Lexo', and half your cash. Oh! And you might want to change the linen if you are going to sleep in your bedroom tonight, homeboy."

As Roman moved towards Casey to hasten his departure, Sage told Casey, "You might want to change your linen because you're the one that's going to be getting a roommate. It's Lia who'll be moving in with you because your girl signed a prenup."

Unable to resist, Roman started rapping, "I ain't saying she's a gold digger, but I know she's gonna be living with a broke, broke.. ."

Caught off guard by the prenup comments, and the sight of Sage joining in with Roman to sing his version of Kanye's hit, Casey left in a state of shock

#

Casey had barely closed the door to his car before he texted Lia a "911" to get a fix on her location.

>"whr ru we nd 2 tlk"

>"Rare Bean"

>"b thr n 5"

Casey made his way through Westside traffic to the Rare Bean in record time. He found Lia sitting at a bistro table in the back of the lounge. He grabbed a chair from another table and joined.

"You see what I have to put up with, baby? I'll be so glad

when he's out of my life, and you and I can be together," Lia said. It struck him that under the circumstances she seemed particular cool.

"Yeah, that's what I wanted to talk to you about. Uh…what's the deal with you having signed a prenuptial agreement?"

"Uh huh. Before he and I got married I had to sign a prenuptial agreement…mainly to protect his foundation, which isn't a problem because I don't care anything about his foundation."

"Did you have a lawyer look over any of the paperwork before you signed it?"

"Of course, I did. In fact, Owen's people insisted I have two separate lawyers look over the paperwork."

"And what did they say?" Casey asked, afraid of her answer.

"They said I would be forfeiting any of the rights I have to go after any assets associated with his foundation or his corporation," Lia answered, clearly not sharing Casey's concerns. "Who told you we had a prenuptial agreement? And why is it such a big deal?"

"It's not. It's just that they made a big deal out of it after you left," he covered.

The truth of the matter is it was a huge deal to Casey whose chance reunion with Lia was everything but a random occurrence. He had heard from one of Lia's best friends that she wasn't happy in her marriage. This friend also confided that she still had unresolved feelings for him. He had been her first love. In reality, the past six weeks was all a part of an elaborate scheme hatched by Casey to get Lia to divorce Owen and take half of his money. Casey's plan was to be there for her after their divorce, to comfort her and to help her spend all Owen's money. It was he who put Lia up to going to The Center to find out when Owen was moving out, how much money he was going to give her, and to ask for the Lexus—which he wanted to drive.

The contents of that prenuptial agreement meant everything to Casey. If she wasn't going to get half of Owen's wealth, there was no way he was going to waste another minute dealing with somebody as damaged and needy as Lia, no matter how fine she was. Without the cash, Casey had no incentive to be with Lia. Just like he said to one of his friends, "I had already served my sentence those first two years we were together in college."

Desperate to find out what was in the prenuptial agreement, but not wanting to push Lia too far, too fast, he turned the tables on her.

"Let me ask you something. How do I know whether you truly have my back?"

"Have your back? What do you mean?" Lia was stunned by his question.

"I mean to have my back, you know ride or die."

"Baby, that's crazy talk. You know I have your back."

"I used to think so, but after today I'm not that sure. First… you don't tell me that Owen is coming home, and then you let me get ambushed by Sage and that 'Planet of the Apes' husband of hers. You then run off and leave me there. I could have been killed for all you know. Oh, and then, if that's not enough, I find out you've been keeping secrets. How do I know you're not just trying to hook up with me because you're tired of Owen?"

Lia was shocked into disbelief. "How could you question my love?" she said.

"Look at it from my perspective. When we were back in college, you and I fall out for a minute, and the next thing I know you and Owen hooked up. You don't know just how much that hurt me at the time. Then, I find out you been keeping secrets from me?" Casey managed to conjure crocodile tears to fortify his charade causing Lia lean forward and grab his hands across the table.

"I've risked my marriage to be with you. How can you treat me this way?" searching his eyes for the answer.

"How do I know what you risked? You've got a prenup agreement that has who knows what written it," Casey countered, laying the fake emotion on thick.

"What if I give you a copy of the agreement? That way you can read it and we can put this behind us."

"That's a start," he sniffled. "When can you get the file to me?"

"I have to find it. It'll probably take me a few days."

"Why are you jerking me around? If you honestly wanted to get this over with you'd just go to your lawyer's office tomorrow and get a copy of the agreement," Casey said, his feigned hurt, but entitled tone was effective.

"You know I care about you. Why would you accuse me of trying to play you? Of course, I'll go to my lawyer tomorrow and get a copy of the agreement. I will call them first thing in the morning and tell them I am coming by to pick it up."

When that seemed to settle Casey down, Lia tried to engage him in conversation to no avail.

"I have to go. I am too hurt and disappointed in you to talk," he said, rising to his feet. He grabbed his old leather coat off the back of the chair and told her to call him when she had a copy of the document. With a bruised body and a bruised ego, he turned and walked out the door without as much as a goodbye.

CHAPTER TWENTY-FIVE

Sage and Roman Debrief

Roman, Owen, and Sage sat in the living room attempting to process what had taken place earlier that evening. Roman and Sage confronted Owen about his reckless behavior, trying to penetrate the 4-ft thick wall of denial he had constructed around everything in his life that was Lia focused.

Sage ever the one to say, "I told you so" was in full "What were you thinking?" lecture mode.

"You do know none of this would have happened if you had just called Lia and told her you were coming home," she scolded.

"None of this would have happened if Lia had not brought another man into my house," Owen fired back in an effort to justify his actions.

Roman asked, "You know what you and Lia's problem is?"

"Yeah. She doesn't appreciate me."

"No, it's that you do not appreciate each other."

"We don't appreciate each other?" Owen said. His words brimmed with indignation. "Ever since we've been together I have done nothing but appreciate her. If anything I've over appreciated her. I bought her the house she wanted, I helped her get her business off the ground, and I traded in her Escalade for the Lexus at a $17,000 loss, just because she needed to drive something that was greener to impress her clients. Not to mention the clothes, trips, jewelry and the two, three, and six hundred dollar random charges on the credit card for God knows what. I think I deserve to get a medal for how much I have appreciated her."

"Spending money is not the type of appreciation Roman is referring to," Sage rebutted. "Forgive me for what I'm about to say but, that's just money and you have plenty of it,"

"I'm talking about who you are, not what you do for each other," Roman said, reinforcing the point.

Owen's arms flailed in frustration. "What do you mean?"

"I'm talking about the way you deal with each other—not what you do for each other," Roman explained. "Like thousands of other couples, ourselves included, the two of you handle each other based on what you think the other 'should' be doing, not what they are doing. By your own admission your wife has a lot of intimacy and boundaries issues. Yet, you're several years into your marriage and you engage her like she doesn't. Then you get frustrated and mad when she reminds you that she does. It's like owning a Ferrari then getting angry every time you take it in for service because the bill is too high. It was high maintenance when you bought it. Dude...get over it," Roman said bluntly.

"Spell it out for me," Owen asked, more out of his commitment to his denial than his need for clarity

Roman challenged Owen to count the number of times Lia visited The Center. Owen confirmed that she had come only four times in all the years he'd worked there, and each of those visits was tied to a celebrity event. Roman then asked how many times had he asked her to attend other events?

"Hundreds! Which proves my point that she is not supportive."

"No Owen, it proves my point. Lia has never been interested in The Center, yet you keep asking her to attend events when everyone knows, including me, she's not coming. Why is that?"

Without thinking about what he was saying Owen tried desperately to justify his repeated invitations with a series of "shoulds" and "oughts:" "I ought to be able to ask..." "Shouldn't a wife support her husband?" "She should realize..." "If a spouse is supportive of his wife, shouldn't the wife be some-what supportive…" etc.

When Owen was done trying to justify himself, Sage jumped in, "O.B. all the 'should' and 'ought' you just mentioned that 'should' take place between a husband and a wife are only valid if the kind of spouse you described married the kind of woman you described. The woman you just described is not the woman you married. The woman you married is, and always has been, too overwhelmed or too into herself to be that kind of wife. The woman you married does drama, which is why she is so good at marketing. Owen, Lia has always had drama in her life. From the time she ran out of your Psych 101 class and you followed her, the orbit of your world tilted away from your parents' stuff toward Lia's stuff. I'm not saying this to put her down, Lord knows I am one to talk. But I'm saying it to get you to see that Lia has not changed. The whole time you've been with her you've been trying to change a woman who is committed to her personality. You ask her to attend an event you know she's not going to attend. Then, you complain for weeks about how unsupportive and selfish she is, when you're the one making things worse."

Sage paused before continuing to search his face to deter-mine if he was still fully engaged or if he'd checked out. "That's what Roman and I mean when we say you don't show her any gratitude and she doesn't appreciate you," she mur-mured, hoping to soften the impact of her words.

"That's it exactly. The type of appreciation we're talking about has nothing to do with please and thank you. The way the two of you engage each other is like the movie 'Groundhog Day': every day, every month, every year, it's the same thing. Heck, you might as well have Digital Underground playing 'Same Song' in the background," Roman chimed in.

Picking up where she left off, Sage said "Lia does some-thing that's typical Lia. You are shocked and appalled by it. You do something that is typical Owen. She feels abandoned and rejected. You feel guilty about the way you handled her, and then you buy her something. The two of you are back in love for a while until it starts over again. The two of you are never going to get out of the parasitic loop unless you wrap your head around the reality that this is who I married. It's not personal– it's personality.

"Bottom line Owen, you married a needy, passive-aggressive woman who struggles with boundaries. And she married a codependent caretaker who also struggles with boundaries. You've got to come to terms with the unrealistic expectations you have for each other or you will keep searching for the marriage you think you 'should' have instead of fixing the marriage you do have," said Roman, in summation.

"This is starting to sound like the coaching stuff you guys have been trying to get me to follow," Owen remarked.

"We are not trying to get you follow anything. All that would do is to get you to replace one should-driven narrative with another. But, we are trying to get you to develop a more mindful approach to the process. What you choose to do with it is entirely up to you. It's not a formula because formulas produce predictable outcomes; it a process that produces different results for different people based on who they are," Roman encouraged.

"What we are trying to show you are the elements of the next phase of the recovery process: the forgiveness phase and the mercy phase as best as we understand it," Sage added.

"Oh, so I'm supposed just to show forgiveness and mercy to Lia for trying to clean me out and move another man into my house?" Owen scoffed.

"No O.B. The forgiveness phase, like the discovery phase, is a process not an event. As I told you at the coffee shop, it's how you move forward. This is not about whether the two of you get back together or not."

"Why would I need to forgive her if we are not going to be together? It just seems like a waste of time."

"Forgiveness benefits everyone involved—especially the

person who forgives. Do you want to become a male version of the Bryant women? Remember when our second cousin Juliann announced her engagement to Christopher at our family dinner about eight months ago? Well, four of us unhappily married Bryant women spent the rest of the evening hating on her happiness because we weren't happy. What we called 'wise counsel' was nothing more than bitterness. The next week I had to call her and apologize for contaminating her joy with my unhappiness."

The thought of the bitterness that seemed to afflict the Bryant women like a genetic heart disease sobered Owen right up. "I see," he conceded

"Good, because there is nothing more pathetic than a bitter man in his thirties, except one in his forties or fifties," Roman added trying to lighten the mood.

"Are we going to need another session on the grease board to work through this phase?" Owen asked, half joking.

"No, this part is more about the heart than steps and categories. I'll give you a copy of the audio file Coach did on the forgiveness and mercy phase."

"There is one thing I think we should talk about that I believe would be helpful. It's one of Coach's core principles: Honor."

"Sage is right," Roman interjected. "Honor is the level of regard you and Lia need to preserve each other's dignity. It's based solely on the fact that she is still your wife, and you are still her husband," Roman explained.

"How can I honor her when she is sleeping with another man?" Owen exclaimed.

"What you are describing is respect, which is reverence, regard, and esteem you would have for her performance, not her position," Roman replied. He read Owen's look of confusion and offered a sports analogy as a means of further explanation. "Let's say that one of the coaches in the league you run at The Center has an exceptionally high basketball IQ and knows the game inside out. Now one of the refs in the league misinterprets a rule and blows a call that could cost that coach a championship. If that coach runs onto the court, grabs the ref, and goes off on him a la Bobby Knight to explain the rule, tell me…what will happen to the ref and the coach when the league reviews the incident?"

"Well," Owen answered with sobriety, "the referee would undergo some retraining and clarification of the rules in the off-season to make sure he, or she, was brought up to speed. As for the coach, that's a different story. There are so many issues involved that would need to be sorted out. I'd say that there's a good chance he would never coach again, at least not in our league."

"Right. Because there are certain things that a coach can't do to a ref even, if the ref's incompetence is so flagrant that it costs his team a championship. You can't play the game if the coaches do not honor the ref's position—no matter how bad the ref performs. Now flip it," Roman said, "and let's say the coach calmly asks the ref to explain his or her interpretation of the rule and the ref goes on a profanity-laced tirade, then tosses the coach for having the nerve to question their-authority. What happens then?"

"That ref is gone. He will never work a game again because he disrespected the coach. We'd be unable to use him moving forward. We'd have no way of knowing if the coaches were coaching scared."

"Owen what you call disrespect, Coach Perkins would define as dishonor. In each of these scenarios it was the dishonoring of the position that got the coach and the ref banned. The role the coach plays deserves a response from the ref. And no matter how right or wrong a person, the position they hold must still be honored…"

"Or the whole thing descends into chaos," Owen finished Roman's sentence.

"That's it," Roman continued. "It is not the presence of conflict that escalates or deescalates the situation, it's the absence of honor. Honor is the foundation every stable relationship rests on. It keeps relationships from going toxic because it protects the dignity of everybody involved.

"If you and Lia knew how to honor one another, you'd be able to discuss your issues without threatening each other's dignity. Even though she violated your marital vows it should not cost her, her dignity. When the two of you get around to negotiating what you need to settle, it is honor that will keep the negotiations from becoming a battle over who has the moral high ground. It will keep Lia from having to worry about being shamed for committing adultery, and you from worrying about being punked in the process."

Sage, who had been listening intently, chimed in to connect the dots. "When you decided this afternoon not to call Lia to tell her you were coming home, you dishonored her position as your wife. Likewise, when Lia did not ask Casey to leave when you arrived, she dishonored your role as her husband. And it's not just a man and wife thing. Casey dishonored you as the homeowner, a man, and spouse by chosing to stay when you arrived."

"I got it. I got it," A light bulb suddenly came on for Owen. "What I have been calling disrespect is really dishonor thrown my way. Lia and Casey's affair violated my position as her husband and the head of our household."

"That's it exactly, O.B."

"Got it, got it. So where does respect kick into the relationship?"

"Respect," Sage answered, "which Coach Perkins defines as 'regard for a person's performance,' focuses solely on behavior regardless of position. The way he explained it to us is to think of honor as the foundation of a relationship and respect as the building blocks. As our admiration for the way our spouses treat us, handle their responsibilities, and stuff grows, so does the intimacy. That is a huge part of what is missing from your marriage. It was a big piece missing from our marriage too," Sage said. Her soft and solemn voice was barely audible.

"The lack of admiration, trust, and intimacy grew out of

the inconsistency in the way we treated one another. When Roman started to treat me consistently in a loving way, my honor for his position rose to respect. My respect for the man he is becoming has taken away my incentive to use manipulation and other dysfunctional behaviors to try to get him to love me."

At that Roman smiled warmly at Sage. "Listen, the bottom line is, it's hard to mistreat a spouse when you have a sincere appreciation for your partnership. However, it's easy to mistreat someone you don't have respect for and do not honor," he said.

"So how does all this connect with forgiveness and mercy?" Owen truly wished to understand all of the dynamics of this process.

Sage took the lead in answering. "When I found out Roman was cheating, or should I say when he admitted it, we had to decide if we were going to try to salvage our marriage. To do that we had to choose between facing the scary elements of putting our relationship back together or the complicated notion of separating—battling it out in court, dividing up our assets, the whole nine—which meant we had to forfeit all the excuses we had for why we weren't present in our marriage including the "It's the other person's fault mindset." Our task was to face the trauma we inflicted on each other that robbed us of our dignity and turned us into people who were incapable of giving love and receiving love. From there we had to confront what we had built, meaning all the stuff we learned about during the discovery phase. I started to come out of the discovery phase around the time the sense of crisis subsided. I began to look at Roman's behavior and his treatment of me over the entire course of our relationship, and that is when I got mad."

"Oh, I remember that season," Owen reminisced. "You were on Roman about everything."

"Yeah, I know. That's also when we first met with Coach Perkins as a couple. I only went to meet with him for two reasons: First, to tell him what kind of dog Roman was, and second, to ask him a question I spent three days formulating: How could any man with a shred of integrity waste his time on a male slut like Roman?" Sage admitted.

"Wow! You said that to his face with Roman sitting there? What did he say?" Owen shifted to the edge of his seat.

"Yeah, tell him what he said," Roman added. Owen thought he detected the beginning of tears in Roman's eyes.

"Coach Perkins broke eye contact with me, turned to Roman and said what I imagine only a loving father could say to his son. He said, 'Because like you I have chosen to love him. The only difference is you are more in love with who he isn't, I'm more in love with who he is. And I have chosen to walk with him based on who he says he wants to become. As long as he's willing to put in the work and run the plays, I'll continue to show him love for who he is and mercy for who he isn't.'"

"Wow, that's powerful," Owen said. He was visibly moved.

"Yeah, I was crushed after that," Sage shared.

"You were crushed? You have no idea how deeply that affected me. For a man of integrity to say the things he said just moments after Sage outlined the awful things I'd done to her, it was..." Roman paused as his voice broke and his eyes welled in earnest. "That's the first time a real man had ever shown me love despite my performance on or off the field. Honestly, I felt a strange combination of conviction and hope. So yeah, that was our introduction to the forgiveness phase."

Sage broke eye contact with Owen in a similar way to look Roman in the eyes, and with the same tenderness said, "It was also my introduction to the man I have fallen in love with all over again, " she slipped her hand in his.

Roman smiled then looked away to keep from losing his composure again.

"If the two of you are done making eyes at one another, could one of you finish telling me about the forgiveness phase?" Owen said as a wave of awkwardness came over him.

Roman having regained his composure offered: "To honor

me as her husband Sage had to forgive me, which meant she had to come to terms with who I was as a person instead of how I measured up to her ideal of what a husband was supposed to be. I was at the point where I was trying to be the best man I could be, and all she was giving me was attitude and a whole lot of sarcasm. It got so bad at one point I was ready to bounce. I started looking for an apartment, asking people about lawyers–the whole nine. It wasn't just that she was sarcastic, she was becoming bitter, which is something I said I'd never live with after watching how my mom, her sisters, and her friends got down. She was mean...half the time for no reason. It was like living with someone who didn't care and didn't want to try."

Owen remembered too well how bad it was. "I remember a couple of times she'd turned that venom on me, and I had to check her and remind her my name tag says, Owen – not Roman," recalling a particularly tense encounter he had with his cousin.

"I wasn't that bad," Sage made a half-hearted effort to defend herself.

"Yes, you were," Roman and Owen said simultaneously.

"Oh well," Sage said with a sheepish grin.

"It wasn't how mean you were that made it so bad, it was how far you'd traveled to get there that made it so dangerous," Roman sighed. "When I met you the one thing that made you stand out from any person I had met was your ability to keep it positive no matter what went down. Your resilience and keep-it-moving attitude changed the way I processed stuff. Even my friends could see that being with you had a dramatic effect on, shall we say, my moodiness. All of them said, "She's a keeper dude, don't blow it," which of course to my distorted way of thinking meant don't get caught. Sorry I digress. The point I'm trying to make is, the one thing about you I loved and admired the most was gone. You'd fallen off your pedestal and I had no interest in saving a marriage with a bitter woman. All my life I operated out of a 'hit it and quit it' mindset. Later I realized the real thing that was driving my desire to leave was the fact I did not want to face the carnage I'd created. I was a hit and run driver who fled the scene to avoid responsibility for my recklessness."

"Not to diminish what you're saying, but again, we're drifting. What does all this have to do with forgiveness?" Owen asked.

"Here's the bottom line. Forgiveness is all about coming to terms with the humanity of a spouse. Sage had to come to terms with my ability to do charming and romantic, but not intimate and transparent. All her anger grew out of her refusal to let go of the 'shoulds,' 'musts' and 'oughts' about me in the role of husband and come to terms with the guy she really married.

"Every time a mate disappoints their spouse, they eventually reach a crossroad where they embrace the discovery process or reject it. The choice to entrench or forgive is always determined by our capacity to embrace the humanity of others, which is determined by our capacity to grieve the loss of some idealized notion about them, and all the unrealistic expectations our idealized view of them birthed.

"Unchecked, unprocessed grief becomes grievances. Our grievances turn into personal mythology through embellishment, and they help us make sense of our internal world by projecting it onto the external world—i.e. our spouses and others. So forgiveness is little more than demythologizing the person you married and grieving it."

"Roman and I call it the choice between 'doing scary' or 'doing complicated,' said Sage.

"I get it. It's not complicated, it's just scary," Owen recalled the adage from his initial meeting with Roman.

"I learned that the real recovering in the recovery process starts in the forgiveness phase," Sage said. "After we began working with Coach Perkins together, he helped me see the necessity of forgiveness for my marriage and myself. That's the time I spent learning to accept Roman as a man—the good, the bad, and the ugly of him. I realized that forgiveness was the only way to soften my heart and be me again."

"To be you again? " asks Owen.

"To be me again meant three things. One, I eliminated the need to act exceptionally. To do stuff that just wasn't me. Even you mentioned on several occasions how I'd changed. I had adapted my behavior to Roman's world. Instead of trying to contend with Roman out of his dysfunctional paradigm, I chose to accept him for who he was and not fight, manipulate or try and control him to get him to change. Forgiveness allowed me to set aside all the delusions I had about my husband and my marriage.

"Two, forgiveness also helped me to stop living in fear. Once I chose to forgive I ceased walking in the fear and intimidation that consumed me. It changed the balance of power in our relationship. When I started walking in forgiveness, I was finally traveling on a path I had chosen for myself and I wasn't responding to Roman's dysfunction. See, he was responding to my love, a love that I had to accept he may not want or know what to do with.

"That was, and is, me doing scary. When you walk in love that is all you got. But when do complicated, you can always add a little more complexity to the mix if something isn't working. In the end, all you are doing is creating the regrettable and avoiding the inevitable."

"You said there were three things forgiveness did for you. What was the third thing?" Owen asked.

"Even though I am still working on it, I'm not as harsh. I don't live on the emotional edge like before. I'm not so *grr*r about everything," Sage said. She pantomimed clawing like an animal for emphasis.

Roman nodded enthusiastically in agreement. "Everything is not a battle."

Sage went on to explain the degree of change in their marriage, how forgiveness established a presupposition of goodwill between the two of them. Instead of thinking everything her husband did was coming from a hostile deceptive place, she learned to see that it was coming from a mostly wounded place in his soul.

Roman added, "When people get married they seldom have a full, let alone an accurate picture of the person they're marrying." He likened it to the recruiting process. Recruiters watch the highlights, check grades, interview the players, talk to people who know them, and check out the profile on social media, but don't know everything there is to know about their prospect.

"You may see and hear things during the recruitment process that lead you to believe the prospect will have no problem acclimating to your system and playing the game at the next level—until you get them on campus and they begin to struggle. At that point you either adjust to who they are, send them home, or try to turn them into something you think they should be but they aren't. And that's when things get toxic. It's the same thing in marriage, you either own the choice you made and adjust, or you live in the delusion of how you think things should be. Forgiveness is all about adjustment."

"Yeah but how much forgiving do you do for a recruit who is a continual disappointment?" Owen asked.

"Owen, you're missing the point. The kid is not a disappointment, the kid is still the same kid. He didn't become a disappointment until expectations were put on him that he was never going to meet. Once those expectations are removed, and we begin to work with who they are, we sometimes find hidden gems. There are a couple of All Pro's in the NFL right now who switched position in college because they were a 'disappointment' in the position for which we recruited them."

"On top of that, there's the adjustment that we need to make as our spouses' grow and change," Sage added. "When it comes to the people you love, you have to update your files regularly to maintain the intimacy between you and them. It's all about honoring where they came from, appreciating where they are, and trying to partner around where you are going.

"Forgiveness helped me get over the hyper-vigilance that distracted me from the work I needed to do on myself. If Roman was the identified sinner in our marriage, I could maintain the moral high ground in our relationship. My unforgiveness allowed me to cover the crazy I was bringing into the relationship. Once all my time and energy was no longer focused on what Roman was doing, saying, or planning, I could direct my attention to the one person I could change–me. The reality was I could not harden my heart towards Roman without first cultivating bitterness. Through forgiveness I learned to address what was missing in him without condemning or making him the scapegoat for my unresolved issues.

"The best way I can describe the process is to say it was a series of painfully disappointing acknowledgments of the unrealistic expectations I had about Roman. I had to let go and grieve those expectation."

"Alright, I see some of the benefits of forgiveness. But what if you are married to someone who takes advantage of the situation and perceives your acceptance as a license? What do you do then? How do you protect yourself from being punked?" Owen still not entirely convinced that he could forgive Lia for her transgressions.

"You don't, because you can't," Sage said. "That's why it's called 'doing scary.'"

"Yeah, all you are doing when you forgive is acknowledging the terrifying truth about being married. There is nothing you or I can do to stop anyone if they're determined to violate their vows—like that stunt you pulled this evening. Not cool," Roman said, one eyebrow raised.

"Yeah O.B., you've got to stop listening to that 'Gangster' crap. Listening to that stuff is like having a gun, it'll only make think you're braver than you are!" said Sage, sounding again like a mother hen.

"How did you know I'd been listening to hip hop?"

"Please, I can always tell when you've been listening to that stuff. You start talking all hard, 'I didn't want people to think I was all M.O.B about my money," Sage mocked.

"C'mon bro, please don't tell me you played the money over b****** card," Roman said, already laughing wiping a tear from his eye.

"That's what he did exactly. If I didn't love his peanut head so much, I would have reached through the phone and popped him upside his head when he said it. Seriously… Don't even."

This sent Roman into a full-on belly laugh.

"Okay, okay, that's enough mocking for one night," Owen pleaded.

"You're right. We're sorry O.B." said Sage, suddenly embarrassed for her cousin.

"I'm sorry, too. I should have never put you guys in the middle our mess."

"Hey, we forgive you, see how it works?" Roman said, wiping laughter induced tears from his eyes.

"Very funny, Roman," Owen said, a faint smile breaking forth on his face.

Sage turned to Roman, "You ready to go?"

"Yep. You going to be okay, bro?" he asked Owen as he stood.

"I'm good. I don't think I am going to have any problems the rest of the night."

"Well, if you do you know who you can call?" placed a firm hand on Owen's slender shoulder.

"Yeah, I got your number on speed dial."

"Oh, I wasn't talking about me. I was talking about the real Mob Deep—the LA County Sheriff Dept., and then you call me so I can watch them load homeboy into the back of the ride," Roman smiled at the thought of Casey being placed in squad car.

"Okay funny man, it's time to get you home. You're starting to lose it," Sage retrieved her jacket from the back of Owen's favorite lounge chair.

"All right man, we're out." said Roman, pulling Owen into an embrace.

"Aw…that's so sweet. You are giving each other the "that's my homie hug," Sage watched the two men perform a one arm handshake, shoulder to chest bump, with a couple of quick pats on the back.

"Who's clowning now?" Roman said as he helped Sage with her coat.

"Sorry, I just think it's so cute the way men hug without hugging."

"Yeah, it's time for us to go because now you're the one that is losing it."

Easy laughter filled the room as they made their way down the hall.

CHAPTER TWENTY-SIX

Lia And Casey Round One

Still reeling from the emotional aftermath of Casey's hasty departure from the Rare Bean, Lia reached into her purse to pull out her iPad. As she scrolled through her calendar, she realized she'd done something that she had never done before. Amid the drama swirling around her personal life, Lia had forgotten she was scheduled to be in and out of town for the next two weeks. One of her clients, a celebrity trainer, was launching a book on CrossFit training while simultaneously opening four CrossFit gyms in San Francisco, Malibu, Carlsbad, and Newport Coast.

Knowing she had only a day to get ready, she texted Casey to let him know she'd forgotten that she was going out of town and did not have time to swing by her lawyer's office.

"Oh, it's like that!" Lia could sense the chill in his text.

She replied, "Like what?" His whole attitude about the recent turn of events both confused and frustrated her.

"You know what I mean—more excuses."

"What are you talking about? I told you I had to go out of town a month ago. I even invited you," her thumbs rapidly moving across the keypad.

"Oh, so it's my fault, I see how you are..."

Seeing Casey's last text, her need to appease got the best of her, She pressed the home button and said, "Call Casey," the phone rang once then instantly went to voicemail.

In an effort not to provoke Casey further, Lia carefully modulated her tone. "Why are you doing me like this? You know I'm under a lot of stress?"

Forty-five minutes later she sent a second message: "I just talked to my lawyer's office manager; she's one of my sorors. She's arranged to have a copy of the agreement ready for you to pick up after 1:30 p.m. Just ask for Tiffany Williams. Please call me to let me know you got this message." Twenty minutes later, a third message was left: "Call me." Thirty minutes passed, then a fourth, and decidedly plaintive message was left after the beep: "It's me again…"

With all the malls closed and nothing to keep Lia from distracting herself, Casey figured it would take two hours for her abandonment issues to kick in, and for her to figure out a way to get him what he wanted. He took his phone off airplane mode. Boom! There they were—four messages in less than two hours. He calculated that she had shaved a whole hour off her personal record. "*Impressive,*" he thought to himself as he quickly keyed in his voicemail code. "*It's good to see that some things never change.*" He grabbed a pen out of a cup sitting on the counter separating the kitchen from the living room of his studio apartment. "That's what I'm talking about," he said out loud.

Feeling proud of himself he began to dance around the room: "Man, I should write a book on how to play these weak-minded chicks. Yeah, 'How to Take Advantage of the Disadvantaged.' How's this female gonna call a player and tell him what she ain't got time to do? Who the hell does this chick think she is? Sometimes you've got to pull some strings to remind these puppets what end of the strings they're on. That's right. It's the Queen's job to make all the moves she can to make sure the King is all right."

The more Casey bragged on his latest conquest, the more his hatred for Lia emerged.

As a form of punishment he decided not to call her back. He would pick up the paperwork and let her miss him for two weeks.

"Then we'll see what kind of attitude she has when she returns."

#

Tired and defeated Lia arrived home wanting only to go to bed. She pushed thoughts of Casey's radio silence aside and focused on getting rested for her upcoming trip. Her cell phone glowed 11 p.m. It was the earliest she'd made it home in weeks, and for the first time in a long time, there were no stories to be spun. The last time she'd come home was the night Owen found out she was cheating on him. Crossing the threshold she wondered if Owen was lurking in the shadows waiting to pounce for round two. Since she was way too exhausted to listen to another one of his lectures, she decided that she would let him have his pound of flesh and be done with it. There was no fight left in this Texas girl.

She took a seat on the upholstered bench in the hallway and crossed her legs to remove the $600+, form-fitting, olivine Tsubo Tarian tall boots with the four-inch heel she called her "stunners." Lia drew stares from both women and men when she wore them. Of all the outfits and accessories she owned that she took pride in, it could be argued that these shoes were her most prized possession. Still, none of that mattered. As each shoe came off, she slung it in a corner like a worn-out pair of work boots.

As Lia sat there rubbing her feet and trying to gear up for the long walk down the hall, she glanced up at the wedding picture on the wall. Staring at the picture Owen had broken the night he left, she realized the only damage to the photo was the broken glass. Neither the picture nor the frame was damaged. She wondered if the only thing broken about her marriage was the facade that she and Owen had put on. She asked herself what would happen if they committed to working on their relationship? Could it be salvaged or was the bond between them so damaged it could not be mended?

Suddenly, she caught herself in mid-thought about Owen and shook her head as if to shake the idea loose. "Whew! Snap out of it girl that ship has sailed. I must be tired, I'm tripping," she reasoned with herself. "I've already made my decision. I love Casey. He and I are going to be together like we were supposed to be."

But Lia wasn't tripping. She was simply being Lia— the same person who, as a girl, got bounced from one relatives house to another until her mother got sober. The strain of living on and off with a mom who was an addict with no boundaries for the first half of her life and a mom who was a recovering addict and a therapist who still doesn't have any boundaries the second half of her life had taken a toll Lia. Having dealt with her mom's addiction and recovery most of her life Lia's sense of self could not have been more damaged even if she had been raised by Cinderella's wicked stepmother. The hole in her soul was broad and deep. No amount of gifts from Owen, or sex from Casey, would ever fill it and bring her peace.

As she sat there wrestling with her thoughts, her trance was broken by the sudden realization that she was being watched. She glanced over one shoulder to see Owen leaning against the wall staring at her.

"How long have you been standing there?" Lia squealed.

"Long enough," Owen answered.

"Long enough for what?"

"Just long enough, just long enough," With that he turned and headed back down the hallway toward their bedroom. "There's some leftover Chinese in the refrigerator if you're hungry," he tossed the words back at her without stopping. "I bought it when I made a Target run to replace the linen throughout the house," he said, getting in the last dig.

"Okay," she sighed, resigned.

"Where do you plan to sleep tonight, our bed or one of the guest rooms?" Owen stops and turns to look at his wife before turning the corner.

"One of the guest rooms I suppose," Lia replied quietly, not making eye contact.

"You don't have to. We are after all still married, and the

Bible says don't let the sun go down on your wrath." Owen said in the hope of having her close even though he lacked the emotional self-awareness to know where the desire to have her near was coming from.

More than a little bit surprised by his invitation to share their bed, Lia looked up at Owen. Given her exhaustion she would love nothing better than to sleep in her own bed. But when she considered his tendency to go over an issue until the wee hours of the morning, Lia thought better of it.

"Thanks, but I think it's best if I just sleep in one of the guest rooms," she answered plainly.

Causing Owen to storm off in a huff and slam the door behind him.

Lia got up and made her way to the guest room at the far end of the house off from their home office. Snapping on the light, the first thing she noticed was the stripped bed. On top of the queen-sized mattress was one of those all-in-one linen bags you buy at a discount department store, and comes with everything you need to make the bed. This one was in a color scheme that could best be described as Disney Princess pink and blue pastel.

Too tired to even try to process what made Owen think this would work, she opened the bag, removed the linen, made the bed, climbed between the scratchy sheets and fell fast asleep.

CHAPTER TWENTY-SEVEN

Lia's Road Trip One

The next morning Lia rose early to avoid a confrontation with Owen. Her plan was to grab a bite and head out. But when she turned the corner to enter the kitchen he was already seated at the breakfast nook drinking a Mountain Dew and eating leftover Chinese food.

"Morning," Lia said, trying to break the ice and establish an atmosphere of civility.

"Good morning. How'd you sleep?" Owen's tone was measured.

"Okay, I guess."

"Just to let you know, today I'm filing a restraining order against Casey. I don't want him anywhere near me,"

"That won't be necessary," Lia mirrored Owen's monotone delivery. "I will not be bringing Casey anywhere near this house or The Center."

"Nevertheless, I am going to file for it anyway just to be on the safe side," he eyed her closely. "In case you change your mind. I just want to be protected."

"Yeah, I know!" she seethed in a loud whisper accompanied by the sarcastic roll of her eyes.

"What's that supposed to mean? he asked.

"All I'm saying is, I won't be bringing Casey anywhere near where you might be if that's what you are worried about. But do what you've got to do to feel safe. I know that's a big deal for you." As far as she was concerned that was the end of matter. There was nothing more to say.

Unable to let that be the end of it Owen tried to goad her into keeping the conversation going to no avail.

"How can I be sure Casey won't try to break in while you are gone, or ambush me in the parking lot at work, or something? Because of you he knows where I work and where I live," he protested.

The whole time Lia pretended to be preoccupied with her iPad. When he stopped to take a breath Lia reminded him that she would be out of town for the greater part of the next two weeks. Anticipating Owen's follow-up question she said, "And before you even ask, I will be traveling alone."

"I didn't forget. It's just that with all your extracurricular activities and getting your needs met, I thought you may have forgotten you have a business to run."

Still not wanting to engage him, Lia ignored his comment like a driver executing a rolling stop. "I'll leave my itinerary on the refrigerator," she tossed the words in his direction.

Again, Owen tried to bait her into an argument. He questioned her motive for leaving her itinerary on the fridge. Not satisfied with the short answers she offered, he decided to make one last effort to draw Lia into a conversation.

"I'm thinking about changing the locks on the door because I don't know whether you gave Casey a set of keys or if he might have grabbed yours and had a copy made."

At this point, Lia had heard enough. She put down her iPad, took off her reading glasses, looked at him and said, "If you want to change the locks and the codes on the house that's fine. Just go ahead and do it! Stop talking about it because I don't want to hear it. Just decide! One minute you're telling me I'm your wife and we should sleep in the same bed, and the next minute you're telling me you don't feel safe because you can't trust me. Look, I've only got today to prepare for this trip, then I'll be out of your hair for the next two weeks. While I'm gone you can do whatever the hell you want with this house: you can build an electric fence around it, put a moat around the place, install a minefield in the backyard. Hell, you can even sell it for all I care! Just stop talking about it!"

"That's not what your man said last night," Owen sniped.

"What are you talking about?" asked Lia.

"Last night, when I put your man out my house after you left, he said the next time he returned it would be with a U-Haul after you took the house in a divorce settlement."

"He told you that?" asked Lia, somewhat surprised.

"Yep, he seemed pretty pleased with himself until I told him I had an ironclad prenuptial agreement," Owen went in for the bonus point.

Clearly wounded, she cut off the conversation, got up, and swiftly headed back to the guest room to get ready. Her mind whirled around the notion that Casey's outrage towards her the night before might not be so genuine. Torn between confronting him and potentially ruining her day, she decided to put off dealing with it until she'd run all her pre-travel errands. After getting dressed, she decided that she would wait for Casey to call her.

\#

Lia finished her final errand around 2:30 p.m. It was then she realized that she had not heard from Casey. Rescinding her decision to call, she made several unsuccessful attempts to get in touch. She called her sorority sister to see whether Casey had come to the office to pick up the documents.

The phone had rung only once when Lia heard Tiffany's voice on the line. She told Lia that she was just about to call to confirm that Casey had been by to pick up the paperwork, and to share a couple of concerns she had. Tiffany began by saying that she wasn't "trying to pry" into her personal business, but there were a few things she was concerned about that she felt she needed to share with her.

"Is everything all right in your marriage?" she asked.

Lia told Tiffany that she and Owen were probably headed for divorce.

"Please don't tell me the guy you had me give the paperwork to is the person you're leaving your husband for?"

"Why?"

"You know how committed I am to my walk with the Lord. What you don't know is that one of my spiritual gifts is the discerning of spirits. I don't talk about it much because people either get freaked out about it or make a big deal out of it.

"But girl, when your friend walked into the office, there was something so dark about him it made the hairs on the back of my neck stand on edge. And when he left, girl…I got my oil out and anointed everything he touched and prayed over everyone he talked to. Something in his eyes seemed deceptive despite all that charm he slung around the office like the smell of that cheap cologne he was wearing. When I got back to my office I started searching scriptures. I needed a word from the Lord about what kind of spirit that brother had on him, and the Lord led me to 2 Timothy, Chapter 3:1–7. After I had read it, the Lord gave me a word to share with you."

Lia was stunned. Tiffany took the sound of Lia's ragged breathing on the other end of the line as permission to continue.

"The Lord told me to tell you 'It's time for you to put away childish things and stop walking in the past.' He wants you to graduate from walking in your burdens and start walking in the truth."

Despite the chaotic environment Lia was raised in, her family still managed to get to church every Sunday. Notwithstanding her traditional Baptist upbringing, nothing in Lia's experience came close to what Tiffany had just shared. She had no clue how to respond. Not wanting to seem rude or insensitive to a friend who'd just done her a favor, she said, "I appreciate your concern, but I haven't been in a church for years. I am sure God has more important things on his mind than my trifling situation."

"Let me tell you something, girlfriend. There is nothing trivial or triflin' about your situation to God. He loves you more than you can imagine; and He wants you to find some peace and joy," Tiffany said with conviction.

Processing what Tiffany had to say Lia thought, *"Finding some peace and joy in my life sure would be nice."* Feeling a little more hopeful, she thanked Tiffany for caring. Before she got off the phone, Lia told Tiffany "If I can find some peace and joy in the middle of my messed-up life, I will be up in somebody's church every Sunday!"

"Okay girl, I'm going to hold you to that."

CHAPTER TWENTY-EIGHT

Lunch 2: The Mercy Phase

While Lia's world was being turned upside down, Roman and Coach Perkins were just being seated for lunch. The last time they had met for lunch Roman was just entering the Mercy Phase. He was eager to share this progress with his mentor.

"Before we get into it, I need to ask you to switch seats," said Coach Perkins.

After the seat switch, Roman asked why he wanted to trade seats.

"I didn't want you multitasking our conversation while watching sports on the monitor over my head like you did the last time we were here. It was like watching a pitcher try to pick off a runner on first base," the older man teased.

"Sorry, I can't help it. It's an occupational hazard," Roman replied feeling a bit embarrassed.

"I know. That's why I asked you to switch seats instead of stopping you. It's me coming to terms with your humanity. Okay so, let's talk about the mercy phase of recovery. Not to get too spiritual on you, but in the Bible everywhere it talks about God's mercy, the emphasis is placed on God's character, and not the worthiness of the person receiving his mercy. When God grants mercy to a person, He is showing them a level of compassion they don't deserve and cannot earn, therefore the compassion being shown must originate with him. It is not a byproduct of His interaction with man. It is offered and sustained by his capacity to resist provocation and show compassion.

"In the same manner that God extends mercy to us, we

have to extend mercy to one another. Being married is a contact sport. Stay together long enough and someone is going to do something that crosses the line and hurts the other in a way that 'sorry' can't fix. Or, they are going to bring some baggage to the marriage that clashes with the baggage brought in by the other spouse. To withstand those seasons of barrenness—seasons where all the goodwill that has been built up is exhausted, a couple needs something a lot stronger than forgiveness. They are going to need mercy. Compassion at this level flows out of the emotional resilience one spouse has in their heart, not the worthiness of the spouse in need of mercy."

Roman sat taking it in as Coach Perkins continued to explain how mercy works.

"Mercy is the one area where things get really complicated in the recovery process, primarily because we try to show mercy at a level that does not match our emotional resilience. Again, not to get all holy on you but scripture says: 'God is the Lord who does not change; His mercy never wavers. His mercy is new every day. What gives Him the capacity to show mercy at this level is his unique nature as God. Despite the anthropomorphic references in scripture, the truth is God is not affected by what we do. He simply does not have a last nerve to get on. We on the other hand do." Coach Perkins laughed as he picked up his menu.

"Boy, do we," Roman said.

"That's because we get old, tired, mad, frustrated, afraid and a whole host of things that affect our ability to bounce back, which in turn affects our ability to show mercy. Ultimately, our capacity to show mercy is capped at our capacity to show compassion and manage provocation without hitting the trip wire that kicks in our fight, flight, freeze instinct.

As Roman took it all in he noticed out of the corner of his eye a man staring at him. The slender man with a permanent tan, and a full head of white hair, appeared to be in his early 60's. He sported blue slacks and pink shirt. Roman turned to look at him directly just as the man got up started towards his table with two friends in tow. As they approached, Roman saw the two-by-two inch square Trojan key ring in the man's left hand and intuitively stood to greet them. After he introduced Coach Perkins, the four men talked Trojan football for next 15 minutes until the food arrived. Another gentlemen in the small entourage grabbed his friend by the arm and said to Roman, "We'll let you eat in peace," before departing back to their table.

"You do know you just made their decade?" said Coach Perkins. "They'll be telling the story about their chance encounter with Trojan royalty for the rest of their lives. You know you need to go over there and take a selfie with them so they'll have proof."

"Yeah, I should. I'll grab them before they leave."

"That'll be good. In today's climate black folks and white folks should take as many selfies together as they can just to stem the tide of all the negativity."

"Amen, Dr. Martin Luther the King, amen," Roman said laughing.

"That is enough from you, young man. Where was I before you had to tend to your adoring fans?"

"You were talking about our limited capacity to show mercy."

"Yes. Mercy requires compassion and compassion requires resilience. Unfortunately, resilience comes in limited supply and varies from individual to individual. The mistake most people make when they try to show mercy is they tie it to the love they have for the person, and not their resilience. They mistakenly equate the amount of love they have for their husband or wife with their ability to endure the time and effort it will take to recover goodwill and see change. Showing mercy requires a level of honesty with ourselves that love tends to obscure. Just because you love someone deeply doesn't mean you can survive being with him or her.

"That's why the mercy phase is all about coming to terms

with yourself. It's about being honest with yourself about your feelings for Sage, your pain threshold for her sharp tongue, her family drama–especially her relationship with Owen–and her insecurities, as well as the fact she makes more money than you, plus a truckload of other things you'll need to endure to build a strong marriage. It's a season of counting the cost of being together which, in my opinion, is something people seldom do before they get married."

"I guess that's what people mean when they say 'I didn't sign up for all this' when things go left in their relationships," Roman added.

"For Sage, the mercy phase started when she began to show you compassion while you struggled to become a connected husband. Throughout the mercy phase, she'll be struggling to come to terms with her capacity to abandon the delusion of control and prevention related to keeping you engaged and accountable as a husband. She must relinquish her good girl narrative that being a good wife is going to 'fix you.' She's got to learn to let you struggle without becoming so anxious to help. She must not try and rescue you from the work you need to do to grow.

"The ultimate question she's going to have to answer is: 'Is there enough mercy in her for you? Is there enough to still be with you, knowing who you are?' She's got to decide if there's something in her that says the two of you have a future together that is important, necessary, and worth it, despite the way you have treated her. To show mercy to you she must give you another opportunity–knowing you have the capacity to blow it, <u>and</u> that she has the capacity to recover from it."

"Man…Now that's some scary stuff. I have to risk being rejected and she has to risk me acting a fool again."

"It is. And to pull it off she must to reach the conclusion that she can handle who you are, process her doubts while at the same time giving you enough space and safety to put in the work you need to put in. The entire process is one big par-adox. At the same time she needs your support, affirmation, and assurance that she can trust you, The process calls for her to cut you some slack to give you the grace you need to grow, even though there is a strong chance you'll continue to engage in some of the non-cheating behaviors that provokes her. Deciding that requires a sober look at one's self.

Roman's eyes had a sheen to them as he said, "That's what I am afraid of, sir. I'm afraid that she'll decide I am too big a project to take on. You know how deep my issues run."

"It's okay to be afraid; it's not okay to act out of fear. At the end of the day, it is her decision to make and you will have to honor it," Coach Perkins' voice was soothing, but firm.

Later, walking to their cars after Roman took photos with the Trojan alumni, Coach Perkins reminded Roman that what he was feeling in the aftermath of his fight with Sage was the kind vulnerability that only comes from authenticity. How having listened to Sage give a detailed account of how his reckless behavior affected her– without being able to rationalize, justify, or minimize what he'd done was bound to have an impact, but to allow himself to feel that and take ownership of it.

It wasn't that Roman hadn't heard the story before, he had, but only as something that happened to Sage. It was something Shelia did to her. He'd never thought of it as something he alone had caused. Instead, he had chalked it up to the bitterness inside of Sheila, not the cowardice inside himself. What he had gone through was genuine conviction followed by genuine grief.

CHAPTER TWENTY-NINE

Lia And Casey Round Two

It was day seven of Lia's series of turnaround trips. The grueling schedule of book and club launchings for her client Brie Anne Swiss, the cheese lady Owen called her half joking and half dismissive, left her looking forward to a break. In that short time she had already pulled off two of the four health club openings—Malibu earlier in the week and San Francisco the day before. Driving home along the coast the sun beamed directly overhead as she crossed the county line into Santa Barbara. In just a little over four hours she'd put 289 miles behind her. The sign up ahead read 'Vandenberg AFB Next Exit.' Calculating LA traffic, Lia figured she was still about three hours out from a husband she had not talked to in six days and the man she was leaving that husband for in seven days. Passing through Lompoc, Lia began looking for a place to stop to get something to eat. When Siri informed her that there was an In & Out Burger up the road in Goleta she decided to stop there for lunch. Of all the things Lia loved about California, In & Out Burger was at the top of the list.

At the halfway point between Goleta State Park and the In & Out Burger she craved, the display screen on her rented Buick Enclave signaled an incoming phone call—it was Casey. A mix of anger, annoyance, and excitement overwhelmed her as she hit the answer button on the touchscreen.

"Hello," a guarded Lia said.

Casey fired the first shot of attitude. "Hello? Is that how you answer the phone?"

"All I said was 'hello.' I didn't think you wanted to talk to me since you haven't answered my calls or text messages."

"Where are you? I need to run something by you," Casey asked.

"I'm somewhere in Santa Barbara County about to stop and have lunch."

"This'll only take a minute. My old girl and I have been doing some serious talking the past few days, and we've decided we are going to get back together for the sake of our son, Trey. So I need you to stop calling and texting me, disrespecting my lady and my situation. Well, that's all I had to say. I need you stop trying to reach me that's all," He said it as though Lia had been stalking him.

Lia's gaze was flash frozen on the road ahead of her. All the anger and frustration she'd built up over the years came to the surface in a perfect storm of rest, perspective, and the sense of achievement she'd gained in the last week of not having to deal with him or Owen. "Release the Kraken," is the best way to describe what followed.

"You don't want me to disrespect your woman? Are you out of your damn mind? How about all the disrespect you showed my situation: riding in my husband's car, sleeping in his bed, spending his money? You got some nerve accusing me of disrespecting your situation. How about the disrespect that she showed me when you got her pregnant in the first place? You and I were supposed to be together and she pops up pregnant? Oh! But I'm disrespecting her? And what the hell do you mean getting back together for the sake of your son? In a few years he'll be a grown freaking man! Hmph...which is more than I can say for his father." Lia said with absolute disdain in her voice.

Casey countered, "That's all you got? Be a grown man and I cheated on you? You got to go all the way back to college to dredge something up? You need to give that a rest!

"You want to know the real reason I was with her back then and why I'm getting back with her now? It's because she's a grown woman who knows how to handle herself. She doesn't get all paranoid and jealous at the drop of a dime."

Enraged at the notion that she was needy—partly because at some level she knew it was true, and partly because Casey was the last person she felt had the right to say it—Lia was all in.

"You're calling me needy with your wannabe trifling behind?! Every time you open your mouth it's 'Hey, ah…Can you let me hold something?…Hey, ah…I need a favor…Hey, ah…can you help me out…? I'm a little short this month ah…' So, how's a man who's always coming up short going to help a boy grow into a man? Oh, and who's the one who had to help who pay their tuition and rent back in the day? Who's the one who helped who pass their classes? They should have given me two and a half degrees when I graduated: half the one I had earned for you before you quit school, the one I achieved despite you, and another one for putting up with your all your drama and foolishness.

"And while I'm thinking about it, who's the one who gave who money and gifts to help prop up their self-esteem in the past few months? I'm also not the one who needs a Range Rover with Lowrider rims to prop up their manhood. Every time I see you it's like dealing with a baby bird, your mouth is open and you're wondering what I brought you because your sorry behind is too afraid to leave the nest and fly. I might be a needy woman, but that's a whole hell of a lot better than being a sorry man. Yeah, I think it is better you get back together with your baby's momma because I think you'll do a whole lot better dealing with someone who's used to dealing with a child, than a woman who expects you to be a man."

Realizing bridges were being burned Casey retaliated. "Trick, don't you know I've never needed anything from you? Everything I have ever asked you for, or said to you, has been straight game. I never loved you, I've just been playing you. You think we ran into one another by accident? The only reason I tried to get with you was to get my hands on some of Owen's paper. Homeboy never paid the necessary penalty and fees for trespassing on my property. Oh well! It looks like I lost out on the cash. But you lost out on your man. I guess we'll call it even. I suppose I should have been the one buying you the Rolex so you'd know what time it is. Trick, to me you just another tit that ran dry.

Stunned by the sudden hostile honesty coming from Casey's mouth, all of which confirmed the warnings she'd received since they first met, Lia didn't see the oncoming car that swerved at the last possible second to avoid hitting her. The combination of relief and adrenaline brought her back into sharp focus. Her flesh and mind now processed Casey's words at their pace which made her heart pound, her palms were sweaty, and her mouth was dry and rendered speechless. Simultaneously, the psychological burden of being with Casey lifted and relieved her of all the soul stealing drama and obligation of being with a parasite. She let Casey's confession set in for a few second and then began to embrace the finality of their relationship. Peace came over her like a rogue wave obliterating all the pain, anxiety and denial Lia had taken on just to be with Casey, and left in its wake a calm resolve she had never felt.

"Well there it is. Finally the truth comes out. Have nice day, and thanks. I needed this," she said as though she were ending a call with a vendor.

"Oh, I will-" was all Casey could get out before Lia pressed the red hang up icon on the dashboard.

A few minutes later, a text came in: "Thanks for the cash, the Rolex, and the wardrobe. Good luck finding a man willing to deal with all your baggage, since the only two brothers on the planet willing to deal with you are done with you Trick."

It was Casey's sadistic need to take one last cruel shot at Lia's self-esteem that severed whatever remaining soul ties that existed between the two of them. Like the In & out Burger she passed while on the phone, Casey was officially in her rear-view mirror. Whatever was next was up the road.

She had finally seen and accepted who and what Casey was—a parasite who had predatorial tendencies.

After asking Siri to give her the next location of an In & Out Burger, Lia began to process her relationship with Casey and all the other men in her life. Thinking about all the time and energy she had wasted with Casey, the peaceful resolve she had felt earlier turned into a haunting sorrow she could not shake. She turned the radio on to distract herself. The old-school station she flipped to played music that was nothing more than a soundtrack of sorrows, a sad reminder of family gatherings gone awry, birthdays, graduations, and other special events that were bigger disappointments than were celebrations. Then there were the songs that had been the score to her break-ups and the lonely nights. "*Oh no, this was not a good idea,*" she thought. By the time Lia fought off the funk coming over her she'd passed yet another In & Out Burger.

"Well, if I had to get dumped, this was as good a time as any," Lia said to herself as she passed a sign that read 'Camarillo Premium Outlets Next Exit.' Camarillo was her happy place, not because it was the best outlet (it was number three on her list statewide), but because it had an In & Out Burger adjacent to the on-ramp and you could drive the coast to get to it.

Parking her car next to the Nike outlet, she planned her strategy. She'd work the stores in a counter-clockwise motion so she'd already know the colors of her new outfit by the time circled back to Nike where she could get a pair of cute shoes to match.

Her mood began to brighten as she considered the prospect before her. "*A little retail therapy and a Double-Double before I get back on the road and this Texas girl is going to be just fine,*" she thought. Since it was a weekday afternoon the stores would be virtually empty. Lia couldn't deny the high she felt as she thought about searching for deals, trying on new clothes and playing dress up without having to fight crowds. And then, of course, there was the affirmation she derived from the salespeople who know her by name from her previous shopping excursions.

After two and a half hours of hanging out with her friends Calvin, Ann, Kenneth, St. John, Brooks, Karen, Coach, Neiman and Saks, Casey seemed like ancient history.

#

After loading the rear compartment of her rental with an endless array of bags, Lia jumped in and headed up the road for the "feast de resistance"—an In & Out Double-Double, fries, and a creamy, thick chocolate shake.

While savoring every bite of her Double-Double, Lia glanced out the window and across the parking lot at the rental car. It occurred to her that the SUV was not half-bad. It was no comparison to her Lexus, she thought, but she could envision herself driving it. She especially appreciated all the room it had in the back.

"A girl could get her shopping on in a vehicle like that," she thought, looking at all the stuff piled in the back. Even with the factory tint on the rear of the car, the stack of bags seemed like a UPS truck leaving the warehouse at Christmas time. But it wasn't— it was $5,200 dollars worth of 40-to-75% off deals.

The more she thought about the stuff she'd purchased, the more Lia realized she had not bought one item she was dying to have. Oh sure there were a lot of things she liked, but there was nothing that she was in love with (except for a cute pair of orange Texas Longhorn Reeboks she planned to ship to her little cousin). Everything else she bought solely because it was discounted. Within moments her shopping high turned to depression.

Coming down from the euphoric feeling opened the door for a resurgence of the sorrow she felt earlier. She contemplated how her shopping habits mirrored her relationships— buying things not because she wanted them, but because they were on sale.

The blueprint she adopted to build her wardrobe turned out

to be the same blueprint she used to build her relationships, which explained how she hooked up with Casey and with Owen. The two relationships bore a striking resemblance to one another. Neither of them happened to be men she found particularly attractive when she first met them. Both men employed the same strategy to work their way into Lia's life. All Casey and Owen had to do to overcome Lia's resistance was to show persistence. Casey wore her down with his persistent aggressiveness, while Owen wore her down with his persistent kindness. Though opposites on the surface, their pursuit of Lia was the same.

Continuing to stare at the stuff in the back of her rental, she wondered, *"What does it say about me if I've never been in a relationship with a man I wanted to be with from the start? Or felt I chose him just as much as he chose me?*

"When did my relationship with Casey go from 'not interested' to 'I want to be with you'? And when did my relationship with Owen go from like a brother to me to let's get married?" she asked herself. *"What kind of 'I'll settle' vibe am I giving off that says 'I'm okay with this'? What's wrong with me?"*

Scrubbing through the video clips in her mind, trying to pinpoint the exact moment her feelings for Casey or Owen blossomed, she became overwhelmed when she could not find one. Things simply evolved through a process fed by obligation, fear, and passivity.

Lia couldn't point to time or place where she said yes to love, she just never said no. It was like her Uncle Charles used to say when people asked him about the length of his beard: "I'm not growing a beard. I'm just not shaving." Lia never opened her heart to Casey or Owen, she didn't have to. They both pried it open and walked in. It had been the perfect scenario for both men as neither of them cared much about what she thought, wanted or needed. Both were driven by their desire for her, not her desire for them. They simply pushed their way into her life because she never pushed back.

One minute she and Owen are kicking it, the next they

are dating, then engaged and ultimately married. All without Owen ever asking her out on a date, to be his girlfriend, or to be his wife. On Sunday he told her he'd spent the previous day fielding questions from his family about their relationship, and on Monday he gave Lia a budget and told her to go to The Jewelry Exchange and pick a ring. Boom, there it was... done. His mother planned the wedding as though Owen was the bride and Lia the groom, right down to the number of guests she could invite. She was even given a list of friends she couldn't invite. At no point in the process did she ever stop to ask herself, "What am I doing?" Let alone, "Is this what I want?" The closest Lia came to setting any boundaries occurred when she chose a ring that exceeded her budget by several thousand dollars. This became her preferred way of engaging in civil disobedience in their marriage.

Every time she was moved from one relative's house to another, Uncle Jr., the family's designated bearer of bad news, would show up and take her for ice cream and then announce, "Something's come up. We're going to have to make some changes." For Lia, "change" was interpreted as she had worn out her welcome. After giving her the when and the where she'd be moving, he'd conclude their conversation with the same closing statement, "Trust me, it's for the best." There was no explanation, just things have changed. It was as though the family had gotten together in some secret place and decided her fate.

The only time Uncle Jr. ever went into detail was the time her mom got sober. Uncle Jr. showed up out of the blue like always and announced, "Your mother has completed rehab and you'll be moving in with her." Once again it was all settled without one word of input from Lia, despite the fact she was staying with an aunt she did not want to leave, and who did not want her to go. None of that mattered. Somewhere the gods had decided her fate once again. The only difference this time is that she was told the family had decided that staying with her mother would be therapeutic and help incentivize her mom to stay sober. This time there was no "trust me it's for the best." Uncle Jr. is a lot of things, but he's not a liar.

Though she didn't know it at the time, Lia was in the midst of transitioning into the third phase of the recovery process—mercy. She'd reached the goal of the forgiveness phase as she came to terms with the real Casey, and to a lesser extent with the real Owen. Now with Casey out of the picture as a scapegoat, Lia was emotionally freed-up to deal with Lia. It was time for her to come to terms with herself.

On the last leg of her drive home, she thought long and hard about the choices she'd made, or failed to make, which led her to this crossroads. *"All of my life I've let other people run my life. I allowed people and circumstances dictate how I would live my life. I let men decide for me who I was going to date. And I let my family decide where I was going to live without saying a word."*

Her mind turned to the stuff crammed in the back of the car. A conviction to return it hit her and grew stronger with each mile she drove. This was nothing short of a miracle. Lia had never returned anything in her life. If it didn't fit, she gave it to someone it did fit. If it didn't work, she kept it until she found the right accessories to make it work, or she'd donate it. Over the years, she'd given away thousands of dollars of retail merchandise. *"Reverse shopping. What a concept,"* she thought as hit her signal and maneuvered toward the exit.

After returning everything but a killer pair of silver and black pointy-toe Kenneth Cole pumps with a buckle that she got 50% off and thought were stunners, and the Reeboks she purchased for her cousin, Lia was back on the road. According to Siri, even with traffic she'd make it home in an hour and forty minutes. Driving with just the hum of the engine in her ear, her funky mood returned. A whole cocktail of thoughts and feelings ran through her mind. She began to ruminate on the mistakes, lapses in judgment, and the sheer volume of the time she'd wasted trying to hold onto one man and meet the standards of another.

As the miles ticked off on her odometer what started off as

grief turned to shame. Similarly, what started off as pain over the loss of relationships quickly became a pain over the loss of life, a life jumping through hoops. A life wasted trying to satisfy everybody but herself. Even as a child, fear and vulnerability led Lia to do things that weren't in her character, and that was the most painful part of all.

Making the transition from the 101 to the 405, she whispered, "Where do you go from here girl?" And like an old friend, there was that feeling again, the same feeling she'd get when Uncle Jr. would give her the "things have changed" speech. The only difference is this time the decision on where to go from here was on her–not on her aunts, uncles, or anyone else who ruled from Mount Olympus. Oh, she could seek their counsel, and they would tell her what she should do, but not without serving it up with a generous dose of shame and judgment.

From the time it took her to get from the Valley to the Westside, panic had set in. All of Lia's abandonment issues had shot to the surface like a geyser. By the time she parked her car and walked into the house, the combination of her fatigue and anxiety on a scale from one to 10 had risen from a four-and-a-half to solid eight. She did not want to talk, process or deal with anybody or anything. Instinctively, she dropped the one remaining shopping bag on the bench in the hallway and headed straight to the bedroom she and Owen shared. Sitting on the edge of their California King-sized bed, she took off her shoes and leaned back on the plush pillows. She remained there for a half hour pondering everything from her break up with Casey to the success of her trip. But before any of her thoughts could pierce the surface of the superficial, she fell fast asleep. Ironically, the only unclothed part of her body dangled off the side of the bed. For the next several hours, she lay on the edge of the bed, fully clothed and perfectly still except for the rhythmic rise and fall of her body produced by the shallow respirations.

CHAPTER THIRTY

Lia's Home

The next morning, Lia awakened in that "where am I?" state of confusion that sets in when you've been on the road too long. It took her a few moments to shake off the cobwebs. The combination of travel, bad dreams, and the hideous safari themed linen that now adorned the bed she and Owen used to share left her with a dry hangover. Another bed-in-a-bag special from some discount store no doubt. She smoothed over the area of the comforter where she had slept then stood back to take in the scene. The bed that was once adorned with color coordinated John Robshaw designer linen was now assaulted by an array of purple and ivory pillows, with a splash of yellow interspersed among four burnt orange, brown and black pillows, all resting on a comforter with a huge black and brown lion in the middle and gigantic leaves running along the border. Lia laughed to herself because if ever something symbolized the differences between her and Owen, it was this bed.

Lia recognized she hadn't cracked an authentic smile in a long time. In fact, it had been about four years. That's when her frustration with the marriage truly began. It was long before her affair with Casey. It could be argued that her affair with him didn't wasn't the start of her stepping out on Owen. There had been several close calls before she hooked up with Casey. These flirtations could have quickly turned into sexual liaisons if she didn't love the attention she garnered from men more than sex. She was not promiscuous to that extent. Casey and Owen were the only two men she'd ever been with intimately. Because of her past, and the way Casey and Owen did intimacy, sex was more of a chore than an act of love. It was something a woman did to please her man; it was not a pleasure to be shared.

As she turned toward the bathroom with a smile still on her face, she realized Owen hadn't come home.

"Where could he be? Is it possible he's...?No, there's no way he's got a chick on the side." Lia thought.

A fierce jealousy rose in her she didn't think she had the right to embrace. Nonetheless, there it was. She grabbed her phone off the nightstand and dashed off a text to Owen: "I got in last night around six. Where are you?" Ten minutes passed and nothing. Lia took the phone into the bathroom with her in case he called.

Mindlessly, Lia stood under the nearly scalding water of the shower until she thought she heard a sound. Unable to see through the fog that filled the bathroom she cast her eyes down at the bar of light across the bottom of the door. The dancing shadows beyond the light told her she was not alone. Someone was pacing the floor in the other room. Heart pounding, she threw on the pink Trojan sweats she'd hung on the door.

"Owen is that you?" she said faintly. No answer. "Owen is that you?" she cried out again with more conviction. Bump, bump went the sound on the other side of the door again and again.

Lia snatched her phone off the sink to dial 911. Before the operator picked up, a high-pitched wail she recognized came from the other room.

She'd barely managed to get the door open when the four-legged bundle of muscle and excitement forced her way into the bathroom like a SWAT Team serving a warrant. Scarlet couldn't contain herself and jumped into Lia's arms without hesitation, her muscular frame in full on spasms. Lia buried her face in the dog's furry mane.

After a few moments of rubs and kisses, Scarlet leaped

out of Lia's arms and did a lap around the bedroom that would have made Ferrari jealous—under the chair, over the bed, past the closet and the dresser back into Lia's arms. Tears fell from Lia's eyes as she experienced Scarlet's unconditional love.

The dog she'd raised then dumped in a kennel, the dog that had not seen her in weeks, was just as excited to see her as the day she brought her home. The unbounded affection coming from Scarlet sent waves of guilt through Lia's heart and turned into tidal waves of shame when she realized she had treated Scarlet just like she had been treated as a child.

Stroking the dog's head, Lia repeated over and over, "Mommy's sorry, Mommy's sorry." Scarlet lay there soaking up all the overdue affection being heaped upon her. Suddenly, the Boykin Spaniel jumped up and made a mad dash for the front of the house. Lia picked herself up from the floor, wiped her eyes, grabbed a handful of her damp hair, rolled it into a bun and made her way to the front of the house. She was startled when she walked by the entrance to the garage and caught sight of Owen bent over pouring dog food into a brand-new dog dish with "Starlet" printed on it.

"Did you hijack some other dog's bowl?" she asked. Stunned, Owen jumped at least three feet spilling dog food all over the floor, which Scarlet quickly licked dry.

"Oh my God! You scared the mess out of me. What are you doing here?"

"Ah…As far as I know, I still live here," Lia answered with the causation of a boxer felling their opponent out in the early rounds of a prize fight.

"I didn't mean what are you doing here? I meant what are you doing home, now, at this moment?" Owen stumbled over his words..

"Did you get my text?" Lia asked still trying to gauge Owen's mood.

"Yes, I did. I texted you right back to tell you I spent the night at Sage and Roman's house. When I didn't see the rental car in the driveway I assumed you'd left," He was careful not to imply this was no longer her home.

"I parked in the garage."

"The garage?" Owen blurted out, unable to hide his astonishment.

"Yes, in the garage."

"Well, well."

"What's that mean?"

"Nothing, nothing," Owen said quickly, trying not to start trouble.

"What's up with the 'Starlet' bowl," Lia said, trying to change the subject?

"It was supposed to say 'Scarlet,' but they spelled it wrong."

"Why didn't you have them print another one?"

"What and have them throw this one in the trash? Not a chance."

For another five minutes, the two of them made small talk reminiscent of two roommates not a husband and wife seeing each other for the first time in over a week. Even the texts they exchanged while Lia was away were succinct. They were in a polite loop that neither one of them would pull out of for fear they would have to deal with the herd of pachyderms in the room. Thinking he was keeping things light, Owen innocently asked, "How was the ride home?"

Lia reflected on the many twists and turns her journey home took and said, "Interesting...Yeah, interesting."

"How so?"

"Mm...I am not sure yet, that's what made it so interesting," Lia said. She wasn't ready to go into details. All she knew was that the break up with Casey had resurrected something in her that softened and emboldened her at the same time. She was feeling things that she'd suppressed and outright denied for years. What it meant for her moving forward she was not sure.

After several seconds of awkward silence, Lia said, "Well I need to dry this hair before it makes its way back to Africa and can't get a work visa to get back in the US." She turned and headed back down the hallway leaving Owen still holding a small bag of dog food in his hand.

Twenty minutes later, Lia found Owen in the kitchen. "I've got errands to run to get ready for the second leg of my trip," she ventured.

"Where to this week?"

"I go to San Diego—Carlsbad to be specific, then Newport Coast."

"Do you want to take the Lexus? It's in the driveway," Owen offered.

"No. I'll take the rental. No need in putting extra mileage on the lease when you can put them on a rental," Lia said as she grabbed her keys.

Wide-eyed, Owen watched her as she exited through the kitchen door leading to the garage. "What the heck just happened?" he whispered to himself. Lia's warm and cordial manner bordered on charming, something he had only seen glimpses of when she was trying to negotiate a bargain. She didn't even want to drive the Lexus. "*Who was this woman?*" he thought. Then it hit him. The Lexus was blocking the rental.

He thought "*She's going to freak!*" Among the many things Owen did that irritated Lia, blocking her in was at the top of the list. He sprinted outside to move the car and made it just in time to witness a real miracle that would rival seeing Santa Claus going back up the chimney. Lia had moved the Lexus out of the way herself.

Getting out of the car, Lia saw Owen standing across from the driveway looking slack-jawed. Assuming he was shocked that she had a key to the Lexus, Lia shouted to him, "I found my key when I was packing for my trip."

All he could manage to formulate was a weak "Great" in response. Owen watched in awe as this new 2.0 grown-up version of Lia drove off with a slight wave. His curiosity now on red alert, he wanted desperately to know what happened on her trip that had her in such an uncharacteristic mood? He wondered if it was some new game plan. Or perhaps, she had been abducted by aliens. He even considered the possibility that she could be taking drugs. These were a few of the wild speculations that ran through Owen's mind as he watched her turn the corner.

CHAPTER THIRTY-ONE

Sage and Roman Spar Over Owen

Owen turned to head back into the house. He grabbed his cell phone out of the left pocket of his tattered gray sweats. The phone rang once.

"How did it go?" Sage said with eager anticipation.

"Surprisingly well, considering," said Owen, still stupefied by the change in Lia.

"What do you mean? What happened? And don't spare any details."

Owen then recounted the morning's events in minute detail with Sage adding her commentary along the way. When Owen was done explaining what had happened between he and Lia, he asked, "So what do you think?"

"Wow, that's different, I would've never expected that from her."

"Yeah, I know. When she moved the two cars around, I thought I was going to lose my mind."

"Oh yeah, something happened to her on that trip. You know what it sounds like to me? Like somebody might have gotten in her head and told her to try to be kind to you to take advantage of your generosity. Either that or the thing with Casey has gone south, and she's trying to work her way back in. Yeah, that's probably it," Sage wondered aloud.

"You know what? That's got to be it," co-signed Owen.

"Remember how upset Casey got when he found out Lia had signed a prenuptial agreement? I'll bet you he figured out that she wasn't getting a dime, and ended it. Now she's trying to be nice just to get back with you," Sage speculated. "You need to realize this is nothing but game on her part, and you need to watch your back. Make sure you don't fall for it. You cannot afford to get soft at this point," she warned.

"Oh, you don't have to worry about me. The truth is there's nothing Lia could say or do that would make me take her back after what went down last week. No sir, you don't have to worry about me. I'm straight. I learned my lesson."

"Good. Right now the best way to handle her is to lay low until she overplays her hand. And you know she will."

#

Sage hung up the phone and turned around to find Roman staring at her from across the gigantic island in the kitchen. The look in his eyes said he heard enough of the conversation to be concerned. She could instantly tell they were about to go into a conversation that was going to last more than just a few minutes.

"Before you say anything, that was Owen," Sage defended, "and all we were talking about is what kind of game is Lia trying to run on him."

"Oh, I heard enough of the conversation to know what the two of you were talking about," Roman said.

The direct no-nonsense tone of his voice rattled her, and in an octave just above her normal speaking voice she shot back, "What do you mean?"

"I'm talking about you and Owen's little strategy session where you're getting him hyped about what Lia may or may not be doing."

"You do know this is straight out of you all's college play-book. The two of you in each other's dorm room spending hours talking about what was going down with Lia and Casey. I know I may not be the one who needs to say this, but the two of you need to let this go. If it's not a good look for a wife to share her business with one of her 'girls' when she and her man aren't talking, then it certainly can't be a good look for a husband to be sharing his business with one of his 'girls.'"

Roman and Sage went back and forth about what role Sage should play in Owen and Lia's situation. On the one side, Sage argued that she could be fair and balanced while on the other side Roman claimed that there was no way that she could be fair and balanced unless she adopted the FOX News definition of fair and balanced.

After about 30 minutes, Roman said, "I just think you need to stand down on this."

"Stand down? What are you talking about?" Sage said. She was offended at the mere suggestion that she not be there for Owen.

But Roman didn't flinch. "Yeah stand down, stand down. Back down, take your hands off it, step aside, surrender your position, and anything else that means to stay out of it or mind your bleeping own business."

"You know I can't do that. Owen needs me."

"What Owen needs to do is figure out what he wants to do with his life moving forward, without being distracted by the input of someone who's helping him walk in denial."

"You expect me just to stand by and let Lia run game on Owen without saying a word?"

"No. I expect you to let a grown man who runs a multi-million dollar charity figure things out with his grown wife who has an IQ higher than both of ours combined," Roman said turning his back on Sage to open the refrigerator.

By the time Roman had retrieved a drink from the refrigerator Sage was standing behind the door when he closed it. "I am not telling him how to run his life. I'm helping him process what's going on from a woman's perspective."

"Oh, is that what you call random speculation about Lia's motives? Sage, he already has access to a woman's perspective—her name is Lia, and her title is wife."

"Random? There's nothing I've said about Lia that was inconsistent with some of the stuff she's pulled in the past. I may not know what she's up to, but I do know she's running some game, that's for sure."

"You mean like getting her to sign a prenup by saying 'My people are forcing me to do this'?" Roman reminded her that Owen had done his fair share of game playing too.

"He had to do that to keep her from gaming him. Don't tell me you're trying to defend her. exactly whose side are you on?"

"I'm not defending anyone, and if I were, wouldn't I be justified in pointing out that he's the one that took the first shot? What if the game is simply her returning fire? Truth is, they're both guilty of gaming each other. You know, a marriage between two consenting adults is more like a conspiracy. It either works or doesn't. In this case, Lia and Owen have conspired with one another and what they've ended up with is a mess of denial and delusion. Look, all I am saying is, let them work their issues out."

"I am supposed just to keep my mouth shut when he talks about his situation?"

"Sage, it's not an all or nothing thing."

"Why are you so Team Lia?"

"I'm not. But I am anti-meddling and pro opportunity. When all my dirt came out into the light, you and Coach Perkins gave me an opportunity to get my crap together. That's all I am asking you to do for Owen and Lia. Bottom line is, when it comes to figuring anything out remotely connected to relationships, Owen hangs on your every word. What you say to him he takes as gospel. Do you want to be the one who makes the decision to end their marriage? If you do we might as well redo the guest room because he's going to have to live with us. She was only gone a day and a half before you, and I, thought he would do better staying with us than being in that big house all alone.

I know we want kids, but this is not the way either of us planned on having one."

Sage sighed, "I'm with you. I just struggle with the notion of her getting over again."

"You mean like when she went the alumnae route to join a grad chapter of a particular rival sorority when she found out the Bryant women were 'four generations of deep purple,' as you all like to say?"

"Well if you want me to show her love then you need not to be bringing up that particular incident," Sage said, wagging her finger at Roman.

"Let me ask you something," Roman asked, "If Lia had gone through the M.P. process and pledged purple instead of gold, would she be sporting 'deep purple' now?"

"For real...? Ah...no. We have our standards."

"What if she had gone the grad route?"

"First off, if she'd gotten an invitation, the Bryant women would have shot that down in a hot second cause that's how we roll."

"So, what you're saying is she was never going to be sporting purple," Roman said again with air quotes, "because your family left her no choice."

"Oh, she had a choice. She could have just left it alone."

"That's right. She could have just accepted the fact that she was going to be the only Bryant woman with no sorority affiliation. Righhhhht...that wouldn't have kept her out of the Bryant women coven," Roman snorted.

"All I'm doing is pointing out that she never had a chance to honor the Bryant legacy because the Bryant women were hell bent on putting her in her place—even though she spent her weekends volunteering at the children's hospital, had a 4.0 GPA, and graduated in three years—and despite the drama of being abused by her college sweetheart and stalked by her future husband. So let me see if I got this straight? The whole Bryant coven is mad because a sister you wouldn't let roll with you went Uber on you all and found a ride anyway.

"All I'm saying is 'paper burns, but sands are forever,'" Sage used a phrase commonly used to distinguish those who go through the pledging process to join a sorority/fraternity, from those who enter by filling out paperwork. "If she was a 'made sister' who had gone through the actual process I could respect that. But to go grad and gold…Hmm, I am not feeling that," Sage balked.

"To quote Charlie Wilson of the Gap Band, 'rubber burns too,' which is what she did after you all hated on her. Hey, don't kill the messenger. You know I have a thing about bullying. All I'm trying to do is not have history repeat itself. And besides, weren't you a legacy candidate?

It was true. Sage had been given preferential treatment because her grandmother and mother were active members. She herself had been able to bypass the usual process of pledging. For all intents and purposes, she wasn't exactly a 'made' sister either.

"You know I hate you right now," said Sage, with a half-smile on her face. But the smile quickly turned to a blank stare of reflection as she remembered the amount of animosity thrown her way by those who knew she went legacy."

"Don't you have a meeting to go to this morning?"

"I just did," said Roman. He kissed her on her forehead and headed back to their bedroom.

"I'll think about what you said, but I cannot make any promises," Sage yelled out as he headed down the hallway.

"As you tell me, I don't need your promises, I need your support," Roman yelled back as he entered their bedroom.

CHAPTER THIRTY- TWO

Sage and Mrs. Hillard
Spar Over Owen

As soon as Sage knew Roman was gone for good, meaning he hadn't forgotten anything, she ran to her cell phone and punched in the number of the one person who would know what was going on with Casey. Her old friend Denise somehow always managed to keep up with everybody's business from back in the day. If anyone could get info on what was going on with Lia and Casey, it would be her.

"Hey girl, what's going on?" Denise said.

"Oh, nothing just checking in." Sage played it cool so as not to overly anxious to get the scoop. It was a sort of cat-and-mouse game she and Denise played even though they both knew the real reason for the call.

"So...what's been happening in your world? How have you and Roman been doing?"

"We're doing great."

"I was sorry to hear about Lia leaving Owen for that black troll doll Casey, especially since that thing ain't gonna work out anyway," Denise said, baiting Sage.

"What makes you think it's not going to work out?"

"Girl, I have it on good authority that he's just playing her to get to some of your cousin's bankroll. That man doesn't love her. He never has. In fact, a little birdie told me he only plans to stick around long enough to help her spend some of that divorce cash. You want to know something else? I also have it on good authority that he may be getting impatient."

"Already?"

"Evidently something happened last week that has him thinking twice about moving forward," Denise said.

Sage heard the bells go off in her head. Now they were getting to it. She decided to do a little fishing of her own. "Really?" she replied innocently.

"Yeah girl, that thing may not make it another month..." Denise continued until the sound of a beep on her end stopped her down.

"Oh, hold on girl, I got somebody on the other line." In only seconds, Denise clicked back and said she had to take the call, but promised she'd talked to her later. Sage was unfazed since she had gotten all the information she wanted. She hung up giddy with excitement.

"I knew something was up," Sage said to herself. "It just didn't make any sense that Lia would go from lion to lamb for no reason."

She was all set to call Owen when there was a knock at the door. "Who can this be?" she said to herself as she made her way to the front door. Through the peephole she saw Mrs. Hilliard adorned in her starched white Capri pants, Wal-Mart tennis shoes, a white jacket with a blue zipper with a fresh from the beauty shop hairdo. In her arms were a couple of canvas grocery bags.

At 5' 5" and little more than 100 lbs., Mrs. Hilliard was a woman from another generation, and she was proud of it. Her dress, her hair, her conversation, and her demeanor said, "You're not from around here are you?"

Raised in Malvern, Arkansas, she had picked cotton to earn enough to come to California, and cleaned hotel rooms to put herself through college. Like Sage's mom, she had taught school for over twenty years in one of the roughest schools in Southern California. She also managed to make choir rehearsal every Thursday night and teach Sunday school, all while raising seven kids. For Mrs. Hilliard, retirement meant turning her house into a childcare center, which she ran with her husband Deacon Eddie, for five of their sixteen grandchildren.

Sage opened the door with excitement because every time Mrs. Hilliard dropped in it was like getting a visit from a sweet old grandmother.

"Hey Miss Hilliard, whatcha got there?" Sage swung the door open wide and beckoned for her neighbor to enter.

"I brought back the containers you sent all that food in last month. Sorry, it took me so long to get them back to you," she replied, her Southern drawl still detectable.

"C'mon in! You didn't have to do that. I have tons of these things you could have thrown them out," Sage took the bags out of the elderly woman's hands and escorted her to the kitchen.

"Oh no daughter, this is that good plastic. You can get four or five uses out of this. Truth is, I didn't want the fact that I had your containers to keep you from sending Eddie and me some more of that good food. I swear you cook like you were born and raised in the south."

Once the meticulously washed plastic ware was stowed, the women sat down with a fresh pot of tea and made small talk. They had been catching up for 30 minutes or so when Mrs. Hilliard finally got around to asking how she and Roman were doing. Sage hedged by saying that except for the occasional disagreement they were doing great. "No biggie," she dismissed the question with a wave of her hand.

But remembering how her young neighbor had used that term several times before whenever the two of them talked during the crisis phase of the couple's struggles, Mrs. Hilliard knew the spat was tied to something that legitimately bothered Sage, and also that she wanted to gloss over it.

Too compassionate to ignore it, and too old to care how uncomfortable it made Sage, Mrs. Hilliard locked on to the comment like a laser guided missile.

"Was this morning's disagreement tied to any of your previous issues?"

"Yes," Sage said, "but not in our marriage. It's my cousin, Owen. Roman wants me to 'stand down'. She mimicked Roman's air quotes.

Sage poured Mrs. Hilliard another cup of tea before continuing. "It's like he wants me to abandon Owen just when he needs me the most. He just doesn't understand how family works. Being raised in a broken home, he doesn't know what it's like when relatives have each other's back."

Mrs. Hilliard listened intently as Sage justified her actions. Her reassuring eyes, warm smile and occasional nods seemed to spur Sage on like a rider with a whip. Decades of child rearing and classroom time had taught her that when someone gets on a roll, let them keep it up until they run out of steam. After all, Sage could only run her no-huddle offense for so long.

Sage paused to glance at her phone to check the text that just came through. "Call me girl you're gonna wanna hear this," Denise's text read. Mrs. Hilliard could tell whoever it was had gotten Sage's attention.

"Do you need to deal with that, daughter?" said Mrs. Hilliard, using a term she assigned to every female at least 30 years her junior.

Not wanting to be rude, Sage said, "No I'll call them back later."

"You sure? You seemed awfully interested in what they had to say."

"No," Sage said. She powered down the phone. "Anyway, it's like I was saying, Roman doesn't understand how close families work."

Mrs. Hilliard cracked a smile, leaned in across the counter and said with a soft voice, "Daughter, I think you might be the one who's struggling to figure out how families work. A person doesn't have to come from a broken home to have a distorted view of family. Look at Ed and me, he and I have been together coming up on 60 years. It took us almost two decades to figure out what we were doing. During that time our family was just as broken as Humpty Dumpty.

"You'd never guess looking at us from the outside, but it wasn't until our two oldest children were grown that Ed and I realized

Ron and Maria were just as damaged with two parents at home as they would have been had we had gotten a divorce. So, don't assume that because he didn't have his father in his life he didn't learn about having someone's back. Some of the most broken families I know are the ones that do not know they are broken."

"I am not saying he doesn't understand family. I'm just saying he doesn't know how close families work," Sage said, feeling cornered.

"Oh, I think he does. He's spent almost twenty years of his life working in sports at one school. Take it from someone who knows, no black man lasts that long, in a system that white, without learning to support and respect others," Mrs. Hilliard said, placing her hand on the table as though she were swearing on a bible.

"Are you saying you think I need to stand down?"

"If that means stay out of grown folks' business? Then yes daughter, you need to stand down. Your cousin is a grown man married to a grown woman. They need to work things out between the two of them," Mrs. Hilliard said, reaching across the table to pat Sage on her hand.

"Yeah, that's what Roman said," Sage whispered, her eyes downcast.

"That Roman is a smart young man."

"Because he agrees with you?"

"No, because he knew enough not to let a fine girl like you get away."

"I cannot argue with Mrs. Hilliard," Sage said with a bashful grin.

"What do I do when Owen asks me for advice about his situation?"

"Isn't he some kind of math genius who worked on Wall Street?"

"Yes Ma' am."

Mrs. Hilliard just smiled and rose to her feet to leave. "Something else you might want to consider the next time you're tempted to butt in."

"What's that?"

"Ask yourself: 'Where would you and Roman be today if someone had given you the same advice you're about to give Owen?'"

Sage knew her neighbor was right. "Before you go, can I ask you a personal question?"

"Sure, Lord knows I have been all up in your Kool-Aid as you kids say."

"What was it that turned Mr. Hilliard around? What made him get it?" Sage asked earnestly.

Mrs. Hilliard sat back down. "Well, you got to understand I come from a different time and place. We lived way out in the country where not too many good Christians resided. When I got tired of his fooling around, I sent for my family. After about a month of staying with us in California they decided to leave. Before they left my dad and a couple of my uncles set Ed and I down for a talk. They told him he needed to get his stuff together, or they were going and move the kids and me back to the country. And they let him know it would be a mistake for him to come looking for us. From then on," she chuckled, "he's been a good husband."

"That's it? That's all it took? Your father and uncles telling him to get his stuff together?" Sage asked, wondering if Mrs. Hilliard was pulling her leg.

"Yeah, that's it. At least that's my version of the story. If you ask Ed, he might tell a slightly different story. In his version there was four Smith and Wessons' sitting on the coffee table and my father used another word for 'stuff' that starts with a 's'."

In shock, Sage's hand flew over her mouth.

"Like I said, daughter, not every broken family is broken up. To be saved you must be saved from something." With that Mrs. Hilliard rose to her feet and made her way to the door.

"Mrs. Hilliard, your family was gangster. All this time I thought Deacon Eddie changed because he found the Lord," Sage teased.

"Oh, it was God. Nobody but Jesus."

"But you just said it was a conversation with your father and your uncles that changed him."

"It was still God who did it. Who do you think told me to send for my family? It was the best answer to prayer God ever gave me," Mrs. Hilliard shot her a knowing wink. She thanked Sage again for the food as the two of them shared a warm hug.

"You're welcome Mrs. H. If there is anything you and Ed need, just call me."

"Thanks, daughter. Don't worry about us. The Lord has kept me and Ed a mighty long time. We'll be just fine."

#

As Mrs. Hilliard made her way down the street, Sage ran back in the house, cut her phone on and hit the home button: "Siri – Call Denise on her cell."

"Calling Denise on the cell," the phone replied.

Just as Sage thought it was going to go to voicemail, Denise answered. Before Sage could say hello, Denise had launched into the story about how she found out that Casey had dumped Lia because he wanted to get back with his "baby momma." Denise told Sage how she got the details from a friend that Casey broke up with Lia while she was on a business trip. According to Denise's informant, Lia was so devastated that she had to cut the trip short.

Knowing that was untrue Sage asked, "Are you sure about that?" But Denise was emphatic. "Yes! I heard she was so distraught that Casey was worried she would harm herself."

"For real?" Sage feigned shock knowing that nothing could be further from the truth. Recognizing how limited Denise's information was, Sage made an excuse to get off the phone.

Sage hit the home button once again: "Call Owen on his cell."

Siri replied, "Calling Owen Bryant on his cell phone." The call immediately went to voicemail.

"Call me I have something to tell you."

When Owen did not call her back promptly, she phoned Roman who was just leaving his meeting with the boosters.

"How's my spice girl?" Roman answered.

"Doing well," Sage said, her smile came through her voice.

"What's up?" Roman sensed her excitement.

"Remember when I said I know Lia is up to something? Well, I was right. She and Casey broke up sometime during her business trip," Sage said, giddy with pride.

Roman paused to catch himself, but it was too late. The anger he felt poured out of him like vapor rising off the heat of a long stretch of highway on a hot summer day.

"That's important because why?" he seethed.

"Don't you get it? It just proves that I was right."

"Right about what?"

"Right about her playing games. Isn't it obvious she is acting nice to Owen to get back with him because Casey kicked her to the curb?"

"That's what you got from Casey and Lia breaking up and her being nice? And how do you know they broke up?"

"Denise called me," Sage said, her exuberance tempered by Romans apparent displeasure.

"I should have known you've been talking to the TMZ of the 'hood. Are you telling me Denise just called you out of the clear blue? That's funny since you haven't connected since the text you sent her months ago to tell her to stop putting our business on blast?"

"Well, I might have reached out to her first. But it still doesn't change the fact Lia is up to something and I was right," Sage said defiantly.

"The only fact it does not change is the fact you need to respect Owen and Lia's marriage."

"I am just looking out for my cousin."

"That's what you are calling it? Do you remember the one

thing Coach Perkins emphasized more than anything about the recovery process: DO NOT SEARCH," Roman raised his voice to drive home the point.

"Technically, Owen wasn't the one searching—I was," Sage said, a hint of arrogance in her voice.

"I'm sure he didn't mean the task of searching should be delegated to one of the spouse's minions," Roman countered.

"Minion? I'll have you know I'm a full-fledged hench-woman," Sage said, hoping to get a laugh and lighten the mood of their conversation.

"Sage, this is no joking matter. Don't you realize you are playing a serious game with other people's lives?" Roman was desperate to get her to see the danger in the game she was playing.

"I know how serious it is, that's why I'm stepping in to end it," Sage said, going from silly to serious. "The last time I stood by, Owen wound up married to a gold digger. This time I'm not going to let history repeat itself. Lia made her decision on who she wanted to be with and it wasn't Owen. I'm just trying to make sure she reaps what she has sown," Sage said, indignation in her voice.

"There they are, those retractable claws I have been waiting to see. You're not concerned about Owen's well being, you're concerned about your own welfare and the need of all the other 'Bryant women' to put Lia in her place and restore the balance of power. And it's all because Owen chose her without you all's approval," Roman summarized his case.

"Since you're trying to psychoanalyze my family, here's what I don't understand: Why the sudden interest in Lia's welfare? Maybe the Bryant women aren't the only ones with unresolved issues about her? Or, perhaps, you identify with her because the two of you come from the same background and have the same problems?"

Sage's tone was superior causing Roman to ponder the number of ways he could react. Whatever he said, he knew it had to come from Roman and not Trojan Man. He took an extra moment to filter through several incendiary things that crossed his mind. Yet, instead of seeing his pregnant pause as an opportunity to defuse the volatile situation, Sage continued her instigation.

"What's the matter, Roman? Did I hit too close to home? Too much authenticity for you to handle?"

The implication made the hair on the back of Roman's neck stand erect. He struggled to reign in his anger and replied through clenched teeth, "Considering my background? What's that supposed to mean? How bad do you want to have the fight you are trying to provoke me into right now?"

"Bring it on brother! Or should I say, Ramón? If you think you've got something to say, then say it, 'cause there's nothing soft about the Bryants," Sage said, further challenging Roman.

"Are you sure you want to go there with me? I'm telling you, just because the water appears calm on the surface doesn't mean the rip tide won't drag all those delusions about your family floating in your head out to sea. And you know me, I'll let you swallow a little water before I save you from drowning just to send the message. Don't test me!"

"Is that a threat or something?"

"No Sage, it's not a threat; think of it as a warning not to embarrass yourself. Because unlike your little comment about my name and my family, which I have heard before, all I have are a series of observations I've never shared. There's no hostility behind what I would say—it's just fact. So, you might want to chill on your comments about other people's families and backgrounds. Especially with the all the stuff going on when your family gets together. Check it, just because I don't talk about the parade of elephants in the room, along with all the costumes, clowns, jugglers, and all the cotton candy being consumed when you all get together, it doesn't mean I don't know a circus when I see one. You think I don't attend your family functions because I 'don't do family'? Naw, it's because I don't do carnivals, I got a thing about clowns!"

"If you got something to say about my family then speak on it," Sage said, confident that nothing Roman could say would have any substance to it.

He took no pleasure in what he was about to do, and took a deep breath to steel himself. "Just remember when you can't sleep tonight, you told me to 'speak on it.' To your first point, no, I do not have any unresolved feelings about Lia —lustful or otherwise. As for your same background remark, I'm not sure where you were going with that. If you were trying to infer there's some dysfunctional bond between Lia and I because we both grew up without fathers, you might want to check into the room adjacent to ours. Because news flash, Lia and I weren't the only ones who grew up fatherless—so did you. The only difference between my upbringing and yours is that my dad was dead and buried by the time I was eleven. Yours was dead long before you were born, you all just never picked a burial site and had a funeral. As much as you brag about his service to our country, your dad was missing in action when it came to you and your mom," Roman said dispassionately.

"What are you talking about?!" Sage screamed. "My father was always there for me. Even when he was deployed overseas, he made sure we were all right. Unlike your dad who was never there for you even when he was living!"

Roman countered Sage's contempt with a pedestal-demolishing arrogant calm: "Oh, don't get it twisted, my dad was there for us if we needed him. My dad made more money hustlin' in a month than your father earned in a year. My mom struggled because she chose to. My mom loved my dad the way your mom loves your dad. She just wasn't willing to marry a drug dealer. And even though he was a hustler, he was old-school Latino who believed in 'Cuidar de la famila.' He was always offering my mom money. It wasn't anything for my Dad to leave a couple of grand in an envelope, in our mailbox or to take me out for ice cream then fill my pockets with hundred dollar bills before he'd bring me home. How do you think my half-brother and sisters went to private school and graduated college without owing a penny? Here's your clue, it wasn't on the GI bill-"

"He still wasn't there for you. Not like my father was there for me," Sage interrupted.

"What are you talking about? Your dad wasn't there for you or your mom. He was just there—straight *Weekend at Bernie's* the sequel. Instead of leaving you and your mom, homeboy went into stealth mode. You talk about your dad like he chose to be with you and your mother. The truth is your dad never chose to stay with your mom, your mom decided to stay with him. She's the one who should have gotten all the ribbons and medals for putting up with dude. Your mom could move out the house right now and I doubt your dad would even know she'd left until he got hungry or one of the utilities got shut off. Otherwise, he'd be posted up in the front room, channel surfing or at his desk surfing the internet for hunting gear."

Caught off guard by Roman's willingness to declare that the emperor isn't wearing any clothes, Sage backed down. He had been emboldened by her accusations. Afraid of what he might say next, she tried to deescalate the situation as quickly as possible. Taking a play out Roman's playbook, she flipped it. "I am not asking you to understand why I have to do this, I am asking you to support me," Sage said.

"I do support you, but not in this," his tone solemn. "This just isn't right. It's the kind of mess that comes back to bite you in the rear."

"I don't see how. Our family has always stuck together."

"Sage, here is something that no one in your family has ever reconciled. But let me spell it out for you in metaphor. Lia beat you guys with backups, on your home field, in a blowout. She married Owen without lifting a finger to pursue him; it was Owen that did the chasing, the stalking, and the wooing. You guys underestimated how much of a host Owen was. What do you think she's going to do if she catches wind that you all are trying to accelerate the break-up of her marriage?"

"Knowing her she might try to get him back just out of spite," Sage answered.

"Let's say she does try to get him back. Then the whole thing escalates to a winner takes all death match, and as much as I respect how deep your family rolls, my money would be on Lia. And to the victor goes the spoils. That means she'd be running things. Take a guess who would have limited access to any children Owen had? Look, I am not trying to hate on the love your family has for one another, I'm just saying you might want to rethink your strategy. As connected as you all think Owen is to the Bryant clan, he has already chosen Lia over the family once. Take it from me, one of the worst things you can do is underestimate your opponent. Ask yourself this: Do you want a rematch with a motivated Lia?

"No, I do not," Sage said, pondering the apocalyptic aftermath of such a defeat. "Do you think he would cut us off for Lia after all she's done to him?"

"In a heartbeat. If Lia tells him she wants to get back together, it's a wrap, game over. Not only is he a good husband, but he would become a martyr too. I could even see a scenario where they move to Texas to start over. Imagine the size of a building he could build in Texas."

"No!" Sage cried out.

"He's a host...what can I say? Owen has three women in his life he cares about: his mom, you and Lia. Two of you can have anything he owns, but only one of you has his heart. If Lia and Casey are broken up, trust me, the only barrier keeping them apart is Lia's pride, not Owen's."

As hard as it was for Sage to hear, she knew Roman's assessment of the situation was on point.

CHAPTER THIRTY-THREE

Lia's Final Road Trip

At the same time, Sage and Owen were having their conversation, Lia was reaching out to her friend Tiffany via text: "Hey Girl, we need to talk. I think you put a spiritual hex on me...LOL. Call me when you get a chance. I need to run some stuff by you."

In a short amount of time Tiffany had become more than sorority sister/friend, she had become something Lia had always longed for, an older sibling she could share with and who would care and lookout for her. And the timing could not have been more perfect considering how many mixed emotions Lia was having about herself, her marriage, and her carrier. She was excited about some things and apprehensive about others.

Thirteen minutes later the phone rang.

"What's up girl? I got your message. What's going on?" Tiffany said in her usual cheerful manner.

"I'm not sure. What did you mean when you said God wants me to put away childish things, he wants me to graduate and start walking in the truth?" Lia asked.

"Girl, I was just sharing what God put on my heart to share with you. I was speaking from a place of burden, not insight," Tiffany explained.

"Can you help interpret some of this?"

"I'll try. Tell me how your week went."

Lia summarized the past week—the success of the trip, the peace she had, the drive back, the fight with Casey, her shopping excursion, and her encounter with Owen. The entire time she was talking, Tiffany had said nothing. There was a pregnant pause when Lia finished.

"Is that it?" Tiffany asked.

"Yes Ma'am."

"It's obvious. Can't you see it?"

"See what?"

"You hear, 'It's time to put away childish things,' then you break up with Casey. He was the childish thing—in more ways than one, I might add. It's time to graduate and start walking in the truth. You find out he's been trying to play you all this time. You try to buy your way out of your bad feelings, and what happens? You wind up taking everything back," Tiffany broke down the events like a color commentator during Bowl season.

In that moment, Lia realized that she had managed to pull off the entire week without Owen or Casey's help or encouragement. The thought rattled her confidence.

"What happens now that it's over, Tiff?"

"Girl, it's not over. This is just the beginning. God has His hand on your life, and He is not about to let it go."

"Then what is my next move? Do I try to put my marriage back together or what?"

"Ah girl," Tiffany said laughing, "this is not about who you're going to be with; this about who are you going to serve. God wants your full and undivided attention that's what this about."

"But doesn't it say somewhere in the Bible that God hates divorce?" Lia asked.

"Yes, it does. It's in the Book of Malachi. But don't get it twisted girl, the Bible also says God hates idolatry a whole lot more. And from the sound of it, that describes the flow of your typical relationships with men."

"Idolatry? You just lost me. I've never placed any man in my life ahead of God. I know it's been a minute since I was in Sunday school, but I haven't forgotten the first commandment. Give a girl some credit."

"All right then, do you want me to call the roll on just the stuff you've told me happened in the past week? Plus, who knows what I would find out if I called your girls Shanna and Kim," Tiffany rebutted.

"Okay, you win," Lia said. "But what do I do next?"

"Listen, this is not about what you need to do next, it's about what God is doing now. You need to stay out of God's way and let Him do what He does best which is run things. He hasn't required your help to get to this point, and I don't think he's going to need your help to do the rest.

"In the meantime, it wouldn't hurt to start praying for guidance. You also need to apologize to Owen's cousin and her husband. Oh, and while you're at it, it wouldn't hurt for you to step foot in somebody's church since God blessed you with peace this week."

There was something in Tiffany's mother tone that caused Lia's eyes to sting.

"I'll start praying and I'll try to reach out to Sage and Roman to apologize, but the church thing...I think I'll hold out for that joy you said would come with the peace."

"That's up to you. Just remember when the Lord does provide you with the peace and joy I said he wants to give you, you might want to follow through...the Bible also has a lot to say about people who test Him."

"Thanks for walking with a sister through this stuff."

"That's what big sisters do. We have each other's back."

#

As her phone screen went black, Lia said aloud to herself, "There's no time like the present." She knew if she didn't call Sage right away she never would. After taking a drawn-out breath, she pressed the phone icon and said the two words she thought she'd never say: "Call Sage." The screen came alive once again. "There's no turning back now," Lia said under her breath.

Sage stared at her phone in shock to see Lia's number come up on Caller ID. Just as it was about to go to voicemail, she answered. In a few awkward moments, Lia told Sage that she needed to talk to her—preferably in person. The two of them arranged to meet at the RB in an hour.

Heading up the 405 freeway in bumper-to-bumper traffic Sage's mind was racing about a hundred miles an hour. What could she want that required a face-to-face meeting? All kinds of scenarios ran through her head. Did she want to fight? Had Lia found out that she had spoken to Denise? Was she going to blame her and Roman for their separation? Sage spent the entire drive prepping potential responses for every possible topic she could imagine: from stay out of my marriage to I need your help. Sage prepared herself for every possible contingency going all the way back to college.

When she wasn't trying to figure out what Lia might want to talk about, she was debating with herself about whom she should call.

"Calling Roman is out. The last thing I want to do is listen to another lecture. If I call Owen he's likely to call Lia and go off, then I'll never find out what's going on." she thought.

Needing to talk to someone, Sage called the safest person she knew, Mrs. Hilliard. Her wise neighbor advised her to stop stressing about it and to keep an open mind. "Don't go into the situation looking for trouble," she had stressed.

"That makes a whole lot of sense. The best way to prepare for anything is to keep an open mind," Sage thought.

Unfortunately, In Sage's world open-mindedness was not seen as Mrs. Hilliard intended it. Instead, it took on a strategic connotation.

"If Lia wants to go toe-to-toe, I'm ready. If Lia wants to take it there, I'm prepared to do that too."

Sage scanned the parking lot as she drove up. When she didn't see the Lexus or the Prius she was relieved. She figured that she could take up a position at the front where she could watch Lia get out of the car and study her mood as she made her way to the coffee shop.

After ordering black iced tea—straight, no lemon, no sugar, no sweetener, just cold and dark like her attitude—she turned to scan the room for a good sniper position. The place she could do recon on Lia as she exited her car. But it was too late. Lia had already taken up a spot in the back. Being waved over made Sage feel ambushed. How could she forget that Owen told her about the rental? He'd even sent her a picture of it.

"So much for the element of surprise," she mumbled beneath her breath.

Given that all the fakeness had drained out of their relationship months ago, they dispensed with the small talk, and after thanking Sage for meeting with her, Lia got right down to business. She told Sage that she wanted to apologize to her in person for what happened at their house a few weeks back. She went on to say how genuinely sorry she was for putting both Sage and Roman in such a potentially dangerous situation. She apologized for all the negative things she'd said to and about Roman citing that it was uncalled for, especially since all he was trying to do was separate Owen and Casey. Lia concluded by saying that no matter what was going on between her and Owen, Sage and Roman did not deserve to be caught up in her drama.

Sage swallowed hard unable to speak.

"Wow, I wasn't expecting this. I accept your apology," said Sage, finding her voice again.

Lia thanked her warmly.

"Well that's all I wanted...to apologize to you in person before I headed out of town tomorrow. I didn't want another week to pass without saying I was sorry..." Lia said, choking up. "So thanks again for meeting with me."

Stunned, Sage whispered, "No biggie."

Not knowing the proper etiquette for saying goodbye to a frenemy, Lia stood and extended her hand. "Take care of yourself."

Sage managed a sincere, "Thanks, you too. Have a safe trip."

And just like that, the war between them had reached a state of détente. Sage spent the next 40 minutes sipping her black tea trying to figure out what had just happened. In all the years that she had known Lia, she had never apologized for anything. Even if this were some trick, the Lia she knew would never humble herself to such a level, she had way too much pride for that. Sage could only surmise that if it wasn't part of some game that she was running there was only one other option...Lia meant it. Lia being honest was such a frightening proposition to Sage that she didn't want to consider it even as a possibility. Instead, she sat there for another 40 minutes pondering what Lia had up her sleeve.

As distasteful as the notion of Lia being sorry might have been to Sage, it was clear that she was changing. She had entered the third phase of recovery—"mercy." This method allows one to account for the weaknesses and imperfections of their spouse. Forgiveness doesn't give them a pass, and it doesn't retest them in areas where they've failed previously. Forgiveness is to stop asking people to be what they've already shown they cannot be.

Lia had come to terms with the real Casey. She now accepted the reality he was not interested in a relationship with her that did not benefit him. Lia could no longer be mad at him for not being the man she wanted him to be. Once Lia could accept the real Casey, she let go of the fantasy the two of them were going to be together. At that point, she could own her role in what happened between Lia and Casey.

As Lia began to take ownership of her role in she and Casey's relationship, she officially began the transition to the mercy phase. Although many of the same factors that govern the forgiveness phase also govern the mercy phase, their focus is different. The forgiveness phase concentrates on the character and behavior of the cheating spouse while the mercy phase focuses on the nature and behavior of the offended spouse. That's because to extend mercy to another person we must be willing and able to manage provocation in such a manner it leaves room for the other person to grow. Mercy touches on a spouse's capacity to show restraint in the face of provocation, compassion in the face of coldness, and patience in the face of frustration just to name a few. To do this requires real not pretend strength. It demands that we come to terms with our authentic self, the good, the bad, and the ugly all must be considered. In mercy, we stop pretending how loving and kind we are, instead we opt to be just as hurt, angry and as sick and as tired as we are. No more walking on egg shells, here is where the rubber meets the road, and it starts with being honest with ourselves about what we can handle and what we can't handle.

For Lia and Casey's on and off again relationship the mercy phase started 18 years after they first met. It occurred the moment Lia dropped her pursuit of the fairytale ending. Took off her glass slippers and put on her work boots and started wading through the crap the two of them had been trying to sell each other. One of the things Lia did that's crucial to the mercy phase is she stopped attempting to avoid the good fight. She started having the fights she needed to have – the ones that address the heart at the reality level of what was bothering her. The growing anger and resentment, the disappointment, the frustration, and the disillusionment that came from being in a miserable marriage.

The mercy phase is also a time of grief where we let go of the delusion of control and prevention about what we can't fix, manage, and sustain for our spouses. Coming out of delusion requires three things, in no particular order. One, we must take off the masks that hides us. Two, we must put down the armor that shields us. Three, we must give up the behaviors that numb us. If we accomplish these things, we can stop pretending, stop defending, and stop avoiding.

#

When Lia returned home later that afternoon Owen was sitting in the same spot he'd occupied when she left. As she walked by the kitchen with bags in tow, she wondered if he'd been sitting there the entire time she was gone. Owen looked up and said "Hey" in a flat tone. Responding out of some primitive reflex Lia said, "Hey" back to Owen.

With the hostility and disappointment she'd felt toward Owen drained out of her, and the specter of Casey dispatched from their lives, it was the first time Lia ever engaged Owen without the ghost of Casey present. Call it discernment or imagination, but Lia could sense a spirit of heaviness hovering over Owen that produced a profound sense of conviction about how she'd handled him, particularly the night he found out about her affair.

She set her bags down in the hallway and walked over to sit at the dining table across from him. She stared at him until he looked up from the paper strewn about the table. When Owen looked up, he cast his eyes back down at once. But Lia continued to stare until the discomfort of her stare was greater than the pain of holding eye contact. Owen forced himself to look up. Lia looked him square in the eyes.

"I'm sorry Owen, I'm sorry."

"Sorry for what?"

"For everything. The whole sordid mess that has become our marriage."

Owen's mouth was open, but no sound came from it. In all the years they had been together Lia had never told him she was sorry for anything. "Only sorry people say they are sorry," she'd once said famously. Realizing that she had rendered him speechless, she stood up from the table and said, "I felt the need to tell you that."

Still reeling from the shock of Lia's apology, Owen made his way down the hallway to their bedroom where he discovered Lia packing. He stood silently watching her as she meticulously folded items and placed them in her Louis Vuitton suitcase.

"Real talk. Did you mean that or are you messing with me?" he said.

Lia did not look up from her task, but said, "Yes, I meant it or I would not have said it."

"What does that mean? Are you trying to get back with me because Casey dumped you?"

Lia chuckled at her husband's cluelessness about her motives. In the back of her mind, she knew that Owen had talked to someone. She continued to pack.

"No, Owen it doesn't mean anything other than I recognize my contribution to the current state of our marriage."

"What exactly are you taking responsibility for?" he asked.

"My role."

"Yeah, I get that. But could you be a little more specific? I'd like to know what you are accepting responsibility for," he said, still fishing.

"Exactly what is it that you're looking for? Is there something specific you want me to own or address?"

"No, I'm just trying to figure out how serious you are about accepting the blame for breaking up our marriage?"

Annoyed Lia said, "I did not say I was taking blame for breaking up our marriage. I said, I was accepting responsibility for the things I've done to contribute to the downfall of our marriage, things which led me to make a choice to have an affair rather than confront some of the more fraudulent aspects of our relationship. That's what I'm apologizing for."

Not satisfied with her explanation, Owen, pressed the issue: "How can you apologize for the stuff you've done to me when you can't, or won't, say what they are?"

Shaking her head in disbelief, Lia exclaimed, "I don't need a list of offenses to know I hurt you and that I need to apologize. If you are expecting me to give you an itemized list of sins and omissions I have committed against you, I'm not. And even if I did, I'm sure I would leave something out. If, on the other hand, you're asking me how much of the blame do I accept for ruining our marriage? I'd say there's enough blame to go around to try the two of us as co-conspirators in the demise of our marriage. Owen, the cheating in our marriage didn't start with my affair. The fraud goes all the way back to our dating and engagement."

"What are you talking about? It was all good between us until you hooked back up with Casey."

Shocked that Owen was unwilling, or unable, to take in what she was saying, Lia employed another tactic. "Is that what you sincerely believe?" she said calmly.

"Yeah, we were doing just fine until Casey resurfaced in our lives."

"Owen, no wife is ever content with a marriage that is 'just cool.' Let me put it in terms you may understand," she chose her words carefully. "Wives are like Wall Street investors. There are two things they want to see in their marriage: a relationship that doesn't just meet expectations but exceeds them, and year-to-year growth. The same two ingredients that define a healthy company, one that people want to invest in, is the same thing that defines a healthy marriage. The fact that you think we were doing well is one of the problems. We've had issues since we first started hanging out. The reality is you don't listen well when people say things you do not want to hear or you think isn't valid—especially when you and Sage get together to co-sign each other's denial."

"What's that supposed to mean?"

"Exactly what I said! I can't break it down any better than that. I will, however, say this: No one steps out of an intimate relationship they find fulfilling to cheat. There is always a reason—even if the spouse thinks it is irrational or immoral and doesn't want to hear it."

Owen raised his voice in indignation. "That makes no sense whatsoever."

"I know. Yet it does..." Lia said. She returned to packing her bag.

"So explain to me what's so bad about being married to me that you had to cheat?" Owen pushed the issue.

Dumbfounded and angered by the question Lia said, "Owen I don't have the time nor the energy to explain it. I have to finish prepping for my trip. But we can certainly pick this back up when I get back, if you can sustain your focus on us long enough to still care when I return," Lia added sarcastically.

Feeling rejected, Owen turned and headed back down the hall. As Lia continued to pack she was hit by several waves of guilt about the way she had just handled Owen. Usually, she wouldn't set boundaries on his behavior with such a straight-forward approach. Even though it was long overdue, it felt like an act of betrayal on her part. For the rest of the night she struggled with the temptation to unravel the boundaries she had set.

#

The next morning, Lia woke up bright and early. By seven o'clock, she'd worked out for 45 minutes, packed up her cosmetics bag, gassed up the rental, and was ready to roll. Her plan was to let the traffic die down and leave around 10:30. In the meantime, she was making phone calls and responding to emails. Seated at Owen's desk, she noticed several CDs that were labeled "Third Annual Worship Conference." Thinking the CDs contained worship music, she grabbed them and placed them in her purse to listen to on the drive to Carlsbad.

After finishing up her last call she went looking for Owen to tell him she was ready to leave. She had not realized that he had already left for work. Slightly annoyed that he did not let her know he was leaving, she headed for the car. Not wanting her irritation turn to anger, she sent a text to ask why he didn't tell her he was leaving. His reply, "Thought you were too busy to be interrupted, so I just left. Have a safe trip," made it clear he was exacting punishment for her "I don't have time and energy" comment the previous night.

"And that's why I didn't want to go into it last night. Because by the time we were through, you were going to be an unap-preciated martyr," Lia said to herself as she put her cell phone in the center console and headed for the freeway. Instead of letting Owen's message slide as she had done in the past, Lia decided to address him directly. When he answered she dove right in asking if what she said the night prior had offended him, and if so, was his text an attempt to address his offense through sarcasm? Even though he denied being offended or sarcastic, Lia still treated it as a potential problem.

"I know we've not addressed our issues in the past, but in the future if I say something you perceive is offensive I would appreciate it if you dealt with it on the spot rather than harbor it and possibly have it spill out in a text."

Thrown off by the matter-of-fact tone of her directness, Owen could only manage, "Okay."

"That's all I had to say. I didn't want there to be any mess simmering between us for the next seven days while I'm gone."

Owen again: "Okay."

"I left my itinerary on your desk in your office. I am staying at the Four Seasons in Carlsbad."

While Lia knew the direct approach was the best way to deal with his indirectness, Owen, on the other hand had been unnerved by her call. He had no clue what the sudden change in Lia's behavior meant. Like Sage, he did not know what to think. Was Lia running some game or were the changes in her for real? His mind racing, Owen did what he always did when he struggled with questions about relationships—he called Sage.

CHAPTER THIRTY-FOUR

Owen And Sage The Main Event

"Hey O.B., what's up?" Sage said, detecting his stress. Owen had called Sage in a state of absolute panic. The conversation he and Lia had left him shaken.

"I need to run something by you."

"If it's about you and Lia, I don't think I am the best person to help you process what's going on."

"What are you talking about?!" He had not anticipated Sage being reluctant to help. Her reply threw him even further into despair.

This was new territory for their relationship. Sage knew she'd have to choose her words wisely. "For a couple of reasons. For starters, you and I are way too close for me to be objective about your wife. Not only that, I'm as confused by her current behavior as you are."

"Why would you say that?"

"Yesterday your wife and I met at the Rare Bean and had a conversation that I'm still trying to process."

"The two of you met yesterday and you didn't call me?" Owen was incredulous. "Whose idea was it to meet? What did you guys talk about? What kind of mood was she in? How could you keep this from me?"

"Slow your roll, slow your roll. She called me to set up a meeting so she could apologize to me in person for what went down the night Roman body slammed Casey. I didn't call you because as a couple of people have pointed out to me, I need to chill where you and Lia are concerned. So, I'm stepping back to give the two of you some space to work through your stuff without me TMZing your situation."

"You're just going leave a brother hanging?"

"No. That's not what I'm saying. I just think it's better for all parties concerned that I take a backseat right through here so the two of you can find your way."

"It sounds like you're bailing on a brotha to me?"

"Owen, don't do this."

"Do what?"

"Play the victim in this after all the years I've had your back. When it comes to your marriage, I just think it's something you and Lia are going to have to work out between the two of you without my interference."

"Did Roman put you up to this? Because this doesn't even sound like you, this seems like some of Roman's handiwork. I knew he didn't want you to help me. He said so out of his mouth. He just pretended to help me so he could drive a wedge between us. And you fell for it."

"If Roman said that I'm sure he didn't mean it in the way you're taking it. In fact, Roman has been more cooperative and supportive of you while you're going through than he was of me while I was going through.

And if you think about it, Roman and I are the ones who've had your back throughout this ordeal more than anyone in or out of our family. And I'm hurt that you would think we're turning on you."

"What else am I supposed to think when out of the blue you tell me you don't want to be bothered?"

"Owen, I hate it when you go to this dark place and start acting like this," Sage warned. Too many times she'd seen the aftermath of his dark moods.

"Like what? Like what? A punk?" Owen challenged.

"I was going to say a victim," replied Sage, now more saddened than angry. "But the way you're acting now, punk works too. I'm going to get off the phone so I don't say something that I'm not going to be able to take back."

"That's right kick me to the curb now that I need you! That's okay. The next time Roman hooks with some tramp, don't sweat it. I'll still be there for you."

Hot tears spilled down her cheeks. Sage tried to tell herself that Owen didn't mean what he was saying. But the high road was out of reach and she fired back, "Owen, I think you need to talk to somebody about your misplaced anger. Call me when you climb down off your high horse and realize what an A-hole you've been."

The last sound Owen heard was the click of the call being disconnected.

#

Enraged by Owen's abrupt callousness, Sage pulled out her laptop and started typing. In less than 10 minutes she had written two resignation letters addressed to the Board of Directors of Owen's Foundation and his enterprise. Before attaching them to emails addressed to other members of the board, she called Roman with a Code Red situation. "Code Red situation" was a failsafe measure the two of them came up with in the event that either one of them was about to send a text, tweet, post, email, direct voicemail or Instagram out of anger that they may regret later. The agreement was that before hitting send they would call the other and share what they're about to disseminate.

Roman was sitting on the 5 Freeway headed to Bakersfield when the letters "CR" popped up on his phone. He hopped off the road and pulled into fast-food parking lot. Sage picked up on the first ring.

Roman, thinking it was job-related, spoke first, "No, you can't quit your job. We got too many bills to pay."

"I wish it was the job," the increased bass in her voice instantly alerted him that a deeper problem was stirring.

"What's going on? I can tell you've been crying."

"Owen and I just had a big fight. I'm about to resign from

the board of his company and his foundation, and I wanted to read it to you before I sent it."

"Hold up, Babe. What happened?"

Sage recited the whole incident complete with voice over imitations of Owen, which is something the refined Sage only did when she was highly upset or deeply hurt, and she was both.

When Sage was done, Roman said," Wow! He went there? He must be in some pain."

"In pain? I just thought he was acting like a selfish butt-hole."

"Yeah, in pain. You know your cousin is just two steps to the right of the autism spectrum when it comes to feeling his feelings," Roman reminded Sage that Owen never put any of the quarantine processes into effect, except in checking his finances. "He hasn't grasped the concept that the best way to communicate when you've been hurt is to share your pain rather than to act out of it. Think about it, Sage. As much sharing as we have done with him he has not taken much of it to heart. Despite that 'good guy got it together' attitude your cousin tries to show everyone, he's a lot more damaged than he looks. Did you forget what happened the last time Lia left for a trip and he had to stay with us? Okay, she's gone? I got four words for you: A...BAN...DON...MENT. Then, you tell him he's on his own and 'Bam' dude's in survival mode."

"I didn't say I didn't want to be bothered with him."

"I'm not talking about what you said; I'm talking about what he heard."

Sage released a heavy sigh. "Oh wow. I see. He hasn't pro-cessed much of anything we shared, so technically he's still in the pre-discovery phase."

"You got it. Trust me you're going to get a phone call before I get home tonight."

"What makes you think he's going to call?"

"If you think he's lonely now, wait until tonight girl," Roman sang, doing his best Bobby Womack impression, "Just wait until those skeletons come out the closet and chase him all around the room!"

Sage sniffled and said, "You mean Jodeci. They're the ones who made that song, and then 50 Cent sampled it and messed it up."

"Baby, please don't repeat that in front of any black folks over forty. In fact, just don't repeat it." Roman chuckled.

"What do you mean? I know what I'm talking about, and Jodeci is the one that recorded that song."

"Baby, trusts me. Do not repeat that to anyone in the office. When you get off the phone, go to Google or YouTube and look up Bobby Womack "If You Think You're Lonely Now," then just text me your apology. I'll read it later. In the meantime, I have to get back on the road. Are you okay?"

"Yes, but what do I do with my resignation letter?"

"Like the Jodeci comment, keep it to yourself. Don't hit send."

"I won't. I'm officially calling off the Code Red. It's a 'No' until further notice.'"

"Good. See you tonight. Love you. Bye."

"Love you too. Be careful. Bye."

Twenty minutes later Roman received a message from Sage: "You were right about the song. How embarrassing! I asked one of the managers who listens to 98.9 old school jams. Just got schooled on R&B by a 35-year old Latino man from East L.A. and his 27-year old Caucasian female assistant from South Dakota, no less. How's that for diversity? Sorry I doubted you. Yes, this is me apologizing."

"You should have used Google. I told you not to mention it to anyone." The heart emojis on his response made Sage smile.

Later that evening, Roman received another text from Sage: "Right again" was all it read. He knew Owen had reached out. Ten minutes later, Sage reached out again: "He wants to talk. What should I hit him back?"

With the speed of a court reporter Roman responded: "About an hour away from home. We can talk when I get there. Text Owen. Tell him you can't talk. You'll get back to him in a couple of hours."

CHAPTER THIRTY-FIVE

Roman Prepares Sage
for Owen Rematch

After Roman got home and settled in, he and Sage set about developing a game plan for the conversation they agreed needed happen with Owen. Roman remembered the notes he took on having an awkward conversation and shared them with Sage to help lay the foundation for their conversation.

"The goal is to produce as authentic a process as possible," Roman began. "To set the stage for that, you need to take as much ownership for what is going on between the two of you as possible. You also need to bring as much clarity as possible."

They agreed that accepting ownership for her role in the process meant Sage had to take responsibility for the weak boundaries and lack of authenticity and accountability on her end. She unwittingly had bred an atmosphere where Owen felt his outburst was justified. It also meant that would have to accept the amount of resistance that Owen may throw at her for changing the rules of their engagement.

"Since you've always been a willing participant in all this drama with Owen, he's probably not going to receive the new boundaries well. More than likely you'll have to demonstrate that things have changed between the two of you. Are you ready for that?"

"I think so," Sage said, not sure if she had the capacity to engage in behavior her mind knew was necessary, but her heart told her was abandonment and betrayal of an unwritten family code.

The next part of the process Roman and Sage spent time on was identifying the feeling the two of them felt about Owen's behavior. A critical component of the process is to not only identify the feelings, but to feel and own them as well.

For a solid hour Roman listened to Sage recount how Owen denied and deflected any responsibility or blame. He grew frustrated as he realized how unwilling Owen had been to put in the work. Roman lost some of the respect he'd gained for who he believed was a brother who handled his business.

But more troublesome was the way Owen had turned on Sage. "A real brother doesn't hate on someone who's had their back the way you've had his. Man! Dude, just flipped the script the moment he didn't get his way. That's not cool," Roman felt the protector in him rise to the surface on Sage's behalf.

"Yeah, even from a women's perceptive that's a...you know what kind of a move," Sage added.

The two strongest feelings Sage identified were disillusionment and anger. "I guess what I am struggling with the most is how I always saw Owen as a loving guy—too nice to turn on anybody—let alone me. Then for him to turn on you, especially after you had gone out of your way to befriend him and walk with him through this, that tells me that he's been sitting on that anger for a while. The fact that he put his pain and pride ahead of my feelings and our marriage, when he knows what we have been through to try to salvage our marriage, Babe... I'm not sure if Owen and I ever had an authentic relationship."

"Yeah," Roman exhaled. While he was inwardly thrilled that Sage was finally seeing the light concerning the weakness of the relationship with her cousin, it pained him to see the hurt of that revelation in her eyes.

"You know the thing that hurt most was his willingness to weaponize the information we shared with him in confidence. He shared with me what you and he talked about on a confidential basis, without any context. And saying you were going to cheat again like he knew something, knowing it would tap into a fear that I have only shared with you and him takes this thing to a whole 'nother level. What Owen did was worse than what that skank Shelia did."

"Yeah, don't think it hadn't crossed my mind," Roman agreed.

Roman and Sage were now tasked with determining how they were going to frame their discussion with Owen. They wanted to support Owen without further enabling him.

"So, we agree Owen needs to talk to someone outside of our circle of family and friends," Roman said.

"Yes, I am convinced he needs to see a counselor, or I am going to hit send on that resignation letter. There is no way I am going through this again. It's just not safe to be around him if he is not going to deal with his issues."

"I think we also need to stop indulging him and go the tough love route. We can't indulge his bashing of Lia, Casey, or his victim narrative anymore. No more rehearsing what Casey or Lia has done to him. No more rehearsal dinners where he talks about how he has been betrayed, abandoned, and what he is going to do about it but never does. From here on out, our conversations with Owen need to focus on his feelings, choices, and behavior. No more scapegoating, excuses or negations for not addressing his issues."

"I agree we need to call him on his stuff on the spot," Sage chimed in. "He's always talking about 'keeping it real,' well, it's time to take keeping it real to a whole 'nother level."

"Yep, it's time to do 'for real', 'for real' with him. Okay so, how do we communicate this to him?" Roman admitted that he was uncomfortable with the thought of Sage talking to Owen on her own. And because Owens accusations were directed at them as a couple, they agreed that she would keep her one-on-one communication with him superficial until such time that they three of them could get together.

Once Sage and Roman finished laying the groundwork for the pending conversation with Owen, it started to feel more like preparation for an intervention. Even though Owen was in a lot of emotional pain, Roman felt like his behavior needed to be checked. The conversation needed to take on an asser- tive tone. Roman reasoned that letting him get away with the kind of behavior he'd been exhibiting was akin to allowing a child have a tantrum simply because you understand their frustration about not getting their way. But it does not help the child nor does it assist the parent, it only prolongs the inevitable. Roman knew from experience that holding Owen accountable for his behavior, even though he's going through, affirms rather than undermines his personal dignity. He wanted to send a clear message that he and Sage expect him to act like a grown man—even though he's hurting.

"Yeah, homie needs to learn how to play with pain," Roman said to himself.

All that was left to do was arrange a time and place to talk. And since Owen had been blowing Sage's phone up with text messages for over an hour, they would be the easy part. It also led them to another conclusion— they would stop reacting to Owen when he was in panic mode. Nothing that transpired in Owen's marriage to Lia was a legitimate crisis. Indulging Owen in this way was only reinforcing the anxiety provoking patterns from his childhood when his mother would need emergency hospitalization and it was off to Sage's house.

Making the switch from a static view of his marital problems—a series of crises to be managed—to an episodic view of his marriage as a lasting state of unresolved issues to be addressed was going to be a real challenge for Owen. Getting him to take a big picture approach to his marriage was all that was keeping him from walking in peace versus walking a state of anxiety.

#

After he received Sage's text saying she and Roman could meet the following evening anywhere he wanted, so long as it was after 7:30 p.m., Owen put on the full court press. He shot off messages one right after:

>"Why can't we do it tonight?"
>"Why does he need to be present?"

>"I just needed to talk to you."

>"What do the two of you want to talk about?"

>"How about I come to your job for breakfast, then the three of us can meet in the evening."

Frustrated, Sage sent the final text of the evening: "I'm cutting off my phone and going to bed. I will see you tomorrow night. Goodnight O.B. Please try to get some rest."

#

The next morning Sage told Roman about Owen's obsessive desire to meet with her last night, and her struggle with telling him 'no.' Roman gave her an encouraging squeeze around the waist.

"You and Owen have co-signed each other's issues for so long, it's going take a lot of energy and focus on your part to establish healthy boundaries. And because of your history, it is going to feel like betrayal, like you are letting him down for a season. You're going to have to endure Owen's disappointment and subsequent acting out until he adjusts to the new boundaries," he encouraged.

"I know. I know…it's just…"

"Hey, no buts," Roman grabbed her hand and looked into her eyes "The success or failure of this process hinges on two things: You consistently reinforcing the new boundaries, so we're not sending mixed messages, and Owen's ability to manage his reaction and adjust his expectations to the new boundaries. If either one of these things does not happen, then the process will go one of two ways: Everything will go back to the way they were, or irreparable damage will be done to your relationship. If you are going to do this, you need to be all in or it won't work," trying to steel his wife's resolve.

"Sage, these changes need to be made out of love not out of hurt or anger. Setting new boundaries is for the good of everyone involved, no matter how things turn out. Although I can't do anything to make you feel better right now, I can assure you we will all get through this just fine. If I can address the issues I have, Owen can too," Roman reassured her.

As Sage listened to Roman talk her focus shifted off the grief caused by her relationship with Owen to her gratitude for the state of her relationship with her husband. Listening to him say things she'd always wanted him to say, but never dreamed he'd would, softening her heart even more toward Roman. A lot of the fear, pain, doubt, anger, and disappointment she felt was fading. She could feel the grip on her heart loosening. It had been a long time coming. Her relationship with Roman had gone through two distinct phases and was heading into a third. In phase one, she realized she walked in delusion. In phase two, illusion turned into disappointment when she was forced to deal with the reality of the man she married. And now, the disappointment she had walked in for most their marriage was turning into hopefulness.

Abruptly Sage jumped from her seat, took the three steps necessary to make her way to Roman's side of the table, and bent over and kissed him on his bald head. She caressed him under his chin and gently tilted his head up until they made eye contact.

Sage, staring deep into his eyes said, "Thank you."

Before Roman could get "For what?" out of his mouth, Sage took him by the hand and led him to their bedroom. It had been so long since Sage had been the initiator, the day before their third anniversary to be precise, Roman didn't figure out what was going on until she turned around and gave him the same smile she gave him when he first asked her for her number and wrote it on his forearm so he wouldn't lose it. Her mannerism was more than a sign Sage was: "in the mood," it was a sign she had a new mindset. Sage felt more than amorous, she felt safe. For the first time in their marriage, she viewed Roman as her partner and not her adversary. Her defenses were down, along with her inhibitions.

Having spent the morning in "Special Fellowship" with her phone powered down, she forgot to text Owen a time and a place for them to meet. It didn't matter the moment she synced her phone to the Bluetooth in her car the dashboard lit up like Times Square. Owen had been trying to reach her since 6 a.m., while her assistant had been trying to get her since 9 a.m. Owen wanted to schedule a time and a place to meet, her assistant wanted to remind her of a 1 p.m. appointment, and to tell her that Owen was looking for her. Sage called her assistant first to say she was on her way in, then called Owen to confirm that she and Roman could meet any time after 7:30 p.m. They decided the best place for them to meet would be The Center where they could order take-out.

Owen tried to get a head start on the conversation. Again, he pressed Sage to divulge what she and Roman wanted to discuss. But by this point it was evident that Sage wasn't talking.

"Have to go. See you tonight," Sage said quickly to get off the phone. *"Boy, have things changed,"* she thought, *"Just a few weeks ago, it was Owen rushing me off the phone."*

By the time Sage and Roman pulled into The Center, the parking lot looked like a ghost town. The only car in the lot was the LS. Passing by the freshly waxed car Roman quipped, "I guess your boy has changed his mind about the whole 'All I need is something to get me from point A to point B' thing."

"Yeah," Sage sighed." He told me the car would sit in the garage until the end of the lease."

Still laughing Roman said, "Looks like the only garage this car has sat in is the one at Seals Detailing Shop. I don't think it was this clean when Lia drove it. One thing for sure, no brother pays two hundred and eighty-five dollars to have a car detailed just to park it in the garage."

"Two hundred and eighty-five dollars?" Sage shook her head. "Oh my goodness! Now that right there? That's next level. Poor baby must be struggling for real if he's spending that kind of money to wash a car."

"As Coach would say, he's not struggling, he's leaking issues."

CHAPTER THIRTY-SIX

Sage and Owen Showdown

Walking through the double doors of The Center, Sage and Roman spotted Owen as he appeared through the door that led to the administrative offices. Sage greeted Owen with a cordial embrace while Roman welcomed him with a full hug. The small group made small talk about traffic and the weather as they made their way back to one of the conference rooms.

"I ordered Chinese, if you don't mind," Owen said.

"Let me guess? Shin Shin," Sage said.

After the 45 minutes it took to eat, Owen escorted them to his office so they could talk.

Roman got the conversation started by acknowledging the issues and concerns expressed by Owen during his conversation with Sage. He explained that since some of the comments were directed at him, he and Sage thought it best that he be present to address Owen's concerns. Sage added that both she and Roman wanted to make sure that Owen felt heard.

She also added that one of the things she hoped would come out of their meeting was a clear set of boundaries and expectations around their level of engagement with Owen regarding the status of his marriage. Having said that, Sage yielded the floor to Owen.

Owen sat for a moment. He was not quite prepared for the directness of Sage and Roman or their openness to hear him out. He started off trying to minimize the significance of the conversation he had with Sage by calling it a misunderstanding, blaming the whole incident on the stress he was feeling. He assured them that there was no problem, that everything was fine, and he only needed to get some rest and to put it all behind him. But toward the end of his explanation added that Lia was also to blame for his response.

Sage and Roman looked at each other in astonishment at Owen's explanation of what happened between him and Sage.

"That's it? That's your take on what went down," Roman asked?

"So let me see if I got this straight. Everything you said in our conversation was a misunderstanding brought about by the stress Lia has put you under," Sage summarized.

"Yeah, yeah, that's pretty much it. I was tired, you were tired, I said some stuff, then you said some things. It got blown out of proportion. No harm, no foul. We're family here. We squash it and that's it," Owen answered with a hand wiping gesture.

Sage tried hard to keep her cool. "Owen, it wasn't a misunderstanding. It was a conversation that escalated to the point where you felt the need to question my loyalty, attack my husband, and further predict he would have another affair. I got so mad I had to hang up on you before I said some things from which neither of us would recover. I don't call that a misunderstanding, I call that a fight. The fact that you're trying to minimize what happened—particularly the things you said to me—is unacceptable. Not only do you put it off on your wife who's been out of town on business for a week and running errands all day, but you also didn't even apologize!"

"I apologize if you were offended by my comments," said Owen, his sarcasm thinly veiled, "but I'm trying to deal with the fact that my life has been turned upside down by my wife! Forgive me if I was looking for a little understanding from my best friend who I helped walk through her crisis!"

Sage stood up, grabbed her purse, and headed for the door. But before she could turn the knob, Roman had caught up to her. He placed his hand on her shoulder and asked her to reconsider leaving.

"Babe, we need to address all this so we can move on," Roman said gently. "I know you're hurt, but we need to hash this out." Roman returned to his seat on the couch. Patting the empty seat next to him he gently said, "Please come back and sit down."

With tears in her eyes, Sage turned and sat back down next to Roman. Her husband placed his massive hand over her two hands clasped in her lap. He then leaned in and kissed her on the cheek. "Thank you." His voice was a safe harbor that comforted Sage. She settled her head on Roman's shoulder.

Channeling his anger in the same focused way he did when he played football, Roman turned his attention to Owen.

"For seven years, I have done enough stuff to the woman sitting next to me to die and be resurrected ten times," he began, "and she'd still be justified to ask for a divorce. But there are three reasons why we are together today. The first is Coach Perkins. He didn't just show me how to be a husband, he helped me realize I could be a good man. The second reason we're still married is because of the depth of undeserved love this woman carries in her heart for me. I know her love for me is real. Lord knows I have tested it. The third reason we are still married is because of you. Had you not been there providing her with a listening ear and all the support she needed while I was out running the streets, I know my marriage would be over. So, I want to say thanks for being there for her. But more than that, thanks for being there for me. From my heart bro, I sincerely mean that. I will always appreciate the fact that you were there for my wife when I wasn't.

"That being said, now that I have stepped my game up she doesn't need you like that anymore. And just because the circumstances have changed, it does not mean her love for you has changed. The only reason you and Sage could have the relationship you had was that neither of you were in marriages healthy enough to demand the focus necessary to be intimate. Now that Sage and I have changed the dynamics of our relationship, the dynamics of the friendship you two share must change as well. It's not fair, but it's the truth.

"Think of this as a chance for you to put yourself in a position to have a healthy marriage, whether it's with Lia or someone else. The reality is no healthy spouse is going to let you and Sage hang out at the level that Lia and I did. That season is over.

"Once I decided to fulfill my role as husband, lover, and friend, I committed myself to spending the rest of my life making up for all the pain I caused Sage by doing two things: Making sure I never knowingly do anything to hurt her. And that I do everything in my power to make sure no one else will hurt her. Owen, you intentionally hurt my wife not once, but twice in the last two days. If you value your relationship with her, you need to grasp what's at stake and fix it. Otherwise, it's 'Thanks for being there homie, and we're out.' That, as you say, is, 'real talk.' Oh, and on another note, you owe Sage a sincere apology for the vulgar and hurtful things you said to her. Not cool, man. Not cool at all!"

\#

What Roman managed to do that no one else had been able to do was penetrate through his layers of denial and defensiveness with straight talk that Owen had no ability to finesse. Owen tried to take in what Roman was saying, but unfortunately, he could not. Owen lived in a black and white world of right and wrong, credit or blame. Within his heart there was no room for even a hint of a gray area. He was either the hero that helped saved their marriage or the guy who hurt Sage. In his mind there was no way he could be both. And there he sat, emotionally locked out of his own heart, unable to reconcile if he was a good or a bad person. He did not know which to take more seriously: Roman's expression of appreciation or his warning.

Not sure how to interpret Owen's silence Sage asked him if he understood what Roman was saying.

"Yeah, yeah, I get it. Things have changed," Owen said, though still confounded.

Sage, not convinced that he understood, asked, "But do you know how they changed and why?"

"Yeah, yeah, it's cool. I get it," Owen said, trying unsuccessfully to mask his confusion.

"Just so there is no misunderstanding moving forward, could you tell me what you think we're saying?" Sage asked.

For the next 15 minutes, Owen rambled on like an athlete at a press conference trying to rationalize a loss—"It is what it is"..."It's a learning experience"..."Take it one day at a time"..."It'll make me stronger"...etc.

Roman, having heard enough shut him down. "Dude, dude! Just stop. Enough with the clichés! What are you feeling right now?"

"I'm good. I'm good. I'm straight," Owen's voice cracked.

"For real, Owen you're not okay," said Sage with both compassion and firmness. "We think you need to see someone... someone other than a friend or a family member."

"You mean like a professional? Oh, hell no!" Owen said, thinking of his mother's depression. "I'm hurt, but I'm not that hurt! I just need a little time to adjust so that I can put this behind me."

"Put it behind you? Owen, do you still love Lia?" Roman asked.

"Of course, I love her, she's my wife."

"I didn't ask about your duty as a husband. I asked if you still love Lia—in your heart, not in your head. What do feel about her in your heart?" Roman probed.

"I'm not sure what you're asking," Owen's eyes had glazed over.

"Let's put it this way. Do you as a man want to lose Lia? Can you answer that question without addressing the roles and duty of a husband or a wife in the abstract?"

Owen slumped down further in his chair. His face took on a reflective look, and finally, in a soft voice he replied, "No.... no.... I do not want to lose Lia. Yes, I love her."

"Then stop pretending like her leaving is something you're

just going to get over when she's gone. That's not how grief works. You can't grieve something you keep pretending isn't a loss," Roman sensed that they were on the precipice of an emotional breakthrough.

"It's just that I don't do the feelings thing well, so it's easier for me to deal with it in my head," Owen offered.

"We know. And that's why we think you need to see someone who sees through your stuff and can call you on it without you taking it personally."

Owen turned to Sage. His eyes pleading with her to help him, "Is this what you think I need?"

More than anything she wanted to be the one to relieve his pain, but knew in her heart that this was best. She mustered all her courage to say, "In the last couple of days, you have lashed out at me in ways I never thought was in you. If that's an indication of how much pain you are in then yes, you need to see someone. Because if you don't get help, I'm going to need to step down from the board of your corporation and your foundation. One Sergeant Major in my life is enough."

Realizing how serious Sage was, Owen agreed to get help. However, Sage, knowing his propensity to put things off that he did not want to do, issued an edict. She and Roman had agreed to give him three weeks to find someone or she would move forward with her resignation.

"I hear you, I hear you, consider it done..." his voice trailed off with feigned confidence.

Having settled the issues between them, they spent the rest of their time discussing Owen's feelings for Lia.

"If Lia said she wanted to work on your marriage would you take her back? Not out of duty, but out of love?" Roman asked.

That's when Owen gave the most emphatic, direct answer he'd given all night: "Yes." Roman followed that question with another: "If that's the way you feel, does she know it?" Right there is where the conversation ended for the night.

Owen left that meeting a man on a mission. He decided

that if his marriage was going to fail, it wasn't going to be because he watched it go down in flames. Owen wanted his wife back, and he was willing to do anything, and he meant anything, to get her back. Whatever he needed to do, say, or buy he was prepared to do. On the way home, he decided there was no time like the present. With his mind made up, he decided to drive to Carlsbad first thing in the morning to tell her. "*Yep, that's what I am going to do,*" he thought.

CHAPTER THIRTY-SEVEN

Let's Talk

Sage was still groggy when her phone rang early the next morning. Owen had rose with the trash haulers and the people delivering newspapers, and now was on the road headed for Carlsbad to inform Lia that all is forgiven. He called Sage to let her know how much she and Roman had inspired him to put his relationship back together.

"This better be worth it O.B." She fluffed pillows behind her back in order to sit up.

"Oh it is! I wanted to say how much I appreciate you and Roman walking with me through all this stuff. I know I can be quite a handful to deal with sometimes. But, I just wanted to thank the both of you." Owen said, sounding refreshed and strong.

"You're welcome. But couldn't this have waited about an hour or so?"

"No. Guess where I'm headed?"

"Guess who doesn't feel like playing the guessing game this morning?"

"Yeah, yeah, I feel you. I'm headed to Carlsbad to reunite with my wife."

Sage shot straight up in the bed. "I'm awake now. When did all this take place?"

"Well, last night got me to thinking. I hadn't told Lia how I felt about her. I was just going to let things happen and deal with it. But after talking with you and Roman, I decided I was going to fight for my marriage."

"What makes you sure the two of you are getting back together? Have the two of you talked?"

"No, that's why I am headed down there now to speak with her."

"You're headed down there without a phone call or text?"

"Yes, it's going to be a surprise."

"O.B., do you remember what happened the last time you surprised your wife? You were the one who got surprised. Not only that, she is on a business trip. Her time for the next two days belongs to her client. Had you thought about waiting until she gets home or at least giving her a call first?"

"I thought about it, but I can't wait. I'm too excited. And what could be more important than us getting back together?"

"I get that, but have you thought about if she could wait or not? Maybe she'd prefer if you'd hold on. You know Lia is not big on surprises. Remember the surprise birthday party you tried to throw? She shut that thing down the moment she found out. Owen, do you have any idea how hard it is for a women entrepreneur to be taken seriously? What's it going to look like to her client when you show up and hijack Lia's focus?

"Yeah, I hadn't thought about that. I'll call Lia and let her know I want to talk when she's done with her assignment."

#

As soon as Sage hung up the phone, Roman came into the bedroom with a shaker full of green goo. "When did you start drinking my stuff?" Sage asked.

"The last time I got on the scale," he said. "Daddy's been slipping."

"You look fine to me."

"Fine is not sufficient. I've got to look like I've been chiseled from marble when I'm wooing these recruits' parents. Ooh, that didn't come out right," Roman said, realizing it wasn't the wisest thing to say considering his past.

"It's okay," Sage smiled at the thought of her husband's physique. "I understood what you meant."

"I'm so sorry.. I did not mean for it to come out like that."

"For real, it's okay. I like you being free to say what's on your mind. It's a sign of progress. And growth is sexy."

"Thanks, so was that Jr. on the phone?"

"Jr.?" she immediately pictured Coach Perkins' son. "Why would Jr. Perkins be calling at this hour."

"No. Our son, Jr....Owen."

"You know you are wrong. But yes that was him," Sage said laughing. "He wanted to thank us for encouraging him to fight for his marriage and to inform me that he was headed to Carlsbad to put his marriage back together."

Roman sat down on the edge of the bed and offered her a sip of his green goo.

"So out of all the stuff we talked about, that was his big take away? Well good for him. At least he's not going down without a fight. Even if they don't get back together he won't have to live with the regrets that go with playing the victim in your home. Yeah, they'll be back together before the weekend is out."

Shocked by Roman's bold prediction, Sage said, "I have two back rubs that say they won't."

"You're on," Roman countered. "Oh, and you might want to pick up some of that massage oil from your job, we're out. You're going to need it."

"You sure you're not going to need it?"

"Positive. Who's the one that said he still loved Lia? And who is also the one that asked him if Lia knew it? Trust me— before the weekend is out."

"What makes you think she'll want him back?"

"Because she never decided to be with Casey and she loves Owen."

"How's that? She was about to leave him for Casey."

"That had been a possibility ever since we were in college, and yet it never happened, which tells me she loves him despite how different they are. Think about it. Every time she's had the chance to choose Casey she chose Owen. Even the night they fought, she did not tell Casey to come with her when she left. She just left him there to potentially be jumped on by Owen and me. If she loved Casey she would have never left him alone in the house after being body slammed."

"Ooh, you are right. Dang it," Sage said, realizing she might be performing a few back rubs in the near future.

"Yeah, don't forget the oil—the spearmint not that lavender stuff," Roman said with a huge smile on his face. "Oh, and I'm going to want that with a happy ending."

"You do know how much I hate you right now," Sage smiled and waved a balled-up fist at Roman.

"Babe, your heart can be as hard as you want it, just make sure those hands stay soft for that back rub," Roman said as he pantomimed rubbing himself.

#

Owen dialed Lia's number and got no answer. His mind began to race. *Why hadn't she pick up? Was she back with Casey?* he wondered. Trying to stay optimistic he pulled into a gas-mart parking lot to text her. The message read "Can we talk?" followed by a white flag emoji.

#

An hour later, at the Four Seasons in Carlsbad, Lia was just waking up. Everything had gone great on the first leg of her trip. Everyone, including her client's hard to please mother, was ecstatic at how well the openings were going.

One more event and it would be a wrap. Lia was experiencing a level of professional success and fulfillment beyond her wildest dreams. Not only were the events a big success, but she had also already picked up several potential clients from the Carlsbad event to add to the others she garnered from the San Francisco and Malibu events. "This Texas girl is on a roll,"

Lia said to herself. That was until she glanced at her phone and saw that Owen had called.

Reading Owen's text flooded her with a whole host of emotions. *What does he want? Is it positive, is it negative? Has something happened?* There was just no way to know. So many mixed emotions: anxiety, fear, dread, excitement, anticipation, and hope. *What did the white flag mean? What was he surrendered to?* Despite the hours Lia was putting in on this trip, she spent lots of time thinking about her marriage. Her thoughts had been inspired by the CDs she brought from home thinking they contained gospel music when, in fact, they were recordings of Coach Perkins delivering a message on recovery. Instead of listening to music on her 3 ½ hour drive to San Diego, she immersed herself in Coach Perkins' outline of the entire recovery process: Limbo, Discovery, Forgiveness, Mercy, and Renegotiation. What she heard intrigued her in a way that left her feeling both affirmed and convicted.

Lia easily identified that she and Owen were in a parasitic relationship with him as the host and she the parasite. Although she struggled with the term "parasite," it helped that Coach Perkins kept repeating that "it's just a survival strategy and not a judgment." She was also able to see how the plan she chose fit the way she was raised. Being bounced house-to-house at an early age, Lia's survival was dependent on her ability to get people to take care of her. It was this strategy that helped her to survive childhood, and it was the same strategy that now undermined her adulthood.

Another concept that she connected with was the emptiness that the parasite feels. Because nothing was ever stable in her life, she had never taken the time to decide who she was, what she was about or what she wanted. This inability to make solid decisions played out in her vacillation between Owen and Casey. One by one, the dots between her emptiness and some of the behaviors connected. She engaged activities like shopping in an attempt to fill the voids in her life. Instead of connecting with people, she connected to stuff. What she called a passion for fashion, truly wasn't a passion. On the contrary, it was pathological—a numbing behavior that was more self-medication than a hobby.

The more she listened to the coach's message, the more she was able to make honest observations about her relationship with Owen, and even more critical observations about the relationship with Casey. The information she got from Tiffany, and Casey's own actions, were enough to expose his true agenda. Coming to terms with Casey's humanity and her limitations, she now understood why their relationship was no more than a liaison that never would have developed into a healthy romance. This new perspective allowed her to turn the page and have real closure on the Casey saga.

Having gone through the process with Casey already, Lia believed it accelerated the process with Owen. It appeared that she and Owen were in a different phase of the process. She found herself vacillating between mercy and forgiveness, while Owen was still struggling with the discovery phase. She found the idea amusing considering how fond he was of telling her, "That's not how the real world works," whenever they got into a debate over something.

As far as she could tell, the reason Owen still struggled with the discovery phase wasn't tied to anything she heard on the CD. Lia based her opinion on an discussion she and several others who'd married into the family had during the first family reunion she attended. Somehow all of them wound up in a hotel lobby together in Chicago, discussing how much of the Bryant Kool-Aid each of them had drunk to fit in. It was said that as close as the Bryant family appears to be, they don't put a lot effort into dealing with the truth; especially when it came to Owen. As the only boy born in his generation, "the chosen one," his cousin Beth called him, Owen was coddled by all his Aunts. And largely ignored by the only male in the previous generation, Sages Father, who thought he was too soft but never said it. Throughout his entire childhood no-one had ever told Owen the truth in love.

That reunion had such a profound impact on Lia, she remembers it like it was yesterday. On that day, all of them made a pact to keep each other grounded in the truth, no matter what. That's the moment she decided she wasn't going to become a "Bryant woman," which is the main reasons she decided she wanted no parts of membership in "four generations of deep purple." Since then all her compatriots that stood with her on that day have fallen. One by one they became little more than arm accessories. Robert, the last soldier to stand with her, fell a year ago when he could no longer take it and divorced his wife. Even so he had drank enough of the Bryant Kool-Aid for it to have a lasting effect on him. Robert still shows up to all the Bryant events on the arm of his ex as though they are still together. Ever faithful to the Bryant code of conduct, no one dares to question the status of the relationship. It simply goes on under the guise of "It's to protect the kids,"— the youngest of whom is a sophomore in college.

Being part of the Bryant clan had a definite influence on all the men who married into the family—except Roman. Early in their courtship Roman made it clear he would not be attending any of the Bryant family's numerous "little events." Drinking the Bryant Kool-Aid wasn't an issue for Roman because he was neither entranced nor intimidated by Bryant mystique (or as he put it mythology.) He didn't care what they thought. At the first, and last, family reunion he attended, he declared to anyone who would listen that it was too much of a chick scene for a brotha in full possession of his manhood to be bothered, and for this he was granted a lifetime waiver releasing him from all Bryant family events, official and nonofficial.

Piecing clues together from the scattered comments made by the older Bryant women, Lia deduced that they did not want Roman riling up the other men with all his seditious talk about sports, man caves, hobbies, and hanging out with the fellas and such. As much as Lia hated to admit it, Roman was the only legitimate hold out and he had not even taken the oath. From Day One he let it be known: Sage was becoming a "Cole." He was not becoming a Bryant.

#

With all this floating in her head, Lia wasn't sure if she should call Owen right away or wait until after her final event in the O.C.. Not knowing what to do she called Tiffany to get her take on what to do.

"Girl, how have you been?" Tiffany answered in usual cheerful manner. "I've been thinking about you for the last few days. What's up with you?"

"I'm not sure. I am down here in Carlsbad finishing up an event for a client and getting ready to head up to the O.C. for a final opening. But I got this text from Owen at 6:10 this morning saying he wants to talk. I wasn't sure if I should call him back or wait till I'm done, so I decided to run it by you first since you obviously have a direct line to the man upstairs," Lia said, only half-kidding.

"You have one, too. It's called prayer."

"I know, but he seems to favor talking to you more than he does me."

"That's not true and you know it. The thing is, God doesn't listen to the prayers of the righteous more intently than others. In fact, the only difference between the prayers of the righteous and others is the righteous wait for God to give them an answer to their prayers. Just call Owen to see what he wants. What do you have to lose?"

"You don't think I should wait? What if it is bad news?" Tiffany encouraged.

"What if it isn't?"

"But what if it is?"

"Girl, I am not going to play this game with you. It's time for you to woman up and deal with this thing. All this double-mindedness on your end has got to stop. If you want to save your marriage, then own it. If you don't think it's worth saving then own that. God has not given you a spirit of fear, so stop walking in all this "what if" fear and start walking in the truth of what you want. And stop settling for what you're left with."

"Okay, so we are just calling a sistah out this morning?"

"It may be early in the morning, but it's late in the game. I wouldn't be doing it if I did not think you and my God could handle it. Stop trying to get answers to questions you won't ask, and ones that only your husband can answer. Call your man, girlfriend. Right now! I'm hanging up. Call me after you talk to him. You know my flesh wants to know what he says. Love you. Believe in you. Bye."

"That's it," Lia thought. She'd called to get comfort and advice, and all she got was the Dr. Phil treatment. Standing on the balcony staring out the window phone in hand she realized Tiffany was right. The best way to deal with this was to confront it directly.

#

"Siri, call Owen on the cell."

The phone rang for what felt like an hour to Lia before Owen picked up.

"Hey."

"Hey, I was just returning your text. You said you wanted to talk." said Lia, bracing herself for his response.

Owen stumbled for a moment to get out what he wished to say. "See, uh, I wanted to tell you that...If uh, you wanted to save our marriage...that's something I would not be opposed to."

Not sure what he meant Lia asked, "Are you saying you wouldn't be opposed to trying to put our marriage back together? Or, are you saying you want to try and put our marriage back together?"

"I'm saying I don't want to lose my marriage, and I would like to save it, but only if you want to keep it too," Owen felt the need to hedge his bet in case Lia did not want to work on their relationship.

Understanding how Owen's mind works, Lia asked, "Is it the marriage you want to save or is it me you don't want to lose? Which is it?"

"What I am saying is, I, uh…I love you and I, uh, don't want to lose you. Okay, there I said it. I still love you," he repeated, relieved he'd managed to overcome the fear of rejection he thought might follow such an open profession of his love.

Wanting to be realistic about the prospects of putting their marriage back together, but feeling a tug on her reawakened heart, Lia quietly said, "I love you too. But are you sure you want to go through what it's going to take to put our marriage back together?"

"I'm sure," Owen said emphatically now that the dam of fear and anxiety holding back his emotions had fallen and Lia had reciprocated.

Assuming they'd follow the guidelines laid out by Coach Perkins on the CDs, Lia said, "Okay, then let's talk about when I get home tomorrow."

"Great I'll see you then."

#

Lia immediately called Tiffany back. While she was excited about this turn events, Tiffany voiced two concerns. The first was now that Lia had begun the worthy pursuit of living from an authentic place, would the painful realness of addressing the truth cause her to buckle and choose her lifestyle over her life? She advised Lia to keep her eyes on God. The other concern was whether Lia was willing to be patient with Owen as he tried to break the gravitational pull of his upbringing that caused him to shut down emotionally. *Could Lia deal with Owen's denial and moodiness?* Tiffany wondered. It was something she was going to add to her list of petitions to bring before the Lord when she prayed for Lia.

\#

That evening, an excited Owen called Lia back and said he would like to meet her in Orange County for breakfast the next morning. Since it was the end of the tour, he suggested they drop off her rental car at John Wayne Airport and drive home together. Lia thought it was an excellent idea because it would give them the entire day to talk.

CHAPTER THIRTY-EIGHT

Owen and Lia Meet

Throughout the breakfast at a Café they found in Newport Coast, Lia waited for Owen to open the dialogue about how they were going to move forward. Despite being a little anxious, she was hopeful they would be able to hash things out. When it didn't seem like he was going to bring it up she attempted to broach the subject to no avail. Every time she brought up a concern of substance, Owen would just say how much he loved her, how great it was they could put this stuff behind them, and how things were going to be different.

Although Owen's apparent reluctance to talk about anything deep concerned Lia, she didn't press him. They had the whole day ahead of them. After dropping off the rental car Owen sprang a big surprise on Lia. He had booked a hotel room. More than just a room, Owen had gone all out and booked a romantic weekend getaway at the Ritz-Carlton Laguna Niguel in one of their 1,600 square foot luxury suites with a breathtaking view of the ocean. Their accommodations included Five-star service equivalent to personal valet service, preferred access to all the hotel amenities, and elegant dining at its finest. And to top it off, Lia was to be pampered with the rosemary reflexology treatment she developed an addiction to when they stayed there for their second wedding anniversary.

What neither Lia nor Sage knew was Owen had hatched a plan to kill two birds with one stone. Since he promised Sage he would seek counsel (even though he did not think he had any issues) he thought why not set up a meeting with Coach

Perkins for both him and Lia when they returned home. That way Lia, who he believed was the one with the issues, could get the help she needed. The goal was to talk Lia into agreeing to see the coach with him. Understanding what was at stake, Owen knew he would have to be at the top of his Lia game when he presented the idea to her. He had only one shot to get her on board. Once Lia soured on something there was no redeeming it. He decided to bring up the topic at lunch after she'd had her reflexology treatment.

Owen's plan included pitching the idea in a style that played to Lia's grandiose sense of self-importance and entitlement. He spun it as though talking to Coach was like getting a reservation at Rao's Italian restaurant in Harlem New York—you must know somebody who knows somebody. He indicated securing an appointment with him was a special privilege only granted to the most deserving of people. While it was true that you needed to know someone to meet with Coach, it had nothing to do with exclusivity or elitism. Walking with people was not a ministry or a business that Coach Perkins set out to build. It had grown organically.

If you followed the breadcrumbs from Roman backward, you would see a recommendation from Roman's longtime friend, Coach Dole, a middle school football coach who was the first to turn him on to Coach Perkins' son as a possible recruit. It was Coach Dole who encouraged Roman to call the coach when Sage found out he was cheating. It was a story of happenstance and random chance that had repeated itself for the past 14 years.

To sweeten his pitch, Owen told Lia that Coach had even helped a few celebrities with their marriages. Upon hearing that, Lia insisted that Owen do whatever it would take to set up a meeting with Coach Perkins immediately. Her urgency was not because she was star struck as Owen assumed, she was desperate to fix her life and her marriage. To add to the hype, he told her he wasn't sure if he could pull it off and that he would try to secure a meeting with Coach Perkins through either Sage or Roman. Again, Lia repeated, "Do what you've got to do to make it happen." At that point, Owen knew Lia wasn't just hooked, she had swallowed the bait whole. The meeting was now a date with destiny for the both of them. Feeling slightly smug by the success of his ploy, what Owen didn't know that it wasn't his elaborate scheme that sold Lia on the idea, it was CDs she'd found on his desk.

#

It took three weeks after returning from their romantic weekend for Owen to set up a meeting with Coach Perkins who been away on a mini vacation with his two daughters. During that time, Owen and Lia settled into a groove and things seem to be back to normal. One week before their meeting, Owen thought things were going so well that there was no need to have the meeting. He didn't see the point in rocking the boat when the situation seemed to have rectified itself. He thought it foolish to dig up stuff from the past when it was clear to him that he and Lia had moved on.

But the two of them had not moved on.

After listening to the rest of the CDs that Sage had given Owen, Lia decided she'd wait until they met with Coach to share some of the things stirring in her soul. At the same time Owen was so busy trying to manage every single issue that might escalate that he hadn't noticed how the usually demanding and needy Lia had become more subdued and reflective than she had ever been. She was no longer angry or passive aggressive as she had been in the past. But she was not satisfied either.

Owen and Lia had simply reached a stalemate in their relationship. With Lia biding her time until they met with Coach Perkins, and Owen's natural reluctance to deal with any real issues no real progress had been made.

So convinced that things were going well, Owen sent a text to Sage and Roman to thank them for all their help, and to let them know he and Lia would not need to meet with Coach after all. He informed them that they had worked things out and did not want to waste Coach's time. Upon receiving the group text, Roman and Sage immediately called each other to see if the other knew what was going on. They quickly determined that two things were clear—Nothing had changed, and it was best for Roman to reach out to Owen to see why he was tripping. It wasn't because they felt Sage would be too soft on him. On the contrary, they both felt it was time for him to hear the man-up message, which sounds better coming from a man who is manning up.

Also, if Owen and Lia did not meet with Coach, Sage would follow through on her threat to resign from the board of Owen's corporation and his foundation. The ball was in his court.

#

When Sage and Roman got off the phone, he instantly called Owen.

"What's up Roman?" Owen answered in an unusually positive mood.

Roman said, "What's up with you? Sage and I just got your text saying you wanted to cancel with Coach Perkins."

"Yes," Owen said. "We just don't see the need for it; It's all good. We don't want to waste his time when he could be helping a couple who needs it."

Stunned by the sheer audacity of Owen's denial, Roman, who was usually quick on his feet found himself at a loss for words. Before he could respond, Owen made another comment that made the hair on Roman's back stand up.

"No offense, but our issues just aren't as deep as yours and Sage," Owen said in a flat tone that underscored the utter cluelessness he was walking in.

"None taken and none sent back your way. But your issues are deeper than mine and Sage's by miles."

A little irritated himself Owen said, "How do you figure that? Lia only had an affair with one guy for a little bit of time because she was feeling neglected. Fast forward to present. I am giving her the attention she needs—problem solved. Not to put your situation on blast, but you had multiple affairs, over multiple years. That doesn't even compare to my situation."

Roman countered Owen's assessment of their marriage in classic Roman style. He absorbed it without getting angry, and then hit Owen with a devastating counter punch.

"You're right, Owen. I have had multiple affairs for nearly the entirety of my marriage. But out of all the women I'd been with, I can honestly say I never thought enough about any of them to ever once considered leaving Sage. Remember, I got caught because I ended the affairs to be with Sage. Like it or not, Lia's relationship with Casey ended because he broke it off when he found out she wasn't going to get half of that 'Robert Dinero' you are sitting on.

"The way I see it, the biggest problem in my marriage was that I was in sin. The main problem with your marriage is your wife never got over the man she was in love with when she met you—a man who, by the way, she was willing to leave you for not too long ago. Add to it the denial you're in, and yeah, I would say your situation is more complicated than ours."

Driving the knife in deeper, Roman continued, "Man, if I were you I'd be wondering if my wife wanted me back or if she just didn't want to be alone? Especially since she cheated on you at a time you thought your marriage was strong. Hey, that just me. I'm sure the two of you have talked all this out and got it squared away."

This time it was Owen's turn to be rendered dumbstruck a mixture of shock and repressed anger.

Done indulging Owen in his denial Roman said, "Here's the bottom line for Sage and me, Owen. All we want is what's best for you. In this case, we firmly believe it's, at least, one meeting with Coach Perkins. As we stated before we feel so strongly about it that if you choose not to do it, Sage is going to have to resign from both boards. Again, that's not a threat or an ultimatum, it's an expression of our conviction. And for the record, personally, I'm not as concerned about how you and Lia are getting along. My priority is Sage and the way you handled my wife."

"I know you guys want what's best for me. I'm just not sure if it makes sense to rock the boat when everything is going so smooth."

"Trust me," Roman said, "We are aware you do not want to risk losing Lia by rocking the boat, but that doesn't mean you should ignore the hole in the boat."

"I don't know how she's going to process spending time with somebody who's so confrontational," Owen conceded.

"Take it from me, you might want to start worrying about yourself. Coach Perkins is an equal opportunity confronter. Your wife is a grown woman; she'll be fine."

CHAPTER THIRTY-NINE

Owen and Lia Meet With Coach Perkins

Owen, Lia and Coach Perkins decided they would meet at Coach Perkins' favorite restaurant, a little out-of-the-way seafood restaurant in Long Beach. There they could secure a table giving them the privacy they needed. Upon their arrival a waiter who bore a striking resemblance to actor-co-median Will Farrell, who starred in the movie Anchorman, greeted them. "Hello, you must be Lia and Owen," the man said with a smile and a voice so reminiscent of the actor they wondered if they'd stumbled into an episode of *Punked*. The two of them nodded in the affirmative. Farrell's doppelganger then motioned for the two of them to follow him. He escorted them past several tables and through double doors that led into an area used for private parties.

There they discovered Coach Perkins seated two tables from the back of the room. He didn't notice them at first as he was busy alternating between writing on a yellow notepad and scrolling through his tablet. Lia and Owen approached the table. Coach grabbed his tablet and his phone off the table and put them both on airplane mode and placed them in his briefcase, then stood and greeted them with a hug and his standard whispered commentary: "It's good to connect with you, finally."

After taking their seats, Owen said, "Before we get started I have to ask—Is it just me or does our waiter look like the actor who was in *Talladega Nights* and *Anchorman*?

Coach smiled and answered, "It's not just you. Everybody I meet here asks the same question. Bill is a celebrity impersonator on the side. And yes, Bill is short for William," Coach chuckled.

For the first 10 minutes Coach engaged them in typical small talk to give Owen and Lia time to catch their breath. Then, it was time to get down to business. Coach opened the dialogue in the same way he always did, "So tell me your story."

Unaware of the changes brewing inside of Lia, Owen was taken back when Lia spoke up, "I'll go first." She then pulled out her Coach 3x5 designer cardholder that up until today was more of a business accessory than a tool. Lia arranged cards marked "Discovery Phase," "Forgiveness Phase," "Mercy Phase," and "Renegotiation" on the table in four stacks. In her hand, she held two more cards marked "Questions" and "Concerns." When she was done arranging the cards, she looked up at Coach.

"Again, I want to thank you for meeting with Owen and I... We need some help."

Coach Perkins nodded and mouthed "You're welcome."

Lia went on. "I've been listening to the CDs from the conference you spoke at last year," Lia continued. "I've brought the notes I took with me to help me stay on track. I hope you don't mind if I refer to them while I'm talking?"

But before Coach Perkins could answer, Owen jumped in. "Honey, I don't think Coach Perkins wants to spend his time listening to us read from cue cards."

Coach Perkins sensed the need to check the controlling spirit oozing from Owen. "Are you speaking on Lia's behalf, answering for me, or were you expressing your personal sentiments, Owen?"

Owen paused for a minute. "I guess I was doing all three. I am sorry," he admitted

"Not a problem," Coach said, "But let's say going forward we will let everyone answer and speak for themselves."

Recognizing Coach could confront Owen's passive aggressive behavior, Lia began to share. "After listening to your

CDs, I realized Owen and I have a parasitic marriage. At first, I thought we were closer to a partnership with predatorial tendencies. Then, I listened to the part where you talked about the four profiles of the cheater. When you read the list of characteristics that defined a parasitic relationship, I was amazed. It felt like you were talking directly to me. Everything you said fit—the abusive background, the chaotic environment—all of it," Lia suddenly felt the kind of relief that comes when someone gets you.

Lia's voice began to crack as she added, "This is all I have ever known." She paused once more to grab five tissues in rapid succession from the box on the table to catch the tears that had started to flow. "For as far back as I can remember I waited for my knight in shining armor to come along, only to be disappointed."

Owen interrupted, "How have I disappointed you? Haven't I always been there for you? Even after everything we've been through? I'm the one who's here!"

Before Lia could answer, Coach said, "Just let her get it out, there will be time for questions later. I want to hear each of your stories unedited and unfiltered, exactly as you've experienced it. Go on, Lia. You were saying?"

"I guess that's it," Lia said, wiping more tears from her eyes as she shrank back into her seat.

"You sure?" Coach Perkins said, trying to draw Lia back out. She collected herself and sat up in her chair and said, "I am certain. That's it."

It was too late. Lia had just checked out. Owen's demand that she justify her feelings sent her into retreat. She knew there was no way he would let her statement stand until she acknowledged her transgression. With all that had happened in the past few months, she just didn't have the energy or the words to endure another one of Owen's crusades to restore his good name.

In hopes of salvaging the lunch, Coach turned to Owen and asked him to share his story. Intent on defending himself from what he believed was Lia's unfounded accusation, he was eager to share.

"Well Coach Perkins, it has been like this ever since my wife and I got together. All I have tried to do is be the best husband I could be. She doesn't want for anything. If I thought she needed or wanted something, and it was within my power, I got it or made it happen. I have been supportive of everything she wanted to do. When she wished to start her business, I hooked her up with some of my business contacts. When she wanted to get in shape, I built a gym off from our bedroom so all she had to do was climb out of bed and hit it. I also bought her a hybrid Lexus when her clients started to complain about her big SUV. I've even helped her family out. I got one of her brothers a job and paid for the other's rehab—that he did not stay in for the full thirty days. And that doesn't even count the number of so-called loans, letters of recommendation and other stuff I have done. Then to top it off, she cheats on me and says I have disappointed her. I'm the one who should be disappointed. All I have asked her to do is be a good wife."

Owen managed to say all of this with no discernible change in his affect or voice. In reality there was no way to measure his frustration, which meant there was no way for Lia, Coach or anyone else to address his feelings at a level that would match his frustration. Owen's blunted affect surrounding his anger and frustration was one of the reasons why Lia and others in his life were so dismissive regarding his concerns. Owen was so concerned about being a "nice guy," he buried his anger and frustration to protect his image.

Coach asked Owen if there was anything else he wanted to share.

"No I just wanted to make it clear I have done my best to be the best husband I can," Owen replied.

"I accept that. But what made you think I questioned it?"

"Well you didn't, but Lia did."

"No, I didn't," Lia said, her voice low and words measured.

"Yes, you did! I heard you with my ears."

"Owen, you heard what you always hear. You heard what the voices in your head tell you, what you always want to hear." Lia crossed her arms and legs and turned her head away from Owen ever so slightly.

Having heard enough, Coach Perkins interrupted their little exchange before it had a chance to escalate.

"Lia, Owen, is this how the two of you communicate most of the time?"

"Yep," said Owen.

"Pretty much," Lia added.

"Okay, I have identified at least two of the issues you are going to have to deal with at some point if the two of you are going to put your marriage back together. Right now, let's get back on topic. Owen, I asked you why you thought I might have questioned your dedication to Lia. You answered by saying you did it because Lia questioned it. But you still haven't responded to the question I asked."

"What do you mean?" Owen asked.

"I asked if there was something you observed, or heard about me, that would cause you to think that I assume you are a bad husband? Here's what I am trying to figure out: Were you responding to me, to Lia, or to something going on with you? If you were responding to me, then you and I would have some issues to resolve. If you were responding to Lia, then you and she have some things to work out. But, if, as I suspect, you were responding to something going on with you, then that is a matter you'll need to deal with on your own. The way you addressed it left it unclear as to who it is you need to address your questions about how good a husband you are.

"If you're concerned about my assessment of whether you are a good man or not, let me put your mind at ease. I am not here to judge either one of you. It gets in the way of authenticity, and it doesn't change behavior. I don't do blame, I do responsibility."

"Got it," Owen said, "Sorry."

"We're alright, Owen. No need to apologize. We're just

getting to know one another," Coach answered, "So relax, you are doing fine."

Feeling vindicated Lia said, "See what I have to deal with Coach Perkins?"

"Yes. And I also see some of what he's dealing with too," Coach Perkins answered, dousing another potential flare up.

"Sorry, Coach Perkins that slipped."

"I know enough about combat to know snipers don't waste rounds. Nothing slips."

"Sorry, sorry. You're right, Coach Perkins."

"I am not the one you took the shot at, Lia. Owen is the one who deserves the apology."

"I'm sorry, Owen."

"Good. Now with that out of the way, let's see if the two of you can tell me the story of Owen and Lia without issuing press releases. How did you meet?"

"I'll go," Owen said. "We met our sophomore year of college in a Psychology 101 class. One day we were watching a video on some subject I can't remember, I looked across the room, and I could see Lia was having a hard time watching the video. At first I thought she was just sleepy because she kept putting her head down. But then she leaned back in her chair and covered her eyes with her hands, you know, the way people do when they're watching a horror movie? A few minutes later she bolted. I waited to see if the teacher was going to check on her, and when no one stepped up I went after her. When I caught up with her in the courtyard, she was sitting on one of the benches crying. I asked her what was going on and if she was ok.

"She said she was fine, just having a rough day. I knew there was more to it than what she was letting on. I sat there to comfort her. After class I took her to lunch, lunch turned into time spent in the library. The next day I called her to see how she was doing. We talked some more, hung out some more. After that we started 'kicking it.' By the end of the semester, I knew she was the one. That summer we began dating.

We broke up after college when I got a job on Wall Street. We'd talk off and on after that. A year later, I showed up at her condo with flowers and a ring. Two months later we were married, and the rest, as they say, is history."

Coach Perkins smiled when Owen finished, nodded and said, "Thanks for sharing that with me." He then turned to Lia and said, "Now Lia, let's hear your version of the Owen and Lia Genesis story?" At first, Lia was caught off guard, especially after Owen had shared his version. The most she'd ever contributed to the telling of their story revolved around her filling in some of the bits and pieces Owen might have left out.

"Wow, I just realized I've never told anybody my version of how we met. I need a second to get my thoughts together." She closed her eyes momentarily and shook her head as if she was shaking loose the memories.

"Here's my version of how we met," Lia began. "It's as Owen said. We had this class together, Psych 101. The week before I walked out in the middle of class, we had to read a chapter on grieving and loss. As fate would have it, that Friday was the fourth anniversary of the death of my three closest friends who were killed by a drunk driver in a car accident. The whole weekend I was out of it, you know, depressed, crying, the whole nine. When Monday rolled around, I dragged myself to class because I had already missed too many classes dealing with all the other drama I was going through with my boyfriend, and my mom was always calling me with her stuff. When the teacher said that we were going to watch a film, I thought I would sneak out in the middle. But halfway through the movie, a pang of sadness crept up on me that I could not shake.

"It was like all the things I had not truly grieved were demanding my attention. It was like a mother bird returning to her nest to find all her baby chicks' mouths open demanding they be fed. Overwhelmed, I grabbed my things and left. I don't remember running out because running is just not my thing. The rest of my version is pretty much the same as Owen's. We started hanging out, then we began dating, broke up, got back together, got engaged, got married, and here we are."

Coach nodded and said, "Thank you for letting me be the first person you shared your version of your story with."

#

"The reason I ask couples to tell me their stories is that it sheds light on the way they view themselves, their partner, and their marriage. I see marriage as a subculture contained within a larger subculture of family and friends. As such, the people within the subculture—the husband, wife, family, and friends—develop their sacred stories. Like the Greeks and Romans, they develop narratives to address phenomena. These sacred stories shape our worldview. Within these mythic stories are all the major assumptions about their marital epic. All of which contain the elements that define them, reinforce their values, promote social order, as well as speak to the psychological fallout of engaging one another. What people choose to share, or leave out, determines the presumptions that restrict or enhance their level of intimacy, the ability to solve problems, trust, sex, and attitude just to name a few."

"You can get all that from the stories we just told?" Owen was intrigued, yet skeptical about the role a couple's story has in resolving their marital issues.

"Yes. And it also provides answers to some of the questions I can use to identify hidden dynamics between the two of you," Coach Perkins responded.

"I just don't see how that's possible when so much of the stories we tell are subjective at best. After all, the facts are the facts."

"I hear you. Let me see if I can explain it this way. As a person who studies math, you use equations to solve problems right?"

Owen nodded.

"And the key to solving an equation is finding the value of the hidden variables in the equation, right?"

Again, Owen nodded.

"A story is nothing more than an equation—a proposition people use to explain their reality. What I like to do is get one side of the equation, your story, and match it to the other side of the equation, Lia's story. I then work through your stories much in the same way you'd do with a math problem. I try to determine the hidden values of the variables. While that's a rough approximation of what I do, I think you get the idea," Coach Perkins concluded.

Excited by the comparison to math Owen said, "I got it, I got it. Man, that's good stuff, Coach."

"So how do you determine what the variables are between Lia and me?"

"The same way I do with every couple. I look at two types of variables in their narrative. The first thing I look for is a particular kind of auxiliary verb called a 'modal verb'."

"I know what those are. You talked about them in one of your audio messages. They are auxiliary verbs that express seven things a speaker believes about the action of themselves and others," Lia said with childlike excitement,

"That's right. They represent the personal beliefs a person has about the probability, necessity, ability, desire, obligation, possibility, and acceptability of a person's actions," Coach Perkins said.

"If I remember correctly you divided them into two categories: the sabotage list of the closed-mindedness, and the support list of the open-mindedness," Lia said.

"That's right. Words on the sabotage list are: should, shall, ought, and must. The support list consists of words like can, could, may, and might. People who tell their story with a lot of 'should,' 'must' and 'ought' have high conflict relationships full of judgment. On the flip side, people who use 'can,' 'could,' 'may' and 'might' create a more supportive and hopeful environment with their open-mindedness," Coach Perkins explained.

"Yeah, yeah, but doesn't the removal of the so-called 'sabotage list' lower the bar? Shouldn't people be held to some standard?" Owen argued.

"The reality is, Owen, you can't hold people to a standard, you can only judge and condemn them for not keeping the standard," Coach Perkins' tone was flat and matter of fact. "Let me ask you something," he added, "How well have the two of you done at holding each other to a standard the other wasn't inclined to or capable of keeping?"

"Not well," Lia said. Owen nodded in agreement.

"That is my point. All the 'shoulds' in the story you have told yourselves and each other about your marriage has created a toxic atmosphere. Now imagine if all those shoulds, musts, and oughts" were replaced by coulds, cans, mays, and mights. Then the story you'd tell yourselves, and each other, about your relationship would be more hopeful and supportive. To survive will have to abandon the closed-minded 'should' places of your marital narrative.""

"Amazing. Just hearing you say could, can, and might in relationship to our marriage makes our situation seem more hopeful," Owen said.

Coach Perkins went on to explain the second group of variables he looks for in a couple's stories. "The main reason people tell stories is not to preserve an accurate account of history, it's to communicate what's in their heart. The Book of Proverbs describes the heart as a well. It says, 'out of which flows the issues of life.' In the Gospels, Christ identifies the heart as a fountain or well when he declares, 'Out of the abundance of the heart the mouth speaks.' While listening to both of your stories, I was trying to discern what's in your heart. In particular, what you hold sacred, the themes you connect with and want others to relate to you. I try to demythologize the stories the two of you have told. Demythologizing is not the same as myth busting, which is proving whether something is true or not. It's about unearthing the authentic and the meaningful.

"I wasn't trying to assess the truth or accuracy of your story. I was attempting to discern what each of you holds to be sacred about yourself, your mate, and your relationship. What I am looking for are the truths within the story, not the facts. The authenticity."

"What have you learned about us from our story?" Lia asked.

"A lot about the questions I think the two of you need to answer to move forward. What the two of you have shared with me this afternoon has provided me with more clues than conclusions, and that's a good thing. It means there are elements of your story yet to be revealed."

Wanting to test Coach's discernment and more detail Owen asked, "What are some of the specific things you got from our stories?"

"The first thing I noticed is that Lia did not have a story, she merely supplemented your yours. The second thing is that Lia's story focuses on the situations going on before she met you, whereas your story focuses on what happened after you met. Your stories are out of sync," Coach Perkins replied.

"What do you mean?" Owen asked.

"Her story started a full week ahead of yours with a story arch that doesn't involve the two of you," Coach answered. "On the other hand, your story arch is solely focused on when you came into Lia's life. Also, nowhere in your narrative the two of you talk about being attracted to one another. The fact that you weren't able to remember what she was going through or what the film was about raised questions for me about your motivations during that time," Coach Perkins explained.

Owen went on the defensive. "That was a long time ago. I just forgot," he responded to the implication that his motives for going after her were not what they seemed.

"I am not condemning you for forgetting. I'm just

wondering out loud why this is the first time Lia's side of the story has been shared between the two of you?"

Fascinated by Coach Perkins observation, Lia asked if there was anything else he'd picked up from their story.

"Yes, as I said a minute ago, I think the climaxes of your stories are out of sync. If I heard both of your stories outside the context of your marriage, I would say Lia's story fits the 'Coming of Age motif', a story about a teenager's transition into adulthood in which the issues of her adolescent life ascend to the adult level. Owen, your story fits the 'always save the girl motif' in which the hero sees himself as the only one who can save the girl and who is willing to do it at all costs.

"The question here isn't whose story reads better or is more accurate," he continued, "the question is what can we learn from each of your stories that might help the two of you get on the same page so you can move forward.

"One of the biggest questions your stories raised for me that the two of you need to answer came from Lia's narrative."

"What's that?" Owen inquired.

"In Lia's story, she talked about her need to grieve the loss of her friends and to deal with the drama created by her relationships with her mother and boyfriend. The man you said was the same person with whom she had an affair. The question then becomes: 'When did you find the time to do your grieving and how did you resolve your issues with your mother and your ex-boyfriend, Lia?'"

Again Owen jumped in to put words into his wife's mouth. "Once we started dating it didn't matter. All these questions are in the past. I told Lia when we got married we were not going to allow other people's drama to affect our happiness."

"Are you answering for Lia because the two of you have had this conversation? Or are you speaking on her behalf? If so, I thought we agreed everyone would answer for themselves to cut down on confusion." Coach Perkins corrected Owen in a soft tone.

He turned pointedly in her direction and said, "Well, Lia?"

"Honestly, I haven't taken the time to do any grieving. At the time, I thought it was a good time to go through the grieving process. I remember planning to get with a grief counselor the following Monday," Lia said.

"Why didn't you?" Coach Perkins asked.

"I don't know. I remember being deeply committed at the time, stuff started happening, and I never got back around to it. I did think about it after school was over, but then I didn't have the money to do it."

"What did you do with all the pain?"

"Half the time I stuffed it and the other half I did a lot of ruminating, running 'what if' scenarios to tone down my guilt," Lia answered as she grabbed several more tissues.

"What's the guilt tied to?"

Lia began to sob harder. "I was supposed to go with them but I had to watch my brothers. If I had gone with them the accident would have never happened. To drop me off they would have had to take a different route," she said through her tears.

Owen put his arm around her and tried to comfort her by repeating, "It wasn't your fault...It wasn't your fault..."

When Lia at last gathered herself, she continued, "As for Casey, you could say we never officially broke up." Her revelation unnerved Owen. He promptly removed his arm from around her.

"What I mean is not officially," she went on. "The whole time he and I dated we were off and on. He'd screw around with some other girl or be a no show for a date, and we wouldn't talk for a week or so. When Owen and I started hanging out, Casey and I were in off status. A friend of his told me when he found out Owen and I were hanging out, he hooked back up with his ex."

"I see. The two of you never had an official break up," Coach Perkins confirmed.

"No, not unless you counted the end of our affair nearly

two months ago. Now that was a formal break up," Lia said definitively.

"Do you love him?"

"I thought I did, I guess. I don't know," Lia responded.

"Would you consider him unfinished?" Coach Perkins probed further.

"I guess you could say he was, but not anymore. That is a closed chapter in my life."

Owen, who had done little to mask the many signs of his discomfort with the direction of the conversation: rolling his eyes, pouting and rocking back and forth, abruptly grabbed the check off the table. The conversation had gotten a little too real for Owen's comfort. He wanted to leave as quickly as possible. He reminded Lia that he had another meeting to attend. The truth is Owen had scheduled the meeting intentionally to limit the time they would spend with Coach. To hasten their exit, he began waving at the waiter. Never the one to waste anything he asked him for some to-go boxes for the entrees he and Lia had hardly eaten.

Discerning Owen's anxiety Coach Perkins said, "We've covered enough for today."

Owen shoved the plates of food to be packed up and the bill at the waiter simultaneously.

Lia asked Coach, "What was the second question you thought was important for us to answer?"

Owen spoke up again, "You heard Coach Perkins, we have covered enough for one day."

"No problem, the second question was a homework assignment," Coach Perkins responded.

Owen pulled out his moleskin notepad and asked, "What is it?"

"One question is for you to answer, Owen, and the other is for you to answer Lia. The question I want you to answer is: 'When Lia ran or walked out of class, did she need you to follow her? Or did you need to support her?'" Turning to Lia, Coach ask, "Did you need help or did you need to be alone?"

Owen read both questions back to Coach to make sure he'd written them down correctly. Anxious for their session to be over, Owen stood up sending Lia and Coach a clear message their time was up. When Coach embraced the two of them, he whispered, "Thanks for sharing your story with me."

CHAPTER FORTY

Owen and Lia Round Three

Lia spent several weeks following their meeting with Coach Perkins trying to engage Owen in a conversation about their meeting and their relationship, but Owen continued to stonewall. Whenever she brought up the issue, he made it seem like going there was something he did for her benefit alone. He still didn't think he needed to talk to anyone. He and Lia were together and that was enough for him. In his mind's eyes, Lia was the one who needed to help in dealing with her emotions around their relationship. He went so far as to tell her that he was glad she had another outlet to help her deal with things. As far as their relationship was concerned Owen did not think there was anything to discuss. In his mind, they were well into the process of putting their mess behind them. Casey was out of the picture—problem solved.

Yet nothing could be further from the truth. Lia was growing more frustrated with Owen. To say there was a storm brewing would be the same as describing Hurricane Katrina as summer rain. Lia was doing everything in her power to engage Owen in an adult conversation about the state and trajectory of their marriage to no avail. To keep herself from going off, she would intermittently call Tiffany to talk her off the ledge and to pray with her. Lia became so desperate that she even began going to church with Tiffany and her family in the hope that God would touch Owen's heart—but even that became a source of frustration.

"So why are you attending church with this Tiffany person and her family and not the Bryant family church?" asked

Owen one Sunday morning as she was dressing for service.

"Why does it matter if my spirit is being fed?" Lia called out from the closet where she was busy selecting a pair of shoes.

"Couldn't your spirit be fed at our church? A church is a church. I just think you going to another church sends the wrong message."

"The wrong message to who and about what? My church attendance doesn't require a press release," Lia stuck her head out of the closet, tilting it to the side wondering where this was going.

"Well, to our family and our friends it's about our unity," Owen sighed his frustration rapidly growing.

"You mean to your family who just so happen to be your only friends," Lia said, feeling the tension in the room rising.

"They're your family too, in case you've forgotten."

"Oh no," Lia said with a smirk, "those are your people. They are Bryants through and through! My people are in Texarkana, Texas and my friends are scattered throughout the southwest." Lia declared.

"I'm just saying," Owen raised his voice slightly, "if we want people to believe everything is fine between us, then we have to do things that let people know everything is alright between us," he reasoned.

"So, I'm supposed to go to a church with weak singing and even more ineffective preaching to appease the Bryants as they watch from their perch among the gods?"

"That's not what I'm saying. I just believe that we must present a united front during this season of our marriage. Besides, what difference does it make which church you go to? You should be able to worship wherever you go. If God is as omnipresent and omniscient as you say he is, why would he care?" Owen waved his hands dismissively to reinforce his point.

Infuriated by content and tone of Owen's comment, Lia stopped defending herself and went on the attack.

"I don't believe you! Your spirituality lies somewhere

between agnostic and atheist, and you're telling me which church I should go to? I know I am not as high class and refined as the other Bryant women, but coming from Texas, I do know a thing or two about doing church.

"Let's just agree you're not going to try to teach me about a God you may or may not believe exists, especially when that little church you grew up in is little more than a glorified book club. They spend more time talking about the books on the Times bestseller list than the books of the Bible. You get off my back about what church I attend and I won't bother you about your forsaking the fellowship of the saints in favor of watching your beloved Saints football instead of attending your precious family church."

"What am I supposed to say when people ask why your wife is going to another church?" Owen asked, clueless.

"Tell them your wife said it is none of their business where I choose to worship. And if they have a problem with where I worship, tell them to pray for me."

"Hypothetically speaking, what would you do if I started attending church? Owen was not content to let it go. "Would you let me go to church by myself?"

"Hypothetically speaking, it would mean you were saved, sanctified and filled with the Holy Spirit. And if that happened I know you wouldn't want to attend the weekly funeral you all call a worship service."

"Are you saying you wouldn't go to church with me if I started attending service on a regular basis."

"No, that's not what I said. I would go with you, and I would be sitting by your side every Sunday. And the moment the Pastor gave the benediction, I'd be headed across town to Tiffany's church to get my praise on and my spirit fed," Lia slid one palm across the other to indicate how fast she'd be out of there.

"You would attend two services in one day?" Owen couldn't believe what he was hearing.

"That's what I mean exactly. You Californians don't know

anything about doing church. Back home we'd be in church all day long: Sunday school, worship service, BTU, and evening service, not to mention Wednesday night prayer. Doing two services. Please, that's nothing," Lia chuckled.

"That's one of the reasons why I'm anti-religion. I don't think anyone should have to spend their entire day, all dressed up, listening to a bunch of nonsense being spewed by some converted pimp in gators to try and please God," Owen said. The contempt dripped from his lips.

"That's what I use to say to myself every time you would come home from church late," Lia murmured, baiting Owen.

"What are you talking about? I attend church about several times a year: Easter, Mother's Day, and Christmas, and that's not counting weddings and funerals. I don't need all that mythology to get me through the day. I live in the real world."

"That's not the church I'm talking about," Lia said, laughing out loud. "The church I'm talking about is your precious Center. That facility is your Crystal Cathedral, your Taj Mahal, your Temple, your Mecca. And like most churches you are always complaining about, it was built with tithes and offerings you collected from the pimps you use to work with on Wall Street. Hmm...I guess that would make you a converted pimp too! Whether you accept it or not The Center is as much a church as First Baptist up the street. You function as the pastor, the people who attend are your parishioners, and all the various programs you run are the ministries. The Board of Directors of the foundation makes up your elder board comprised of the people close to you. That place couldn't be more like a church if you put a 20ft cross at the top of it and replaced the windows with stain glass." To Owen's chagrin, Lia was now in full on laughter.

"How can you compare the work I do for the community to the self-serving practices of most churches?" Owen said indignantly.

"Sorry if I offended you, Apostle Bryant. I didn't mean to blaspheme the sanctity of your position nor demean the good works of your congregation," Lia said, bowing her head in mock humility. "I was merely making an observation based on the writing of theologian and philosopher Paul Tillich, who said, 'A person's faith is defined by their ultimate concern,' Lia said with a smirk of scholarly condescension that trumped the mere arrogance coming from Owen.

"That's not true, I'm concerned about a lot of things," Owen fired back.

Taking pleasure in watching Owen squirm for a change, Lia continued.

"Yeah, but only one of them can be your ultimate concern."

"You're an ultimate concern," Owen said, thinking it would get Lia to back down.

Instead, Lia went at him harder. "I know anything outside of the hard sciences of logic and reason is beneath you, but let me see if I can spell it out for you. An ultimate concern is by definition a single concern, hence the word 'ultimate.' Therefore I cannot be an ultimate concern—I would have to be the ultimate concern, which we both know I am not," Lia said, her tone suddenly turned somber.

"That's not true. You have always been my ultimate concern," Owen said, trying to adjust to the sobriety in Lia's voice.

"Really? Always? Is that's why you had me sign a prenuptial agreement because you were more concerned about me than your god?" Lia asked.

"That was forced upon me by my lawyer—" Owen started before Lia cut him off.

"Save it Owen! Save that crap for someone who doesn't know better. I had known before we were married it was your idea, not theirs," Lia said, again in a defeated tone.

"Wha…, what are you talking about…it was their idea…" a stunned Owen tried to claim.

"Are you saying it wasn't your idea because you've said it so many times you have become so steeped in denial that you believe it, or are so sure your game is so tight that you think I couldn't possibly know the truth? Well, here's a press release for you—I 've always known it was you who wanted me to sign a prenup. So, you can stop with the charade. You're straight busted. Your lawyer let it slip out when he was talking to my lawyer when they were going back forth about the language. And before you get all hot about your confidentiality being violated, I also saw the email you sent telling him you were thinking about getting married and wanted him to draw up an iron-clad contract to protect yourself in case things didn't work out. Imagine my shock when I discovered you had a 'Lia file' on your computer. You know, you really should wipe your hard drive clean before you gift someone your old computer. You want to know what my lawyer advised me to do when she found out? She advised me not to sign it—not because it was an evil document, but because she thought you lacked character.

"Funny huh? Even a lawyer thought you lacked character. Yet I married you anyway, knowing I was not your ultimate concern. Yes, it was partly out of love, but partly out of denial. For years, I told myself it didn't matter because I loved you. But it did bother me on several levels. That's why I didn't like going anywhere near The Center. I was jealous of your mistress—your god."

"Believe me, you are my ultimate concern," Owen's plea was to meant to cover his shame more than to address Lia's accusation.

"No Owen, I am not. I am not even your second, or third concern. Protecting your money is your first concern, followed by caring for your mother, The Center, and Sage's approval. The more I think about it, you do have an ultimate concern—it's your concern about keeping your reputation as a nice guy, even at the expense of the truth. That's why you're still clinging to the lie about the prenup."

"But you are important to me," Owen again protested.

"I'm not saying I'm not important to you. I'm just saying I had to come to terms with where I rank on the list. Owen, the truth is being with you was so important to me that I let our marriage be built on the foundation of lies, thinking things would get better down the road. You chose to marry me in deception, and I allowed it," Lia said, trying to wrap her head around how everything between them had become so messy.

"But what about you? I've not always been your ultimate concern either," Owen countered to get some of the pressure he was feeling off him.

"You're right. Up until this point, my ultimate concern had been filling the dark hole inside my soul created by my fear of abandonment. That's the god I've served. I confess that and I own it. It still doesn't provide an answer to the million-dollar question: Where do we go from here? Do we want to partner with one another and work things out, continue to play the game, or call it a wrap?"

It had taken thirteen years, two months, five weeks, six days, five hours, and forty-two seconds from the time they met for all their cards to be placed on the table, face up for both to see. In doing so, Lia had done something for Owen she hadn't been able to do their entire marriage—she told him the truth in love. Not out of frustration, anger, or manipulation. She'd unmasked his manufactured "nice guy" façade, without being judgmental. In addition, she owned the role she'd played in the process without sinking into defensiveness or denial. All the moment required was for Owen to receive what she said in the spirit of love and cooperation it was sent in, and to take advantage of the opportunity for them to move forward.

But there was one problem: Owen wasn't ready or able to deal with how things worked in the real world. He was too wedded to his sense of self to seize the moment. In an instant, he countered her truth in love with judgment.

"You are still living in the past. That's the difference between you and me. I'm able to move on while you keep getting stuck in the past, your childhood, the death of your friends, what I've done. You don't know how to let stuff go. I, on the other hand, have been able to put your affair with

Casey behind me. I forgave Sage and Roman for giving me an ultimatum, along with a whole host of other things you and others have done to me. I can't understand why you aren't tougher mentally considering all the drama you claim to have gone through?"

"Mentally tougher? You have got to be kidding me! You can barely handle someone telling you anything remotely critical without becoming dismissive or shutting down."

"I'm not dismissive! I'm just tougher mentally than most people, so I tell it like it is. Truth is I'm surrounded by weak-minded individuals who don't know how to keep it 100 like me. They don't know how to hang when I break them off with logic and reason," Owen pounded his chest with one hand.

Watching Owen as he bragged about his intellect, Lia didn't know whether to laugh or cry. "Do you hear yourself right now? I swear, sometimes I think I married into a family of vampires. You all want your spouse to act like they are under a spell. You don't know how to let anything go because you need the blood of others to survive. It's impossible to get any of you to look at yourselves in the mirror. You are so emotionally unavailable that you are dead on the inside; and you act like you're immortal. Yep vampires.

"Why are you attacking my family? This is between you and me!"

"No, it's not. Have you forgotten how this conversation started and why it went left? Because I haven't! Let me summarize it for you: You asked me why I wasn't going to the Bryant family church so you wouldn't have to answer any of their questions? Face it, Owen—your family is a part of everything we do or don't do. Their fingerprints are all over our lives. How many vacations have you taken that weren't tied to a Bryant event?"

"What about the trip to Texas last year? Huh? That's your home state," Owen said.

"You mean the trip where I flew in to be with you for three days after you'd already been there a week with members of your family? If I recall you were meeting with the planning committee for—wait for it—the Bryant Foundation."

"Still I arranged it where you could spend some time with several of your friends and family. I even picked up the tab for the meal."

"Oh yes, there was lunch at Pappadeaux in Dallas, a mere 180-mile drive from Texarkana. Yes, who could forget four hours of you droning on about the incompetence of your board, staff, the waitress, the cook, the Uber driver, and anyone else who did not live up to your standard of excellence—a standard, by the way, that you have set for everyone but yourself. The whole while me and my crew were trying to break bread, you fussed and pouted because you weren't the center of attention," Lia replied.

"If it was such an inconvenience then why did you even come?"

"You know I asked myself that before, during, and after that trip. You acted like such a douche my friends flew out here a month later to see me just to spite you. You know what one of them told me before they left? 'Proverbs says it is better to dwell on the rooftop of a house in the cold than to live in a big house with a needy, insecure, little man.' I had to check her for her comment, even though it wasn't that far off the mark."

Back and forth, tit for tat, Owen and Lia carried on until he got up to leave. "There is no reasoning with you. I am done with this conversation," Owen headed for the door.

"Owen, at some point you got to stop shutting down and running if you want this marriage to work," Lia said. There was a soothing quality in her tone that caused him to stop short of the door.

"If I don't stop shutting down and running what?" he turned to look at her, "you cheat on me, then try to move another man in my house? And I'm the one who is shutting down and running? Please...

"This marriage isn't going to work till you stop being so emotional about everything. Everything in life doesn't have to develop into an issue to be discussed and dissected forever. How about you learn to accept things as they are and grow the hell up?" Owen poked his finger on the nightstand repeatedly.

Lia slowly rose to her feet from the edge of the bed where she'd been perched. With erect posture and steady eye contact she made a proclamation:

"Owen William Bryant, if you walk out on me right now, I won't be here when you get back. I'm not going to live with a man who doesn't take our marriage or me seriously, not another day, hour, or minute. You either stay and we hash this out, or I'm gone. You've trivialized our issues, and me, for the last time. Leave, and I'll assume you just don't have it in you to put in the work. I'm done living with you in the shadows. I mean it, Owen. You leave, and I won't be here when you get back. There, is that grown up enough for you?"

"See that's what I mean, you're emotional. Look at yourself, overreacting. I'm going out to get some air to give you a chance to pray, meditate or call your pastor, prophet, priest friend or whatever you need to help you calm down. And you can't even appreciate the fact I'm one of those rational brothas who doesn't get upset and put his hands on his woman," Owen said with a wave of his hand.

"Yeah, you are right. You are not the type of brother who would put his hands on his woman in anger, because you are the kind of brother who won't put his hands on his women for months just to show her who's in charge. What was it almost eleven months since we'd made love before I started the affair?" Lia said, her heart suddenly softened and eyes welling up.

Before Owen could take a breath, Lia walked over to Owen, kissed him on his forehead and said, "Baby, you do what you got to do to soothe the shame you are carrying. But, don't forget I told you what I was going to do. I know I do not have the best record of following through, but don't test me; because I might surprise you. My heart is broken, and I am willing to do anything to save this marriage—anything but give up my dignity. That I won't do," Lia said softly."

"You're just acting ridiculous now," Owen moved away to put some distance between them.

"If you want to finish this I'm right here. Otherwise, I'll call you when I figure out where I'm going to stay." Lia then turned and walked down the hall.

Owen paced for a minute, then sat back down. He leaned back in his seat and rubbed his chin thoughtfully. Assuming Lia was trying to manipulate him into staying, her reasoned to himself, *"If I give into her demands, she'll believe she's running the show. I can't stay even if I wanted to. I need to show her these emotional outbursts of hers don't work on me."* Believing that Lia did not have the courage or the focus to follow through on her threat, he grabbed his keys, wallet, and cell phone and headed for the front door. *"I'll go off for a little while then come back just to show her she can't run game on me."*

CHAPTER FORTY-ONE

Doing Scary Aftermath

Like the sudden appearance of Uncle Jr. when Lia was little, the three beeps from the alarm system triggered by Owen's departure made the grim announcement that "things had changed." This time she wasn't worried about the back-story; she knew what had changed because she had just lived through it. Being someone's girlfriend or wife just to be part of a family wasn't going to cut it anymore. Having learned the difference between predatorial, parasitic and partner-ships relationships, she decided she wanted nothing less than a full partnership. Owen's insistence that she attend his family church helped Lia see the other dominant feature within their parasitic relationship. Aside from the obvious parasitic dynamic within the financial realm of their marriage, which Owen played the role of host to her parasitic spending, Lia had identified a subtle dynamic in their parasitic relation-ship. Within the emotional realm of their relationship, she'd picked up on Owen's desire for her to play the role of host to his parasitic need to maintain his image.

She wiped the trail of tears from her cheeks as she sat on the side of the bed. She then leaned to grab her phone off the nightstand. Within a span of 10 minutes and 48 seconds, she placed three phone calls. The first was to her friend Tiffany, asking if she could spend the night at her house, the second was to an area code in Texas, and the third was to American Airlines. Still adept at leaving things behind and packing on a moment's notice from a childhood of being bounced around, Lia loaded her suitcases then left.

There were two errands she needed to run before hooking up with Tiffany. The first was a swing by The Center. Sure enough, just as she'd figured, there was Owen's car parked out front. He'd gone to church to meet with his god and to be comforted. Her second stop took her by Roman and Sage's house. After their initial shock of her appearance, she brought them up to speed on everything that had transpired over the past several months between she and Owen. Lia poured out her heart and apologized once more for involving them in her drama. She sincerely thanked them for their support. Sage apologized to her for not being a more positive influence on her marriage to her cousin. Lia then asked if she could stay at their house while she waited for her ride.

#

An hour and a half later her ride was at the gate.

Lia hugged Sage, and with tears in her eyes said, "Please take care of my Owen. I know he thinks he's got his stuff altogether, but he doesn't. He's the same frightened boy he was when he was being hurried out the house every time his mom had an episode."

"Don't worry I have been looking out for him all his life. He'll be all right. You just focus on letting God do in you what he needs to do," Sage promised tearfully.

"Is it okay if I occasionally call you to check in?" Lia asked.

"Sure, I'd like that. I'm sorry we got off on the wrong foot." With tears streaming from her eyes Sage added, "Here we are just getting to know one another and you're leaving."

After another round of goodbyes, she was gone.

"How are we going to tell him his pride and denial may have cost him his marriage?" asked Roman as he and Sage stood in the driveway watching the black and gray SUV disappear into the evening mist.

"We don't have to, Lia left a 'Dear Owen' letter on his windshield when she drove by The Center."

"Oh man, that's going to leave a mark. How do you think he's going to take it?"

"Hopefully like a man who is ready to step up because he wants his wife back."

"Is that what you think he'll do?"

"No, I think he's going to remain in denial for some time. He'll probably claim that this is just a phase Lia's going through and all he needs to do is hold out until she comes back, and everything will be back to normal."

"Do you think she's going to crack under the pressure of waiting for him to get it?" Roman asked.

"No!"

"Why not?"

"Because..." Sage thought a moment, "because through her tears I saw something in her eyes tonight I've never seen before."

"What's that?" Roman asked.

"Resolve," Sage said, staring down the block.

Roman and Sage clung to one another in the driveway, neither wanting to let go of the other. It was evident that neither of them wished to suffer the same fate as Owen and Lia. They wanted to grow old together more than anything. While holding Sage in his arms, all the dots began to connect.

"Hmm, that's what he meant," Roman muttered under his breath.

"What'd you say?" Sage asked sweetly.

"I'll tell you inside," Roman took Sage by the hand.

#

"Once Coach Perkins told me it wasn't complicated, it was just scary, I didn't understand what he meant, that is until tonight when I saw that SUV drive off. Life is just scary. It's the stuff we do to avoid, control, and prevent the scary things from happening that makes life complicated.

"I see it now. In the same way I avoided telling you about

my cheating, Owen made a big deal out of Lia's 'emotionalism' to avoid the work, and now it may have cost him his wife. He didn't solve anything; he just made things more complicated. Sage, I don't want to do complicated anymore. I want to do scary, with you," Roman was close to tears.

Sage was caught off guard by Roman's sudden display of brokenness. "What do you mean?"

"Let's redo our vows this anniversary, and then let's sign up with an adoption agency," Roman said, his chest sticking out with childlike enthusiasm.

"Roman Cole, don't play with me! Are you sure? Are you sure, seriously?" Sage squealed.

"I'm positive. I want to renew our vows in the same garden at the same altar. That's if you're cool with it? Why should we let someone defile our Garden of Eden? Like Mrs. Hilliard always says, 'let's take back what the devil stole,'" Roman said defiantly.

"Amen, preacher. Let's!" Sage leaped into Roman's arms and kissed him with a level of passion she had suppressed since their honeymoon.

What followed did not arise from a place of guilt, obligation, manipulation or desperation; it emerged from a place of love. It was not driven by the short term intoxicating effects of romance, or the short-sided recklessness of lust, but by the profound impact of a real commitment. The kind of love the Bible describes as patient and kind: free from envy, boasting, arrogance or rudeness. Never demanding, irritable or resentful; does not try to maintain the moral high ground but rejoices in the truth. It is mentally and emotionally tough enough to bear, hope, and endure all things at such a level; it marks a bond that can only exist between a grown man and a grown woman who have put away childish things.

That night, Sage and Roman reaped the spiritual fruit that only a union that has endured its fair share of attacks, sabotage, droughts, famines, and misfortunes could have produced.